D1362832

books in print, she is indisputably one of the most ... and popular writers in the world. She has achieved numerous top five bestsellers in the UK, including number one for *Savour the Moment*, and is a *Sunday Times* hardback bestseller writing as J. D. Robb.

Become a fan on Facebook at
www.facebook.com/norarobertsjdrobb
and be the first to hear all the latest from Piatkus
about Nora Roberts and J. D. Robb.

www.noraroberts.com
www.nora-roberts.co.uk
www.jd-robb.co.uk

By Nora Roberts

Homeport	Northern Lights	Black Hills
The Reef	Blue Smoke	The Search
River's End	Montana Sky	Chasing Fire
Carolina Moon	Angels Fall	The Witness
The Villa	High Noon	Whiskey Beach
Midnight Bayou	Divine Evil	The Collector
Three Fates	Tribute	The Liar
Birthright	Sanctuary	

The Born In Trilogy:
Born in Fire
Born in Ice
Born in Shame

The Bride Quartet:
Vision in White
Bed of Roses
Savour the Moment
Happy Ever After

The Key Trilogy:
Key of Light
Key of Knowledge
Key of Valour

The Irish Trilogy:
Jewels of the Sun
Tears of the Moon
Heart of the Sea

Three Sisters Island Trilogy:
Dance upon the Air
Heaven and Earth
Face the Fire

The Sign of Seven Trilogy:
Blood Brothers
The Hollow
The Pagan Stone

Chesapeake Bay Quartet:
Sea Swept
Rising Tides
Inner Harbour
Chesapeake Blue

In the Garden Trilogy:
Blue Dahlia
Black Rose
Red Lily

The Circle Trilogy:
Morrigan's Cross
Dance of the Gods
Valley of Silence

The Dream Trilogy:
Daring to Dream
Holding the Dream
Finding the Dream

The Inn Boonsboro Trilogy:
The Next Always
The Last Boyfriend
The Perfect Hope

The Cousins O'Dwyer Trilogy:
Dark Witch
Shadow Spell
Blood Magick

Many of Nora Roberts' other titles are now available in eBook and she is also the author of the In Death series using the pseudonym J.D. Robb. For more information please visit www.noraroberts.com or www.nora-roberts.co.uk

NORA ROBERTS

KEY OF VALOUR

piatkus

PIATKUS

First published in the United States in 2003 by the Berkley Publishing Group
A division of Penguin Group (USA) Inc.
First published in Great Britain in 2004 by Piatkus
This edition published in 2016 by Piatkus

1 3 5 7 9 10 8 6 4 2

A CIP catalogue record for this book
is available from the British Library.

ISBN 978-0-349-41165-1

Typeset in Garamond by M Rules
Printed and bound by CPI Group (UK) Ltd, Croydon CR0 4YY

Papers used by Piatkus are from well-managed forests
and other responsible sources.

MIX
Paper from
responsible sources
FSC® C104740
www.fsc.org

Piatkus
An imprint of
Little Brown Book Group
Carmelite House
50 Victoria Embankment
London EC4Y 0DZ

An Hachette UK Company
www.hachette.co.uk

www.piatkus.co.uk

To my mom,
who was brave enough to raise five of us

Courage, the footstool of the Virtues,
upon which they stand.

ROBERT LOUIS STEVENSON

One

ZOE MCCOURT WAS SIXTEEN WHEN SHE MET THE BOY
who would change her life. She'd grown up in the mountains of
West Virginia, the oldest of four. By the time she was twelve, her
father had already run off with the wife of another man.

Even then, Zoe hadn't considered it any great loss. Her daddy
was a short-tempered, moody man who preferred drinking beer
with the boys or banging his neighbor's wife rather than seeing
to his own.

Still, it was hard, since most weeks he had at least brought
home a paycheck.

Her mother was a thin, nervous woman who smoked too
much and compensated for her husband's desertion by replacing him, with some regularity, with boyfriends cut from the
same cloth as Bobby Lee McCourt. They made her happy in
the short term, angry and sad in the long, but she'd never been
able to do without a man for more than a month straight in
any case.

Crystal McCourt had raised her brood in a double-wide,
slotted into a lot in the Hillside Trailer Park. After her husband
ran off, Crystal got shit-faced drunk and, leaving Zoe in charge,

hopped in her thirdhand Camaro to head out in pursuit of, in her words, "the cheating son of a bitch and his godforsaken whore."

She'd been gone for three days. She hadn't found Bobby, but she came back sober. The chase had cost her some of her self-respect, and her job at Debbie's House of Beauty.

Debbie's House might have been more of a hut, but it cut deep to lose the regular pay.

The experience toughened Crystal considerably. She sat her children down and told them things were going to be rocky and things were going to be hard, but they'd find a way.

She nailed up her beautician's license in the trailer's kitchen and opened her own house of beauty.

She undercut Debbie's prices, and she had a talent with hair.

So they'd gotten by. The trailer had smelled of peroxide and permanents and smoke, but they'd gotten by.

Zoe shampooed heads, swept up shorn hair, and minded her three siblings. When she showed an aptitude, she was given comb-outs or allowed to trim.

And she dreamed of better, of more, of the world outside that trailer park.

She did well in school, especially in math. Her skill with numbers put her in charge of her mother's books, the taxes, the bills.

She was an adult before her fourteenth birthday, with the child inside yearning for something more.

It was no surprise that she was dazzled by James Marshall.

He was so different from the boys she knew. Not just because he was a little older—nineteen to her sixteen—but because he'd been places and seen things. And God, he was so handsome. Like Prince Charming out of the storybook.

His great-grandfather might have worked the mines in those hills, but there was no coal dust on James. The generations between had scrubbed it all away, and added a sheen of polish and gloss.

His family had money, the kind of money that bought class, and education, and trips to Europe. They had the biggest house in town, as white and showy as a bridal gown, and James and his younger sister were both sent to private schools.

The Marshalls liked to give parties, big, splashy ones with live music and fancy catered food. Mrs. Marshall would always have Crystal come right to the house to do her hair for a party, and Zoe often went along to do Mrs. Marshall's nails.

She would dream about that house, so clean and full of flowers and pretty things. It was so wonderful to know people lived that way. Not everyone was crowded into a trailer that smelled of chemicals and stale smoke.

She promised herself that one day she would live in a house. It didn't have to be big and grand like the Marshalls's, but it would be a real house, and it would have a little yard.

And one day, she would travel to the places Mrs. Marshall spoke of—New York City, Paris, Rome.

She saved her pennies for it from her tip money, and the pay she earned from the odd jobs she took. Well, the pay that didn't go to helping Mama keep the wolf from the door.

She was good with money. At sixteen she had four hundred and fourteen dollars tucked away in a secret savings account.

In April, when she turned sixteen, she made some extra money helping to serve at one of the Marshalls' parties. She was presentable enough, and eager for the work.

She wore her hair long back then, a straight stream of black down her back. She'd always been slim, but she'd blossomed in a way that had the boys sniffing around her. She had no time for boys—or not very much.

She had long-lidded eyes of golden brown that were always looking, watching, wondering, and a wide, full mouth that was

3

slow to smile. Her features were sharp and angular, adding a touch of the exotic that was a contrast to her innate shyness.

She did what she was told and did it well—and kept, as much as it was possible, to herself.

Maybe it was the shyness, or the dreamy eyes, or the quiet competence that attracted James. But he flirted with her on that early-spring evening, flustered her, and ultimately flattered her. And he asked to see her again.

They met in secret, which added to the thrill. The sheer romance of having the attention of someone like James was overpowering. He listened to her, so her shyness dropped away and she told him her dreams and hopes.

He was sweet to her, and whenever she could slip away they went for long drives or simply sat and looked at the stars and talked.

Of course, before long, they did more than talk.

He said he loved her. He said he needed her.

On a soft night in June, on a red blanket spread out on the floor of the summer woods, she lost her innocence to him with the eager optimism that belongs to the young.

He was still sweet, still attentive, and promised they'd always be together. She imagined he'd believed it. She certainly had.

But there was a price to pay for being young and foolish. She had paid it. And, she thought, so had he. Maybe he'd paid much, much more than she had.

Because while she had lost her innocence, James had lost a more precious treasure.

She glanced over at that treasure now. Her son.

If James had changed her life, Simon had righted it again. In a new way, a new place. James had given Zoe her first taste of what it was to be a woman. The child had made her one.

She'd gotten her house—her little house with its little

yard—and she'd gotten it by herself. Maybe she'd never traveled to all those wonderful places as she'd once dreamed of doing, but she'd seen all the wonders of the world in her son's eyes.

And now, nearly ten years after she'd first held him, first promised him she would never let him down, she was moving forward again, with her son. She was seeing to it that Simon had more.

Zoe McCourt, the shy girl from the West Virginia hills, was about to open her own business in the pretty town of Pleasant Valley, Pennsylvania, with two women who'd become as much sisters as friends in two short months.

Indulgence. She liked the name. That was what she wanted it to be for the clients and customers. It would be work, hard work, for her, for her friends. But even the work was a kind of indulgence, as it was labor they'd all dreamed of doing.

Malory Price's arts and crafts gallery would occupy one side of the main level of their sweet new house. Dana Steele's bookstore would stand on the other. And her own salon would spread over the top floor.

Just a few more weeks, she thought. A few more weeks of remodeling and freshening up, of setting up supplies, stock, equipment. Then they would open the doors.

It made her belly jump to think of it, but it wasn't only fear. Some of those jumps were pure excitement.

She knew exactly how it would look when it was done. Full of color and light in the main salon, then softer, relaxing tones in the treatment rooms. She would have candles set around for fragrance and atmosphere, and interesting pictures on the walls. Good lighting to flatter and to soothe.

Indulgence. For the mind, the body, the spirit. She intended to give her customers a bit of all three.

On this evening, she drove from the Valley where she made her home, and would make her business, into the mountains.

Where she would face her fate. Simon brooded a little, staring out the window. He wasn't happy, she knew, that she'd made him wear his suit.

But when you were invited to dinner at a place like Warrior's Peak, you dressed for the occasion.

Absently, she tugged at the skirt of her dress. She'd gotten it at the outlet for a good price, and hoped the deep purple jersey was appropriate.

Probably should've gotten something black, she mused, to be more dignified and sober. But she so enjoyed color, and for this event she needed the punch of it for confidence. Tonight was one of the most momentous nights of her life, so she might as well go outfitted in something that made her feel good.

She pressed her lips together. Now that her thoughts had circled around to what she'd tried to avoid thinking about, she had to deal with it.

Just how, she wondered, was she going to explain to a nine-year-old boy what she'd been doing—and more, what she was about to do?

"I guess we'd better talk about why we're going up here to dinner tonight," she began.

"I bet nobody else is wearing a suit," he muttered.

"I bet you're wrong."

He turned his head, slanted her a look. "Dollar."

"Dollar," she agreed.

He looked so much like her, she thought. Sometimes it just struck her with a kind of fierce and possessive joy. Wasn't it funny that there was nothing of James stamped on that face? Those were her eyes, that was her mouth, her nose, her chin, her hair, all tipped just the slightest bit to make them Simon.

"Anyway." She cleared her throat. "You know how I got that invitation to go up there, a couple months ago? And that's where I met Malory and Dana."

6

"Sure, I remember, because the next day you bought me PlayStation 2, and it wasn't even my birthday."

"Unbirthday presents are the best." She'd been able to buy Simon his heart's desire with part of the twenty-five thousand dollars paid to her for agreeing to ... the fantastic.

"You know Malory and Dana, and you know Flynn and Jordan and Bradley."

"Yeah, we hang with them a lot now. They're cool. For old people," he added, with a smirk he knew would make her laugh.

But she didn't laugh.

"Something wrong with them?" he asked quickly.

"No. No. Absolutely nothing's wrong." She chewed her bottom lip as she tried to find the right words. "Um, sometimes people are sort of connected, without even knowing it. I mean, Dana and Flynn are brother and sister—well, step-brother and stepsister, then Dana gets to be friends with Malory, and Malory meets Flynn, and before you know it, Malory and Flynn fall in love."

"Is this going to be a sloppy love story? Because I might get sick."

"Be sure to lean out the window if you do. So, Flynn's oldest friends are Jordan and Bradley, and when they were younger, Jordan and Dana used to ... date." It was the safest word a mother could think of. "Then Jordan and Bradley moved out of the Valley. Then they came back, partly because of this connection I'm getting to. And Jordan and Dana got back together and—"

"Now they're going to get married, and so's Flynn and Malory. It's like an epidemic." He was turned to her now, and his face mirrored preadolescent pain. "If we go to those weddings like we did Aunt Joleen's, you're probably going to make me wear a suit, aren't you?"

"Yes, it's one of my quiet pleasures, this torment of you.

What I'm trying to show you is that each of us turned out to be connected, one way or another—to the others. And to something else. I haven't told you much about the people who live at Warrior's Peak."

"They're the magic people."

Zoe's hand jerked on the wheel. Slowing, she pulled off to the shoulder of the winding road. "What do you mean by 'magic people'?"

"Jeez, Mom, I hear you guys talk when you have those meetings and junk. So are they like witches or what? I don't get it."

"No. Yes. I don't know exactly." How did she explain ancient gods to a child? "Do you believe in magic, Simon? I don't mean the card trick kind, but the kind of thing you read about in stories, like *Harry Potter* or *The Hobbit.*"

"If it wasn't real sometimes, how come there are so many books and movies and junk about it?"

"Good point," she said after a moment. "Rowena and Pitte, the people who live at the Peak, the people we're going to see tonight, they're magic. They come from a different place, and they're here because they need our help."

"For what?"

She had his attention and interest now, she knew. The interest that took him into the stories she'd mentioned, *X-Men* comics, and the role-playing video games he loved.

"I'm going to tell you. It's going to sound like a story, but it's not. But I have to start driving again while I tell you, or we'll be late."

"Okay."

She took a long, quiet breath as she pulled back onto the road. "A long time ago—a really, really long time ago, in a place behind what they call the Curtain of Dreams, or the Curtain of Power, there was this young god—"

"Like Apollo?"

8

"Sort of. But not Greek. He was Celtic. He was the son of the king, and when he was of age, he visited our world and he met a girl and fell in love."

Simon's mouth twisted. "How come that always happens?"

"Can we get into that area of things later? We're a little pressed for time. So, they fell in love, and even though it wasn't really allowed then, his parents let him bring the girl home with him so they could be married. This was okay with some of the gods, but it wasn't okay with some of the others. There were battles and—"

"Cool."

"The world split into two kingdoms, I guess you could say. One with the young god becoming ruler with his human wife, and the other ruled by, well, a wicked sorcerer."

"Way cool."

"The young king had three daughters. They call them demi-goddesses because they're part human. Each of the daughters had a special gift. One was music, or art, another was writing, or knowledge, and the third was courage, I guess. Valor."

It made her mouth a little dry to think of it, but she swallowed and went on. "She was a kind of warrior. They were very close to each other, the way sisters should be, and their parents loved them. To keep them safe while there was this trouble going on, they had them guarded and taught by a warrior and a teacher. Then—try not to groan—the warrior and the teacher fell in love."

He let his head fall back and stared upward. "I just knew it."

"Not being sarcastic nine-year-old boys, the daughters were happy for them, and covered for them when they slipped off a little way to be alone. So these girls weren't guarded as well as maybe they should have been. The wicked sorcerer took advantage of that, and he snuck close and cast a spell. The spell stole the souls of the daughters and locked them in a glass box with three locks and three keys."

"Man, that sucks for them."

"It sure does. The souls are trapped there, in the box, and can't get out until the keys are turned in the lock—one by one—and only by the hand of a mortal. A human."

Because her fingers tingled, she rubbed them on the skirt of her dress. "See, because they were half human, this sorcerer made it so only someone from our world could save them. Because he didn't think it could be done. The teacher was given the keys—but she can't work them—and she and the warrior were cast out, and into this world. In every generation they have to ask three humans, the three humans who are the only ones who can unlock the box, to find the keys. They have to be hidden and found as part of the quest, part of the spell. And each one of the chosen has to go in turn, and has just four weeks to find the key and put it in the lock."

"Wow, are you one of the ones who has to find a key? How come you were chosen?"

She let out a little breath. Her son was a bright and logical boy. "I don't know exactly. We look—Mal, Dana, and I—we look like the daughters. The Daughters of Glass, they're called. Rowena's an artist, and she has a painting of them at the Peak. It's connections, Simon. There's something that connects us to each other, to the keys, and to the daughters. I guess you could say it's fate."

"If you don't find the keys, they're just stuck in the box?"

"Their souls are. Their bodies are in glass coffins—um, like Snow White. Waiting."

"Rowena and Pitte, they're the teacher and the guard." He nodded. "And you and Malory and Dana have to find the keys and fix everything."

"Pretty much. Malory and Dana have already had their turns, and they each found the key. It's my turn now."

"You'll find it." He gave her a solemn nod. "You always find stuff when I lose it."

If only, she thought, it was as simple as finding her son's favorite action figure. "I'm going to try as hard as I can. I have to tell you, Simon, the sorcerer—his name is Kane—he's tried to stop us. He'll try to stop me. It's really scary, but I have to try."

"You'll kick his butt."

The laugh eased some of the knots in her stomach. "That's my plan. I wasn't going to tell you all this, but then it didn't seem right not to."

"Because we're a team."

"Yeah, we're a great team."

She paused at the open gates of Warrior's Peak.

The gates were flanked by two stone warriors, hands ready on the hilts of their swords. They looked so fierce to her, so formidable. Connections? she thought. What connection could someone like her have to warriors at the gate?

Still, taking a deep breath, Zoe drove through.

"Holy cow," Simon said beside her.

"And then some."

She understood his reaction to the house. Hers had been the same wide-eyed, slack-jawed stare the first time she'd seen it up close.

Though "house," she supposed, was too ordinary a word for the Peak. Part castle, part fortress, it stood high over the Valley, rose up like the majestic hills and ruled them. Its peaks and towers were made of black stone with gargoyles perched on eaves as if they might leap, not so playfully, at their whim. It was a massive place, surrounded by lush lawns that slid into thick woods gone shadowy with evening.

High on the topmost tower flew a white flag with the emblem of a golden key.

The sun was setting behind it, so the canvas of the sky was streaked with red and gold, adding yet another layer of drama.

Soon the sky would be black, Zoe thought, with only the

thinnest sliver of moon. Tomorrow was the first night of the new moon, the beginning of her quest.

"It's really something inside, too. Like something you'd see in a movie. Don't touch anything."

"Mom."

"I'm nervous. Give me a break." She drove slowly toward the entrance. "But, really, don't touch anything in there."

She stopped the car, and hoped she wasn't the first, or the last, to arrive, then took out a lipstick to replace what she'd worried off since leaving home. Automatically, she flicked her fingers over the ruler-straight ends of the hair she now wore shorter than her son's.

"You look good, okay? Can we go?"

"I want us to look great." She caught his chin in her hand, and used the comb she'd plucked out of her purse to tidy his hair while he crossed his eyes at her. "If you don't like what they give us for dinner, just pretend to eat it, but don't say you don't like it, or make those gagging noises. I'll fix you something else when we get home."

"Can we go by McDonald's?"

"We'll see. We're fine. We're great. Okay." She dropped the comb back in her purse and started to open the car door.

The old man who greeted guests and took care of their cars was there to do it for her. He always made her jump. "Oh. Thank you."

"My pleasure, Miss. Good evening to you."

Simon gave him a long study. "Hi."

"Hello, young master."

Liking the title, Simon grinned at him and walked closer. "Are you one of the magic people?"

The creases in the old face deepened and shifted into a broad smile. "It might be I am. What would you think of that?"

"Sweet. But how come you're so old?"

"Simon."

"It's a good question, Miss," he said in response to Zoe's horrified hiss. "I'm so old because I've had the pleasure of living a long time. I wish you the same pleasure." He leaned down with a creak of bones until his face was level with Simon's. "Would you like to know a true thing?"

"Okay."

"We're all of us magic people, but some know it and some don't."

He straightened again. "I'll see to your car, Miss. Have a nice evening."

"Thank you." She took Simon's hand and walked to the portico and the twin entrance doors. They opened before she could knock, and there was Rowena.

Her flame-tipped hair tumbled gloriously over the shoulders of a long dress the green of forest shadows. A silver pendant hung between her breasts, its clear center stone winking in the sparkling light of the entrance hall.

As always, her beauty was a quick shock, like an electric jolt.

She held out a hand in welcome to Zoe, but her eyes—a bolder, richer green than her gown—were all for Simon.

"Welcome." There was a lilt to her voice, echoing those of the foreign lands Zoe had once longed to see. "It's good to see you again. And such a pleasure to meet you, Simon, at last."

"Simon, this is Miss Rowena."

"Just Rowena, please, for I hope we'll be friends. Come in, won't you?" She kept Zoe's hand in hers, and touched the other to Simon's shoulder.

"I hope we're not late."

"No, not at all." Rowena stepped back, leading the way over the tile floor with its colorful mosaics. "Most of the others are here, but Malory and Flynn haven't yet arrived. We're in the parlor. Tell me, Simon, do you like calf's liver and brussels sprouts?"

He made gagging noises before he remembered his mother's order, but even as he caught himself Zoe was flushing. And Rowena's laugh flowed around them. "Since I feel exactly the same, it's fortunate they're not on the menu tonight. Our latest arrivals," she announced as she stepped into the parlor. "Pitte, come meet young Master McCourt."

Simon slid his gaze up to his mother, nudged her with his elbow. "Master," he said with great satisfaction, out of the corner of his mouth.

Rowena's lover matched her in looks. His powerful warrior's build was garbed in an elegant dark suit. His mane of black hair swept back from a strong face where the bones seemed carved under the flesh. His eyes, a brilliant blue, studied Simon as he lifted one elegant brow and extended a hand.

"Good evening, Mr. McCourt. And what can I offer you to drink?"

"Can I have a Coke?"

"Certainly."

"Please, be at home." Rowena gestured.

Dana had already risen to cross the room. "Hey, Simon. How's it going?"

"Fine. Except I lost a buck because that guy and Brad are wearing suits."

"Bad luck."

"I'm going to go talk to Brad, okay, Mom?"

"All right, but—" She sighed as he dashed off. "Don't touch anything," she added under her breath.

"He'll be fine. How about you?"

"I don't know." She looked at her friend, one of the people she'd come to trust completely. The dark brown eyes looked back at hers with an understanding that only one other person could have. "I guess I'm a little wound up. Let's not think about it yet. You look great."

14

It was perfectly true. The dense brown hair fell in a sleek, swinging bell two inches below Dana's strong chin. It was a good look for her, if Zoe, who'd styled it, said so herself.

It relieved her that Dana had chosen a brick-colored jacket over the more formal black.

"Even better," she added, "you look happy." She lifted Dana's left hand to admire the square-cut ruby. "Jordan has great taste in jewelry, and in fiancées."

"Can't argue with that." Dana glanced back toward the sofa, where Jordan and Pitte were talking.

They looked, she thought, very much like the warriors who flanked the gates. "I got me a big, handsome guy."

They looked wonderful together, Zoe thought. Dana's sexy amazon build, Jordan's tall, muscled frame. Whatever happened, or didn't, Zoe was glad they'd found each other again.

"I thought you would enjoy a glass of champagne." Rowena stepped over, offering Zoe bubbling wine in a carved crystal flute.

"Thanks."

"Your son is beautiful."

Nerves took a backseat to pride. "Yes, he is. The most beautiful thing in my life."

"That makes you a wealthy woman." Rowena touched a hand to her arm and smiled. "He and Bradley appear to be fast friends."

"They hit it off," Zoe agreed.

She didn't know what to think about it; it seemed so unlikely. Yet there they were, huddled together across the room, obviously in some deep discussion. The man in the elegant slate-gray suit and the boy in his dark brown one that was already—God—a smidgeon too small for him.

It seemed odd that Simon should be so easy with the man while she was so uneasy with him. She and her son were usually in tandem.

Then Brad glanced over and his eyes, nearly the exact color of his suit, met hers.

Oh, yeah, she thought, there was the reason. This was the only person of her and Simon's acquaintance who could have bats doing cartwheels in her stomach with just one look.

He was too handsome, he was too rich, he was too *everything*. Way, way out of your league, Zoe, and we've already been there once.

Bradley Charles Vane IV made James Marshall look like a yokel, in every possible way. The Vane fortune, built with lumber, spreading its commerce across the country with its top-rated HomeMakers chain of stores, made Brad a powerful and privileged man.

His looks—the dark gold hair, the sooty eyes and sorcerer's mouth—made him, in her opinion, a dangerous one. He had the toned, rangy build made for those designer suits. Long legs that she imagined could eat up ground quickly on his way out the door.

Plus, she found him unpredictable. He could be arrogant and cool one minute, hot and bossy the next, then surprisingly sweet.

She didn't trust a man she couldn't predict.

Yet she trusted him with Simon, so that was another puzzle. He would never hurt her boy. She was down to the gut certain of that. Nor could she deny that he was good with him, good to him.

Still, when Brad rose to walk toward her, every muscle in her body went tight.

"Doing okay?"

"I'm fine."

"So, you told Simon what was going on."

"He has a right to know. I—"

"You might want to stop the leap down my throat so I can tell you I agree with you. He not only has the right, but his mind's bright and agile enough to deal with it."

"Oh." She stared down into her glass. "Sorry. I'm a little nervous."

"Maybe it'll help to remember you're not in this alone."

As he spoke there was a commotion in the hall. An instant later, Moe, Flynn's big black disaster of a dog, bounded into the room. He gave a delighted bark, then charged toward the tray of canapes on a low table.

Flynn and Malory rushed in in his wake, followed by a laughing Rowena. There were shouts, more barks, and one unfortunate crash.

"In fact," Brad added as he watched the ensuing chaos, "you'll be lucky to find five minutes to be alone with this crew."

Two

IT TURNED OUT THAT ZOE WAS THE ONE WHO HAD TO pretend to eat. Not because of the food, but because she simply couldn't relax. It was difficult to swallow when your stomach was tied up in one hard and messy knot.

She'd eaten in this dining room before, with its soaring ceilings and roaring fire. She knew how lovely everything looked under the lights of the chandeliers and the glow of candles.

But this time she knew without a doubt the way the evening would end. It wouldn't be a matter of a lottery. It wouldn't be the luck of the draw, with her and Malory and Dana reaching into the carved box to see which one of them pulled out the disk with the emblem of the key inscribed on it.

Both Malory and Dana had taken their turns, and had succeeded, against what Zoe had come to realize were astronomical odds. They had found their keys. They'd triumphed, and two locks had been opened.

She'd helped them. She knew she'd contributed ideas, support, even comfort. But when push came to shove, she understood that the burden had been on each of them, in turn. In the end, both Malory and Dana had had to reach deep inside themselves every bit as much as they'd had to reach for the tangible key.

Now it was her burden, her risk. Her chance.

She had to be brave enough, smart enough, strong enough, or everything they'd done before her would be for nothing.

It was difficult to swallow even wonderfully prepared roast pork when that was stuck in her throat.

Conversation flowed around the table, as if it was just a normal dinner party with sociable friends. Malory and Flynn sat directly across from her. Malory had scooped her hair up and back so that the burnt-gold curls tumbled behind and left her girl-next-door face unframed. Her big blue eyes were full of excitement and laughter as she spoke about the work they were doing on Indulgence.

Every now and again Flynn would touch her—the back of her hand, her arm—in a casual glad-you're-here, glad-you're-mine kind of way that warmed Zoe's heart.

To keep her mind occupied with easier things, she decided she would have to talk him into letting her have a go at his hair. It was a great, rich brown with hints of chestnut, very full and thick. But with a few snips here and there, she could improve the cut and still leave him with that easy, tousled look that suited the lean lines of his face, the shape of those dark green eyes.

Letting her mind wander, she mentally clipped and styled her way around the table.

She jolted when Brad nudged her foot under the table. "What?"

"You're needed on this planet."

"I was just thinking, that's all."

"And not eating," he pointed out.

Annoyed, she stabbed a bite of pork. "Yes, I am."

Her voice was tight, her body stiff. He couldn't blame her.

But he thought he knew one sure way of loosening her up again. "Simon seems to be having the time of his life."

She glanced over. Rowena had placed Simon beside her, and even now they were holding what appeared to be an intense, almost intimate conversation while Simon plowed through the food on his plate.

There'd be no need for that stop at McDonald's, Zoe thought with a smile.

"He makes friends easily. Even with magic people."

"Magic people?" Brad repeated.

"That's how he thinks of them. He's taken all this in, and thinks it's cool."

"It is cool. Nothing much cooler for a kid than the battle between good and evil. A little more problematic for you."

She stabbed another slice of pork, moved it from one side of her plate to the other. "Malory and Dana did it. So can I."

"That's my take." He continued to eat as she frowned at him. "So, have you ordered the replacement windows for Indulgence yet?"

"Yesterday."

He nodded as if that were news to him. He didn't think she would care for the fact that he'd given instructions at HomeMakers that he was to be notified whenever she came in or placed an order. "Some of the trim's going to have to be replaced. I can swing by and help you with that."

"You don't have to bother. I can do it."

"I like to work with wood when I have a chance." He smiled easily, in a look that was casual, friend to friend. "It's in the blood. How about the lighting? Did you decide?"

He'd succeeded in distracting her, he noted. She might not have been thrilled to have been hooked into a conversation with him, but she wasn't thinking about the key right now. And she was eating.

He was crazy about her. Or maybe just plain crazy. It wasn't as if the lady gave him any encouragement. She'd been prickly and cold since the first time he'd met her, nearly two months ago. Except for the single time he'd managed to catch her off guard and kiss her.

Nothing cold or prickly about that interlude, Brad remembered, and hoped she'd been just as surprised and unnerved by the experience as he had been.

Even now, if he let himself, he could build a very entertaining fantasy about doing little more than pressing his lips to the base of that lovely, long neck.

Then there was the kid. Simon had been the big bonus prize in this particular box of Cracker Jacks. Fun, bright, interesting, the boy was a complete pleasure. Even if he hadn't been attracted to the mother, Brad would have spent time with the son.

The problem was, Simon was a lot more cooperative about spending time with him than Zoe was. So far. But Bradley Charles Vane IV had never given up on anything he wanted without a fight.

As he saw it, there were a number of battles about to be waged, and he intended to take an active part in all of them. He was here for her, and she'd just have to get used to it. He was here to help her. And he was here to have her.

Her brows drew together, and whatever she'd been saying about wiring and lighting systems dribbled to a halt. "Why are you looking at me like that?"

"Like what?"

She leaned toward him just a tad—away, Brad noted, from her son's sharp ears. "Like you're about to take a bite out of me instead of what's left of your scalloped potatoes."

He leaned toward her, close enough to see her flinch. "I am going to take a bite out of you, Zoe. Just not right here and now."

"I've got enough to think about without worrying about you."

"You'll have to make room." He laid a hand over hers before she could draw away. "And think about this. Flynn was part of Malory's quest. Jordan was part of Dana's. Do the math, Zoe. We're the only ones left."

"I'm really good at math." She tugged her hand free because the contact made her twitchy. "And the way I count it, I'm the one who's left."

"I guess we'll see who's better at adding and subtracting very soon."

He left it at that and finished his wine.

BACK IN THE PARLOR, where they found coffee and wedges of apple pie thick enough to make even Simon's eyes bug out, Malory rubbed a comforting hand up and down Zoe's back. "Are you ready for this?"

"I've got to be, don't I?"

"You've got us all with you. We're a good team."

"The best. It's just that I thought I'd be prepared. I've had the most time to get prepared. I didn't think I'd be this scared."

"It was easiest for me."

"How can you say that?" Baffled, Zoe shook her head. "You went into this knowing almost nothing."

"Exactly. And you've got everything we've learned and experienced in the last two months running around in your head." Her smile sympathetic, Malory gave Zoe's hand a squeeze. "Plenty of it's scary. And there's more. When we started this we weren't as involved. With each other, with Rowena and Pitte, with the daughters. Everything matters more now than it did two months ago."

Zoe let out a shaky breath. "You're not making me feel any better."

"I don't mean to. You've got a big load to carry, Zoe, and

sometimes you're going to have to carry it yourself, no matter how much we want to take some of it off your hands."

Malory looked up, pleased to see Dana coming toward them.

"What's up?" Dana asked.

"A quick pep talk before we get started." Malory took Zoe's hand again. "Kane will try to hurt you. He'll try to trick you. In fact—and I've thought a lot about this—because this is the last round, win or lose all, he's going to be only more determined to stop you."

Dana took Zoe's other hand. "Feeling peppy yet?"

"I've thought a lot about it, too. I'm afraid of him." Zoe squared her shoulders. "I think you're telling me I should be afraid. That if I'm really going to be prepared, I should be afraid."

"That's exactly it."

"Then I guess I'm as ready as I'm going to get. I need to talk to Rowena before she takes us into the portrait room. I've got one stipulation before we move to the next stage."

She looked over, hissed under her breath as she saw Rowena already in deep discussion with Brad. "Why is he everywhere I want to be?"

"Good question." Dana gave her a quick pat on the back.

Malory waited until Zoe started across the room. "Dana? I'm scared, too."

"Well, that makes three of us."

Zoe stopped in front of Rowena, cleared her throat. "I'm sorry to interrupt. Rowena, I need to speak to you for a minute, before we get started on the next ... thing."

"Of course. I imagine it concerns what Brad and I were just discussing."

"I don't think so. It's about Simon."

"Yes." In invitation, Rowena patted the cushion beside her. "Exactly. Bradley's been very insistent that I do something tangible, something specific, about Simon."

"Kane's not going to touch the boy." There was steel, cold and immovable, in Brad's tone. "He's not going to use the boy. Simon is to be taken out of the mix. That's not negotiable."

"And you are setting terms now for Zoe, and her son?" Rowena asked.

"No." Zoe spoke quickly. "I can speak for myself, and for Simon. But thank you." She looked at Brad. "Thank you for thinking about Simon."

"I'm not just thinking about him, I'm making this crystal clear. You and Pitte want the third key," he said to Rowena. "You want Zoe to succeed. Kane wants her to fail. There were rules, you said, about causing harm to mortals, shedding their blood, taking their lives. He broke those rules last time, and would have killed Dana and Jordan if he could have. There's no reason to think he'll go back to fighting fair this time. In fact, there's every reason to believe he'll fight even dirtier."

The muscles around Zoe's heart seemed to clench, leaving her breathless. "He's not touching my boy. You have to promise. You have to guarantee it, or this ends now."

"New terms." Rowena lifted her eyebrows. "And ultimatums?"

"Let's put it this way." Before Zoe could speak again, Brad silenced her with one sharp look. "If you don't do something to remove Simon from the board, if you don't shield him from Kane, he could be used against Zoe and cause her to fail. You're close, Rowena. Too close to let one stipulation stand in your way."

"Well played, Bradley." Rowena patted his knee. "Simon has a formidable champion in you. And you," she said to Zoe. "But it's already been done."

"What?" Zoe looked across the room at Simon, who was sneaking Moe a bit of crust from his pie.

"He's under protection, the strongest I can make. It was done while he slept, the night Dana found the second key. Mother," she said gently, touching a hand to Zoe's cheek, "I would not ask you to risk your child, not even for the daughters of a god."

"He's safe, then." She closed her eyes against the sting of relieved tears. "Kane can't hurt him?"

"As safe as I can make him. Kane would have to go through me, and Pitte. I can promise you, such an attack would cost him dearly."

"But if he got through—"

"Then he'd come up against us," Brad put in. "All six of us—and a big dog. Flynn and I talked about it earlier. You should take Moe with you, keep him around the way Dana did. An early-warning system."

"Take Moe? Home?" That big, clumsy dog in her tiny little house? "I'd think you'd consult with me before you made such decisions."

"It's a suggestion, not a decision." He angled his head, and though his voice was mild again, his face was set. "It's just a sensible and reasonable suggestion. Besides, a kid Simon's age ought to have a dog around."

"When I think Simon's ready for a dog—"

"Now, now." Swallowing a laugh, Rowena patted Brad's knee again, and Zoe's. "Isn't it silly to argue when you're both only thinking of what's best for Simon?"

"Can we just do what comes next? I'm getting all twisted up waiting for it to be official."

"All right. Perhaps Simon could take Moe out for a walk around the grounds. He'll be watched," she assured Zoe. "He'll be safe."

"Okay."

"I'll arrange it. Then we'll move into the next room."

Zoe found herself sitting on the sofa with Brad, without Rowena as a buffer between them. She linked her hands in her lap as he picked up his coffee cup.

"I'm sorry if I sounded ungrateful and rude," she began. "I'm not. Not ungrateful."

"Just rude?"

"Maybe." Knowing she had been brought heat to her cheeks. "But I didn't mean to be. I'm not used to anybody—"

"Helping you?" he prompted. "Caring about you? About Simon?"

There was a bite in his voice, but there was something both careless and cool about it that made her feel small. She countered it by shifting and looking him dead in the eyes. "That's right, I'm not. Nobody helped me raise him, or feed him, or love him. Nobody helped me put a roof over his head. I've done it myself, and I've done a decent job of it."

"You haven't done a decent job of it," he corrected. "You've done an extraordinary job of it. So what? That means you have to slap away every helping hand?"

"No. No, it doesn't. You get me so mixed up."

"Well, that's a start." He took her hand, and had it to his lips before she could protest. "For luck."

"Oh. Thanks." She got quickly to her feet when Rowena came back into the room.

"If everyone's ready, we'd like to continue the tradition of beginning the quest in the next room."

Brad kept his attention on Zoe. She was a little pale, but she was holding her own. Still, as they started down the wide hallway, he noted how Malory and Dana moved in to flank her.

They'd become a team, a triad, even a family over the last two months. He didn't think anything would change that now. They would need that unity through what was coming.

His heart took a bump when he stepped into the next room and looked up at the portrait that dominated it.

The Daughters of Glass, moments before their souls were

stolen, gathered close. Just as the three women who shared the faces of those tragic demigoddesses now gathered close.

Venora, with Malory's vivid blue eyes, sat with a lap harp in her hands and a smile just blooming across her face. Niniane, with Dana's strong features and dense brown hair, sat beside her on a marble bench and held a scroll and quill.

Standing, a sword at her side and a small puppy in the crook of her arm, Kyna looked back at him. Her hair was a long fall of inky black rather that the short, sharp, sexy style Zoe wore. But the eyes, those long, topaz eyes, were the same.

They pulled at him, as if they'd dug hooks into his heart.

The three daughters radiated beauty, joy, innocence, in a world sumptuous with color and light. Yet, a closer look showed the hints of darkness to come.

In the thick green forest was the shadowy shape of a man. Just slithering onto the bright tiles was the sinuous figure of a snake.

In the corner, the sky was bruised with a brewing storm that the daughters were yet unaware of. And the lovers who embraced in the background were too wrapped up in each other to sense the danger edging close to their charges.

To look closer yet was to see the three keys worked cleverly into the painting. One, disguised in the shape of a bird, seemed to fly through the cerulean sky. Another hid itself within the lush green leaves of the forest. And the third reflected deep in the pool behind the daughters who were sharing their last moment of peace and innocence.

He'd seen how they'd looked after the spell. White and still as death in the crystal coffins as Rowena had painted them.

He'd bought that painting, titled *After the Spell*, months before he'd even come back to the Valley or known of this guest and these women. Been compelled to buy it, he thought now, as he'd fallen in love, or into fascination or obsession—he wished to God he knew—with Zoe's face.

"Two keys are found," Rowena began. "Two locks are opened. Now there is but one." She moved to stand under the portrait as she spoke, with the fire snapping gold and red flames behind her.

"You agreed to this quest because you were curious, and you were each at a point where aspects of your life were unsettled and dissatisfying. And," she added, "because you were paid. But you've continued to quest because you're strong and you're true. No one else, not in three millennia, has come so far."

"You've learned the power of art," Pitte continued, and stepped over to join Rowena. "And the power of truth. The first two journeys bring you to the third."

"You have each other," she said to the women. "And you have your men. Together you make a chain. You must not let him break it." She stepped forward and spoke to Zoe as if they were alone in the room. "It is for you now. It was always for you to finish."

"For me?" Panic wanted to gush into her throat. "If that's true, why did we pick before? With Mal and Dana?"

"There must always be choice. Fate is the door, but you choose to walk through or turn away. Will you walk through?"

Zoe looked up at the portrait, and nodded.

"Then I'll give you your map, your clue to the key, and pray that it guides you." She walked over and took up a scroll.

"Beauty and truth," she read, "are lost without the courage to hold them. But one pair of hands can grip too hard, so that the precious slips through the fingers. Loss and pain, sorrow and will, blaze the rough path through the forest. Along the journey there is blood, and there is the death of innocence and the ghosts of what might have been.

"Each time the path forks, it is faith that chooses the way or doubt that blocks it. Is it despair, or will it be joy? Can there be fulfillment without risk of loss? Will it be an end, or a beginning? Will you move into the light, or return to the dark?

"There is one who stands on either side, with hands held out. Will you take one, the other, or close your hands in fists to hold what is already yours until it's ground to dust?

"Fear hunts, and its arrow strikes heart, mind, belly. Without tending, wounds fester, and scars too long ignored harden into shields that block the eyes from what needs most to be seen.

"Where does the goddess stand, her sword in hand, willing to fight each battle in its time? Willing, too, to lay down the sword when the time comes for peace. Find her, know her power, her faith, and her valiant heart. For when you look on her at last, you will have the key to free her. And you will find it on a path where no door will ever be locked against you."

"Oh, boy." Zoe pressed a hand to her stomach. "I can keep the paper, right? I'm never going to remember all that."

"Of course."

"Good." She worked hard to keep her voice calm and even. "It sounded a little ..."

"Violent," Dana put in.

"Yeah, that." Zoe felt better, considerably, when Dana's hand came to rest on her shoulder. "But, it seemed, compared to the others, that my clue was more a lot of questions."

Rowena held out the scroll. "Answer them," she said simply.

WHEN THEY WERE ALONE, Pitte stood beside Rowena, studying the portrait.

"He'll come after her quickly," Rowena said. "Won't he?"

"Yes. He's had more time to study her, to learn her weaknesses, to understand her fears and her needs. He'll use them against her."

"The boy is safe. Whatever we do, whatever it costs us, we must keep him so. He is a sweet boy, Pitte."

Hearing the pain, the longing in her voice, he drew her close.

"He'll be safe. Whatever the cost." He pressed his lips to the top of her head. "He won't touch the child."

She nodded and, turning her head, stared into the fire. "Will she trust, I wonder, as completely as I trust you? Can she, with all that has gone before, and all she has to risk?"

"Everything comes down to the courage of one woman." He tipped her head up, let his thumb graze her jawline. "If she has even a glimmer of yours, we will win this thing."

"She hasn't had you. She's had no one. They've all come to touch my heart, Pitte. I never expected to feel this ... " She laid her fingers to her breast. "Attachment. But she most of all, brave little mother, she touches me."

"Then trust in her, and her army. They are ... resourceful and clever. For mortals."

With that he made her laugh, and lifted her mood again. "Three thousand years among them, and still you find them a curiosity."

"Perhaps. But unlike Kane, I've learned to respect them—and never to underestimate a woman. Come." He swept her up in his arms. "Let's to bed."

LONG AFTER SHE'D PUT Simon to bed, Zoe found dozens of things to occupy her around the house. Long after Simon stopped whispering to the dog, long after Zoe heard Moe clamber up on the bed and Simon's desperately muffled laughter, she wandered around, looking for something to occupy her hands, her mind.

Her quest started at sunrise, and she was afraid she was going to be awake to see it, and the day, begin.

It was hardly her first sleepless night, she reminded herself. She had countless others to her credit. Nights Simon had been fussy, or sick. Nights she'd tossed and turned, worried about bills. Nights she'd filled with a dozen chores because the day simply hadn't been long enough to get them finished.

There had even been times she hadn't been able to sleep because she was too happy to close her eyes. Her first night in this house, she remembered, she'd spent hours walking around, touching the walls, looking out the windows, making plans for all the work she wanted to do on it, to make a home for Simon.

This was another big occasion, so there was no point in complaining about a few hours of lost sleep.

At midnight she was still too restless to settle, and decided to indulge in a long, hot shower—one that wouldn't be interrupted by a young boy wanting her attention.

She hung her best sleep shirt, a poppy red one, on the back of the door, then lit one of the jar candles she'd made herself so the room would fill with fragrance as well as steam.

Little rituals, she believed, set the tone for sleep.

She soothed herself with the pulse of water, and the silky feel of the peach blossom shower gel she was considering as stock for her salon. She would let the clue roll around in her head, she decided, try to see it as a whole first. Then as pieces of the puzzle. One piece was bound to lodge itself, and she would pursue that until . . . until the next, she thought.

Step by step, until she began to see the picture. A painting for Malory, a book for Dana. What did that leave for her? Shampoo and face cream? she wondered with a half laugh. Those were the kinds of things she knew. Those and what was important in a young boy's world. She knew how to make things, she considered. How to build or transform.

She was good with her hands, she reminded herself, and turned them under the water while she studied them. But what did any of that have to do with paths in a forest, or a goddess with a sword?

A journey, she thought as she turned off the water. That had to be a kind of symbol, as she'd never actually been anywhere. And that didn't look to be changing anytime soon.

Maybe it had to do with her coming to the Valley in the first place, or starting her business with Malory and Dana. Or, she mused as she toweled off, maybe it was just life.

Her life? The daughters' lives? It was something to work out, she decided as she smoothed peach-scented cream over her skin. Nothing all that interesting about her life, but nothing said it had to be. She recalled that Dana had taken specific words from her clue and worked with them. Maybe she would try that.

The goddess with the sword—that was easy enough. Kyna had the sword, and Kyna was hers. But that didn't explain how she was supposed to *know* her in order to find the key to free her.

With a shake of her head, Zoe turned, glanced at the steamy mirror over the sink.

Her hair was long, a spill of black over her shoulders that made her face look very, very pale. Her eyes were direct, intense, and golden. The mists, warm from the shower, drifted between Zoe and the glass, shimmered like a curtain as she lifted her hand to reach with fingers that trembled toward a reflection that wasn't her own.

For a moment, it seemed her fingers would pass through the curtain, through the glass, and touch flesh.

Then she was standing, alone, in a steamy bathroom, her fingers pressed to the streaked mirror. And staring at her own face.

Imagining things already, she thought, and let her hand fall. Projecting, that's what it was called. Trying to see herself in the young goddess, and just tired and worked up enough to think she could. Another angle to consider, she decided. In the morning when her mind was sharper.

She got into bed with her files, and went over her supply lists. For the salon, for the day spa she planned to attach to it. For the house itself.

She toyed with some new ideas, made some notes, tried to concentrate.

But the key and the clue kept winding back through her mind.

A forest. There were lots of forests in the Laurel Highlands of Pennsylvania. Did it mean a literal forest, like with trees, or was it a metaphor?

She wasn't good with metaphors.

Blood, what did the blood mean? Did it refer to Jordan's blood when he'd been hurt? Or was it someone else's? Was it hers?

She'd certainly had her cuts and scrapes over the years. She'd sliced her thumb once, when she was, what, eleven? Cutting tomatoes for sandwiches. Her brother and sister had been fighting, and one of them had bumped her.

The knife had cut right along the side of her thumb, from the tip past the knuckle, and the gash had bled like a fountain. She still had a scar, she mused, turning her thumb up to trace the faint line.

But the scar wasn't hard, and it certainly wasn't any kind of shield. So that probably wasn't it.

Pain and loss and blood and despair. Christ, why did her clue have to be so depressing?

She would just have to make the best of it, she decided, and picked up her notes again. She blinked when her vision started to blur, and slid into sleep with the light still burning.

She dreamed of her blood, dripping steadily on a dull brown linoleum floor while children screamed around her.

Three

SHE OVERSLEPT. ZOE COULDN'T REMEMBER THE LAST time she'd done that. Certainly not in the past decade. As a result, it was nearly ten by the time she arrived, boy and dog in tow, at Indulgence.

She parked on the street, as the driveway was already loaded. Flynn's car, Jordan's. And one of Brad's. He had two that she knew of, and probably more.

She managed to snag Moe's leash before he leaped out of the car, and with a mother's skill for juggling, grabbed her purse and her cooler, controlled the dog, and kept a sharp eye on her son as she loaded everything up.

"You keep a good hold of this dog," she told Simon as she passed him the leash. "You make him mind you. We have to find out what Flynn wants to do about him today."

"He can stay with me. We can fool around out back."

"We'll see. You go on, but stay where I can see you from the house until I get sorted out."

They bounded off while she walked toward the front door.

She loved to look at the place, the big old house with all its possibilities. They'd already put their mark on it, painting the front porch a bright, celebrational blue and arranging pots of mums to flank the front steps.

As soon as she got around to it, she was going to pick up some old pots at the flea market. Clean them up, paint them. Maybe she'd search out half a whiskey barrel as well, and they could plant seasonal flowers in it.

She glanced up at the window above the front door. Malory had hired a glass artist to create a stained-glass panel for that space, using the design from their logo.

That was just the sort of touch that was going to make their place unique.

She set the cooler down, opened the door.

She heard the music. It wasn't set up to blast, but it was close. Through it, she heard hammering, sawing, voices. The good noise of work in progress.

She stood absorbing it for a moment, looking up the stairs that neatly bisected the main level. Dana's bookstore on one side, and Malory's gallery on the other. With my salon over them, she thought. The communal kitchen in the back, then the nice little yard where one day, she hoped, they would set up tables where customers could sit and enjoy refreshments during good weather.

Though it would be weeks before Indulgence could open, it was already a dream come true for Zoe.

"Hey. Where's the rest of your crew?"

Zoe brought herself back and looked over to see Dana stroll into the little foyer. "Out in the back. I'm sorry I'm late."

"We've already docked your pay. Or we will, once we get a time clock. Jeez, lose the guilty look, Zoe. Nobody's set hours yet, especially on Saturday."

"I meant to be here an hour and a half ago," she said as she shrugged out of her coat, "but I slept late. I didn't get up until nearly eight."

"Eight!" Dana exclaimed in horror "Why, you lazy bitch!"

"I don't know how Simon kept that dog quiet—or vice versa—but when I got up they were in the backyard. By the time I made them presentable, got them breakfast, pulled myself together, I was way behind. Then I stopped by Flynn's, thinking I would drop Moe off, but nobody was home, which made Simon's day."

She let out a sigh. "Dana, I'm going to end up getting him a dog. I just know it."

Dana's dimples appeared in her cheeks as she grinned. "Sap."

"That's the God's truth. I didn't know everybody was coming over here today."

"Figured we'd give it a nice big Saturday push."

"That's good." Ready to dive in, Zoe strapped on her tool belt. "What are you up to?"

"I was up to putting the second coat of varnish on my floors, but Jordan claims I don't do it right. So he's putting it on, which leaves me painting the kitchen, as the unanimous opinion around here is that painting's all I'm good for."

"You're an excellent painter," Zoe said diplomatically.

"Hmm. Malory and Flynn were doing the varnish in her spot, but *she* claims *he* doesn't do it right, so he was sent upstairs to work with Brad."

"Upstairs? In my place? What's Bradley doing upstairs in my place?"

"I think he was . . . " Dana decided to save her breath as Zoe was already sprinting up to see for herself.

The walls of the salon area had already been painted by her own hand. They were a deep pink that edged toward purple. A rich color, she'd thought, a feminine one, but not so girly that a man would be put off by it.

For contrast, on the trim and for the counters she'd begun

to build, she was going to go with a bold green, then take these same colors, in softer hues, into her treatment areas.

The floors were already sanded and sealed—a chore she'd taken care of personally, then protected with drop cloths.

She had plans for displays, and had already picked out the fabric to make slipcovers for a secondhand couch and a couple of chairs she had on hold.

She'd decided on the lighting, on the treatment tables, even on the color of the towels she would use. Everything in her salon would have her touch, reflect her vision, and be created by her own two hands.

And there was Bradley Charles Vane IV busily sawing the board for one of her counter stations.

"What are you doing?"

Nobody heard her, of course. Not with Brad's saw buzzing, and Flynn's nail gun popping, and the damn music blaring.

She might as well not even be there. Well, she would fix that, right this minute.

She marched over until her shadow fell across the board and the template Brad was following. He glanced up, gave her a little head jerk to indicate she was in his light.

She stood her ground.

"I want to know what you're doing."

"Hold on a minute," he shouted right back at her, and finished running the blade through the board. He turned off the saw, shoved up his safety goggles.

"Your laminate came in."

"I want—my laminate?" The thrill of that had her spinning around in the direction he pointed. And there it was, that wonderful bold green. "It's perfect. I knew it would be perfect. It wasn't supposed to come in until next week."

"Got in early." He'd put a rush on it. "We ought to be able to have a couple of these done today."

"I don't expect you to—"

"Hi, Zo." Flynn set the nail gun down, grinned up at her. "What do you think?"

"I think it's really nice of you to pitch in this way. Give up your Saturday and all. But I can do this if you want to ... do something else."

"We've got a good start on it." He glanced past her. "Where are the big dog and the small boy?"

"They're out back. I didn't know what to do with them."

"Plenty of room to run around out there. I'll go check on them." Flynn got to his feet. "Want coffee when I come back?"

"Only if you didn't make it," Brad told him.

"Ingrate." Flynn gave Zoe a wink, then left them alone.

"I don't want you to—"

"You've got a good design," Brad interrupted. "For your stations. Neat and simple. It's easy to follow your plans, get a good sense of what you have in mind."

She folded her arms. "I didn't expect anybody would have to follow them."

"You do good work." He paused a beat while she stared at him. "Careful planning, good choices, a flair for design. Any reason why you have to do everything yourself?"

"No. You just shouldn't feel obligated, that's all."

He lifted an eyebrow. "Ingrate."

Defeated, she let out a half laugh. "Maybe it's more that I know what kind of work I do, but I don't know if you're any good." She walked around the base of the counter he was finishing for her. "I guess you do okay."

"My granddaddy'd be so proud to hear that."

With the wood between them, she gave him a quick, easy smile. "I want to cut the laminate myself. I just want to be able to ... "

"To look at it when it's finished, to look at it a year from when it's finished and say, Hey, I did that."

"Yes. That's it exactly. I didn't think you'd understand."

He shifted, stood hip-shot, and angled his head. "Do you know why I came back to the Valley?"

"I guess I don't. Not really."

"Ask me sometime. You want to get that nail gun? We'll knock this thing out."

SHE HAD TO ADMIT they worked well together, and he didn't, as she'd assumed he would, treat her as if she wasn't capable of handling tools. On the contrary, he took for granted that she was capable.

He did tend to be bossy about certain things. If she started to lift something he deemed too heavy, he snapped out an order for her to leave it be. And he insisted on going down himself to haul up her cooler.

But she overlooked it in the thrill of spreading the glue for the laminate on her first station.

Even with the windows open for ventilation, the fumes were strong.

"Good thing we're working in small sections," Brad commented. "If we were doing long stretches of this, without a fan in here, we'd be buzzed before we were finished."

"I got carried away redoing my kitchen counters at home a couple years ago. Got giddy as a Saturday night drunk and had to go outside and lie down on the grass."

He studied her face, noted that while she was a little flushed, beautifully so, her eyes were clear. "You start feeling it, let me know."

"I'm fine." She touched a fingertip to the glue. "Nearly done here."

"Too bad. I wouldn't mind seeing you giddy."

She shifted her gaze to his as she straightened up from the counter. "Plenty of fresh air in here."

"You're a little flushed, though." He stroked the side of his finger over her cheek. "You have the most incredible skin."

"It's, ah, like advertising." She didn't know if she'd been flushed before, but she could feel the heat rising now. "I use a lot of the products I'm going to carry. There's this wonderful serum. It's time release."

"Is that so?" His lips curved a little as he trailed that finger down her throat. "Seems to be working."

"I don't want to carry anything I don't believe in."

"What do you do with your mouth?"

At the question, it dropped open. "What?"

"What do you use? Your lips are soft." He rubbed the pad of his thumb over them. "Smooth. Tempting."

"There's a balm that I—don't do that."

"Do what?"

"Don't kiss me. I can't get mixed up this way. And we've got work."

"You're right about that. But work has to stop sometime. Glue's probably set up enough. You ready?"

She nodded. Fresh air or not, she was just a little light-headed now. And could put the cause of it solely on him. She imagined he knew it—knew just how those long, deep looks, those casually intimate touches affected a woman.

So she would just have to toughen up against them before they got her in trouble.

Together, they lifted the laminate. It was an exacting process, one that required teamwork and precision to create a smooth surface. Once glue hit glue, there was no turning back.

When it was down, the edges routed smooth, and the clamps tightened every few inches to hold it in place while it set hard, she stepped back.

Yes, it was right, she'd been right to curve the edges, to give it that subtle flow. Simple, practical, yet with a fluidity that gave it a touch of class.

The clients might not notice the details, but they would notice the effect.

"It's a good look," Brad said from beside her. "Smart to put the holes in for the cords of those gizmos you people use."

"They're called hair dryers and curling irons."

"Right. The way you've got it, the cords won't be dangling everywhere, tangling up. Gives you an uncluttered look."

"I want it to seem upscale but relaxed."

"Just what do you plan to do to people in the other rooms?"

"Oh, secret rituals." She gave an airy wave of her hand that made him smile. "And when I earn enough to pump some real money back into the place, I'm going to put a Swedish shower and a hydrotherapy tub in the bathroom. Turn it into a kind of water therapy space. But that's down the road. For now, I'm going to set up to build the second station."

SHE WORKED LIKE A Trojan, Brad thought. It was more than knowing what she wanted and how to get it, more even than a willingness to sweat to get it.

It was, under it all, a belief that she had to.

She stopped only to check on her son, to see that he was fed and safe.

By the time they were preparing the laminate for the second station, the others were packing up to call it a day.

Malory popped upstairs and fisted her hands on her hips. "Wow! Every time I walk around this place, there's something new. Zoe, this is looking great. The colors are just fabulous. This is the station, right?" She walked over to study the completed one. "I can't believe you built it."

"I had some help with that." Absently, she rolled her stiff

shoulders as she moved over to join Malory. "It really looks fabulous, doesn't it? I know I could have bought something for about the same cost, but it wouldn't have been exactly right. How's it coming downstairs?"

"Floors are done, kitchen's painted." As if she'd just remembered she was still wearing it, Malory tugged off the bright blue kerchief she used to protect her hair. "First coat's on the cabinets, and the appliances have been scrubbed to within an inch of their lives."

"I got so involved up here. I should've given you and Dana a hand with the kitchen."

"We had plenty of hands, thanks." She combed her fingers through her dark blond curls to fluff them. "We're all heading back to our place for some bucket chicken. You ready to pack it in?"

"Actually, I'd just like to finish this. Just send Simon up here, and we'll come by a little later."

"Why don't I take him with me? He's already outside fooling around with Flynn and Moe."

"Oh. Well. I don't—"

"He's fine, Zoe. Just come by when you're done. I'll try to save you a drumstick. You, too, Brad."

"Oh, you don't have to stay." As Zoe turned, Malory winked at Brad, then headed downstairs again.

"You want to finish this station."

"Yeah, but I didn't mean to put you on the spot."

"When you put me on the spot, I'll let you know. Ready to glue this up?"

To save time, she didn't argue.

The second station was finished and clamped, left to stand by the first while they picked up and put away tools. They left the windows open an inch.

Before she could do so herself, he picked up her cooler. "That should do it for today."

"I really appreciate the help. If you'd just leave that on the porch, I'm going to take a look at the floors, and the kitchen, and make sure everything's locked up before I head out."

"I'll wait. I'd like to see the work myself."

She started down the stairs, then stopped, turned around. "Are you looking out for me? Is that what this is? Because I can take care of myself."

He shifted the cooler. "Yes, I'm looking out for you. Though there's no doubt you're capable of taking care of yourself, and your son, your friends, and perfect strangers, should it be called for."

"If I'm so damn capable, then I don't need you looking out for me. So why are you?"

"I enjoy it. In addition I enjoy just looking at you, period, because you're a beautiful woman and I'm very attracted to you. Since you've shown no signs of being slow or stupid, I'm sure you're aware I'm attracted to you. But if there's any doubt in your mind, you could keep going down these damn stairs so I can set this cooler down and demonstrate."

"I asked a very simple question," she returned. "I didn't ask for a demonstration of anything."

She marched down the steps, and had just turned sharply toward the kitchen when she heard the thump of her cooler hitting the floor.

She didn't have time to react, not when her feet cleared the floor, then slapped down again as she was spun around and pushed back against the wall.

She caught the temper in his eyes, turning them hot and almost black. It brought an equally hot tickle to her throat that was both fear and anger and just enough arousal to confuse the mix.

"Take care of yourself," he challenged. "Then we'll move on to the demonstration."

She stared into his eyes, waiting until he'd eased in just a little more. Then she brought her knee up between his legs, lightning swift, and stopped a hairbreath from doing serious damage.

He flinched, and she found it immensely satisfying.

"Okay. First let me commend you on your really exquisite control." He didn't move. They both understood it would take only one quick jerk to drop him to his knees. "Second, let me thank you, sincerely, for using it in this case."

"I'm not some helpless hick."

"I never thought of you as either helpless or a hick." Abruptly, the situation, and his position in it, struck him as ridiculously funny. He started to grin, then to laugh until he simply lowered his forehead to hers. "I don't know how you manage to piss me off, but you do."

He gentled his grip on her shoulders, then released her to brace his hands on the wall on either side of her head. "Would you mind lowering that knee? At least a few inches. It's making me nervous."

"That's the idea." But she complied. "I don't know why this is funny."

"Neither do I. Jesus, Zoe, you wind me up, one way or the other. Tell me something. Am I not supposed to find you beautiful? Am I not supposed to be attracted to you?"

"How am I supposed to answer that?"

"It's a puzzler, isn't it?" His gaze skimmed over her face, down to her mouth. "Try thinking about it from my end."

"Move back some." Because the breath was backing up in her lungs, she tapped her fingers against his chest. "I can't talk to you like this."

"Okay. Just one second." He brushed his lips over hers in a kind of whispered promise that had her stomach fluttering.

Then he stepped back.

"It'd be easy to let you." Not sure if she was steady yet, she stayed leaning against the wall. "To let myself. I've got needs, normal needs, just like anyone. And I haven't been with a man in over a year—going on two."

"I don't care if you were with a man yesterday. I'm interested in now."

"Well, I haven't been. There are reasons for that."

"Simon."

She nodded. "He's the big reason. I'm not going to let any man into my life that I wouldn't let into his."

"You know I wouldn't hurt him." Temper began to edge back. "It's goddamn insulting for you to imply that I would."

"I know you wouldn't, so there's no point in you getting fired up over that. But I'm a reason, too, and I've got a right to be careful with myself. You're not looking to hold my hand or give me a couple of sweet kisses in the moonlight, Bradley."

"It'd be a start."

"That's not where it would end, and we both know it. I don't see the point in starting something if I don't know I can finish it. I don't know if going to bed with you is going to be good for me. I don't know if going to bed with you, if you wanting me to, is because of those normal needs or because of what's going on around us."

"You think I'm attracted to you because of the key?"

"What if you are?" She lifted her hands, palms up. "How would you feel about being used that way? The fact is, Bradley, you and I wouldn't be here if it wasn't for the key. We don't come from the same place. And I don't mean the Valley."

"No."

"We don't have anything in common, except for the key."

"The key," he agreed. "Friends who matter to both of us, a place that holds my roots and where you've set yours. A need to build something for ourselves. Then there's a young boy. He

45

happens to belong to you, but he's hooked me. With or without you, he'd have hooked me. Do you get that?"

She could only nod.

"There's more, but let's just toss in the sexual chemistry for now. Add all that up, it seems like some fairly solid common ground."

"I don't know what to say to you half the time, or how to say it."

"Maybe you shouldn't think about it so hard." He held out a hand. "Let's go look at the kitchen. If we don't get out of here soon, there's not going to be anything left in that chicken bucket but crumbs."

SHE WAS GRATEFUL HE'D let the subject drop. She just couldn't separate her thoughts and feelings, her concerns and her needs into separate areas. Not right now.

She was grateful, too, that the time she'd spent at Flynn's had involved fried chicken and relaxation without focusing on the key.

She had nothing to offer yet, and there was too much information, too many questions, circling around in her mind to line up in an intelligent conversation.

They would need to have a meeting soon, all of them, but she wanted a little time to sort through everything first.

Both Malory and Dana had come up with theories quickly. Those theories had been refined and re-angled and changed over the four weeks, but they'd formed a foundation.

And, Zoe thought, she had nothing.

So she would spend the evening going over the clue, all of their notes, taking herself back, step by step, through the first two quests. Somewhere in there were answers.

Once Simon and Moe were settled down and the house blessedly quiet, she sat at her kitchen table. Notes, files, books were arranged in piles. She'd decided she'd gone over her coffee quota for the day, so she brewed a pot of tea.

Sipping the first cup, she read over the clue again and wrote down on a fresh page of her notebook what she thought might be important words.

Beauty, truth, courage

Loss, sorrow

Forest

Path

Journey

Blood and death

Ghosts

Faith

Fear

Goddess

Valiant

She was probably missing some, but the list gave her a start. Beauty for Malory, truth for Dana. Courage for herself.

Loss and sorrow. Hers, or did it refer to the daughters? If she took it personally for this round, what was her loss, what was her sorrow? Most recently, she'd lost her job, Zoe mused and jotted that down. But that had turned out to be an opportunity.

Forests? They were plentiful, but some meant more to her than others. There were woods at Warrior's Peak. There were woods back home, where she'd grown up. There were woods along the river by Brad's house. But if forest was symbolic, it could mean not seeing it for the trees. Not seeing the overall scope of something because you were too busy worrying about the individual details.

She did that sometimes, that was true. But, God, there were so many details, and who was going to worry about them if she didn't?

She had a parent-teacher meeting coming up. Simon needed new shoes and a new winter coat. The washing machine was starting to make grinding noises, and she hadn't gotten around to cleaning out her gutters.

She needed to buy the towels for the salon *and* spring for a new washer and dryer over there. Which meant the one at home would have to grind for a while.

She rested her head on her fisted hand, closed her eyes for just a minute.

She would get it all done; that was her job. But one of these days, she was going to stretch out in the shade for an entire afternoon with nothing but a book and a pitcher of ice-cold lemonade.

The hammock swung, gentle as a cradle, and the book lay, neglected and unread, on her belly. The taste of tart lemonade was still on her tongue.

Her eyes were closed behind shaded glasses, and she could feel the breeze blowing sweetly over her face.

She didn't know the last time she'd been so relaxed. Mind and body totally at rest. There was nothing to do but bask in the quiet and peace.

She drifted along with a sigh of perfect contentment.

And was standing in the trailer, sweating in the vicious heat. It was like living in a can, she thought as she swept shorn hair into a pile on the floor.

She could hear her brother and younger sister arguing, their voices spilling through the stingy windows. High and tight and angry. Everyone always seemed so angry here.

It made her head pound, viciously.

Moving to the door, she shoved it open to shout out to them.

Be quiet! For God's sake, be quiet for five damn minutes and give me some peace.

And found herself wandering in a forest, with winter snow thick under her feet. Wind screamed through the pines, whipped the branches toward a sky the color of stone.

She was cold, and lost and afraid.

As she began to trudge, hunched into herself against the blizzard, she wrapped an arm under her swollen belly to anchor the baby.

He was so heavy, and she was so tired.

She wanted to stop, to rest. What was the point, what was the use? She would never find her way out.

Pain vised her belly, doubled her over in shock. She felt a gush between her legs, and stared down in horror at the blood spilling onto the snow.

Terrified, she opened her mouth to scream, and found herself back in the hammock, in the shade, tasting lemonade again.

Choose.

She bolted up from her own kitchen table, shivering while Moe stood beside her snarling at thin air.

Four

IT WAS TRICKIER THAN ZOE HAD EXPECTED TO TALK Simon into spending the day with one of his school friends instead of coming with her to work at Indulgence.

He *liked* hanging out with the guys. He wanted to play with Moe. He could help with stuff. He wouldn't get in the way.

In the end she fell back on the most successful parental ploy of all. Bribery. They would stop by the video store on the way and rent two games and a movie.

When it turned out that Moe was welcome to join the play date and romp in the backyard with young Chuck's yellow lab, Simon wasn't only satisfied, he was in heaven.

It alleviated a big chunk of the guilt, and the worry, and gave Zoe the opportunity to explore her first theory.

If the journey in the clue was hers, and the forest a kind of symbol, maybe it referred to her life in the Valley. The paths she'd taken in the place she'd made her home.

She'd been drawn here, to this pretty little valley town, and had known it was her place the moment she'd driven through it nearly four years earlier.

She'd had to work, to struggle, to sacrifice to find the joy and the fulfillment. She'd had to choose her paths, her directions, her destinations.

She reacquainted herself with them now, driving along the streets she knew so well. Quiet streets, she thought, on this early Sunday morning. She cruised the neighborhoods, as she had years before when her mind had been set on finding a house for herself and Simon. She'd done that first, she remembered, to give herself time to find the rhythm of the town, to see how the houses struck her, how the people made her feel as she watched them walk or drive.

It had been spring, late spring. She'd admired the gardens, the yards, the settled feel of the place.

She'd spotted the For Sale sign on the scrubby lawn in front of the little brown house. And with a kind of inner click of recognition, she'd known it was the one. She stopped at the curb, as she had then, studied what was hers while trying to see it as it had been.

The houses on either side of it were small, too, but well tended. Nice trees offering shade. There'd been a young girl riding a bike along the sidewalk, and a teenage boy down the block, washing his car while music blasted.

She recalled the thrill of anticipation that had bubbled through her as she'd jotted down the name and number of the realtor on the For Sale sign.

And that's where she'd gone next. So she followed the same route now. The asking price had been too high, but that hadn't discouraged her. She'd known she probably looked like a mark, in her inexpensive shoes and clothes. She probably sounded like one, with that hint of rural West Virginia in her voice.

But she hadn't been a mark, Zoe thought with satisfaction.

She parked, as she had parked then, and got out to walk.

She'd made an appointment to see the house—one she would, shortly, bargain fiercely for—and had walked along this downtown street and straight into the beauty salon to see if they were hiring.

The real estate office was closed for Sunday, as was the salon, but she walked to both, seeing herself as she had been. Full of nerves and excitement, but putting on a cool front, she remembered. She'd bagged the job—maybe quicker, maybe easier than she should have, she thought now. Another one of those things that were meant to be? Or had it just been a matter of taking the right path at the right time?

Better than three years she'd put into that salon, Zoe mused as she stood outside the display window with her hands on her hips. She'd done good work there. Better work than the bitchy owner, Carly. Which had been part of the problem.

Too many of the customers had begun to request Zoe specifically, and her tips had been solid. Carly hadn't liked that, hadn't liked having one of her operators take the spotlight in her own place. So she'd begun to make things difficult—cutting Zoe's hours here, or loading them on there. Complaining that she talked to the customers too much, or didn't talk enough. Anything that would demoralize or scrape away at her pride.

She'd tolerated it, hadn't fought back. Should she have? she wondered. She'd needed the job, the steady clientele and the pay, the tips. If she'd stood up for herself, she'd have been fired all the sooner.

Still, it was demoralizing to realize how much crap she'd put up with for a lousy pay stub.

No. She took a deep breath and pulled back the anger and the shame. No, she had put up with it for her home, her son, her life. It wasn't a battle she could have won. In the end she'd been fired in any case. But it had been the time for her to be fired, to be at one of those crossroads.

And hadn't that anger, that shame, that sense of despair, even panic, when she'd walked out of Carly's for the last time, pushed her toward Indulgence? Would she have begun to build her own as long as she'd been drawing a salary, as long as the bills were being paid and the house was secure?

No, she admitted. She would have dreamed it, but she wouldn't have done it. She wouldn't have found the courage. It had taken a kick in the ass for her to risk the next path.

She turned away, stared out at the town she'd come to know as well as her own living room. That way to the grocery store, turn there toward the post office, head left and past the little park, hang a right toward Simon's school.

Up the block to the Main Street Diner and the milk shakes Simon loved. Straight out of town and up the mountain road to Warrior's Peak.

She could find her way from here, blindfolded, to Dana's apartment, to the house where Flynn and Malory lived. To the library, the newspaper, the drugstore, the pizza parlor.

She could follow the river to Bradley's.

Different paths, she thought, walking back to her car. Different choices, different destinations. But they were all part of the whole. All, now, part of her.

If the key was here, somewhere in what was her home, she would find it.

She got in the car and took a winding path, the long way around, to Indulgence.

ZOE SAID NOTHING TO her friends through the morning. She needed to work first, not only physically but mentally, to sort through her theory and to decipher exactly what had happened to her the night before.

She couldn't talk about it until she had it all straight in her head. And it was, she admitted, a different sort of dynamic when the men were around. There were things she could say, and a way she could say them when it was just Malory and Dana that didn't fit the same way when you added men.

Even men she'd come to trust.

She left Brad to the carpentry, and spent her Sunday morning regrouting bathroom tiles. It was the kind of work that left her mind free to tinker with what had happened to her, and what it might mean.

Was it odd that her experience hadn't been like what had happened with Malory or Dana on their first encounters with Kane? Or was it significant?

Choose, he'd told her. That, at least, followed the pattern. Each one of them had had to make a choice. And apparently the risk increased with each key.

He hadn't really hurt her. There'd been that moment of pain in the blizzard, but she'd had worse. Why had he shown her three different scenes, barely giving her time to settle into one illusion before tossing her into the next?

The first had been a harmless little fantasy, hardly anything huge and life-changing. The second, more tedious and familiar, and the third . . .

The third, she thought as she spread grout on the floor, was scary. To frighten her. You're lost, you're alone, you're pregnant.

Been there, she reflected.

Then the pain, the blood. Like a miscarriage, she realized. Losing the baby. But she hadn't lost her baby, and he was protected.

What if Kane didn't know? Struck, she sat back on her haunches. What if he didn't know Simon was protected? Wouldn't his first threat to her revolve around the most precious thing in her life, the one thing she would die to keep safe?

"Zoe."

The sponge she'd been using to spread the grout fell on the tiles with a plop.

"Sorry. Didn't mean to startle you." Brad stayed in the doorway, one shoulder resting on the jamb. As he'd been standing for the last several minutes, watching her.

A lot going on inside that head, he knew. He'd seen all of it run over her face.

"No, that's okay." She bent back to the work. "I'm nearly finished here."

"The rest of the crew's about to break for lunch."

"Okay. I'll be down as soon as I'm done. It'll give the grout a chance to dry."

He waited until she'd worked her way over, was half in, half out of the doorway. Then he crouched. "Are you going to tell me what happened?"

Her hand hesitated, then picked up the rhythm again. "What do you mean?"

"I've spent enough time looking at you to know when something's going on inside. Tell me what happened since yesterday, Zoe."

"I will." She put the sponge in the bucket she'd set just outside the room. "But not just you."

"Did he hurt you?" He grabbed her hand, used his free one to tilt her face around.

"No. Let go. My hands are all covered with grout."

"But he did something." His tone had chilled, the way it did when he was chaining down temper. "Why haven't you said anything?"

"I just wanted some time to think about it, work some of it out, that's all. It'll be easier for me to tell everybody about it all at once." His hand was still cupping her cheek. And his face was very close. "It'd be easier for me, too, if you wouldn't touch me that way right now."

"Right now?" He trailed his fingers back to the nape of her neck. "Or ever?"

She wanted to stretch into that hand and purr. "Let's start with now."

She started to push to her feet, but he was already up, her hand still caught in his as he drew her up beside him. "Just tell me this—Simon's okay?"

She could fight attraction. She could even fight the sexual buzz. But she was going to have a very hard time fighting his obvious and deep concern for her son.

"Yes. He's fine. He really wanted to come today. He likes being with you—with all of you," she added quickly. "But I didn't want to talk about this in front of him. At least, not yet."

"Then let's go down and talk about it, and I'll come by and see him later this week."

"You don't have to—"

"I like being with him, too. With both of you." He brushed the side of her throat, her shoulder. "Maybe you could invite me to dinner again."

"Well, I . . . "

"Tomorrow. How about tomorrow?"

"Tomorrow? We're just having spaghetti."

"Great. I'll bring some wine." Obviously considering the matter settled, he tugged her out of the doorway. "We'd better go down and clean up."

She wasn't sure when she'd lost her footing, or why it seemed so impossible to refuse. He'd boxed her in, Zoe realized as she scrubbed up for lunch. There was no question about that, but he'd done it so neatly the lid was on before she'd seen it coming.

Besides, that was tomorrow. She had enough to worry about today without getting worked up about a plate of spaghetti.

It might have been a work in progress, but the kitchen was the best gathering place. A sheet of plywood on two sawhorses served as a table, and there were buckets and ladders for chairs.

Dana scooted a bucket over to her. "Is that peanut butter and jelly?" she demanded, eyeing the sandwich Zoe had unwrapped. "Chunky peanut butter and grape jelly?"

"Yeah." Zoe started to lift one of the triangular halves to her mouth, and noted Dana practically salivating for it. "You want it?"

"It's been much too long since I had a good pb and j. Half of yours for half my ham and swiss on rye."

They made the exchange, then Dana took a test bite. "Excellent," she said around a mouthful. "Nobody makes these like a mom. So, are you going to tell us what's going on, or do you want to eat first?"

Zoe glanced up, then shifted her gaze around the room. Everyone was watching her. Waiting. "Am I wearing a sign?"

"Might as well be." Malory dipped a spoon into her carton of yogurt. "You looked upset when you came in this morning, but more like you were trying not to look upset. Then you shot straight upstairs. Plus you haven't said anything about how the kitchen looks now that it's painted."

"It looks great. I meant to tell you." Never easy with being the center of attention, Zoe tore her half sandwich in two. "And I wanted to wait until everybody was taking a break before telling you what happened last night."

"We're taking a break now." Dana rubbed a hand over Zoe's thigh. "What gives?"

She took her time in the telling, wanting to make it clear, wanting to be sure she didn't leave out any details. "It was different than it was with you. With everybody here who's had an experience with Kane. Even different than what happened to us here in the house, the first month."

"Did you know it was him?" Jordan asked her.

"That's the thing. I never stayed in any one of the three ... places"—she supposed she should call them that—"long enough

57

to feel it. And I don't think I pulled myself out, the way some of you were able to. There wasn't time for that. It was more like being somewhere, then closing your eyes for a second and being somewhere else."

"Let's take them one at a time." Flynn had already pulled out a notebook. "Swinging in a hammock." He tapped the page. "Were you in your yard?"

"No. I don't have a hammock. I've never actually lain around in a hammock in the shade with a pitcher of lemonade and a book. Who has the time? It'd be nice, and I was thinking about not having much breathing room over the next few weeks, then, pop, I'm swinging in a hammock and drinking lemonade."

She frowned, and didn't notice the narrowed look from Brad. "I don't know where I was. I don't think it mattered, that's what I've figured out thinking it over. It didn't matter where the stupid hammock was, it was just symbolic of having nothing to do for an afternoon. Or, I guess, as long as I wanted to have nothing to do."

"I think you're right," Malory agreed. "He clicks into fantasies, lets us get a look at them, experience them. Mine, being an artist and married to Flynn. The perfect house, the perfect life." She gestured across the table. "Dana's, being alone on a tropical island without a care in the world. And for you, a lazy afternoon."

"Pretty pitiful fantasy, compared to yours." But Zoe smiled, relieved that her conclusion seemed valid.

"But he yanked you out of it, instead of giving you time to wallow," Jordan pointed out. "Maybe he didn't want to give you the chance to see it as false. Just give you a quick taste, then move on. A new strategy."

"I think that's part of it. But, well, take the second part. That was my mother's trailer, and God knows I swept up plenty in there. I recognized the way it looked, smelled, the way my brother and sister were arguing outside. But I don't know how old I was. Was I the way I am now? Was I a kid? Somewhere between?"

Thoughtfully, she shook her head. "What I mean is, I didn't get a sense of myself, just the heat and the fatigue and the annoyance of it all. I just felt like this is all I ever do, clean up around this place, mind the children, and I'm so tired of it. I felt, you could say, particularly put upon and bitchy. I think it's sort of symbolic, too."

"Being trapped in a loop," Brad supplied. "Always doing what needs to be done, and for somebody else, and never seeing an end to it."

"Yes. Mama did her best, and she needed me to help out. But you get to feeling trapped. You get so you feel it's not going to get any better, no matter what you do."

"So you can lie around in a hammock and enjoy life, or you can sweat and run the same loop over and over." Dana pursed her lips as she considered. "But those aren't the only choices. It's not that cut and dried. You've proven that yourself."

"Some people might look at my life and think I'm just running a different loop now. I don't feel like that, but it could seem that way. Then there's the third part."

"He wanted to scare you," Malory said.

"Oh, yeah, and boy, mission accomplished. It was cold, and I was alone. It wasn't one of those pretty wonderland snows. It was vicious and mean, the kind that kills you. And I was so tired, the baby so heavy inside me. I just wanted to lie down somewhere and rest, but I knew I couldn't. I'd die if I did, and if I died, the baby died."

Unconsciously, she pressed a hand to her belly, as if to protect what had lived there.

"Then the contractions. I knew what they were, you remember

that pretty quick. But this was meaner, it wasn't progress. The way labor pains are. It was an ending, an ending with all that blood on the snow."

"He wanted to threaten you, through Simon." Flynn's face hardened. "It's not going to happen. We're not going to let him."

"I think that's part of it. Trying to scare me, using Simon to do it. And I think that's one of the reasons he yanked me out of the last one, too, and told me to choose. I can tell you, as soon as I came back, saw Moe standing there growling, I was up and in Simon's room like a shot."

And shaking like a leaf, she remembered now. "But he was just all sprawled out the way he gets, one leg hanging off the bed and the blankets all wrapped around the other. I swear, that boy can't be still even when he's sleeping."

"He was using Simon as another symbol." Brad poured coffee, and since she hadn't taken any for herself as yet, handed a mug to her.

Her gaze met his as she nodded, as the fear fluttered at the base of her throat. "That's what I worked out of it, too."

"A symbol for what?" Dana demanded. "Her life?"

"Her life, yeah," Brad replied. "And her soul. Choose. Comfort, tedium, or the loss of everything she is. He threw down the gauntlet."

"He did. But I think—I wonder if he doesn't know Simon's safe. Maybe he can't see that he's protected and that it won't do him any good to try to threaten me that way."

"You could be right. But," Brad continued, "I'd say he'll find out soon enough, then look for something else to use on you."

"As long as it's not my baby. Anyway, what happened made me think harder about the clue. It pissed me off," she said with a quick laugh. "So I spent more time trying to work it out. I had this idea that maybe the Valley's like my forest. The different things I've done or selected are like the paths."

"Not bad," Dana told her.

"It was something to work on. I took an hour early this morning and drove around, sort of tripping down memory lane. Trying to see it the way I did when I first came, and track how things changed for me."

"Or how you changed them," Brad put in.

"Yes." Pleased, she gave him one of her rare smiles. "I don't know if it's the right direction, but I'm putting together places and, well, events, I guess, that seem important to me personally. If I gather them up in my head maybe one will stand out. If I start heading the right way, it seems to me Kane won't like it. Then I'll know."

IT WAS HARD TO imagine herself in a pitched battle with anyone, much less a sorcerer. But she wasn't going to back down at the first punch. If there was one thing she knew how to do, Zoe determined, it was how to stick it out.

Maybe she wouldn't find the key, but it wouldn't be because she hadn't looked.

She spent Sunday evening plowing through notes, scanning the books they'd collected on Celtic myths, and tiptoeing her way around the Internet on the laptop Flynn lent her.

She didn't know if she learned anything new, but the exercise helped line up what she did know.

The key, wherever it was, would be personal to her. It would relate to her life, or to what she wanted out of life. And in the end, it would come down to a choice. Though her friends, one or all of them, might be connected to it, she would be the only one able to make the choice.

So what did she want? Zoe asked herself as she prepared for bed. An afternoon in a hammock? Sometimes it was just as simple as that. To know she'd shoved her way out of the door of that trailer and moved on? No question about that. And that she'd found her way out of that terrifying forest, and given her child not only life but a good life.

She needed to know those things, and to know that she would keep building that life for Simon, and herself. She needed Indulgence to be a success. That was partly pride.

Her mother had always said she was too proud.

Maybe she had been, and maybe that pride had made things harder than they might have been. But it had also carried her through the hard times.

She hadn't gotten everything she'd dreamed of, but what she had would do just fine.

She turned off the light. If there was a pang that there was no one there, in the dark, she could turn to, there was the satisfaction, even the pride, of knowing she could always rely on herself.

SHE WAS WORKING UPSTAIRS at Indulgence the next day, screwing the hardware onto her completed stations, when she heard the shouts from below. Excited shouts, she noted immediately, not distressed ones. So she finished the station she was working on before going down to see what was causing the commotion.

Following the voices, she walked into Dana's section, then let out a shout of her own when she saw the book display rack lining one wall and the two huge cartons in the middle of the floor.

"They came! Your shelves came. Oh, they look great. You were right to go with these. They look so good with your colors."

"They do, don't they? I've got the diagram I worked out, the one I changed six dozen times. But I'm wondering if I should switch the kids' section with the nonfiction."

"Why don't we just open the next one, put it where you have it planned, then see?" Malory wielded her box cutter.

The deliveryman wheeled in the next carton. "Lady, where do you want this one?"

"Oh, God," was all Dana could manage.

"Just leave it here," Zoe told him. "We'll figure it out. How many did you get?" she asked Dana.

"A lot. Maybe too many, but I wanted to be sure I could showcase everything the way I had in my head. But now . . . Jesus, my heart's pounding. Is it excitement? Is it terror? You be the judge."

"It's excitement." Gleefully, Malory ripped open another carton. "Come on, let's get this one set up, too. Let's get them all set up, then you'll see how wonderful it is."

"It's real," Dana murmured as yet another carton was wheeled in. "It's really real. It's not just going to be empty rooms now."

"Shelves, books, tables, chairs." Zoe tore cardboard away. "In a few weeks we'll sit down in here and have our first cup of tea."

"Yeah." Bracing herself, Dana helped them move the next section into place. "Then we'll wander over and admire all the pretty things in Malory's gallery."

"And finish it off with a tour of Zoe's salon." Malory stepped back. "Look what we've done already. Can you get over what we've done?"

Zoe looked at the next carton to come in. "Right now, I can't get over what we're about to do. Get that box cutter going, Mal. We've got work to do."

They were still carrying bookcases when the next delivery truck pulled up.

"It's from HomeMakers." Malory looked back at them from the window. "Are we expecting a delivery from HomeMakers today?"

"We've got some things on order," Zoe told her. "I didn't think any of it was in yet. I'll go check."

She went to the front door and met the driver on the porch. "This Indulgence?" he asked her.

Hearing someone else say the name made her feel so good inside. "It will be."

"Got some windows on the truck." He handed her the invoice

to check. "Got a list here, which one's we're replacing. If that's right, we'll get started. We'll have them in for you today."

"In? We didn't order installation, just the windows."

"Installation comes along with them. Got a note here." He dug into his pocket. "From Mr. Vane for a Ms. McCourt."

"I'm Ms. McCourt." Frowning, she took the envelope, ripped it open. Inside was a single sheet of letterhead, with a single line of message.

Don't argue.

She opened her mouth, shut it again, then looked back at the driver. She saw two other men now, getting out of the truck to lean against the hood.

"Mr. Vane, he said you should give him a call if there was any trouble with this. You want us to get started, or you want us to wait?"

"No. No, go ahead and get started. Thank you."

She walked back inside, rubbing the back of her neck as she watched Dana and Malory set another section in place. "The replacement windows are here."

"That's great. Maybe we should angle this," Dana suggested.

"There's a crew here to install them," Zoe continued. "Bradley—HomeMakers—included installation."

"Brad's such a sweetie," Malory commented.

"Pays to know the owner." Dana stepped back, shook her head. "No, let's keep this one flush."

Unsettled, Zoe nudged a sheet of cardboard with her toe. "Don't you think we should pay for it?"

"Gift horse, Zoe." Huffing a bit, Dana muscled the shelf into position. "I'd rather kiss it on the lips than look it in the mouth." She glanced back, added a quick leer. "Of course, this particular horse would rather you be the one giving out the smoochies."

"He's coming to dinner tonight."

"Good. Give him a big, wet one."

"I'm afraid."

Malory set the box cutter aside. "Of Brad?"

"Yes. Of him, of me." She rubbed a fist between her breasts as if something inside ached a little. "Of what's going to happen."

"Oh, honey."

"I don't know what to do, or what to think. It's one thing if it's just for the fun, the excitement. But I'm not looking for fun and excitement. Not this kind."

"You think he is?"

"I don't know. Well, I mean, sure he is. He's a guy. I don't hold that against him. And I think maybe he's caught up in the romance of the whole thing. How we're supposed to link up and slay the dragon. But see, I have to think about what happens after that."

"He isn't careless with people, if that's what you're worried about." Serious now, Dana shook her head. "I've known him most of my life. He's a good man, Zoe."

"I think he is. I can see that he is. But he's not my man, and he's not likely to be. Still, if he keeps on the way he is, he's going to wear me down. I'm afraid, if that happens, I'm going to start wishing for something I can't have."

"I don't think there is anything you can't have," Malory told her. "We wouldn't have this place if it wasn't for you."

"That's silly. Just because I found the house—"

"Not just the house, Zoe. The idea, the vision, the faith." Impatient, Malory laid a hand on Zoe's shoulder, gave it a little shake. "You started this. So I think when you figure out what you really want, you'll figure out the way to get it."

To keep her hands busy, Zoe picked up the box cutter and started on the next carton. "Were you ever in love, really in love, before Flynn?"

"No. I've been in lust. Experienced infatuation, had some very heavy like. But I've never loved anyone the way I love Flynn."

Zoe nodded. "And it was always Jordan for you, Dana."

"Whether I wanted it to be or not, yeah."

"I've been in love." She spoke quietly as she worked. "I loved Simon's father. I loved him with everything I had. Maybe some people think you don't have a whole lot when you're sixteen, but I had so much love to give. I gave him all of it. I didn't think, I didn't hesitate, I just gave it."

She pulled the cardboard away, let it drop to the floor. "I've known men since. Some good men, some who didn't turn out to be so good. But none of them ever came close to touching me the way that boy did when I was sixteen. I wanted him, Mal, almost more than I wanted to live."

"He didn't stick by you," she replied.

"No, he didn't. He did love me, I believe that, but not enough to stick by me. Not enough to make the choice to be with me, or even to acknowledge what we'd made between us. He just walked away and went back to living his life, while mine was torn to pieces."

To vent some of that old, old anger, she sent the knife whizzing through the carton. "He got engaged just a few months ago. My sister sent me the clipping from the newspaper. Got a big wedding planned in the spring. I got mad when I read that. I got mad because he's planning a big, fancy wedding in the spring, and he's never once laid eyes on his son."

"His loss," Malory said.

"Yes, that's true. It is his loss. But still, I loved him, and I wanted him. I couldn't have him, and that almost broke me." With a sigh, she rested her head on the side of the unit. "I'm not going to want what I can't have again. So I'm afraid of Bradley because he's the only one who's come along in ten years who makes me remember, just a little, what it was like to be sixteen."

Five

THE IMPORTANT THING TO KEEP IN MIND WAS THAT SHE was a grown woman, and grown women often had men over for a meal without falling apart, or falling in love.

It was just a little twist to her Monday routine.

It meant she picked up some fancy bread and fresh makings for a salad on the way home. And made extra sauce. She had to get Simon started on his homework earlier than usual. And that was a battle, even with the bribe of his good pal Brad coming over for dinner.

She had to clean herself up, change her outfit twice and retouch her makeup. Then she had to clean Simon up, which caused another battle, then light fragrance candles so everything looked pretty and the air wasn't tinged with Eau de Moe.

There was the salad to make, the table to set, arithmetic and spelling to check and a dog to feed.

All this had to be done between three-thirty-five and six-thirty.

He probably wasn't used to going out to dinner so early, she thought as she stirred sauce. The richer people were, the later they ate. But Simon had to be in bed by nine o'clock on a school night. That was the law around here, so Bradley Vane would just have to adjust, or he could go eat his spaghetti somewhere else.

She hissed out a breath. Stop it! He hadn't complained, had he? She was the one making all the trouble.

"Simon, you really need to finish that up."

"I hate fractions." He bumped his heels against the leg of his chair and scowled down at the math assignment. "Fractions blow chunks."

"Some things don't come in wholes. You need to know the pieces that make them up."

"Why?"

She took out the cloth napkins she'd run up on her sewing machine. "So you can put things together, take them apart, understand how it all works."

"Why?"

She folded the napkins into triangles. "Are you trying to irritate me, or is it a natural gift?"

"I don't know. How come you're using those things?"

"Because we're having company."

"It's just Brad."

"I know who it is. Simon, you've only got three more problems there. Get them done so I can finish setting the table."

"How come I can't do it after dinner? How come I always have to do homework? How come I can't take Moe outside and fool around?"

"Because I want you to do it now. Because that's your job. Because I said so."

They sent each other mutual looks of heat and annoyance. "It's not fair."

"Bulletin for Simon: Life isn't always fair. Now get the rest of that done, or you'll lose your hour TV-and-video privilege tonight. And stop kicking that chair," she snapped.

She hauled out her cutting board and began chopping

vegetables for the salad. "You keep making those faces at my back," she said, coolly now, "and you'll lose those privileges for the whole week."

He didn't know how she knew what he was doing behind her, but she always did. In a small rebellion, he took three times as long to solve the next problem as he needed.

Homework sucked. He glanced up quickly just in case his mother could hear what he was thinking. But she kept on cutting junk for the stupid salad.

He didn't mind school. Sometimes he even liked it. But he didn't see why it had to follow him home every single night. He thought about kicking the chair again, just to test her. But Moe bounced into the room and distracted him.

"Hey, Moe. Hey, boy, whatcha got there?"

Zoe looked around, and dropped the knife. "Oh, my God."

Moe stood, tail thumping, whole body wagging, and what was left of a roll of toilet paper clamped in his teeth.

When she leaped toward him, it was a signal in Moe's mind for the game to begin. He charged left, zipped around the table, then bolted back through the kitchen doorway.

"Stop! Damn it. Simon, help me get that dog."

He'd already done his work. Shredded bits of paper, streams of mangled paper, were sprinkled and spread all over her floors like snow. She chased him into the living room while he growled playfully around the crushed tube. Giggling in delight, Simon streaked past her and dived.

Boy and dog rolled over the rug.

"Simon, it's not a game." She waded in, managed to get a hand on the wet roll. But the harder she tugged, the brighter Moe's eyes became.

He bore down, with happy snarls.

"He thinks it is. He thinks you're playing tug. He really likes to tug."

Exasperated, she looked at her son. He was kneeling beside the dog now, one arm thrown over Moe's back. Some of the shredded paper had attached itself to Simon's clean pants, Moe's fur.

Both of them were grinning at her.

"I'm not playing." But the words choked out over a laugh. "I'm *not*! You're a bad dog." She tapped a finger on his nose. "A very bad dog."

He plopped on his butt, lifted a paw to shake, then spat the roll onto the floor at her feet.

"He wants you to throw it so he can fetch."

"Oh, yeah, that's going to happen." She snatched the roll up, put it behind her back. "Simon, go get the vacuum cleaner. Moe and I are going to have a little chat."

"She's not really mad," he said in Moe's ear. "Her eyes get sorta dark and scary when she's really mad."

He bounded up. Moving fast, Zoe grabbed Moe's collar before he could follow. "Oh, no, you don't. Look at the mess you made. What do you have to say for yourself?"

He collapsed and rolled over to expose his belly.

"The only way that's going to work on me is if you know how to run a vacuum cleaner."

She let out a little sigh when she heard the knock on the door, and Simon's shouted "I'll get it!"

"Perfect. Just perfect."

She stared after Moe as he raced away, and heard Simon's excited voice telling Brad about Moe's latest adventure.

"He ran all over the house. He made a real mess."

"So I see." Brad turned into the living room where Zoe stood, surrounded by shredded toilet paper. "The fun never stops, huh?"

"He must've nosed his way into the linen closet. I just have to clean this up."

"Why don't you take care of these?" He crossed to her, held

out a bottle of wine and a dozen yellow roses. "Simon and I can clean it up."

"No, really, you can't—"

"Sure I can. Got a vacuum cleaner?" Brad asked Simon.

"I was getting it." He dashed off.

"Really, you don't have to bother. I'll . . . get it later."

"I'll take care of it. You don't like roses?"

"Yes. I do. They're beautiful." She started to take them, then looked down at her hand, and the soggy remains still gripped in it. "Oh," she said on a very long sigh, "well."

"Trade ya." He plucked it out of her hand before she could stop him, then filled hers with the flowers. "You'll want to take this, too." He passed her the bottle of Chianti. "You might want to go ahead and open that, so it can breathe."

He turned away from her when Simon hauled in the vacuum. "Plug her in, Simon, and let's get this done because something smells really good around here."

"Spaghetti sauce. Mom makes the best. But we gotta have salad first."

"There's always a catch." He smiled at Zoe as he rolled up the sleeves of his dark blue shirt. "We've got this covered."

"All right. Well. Thanks." Not knowing what else to do, she carried the roses and wine back into the kitchen. She could hear Simon still chattering away, then the quick roar of the vacuum, followed immediately by Moe's insane barks.

She'd forgotten Moe considered the vacuum a mortal enemy. She should go back and get him. Then she heard Simon's peal of laughter, the deeper, but equally delighted sound of Brad's, and the increasingly frantic barking that meant man and boy were only encouraging Moe to go postal.

No, they were fine. She should leave them alone.

And it gave her the opportunity to simply bury her face in the flowers. No one had ever given her yellow roses before. They were so sunny and elegant. After some debate, she settled on the slim copper urn she'd rescued from obscurity at a yard sale. With the brilliant shine she'd given it, it was a suitably bright home for yellow roses.

She arranged them, opened the wine. After putting a pot of water on to boil for the pasta, she went back to the salad.

It was going to be okay, it was going to be fine. She had to remember he was just a man. A friend. Just a friend who'd dropped by for dinner.

"Back to normal," Brad said as he strolled in. He noted the arranged bouquet she'd set on the counter. "Nice."

"They're really beautiful. Thank you. Simon, why don't we put Moe out back for now? You can take your books in the other room and finish those last couple of problems. Then we'll eat."

"What kind of problems?" Brad asked as he wandered around to Simon's books.

"Stupid fractions." Simon opened the back door for Moe and sent his mother a long-suffering look. "Can't I do them later?"

"Sure, if you don't want your hour after dinner."

Simon's mouth curled in what his mother recognized as the onset of a serious snit. "Fractions bite. It all bites. We got calculators and computers and junk, so how come I have to do it?"

"Because—"

"Yeah, calculators make it easy." Brad spoke casually over Zoe's heat, and traced a finger over Simon's work-sheet. "These are probably too tough for you to figure out by yourself."

"No, they're not."

"I don't know. Look pretty tough to me. You've got to add this three and three-quarters to the two and five-eighths. Heavy stuff."

"You just have to change the quarters to eighths, that's all. Like this." Simon grabbed the pencil and, clamping his tongue in his teeth, did the conversion. "So, see, now you can add up the six-eighths and the five-eighths, then you take it down again to one and three-eighths, plus the whole number jazz. So altogether you get six and three-eighths. See, the answer's six and three-eighths."

"Ha. How about that?"

"Was that a trick?" Simon asked suspiciously.

"I don't know what you're talking about." He ruffled Simon's hair. "Do the last one, smart guy."

"Man."

Zoe watched Brad lean over her son's shoulder, felt her system start to slide toward melting when he looked up, smiled into her eyes.

No, she was afraid he wasn't just a man, not just a friend who'd dropped by for dinner.

"Done!" Simon slapped his book closed. "Do I get parole, warden?"

"You're out of the slammer for now. Go ahead and put your books away, and wash up for dinner." Zoe poured two glasses of wine as Simon bolted out of the room. "You're good with stubborn little boys."

"It probably helps that I used to be one." He took the glass from her. "He's quick with numbers."

"Yes, he is. He does really well in school. He just hates homework."

"He's supposed to, isn't he? What are you wearing?"

"I ..." Off center again, she looked down at her navy blue sweater.

"Not the clothes, the perfume. You always smell fabulous, and never quite the same."

"I'm trying out a lot of different products. Soaps and creams and ..." Catching the gleam in his eye, she lifted her wine to her lips before he could lean in and take them with his own. "Scents."

73

"It's funny. A lot of women have a favorite scent, like a signature. And it can haunt a man. You make a man wonder what it'll be today, so he can't stop thinking about you."

She'd have backed up, but there wasn't enough room in the kitchen to do so without making it obvious. "I don't wear scents for men."

"I know. That only makes it more seductive."

He caught her panicked glance toward the doorway when they heard Simon coming back. Casually, Brad moved aside and let Zoe turn back to the stove.

"Are we going to eat now?" Simon demanded.

"Just putting the spaghetti in. Go ahead and sit down. We'll start on the salad."

She set a pretty table, Brad thought. Colorful plates, festive bowls, linens in a cheerful pattern. There were candles burning, and since Simon made no comment about them, Brad concluded they weren't unusual at the McCourt table.

He thought she was relaxing into it, by degrees. The boy was responsible for most of that, of course. He was full of chatter, questions, comments, all of which he managed to get out even though he ate like a stevedore.

Not that Brad could blame him. Simon's mother made a hell of a plate of spaghetti.

He had a second helping himself.

"I like your pictures in the living room," Brad said to Zoe.

"The postcards? I collect them from people I know who go places."

"We make the frames," Simon put in. "Mom has a miter box. Maybe one day we'll go places, and we'll send people postcards. Right, Mom?"

"Where do you want to go?"

"I don't know." She twirled pasta absently around her fork. "Somewhere."

"We're going to Italy one day, and eat spaghetti over there." Grinning, Simon stuffed more in his mouth.

"They don't make it any better than your mom does."

"You been over there and stuff?"

"Yeah. The picture you have of the bridge in Florence? I've stood there."

"Is it really cool?" Simon wanted to know.

"It's really cool."

"They've got a place over there that's got water for streets."

"Venice, Simon," Zoe reminded him. "They're canals. Have you been to Venice?" she asked Brad.

"Yes. It's beautiful. You go everywhere in boats," he told Simon. "Or you walk. They have water taxis and water buses."

"Get out!"

"Really. There aren't any cars in Venice, and no roads for them. I've got some pictures somewhere. I'll dig them out and show them to you."

He shifted his attention back to Zoe. "How's the work progressing?"

"Dana's bookshelves came in today. We dropped everything to set them up. It was a real moment for us. And the windows came in." She cleared her throat. "I want to thank you for arranging the installation. It was very generous of you."

"Uh-huh. Did you get my note?"

She twirled the last of her pasta on her fork. "Yes. Despite that, it was generous of you."

He had to laugh. "Think about it this way. Indulgence has brought considerable business into HomeMakers over the last couple of weeks. This was our way of thanking you for your patronage. So, did they get all the windows in?"

"I imagine you know the answer to that already." He was a man, she was sure, who knew that whatever he ordered done was done.

He acknowledged that with a tip of his glass. "The crew said they looked good—and that they got cookies and coffee out of the deal."

Amused, she looked down at his plate. "Looks like you got two helpings of spaghetti out of it."

He grinned at her, and lifted the bottle to pour more wine into her glass.

"I'm stuffed," Simon announced. "Can we go play a video game now? Me and Brad?"

"Sure."

Simon popped up, and Brad noted that he took his dishes and set them on the counter by the sink.

"Can I let Moe back in?"

Zoe drilled a finger into Simon's belly. "Keep him out of my closets."

"Okay."

"I'm going to give your mother a hand with the dishes first," Brad said.

"You don't have to do that. Really," she insisted even as Brad cleared his plate like Simon had done. "I've got a system in here, plus Simon's been looking forward to the match all day. He's only got an hour before he has to get ready for bed."

"Come on. Come on." Simon grabbed Brad's hand and tugged. "Mom doesn't mind. Right, Mom?"

"No, I don't mind. Everybody out of my kitchen, and that includes the dog."

"I'll come back and dry as soon as I beat the midget," Brad told her. "It won't take long."

"In your dreams," Simon sang out as he pulled Brad from the room.

It did her heart good to hear her son enjoying himself while she went through the routine of straightening the kitchen. Simon had never had an adult male take a sincere interest in him. Now, with Flynn and Jordan and Bradley, he had three.

And, she had to admit, Bradley was his favorite. There'd been some click between them, she thought. Some mysterious male chemistry. It was something she not only had to accept, but also should encourage.

Before she did so, though, she had to make certain Brad understood that whatever happened, or didn't, between them, Simon wasn't to be shrugged off.

She finished the kitchen, then brewed a pot of coffee and arranged a tray for it and a plate of chocolate biscotti.

When she carried it in, there was Brad, sitting cross-legged on the floor beside Simon. The dog was snoring away with his head propped on Brad's knee.

The room was reverberating with the sounds and sights of WWE Smackdown.

"Meat! You are meat!" Simon chanted as he frantically worked the controls.

"Not yet, buddy boy. Take that!"

Zoe watched an enormous blond wrestler heave his burly opponent onto the mat and deliver a punishing body slam.

Next came grappling, grunts, horrible shrieks—and not all of them from the speakers.

Then Simon collapsed onto his back, arms spread, mouth gaping.

"Defeat," he groaned. "I have tasted defeat."

"Yeah, get used to it." Brad reached over, drummed a hand on Simon's belly. "You've met the master and now know his greatness."

"Next time you die."

"You'll never take me in Smackdown."

"Yeah? Here's a sample of what's to come."

He flipped over, and with a whoop leaped onto Brad's back.

There was more grappling, Zoe noted, more grunts, and the

kind of shrieks that warmed her heart. She didn't even flinch when Brad flipped Simon over his head and pinned him on the rug.

"Yield, small, pathetic challenger."

"Never!" Simon hooted it out, and laughed from the gut, being ruthlessly tickled while he tried to twist his face away from Moe's slurping tongue. "My ferocious dog will chew you to pieces."

"Oh, yeah, I'm trembling with fear. Give up?"

Breathless, tears of laughter streaming, Simon wiggled and squirmed another ten seconds. "Okay, okay. No more tickling, or I'll puke!"

"Not on my rug," Zoe said.

At her voice. Brad turned his head, Simon squirmed. And his elbow connected, point first, with Brad's mouth.

"Oops." Simon sucked in a snicker.

Brad dabbed at the little cut with the back of his hand. "You're going to pay for that," he said in a dangerous tone that had Zoe's fingers jerking on the tray.

In a blur, Brad was on his feet, and horrors flashed into her mind. She was already opening her mouth to shout, already moving forward to protect her son, when Brad hauled him up, hung him upside down, and had him howling with laughter again.

As her knees went weak and the muscles in her arms began to tremble, she set down the coffee tray with a clatter of dishes.

"Look, Mom! I'm upside down!"

"So I see. You're going to have to get right side up again and go brush your teeth."

"But can't I—" He broke off, as Moe licked his face.

"School night, Simon. Go on, get ready for bed. Then you can come out and say good night to Bradley."

Though he was watching Zoe now, Brad rotated Simon until

the boy's feet hit the ground. "Get going. I'll give you a rematch soon."

"Sweet. When?"

"How about Friday night? You can come over, bring your mom along. We'll have dinner at my place, then suit up in the game room."

"All right! Can we, Mom?" Anticipating her answer, he flung his arms around her waist. "Don't say we'll see. Just say yes. Please!"

Her knees were still knocking. "Yes. Okay."

"Thanks." He gave her a fierce hug. Whistling for the dog, he danced out of the room.

"You thought I was going to hit him." It was said with such complete astonishment that Zoe felt her stomach pitch.

"I just—you sounded so . . . I'm sorry. I know better."

"I don't make a habit of knocking kids around."

"Of course you don't. It was knee-jerk."

"Did somebody else hurt him? Were you involved with someone who hit him?"

"No. No," she repeated, struggling for calm now. "There's never been anyone who's paid him enough mind for that. And I'd like to see somebody try to raise a hand to him when I'm around."

Apparently satisfied by that, he nodded. "Okay. You can rest assured it won't be me."

"I insulted you. I don't like to insult anyone—well, not by mistake anyway. It was just that it happened so fast, and you sounded mad, and . . . your lip's bleeding."

"I was just messing with him. And as I recall, my own mother used to say if you start all that horseplay, somebody's going to get hurt." He tapped a finger on his sore lip. "You people are always right, aren't you?"

"And now you're trying to make me feel better." Following her instincts, she picked up a napkin from the tray. Without thinking, she put a tip of it in her mouth to dampen it, then dabbed it on his lip. "When I walked in just now and saw the two of you together, it was nice. You could've let him win, too, but you didn't. And that's nice, because I don't want him growing up thinking he should always win. You've got to know how to lose, too, and ... "

She trailed off, looked down in mild horror at the cloth. She'd spat on it, for God's sake. "Lord." She crumpled the napkin in her hand. "That was stupid."

"No." Ridiculously touched, he took her hand. "That was sweet. So are you."

"Not really. Not especially. It stopped bleeding anyway. It might be a little sore for a bit."

"You forgot a step." He put a hand on her waist, slid it around to the base of her spine. "Aren't you supposed to kiss it and make it better?"

"It doesn't look so bad." In fact it looked beautiful. He had a beautiful mouth.

"Hurts," he murmured.

"Well, if you're going to be a baby about it."

She leaned in, intending to give that beautiful mouth a light brush. Friendly, casual. She gave it a little peck, and tried to ignore the stirring in her belly.

He didn't draw her closer, didn't try to lengthen the kiss, but only held her where she was, kept his eyes on hers. "Still hurts," he told her. "Can I have another?"

Alarm bells were ringing, but she ignored them. "I guess."

She touched her lips to his again. So warm, so firm.

With a little sound in her throat, she gave in to that stirring and traced those lips with her tongue, combed her fingers through his hair.

Still he waited. She could feel the tension toughen his body, she could hear his breath draw in. But he waited.

So she wrapped her arms around him and let herself sink into that warmth, that firmness, that slow and steady seduction.

It felt so good to ride that long, liquid wave, with all those tastes and textures. The shape of his mouth, the sensation of tongue sliding over tongue, the press of body to body.

So many things inside her that she'd ruthlessly shut down began to churn into hot life again.

"Oh, God." She moaned it, and all but slathered herself against him.

He'd have sworn he felt the ground begin to quake under his feet. He was damn sure the world took a hard tilt that left him reeling. Her mouth had gone from light and sweet to hot and greedy, in one lurching beat of the heart.

Desperate for more, he changed the angle of the kiss, then nipped restlessly at her bottom lip just to hear her low, throaty moan.

When he ran his hands up her body, she stretched under them like a woman waking from a long sleep.

Then jerked back, stared with shocked eyes toward the doorway. "Simon," she managed, and brushed at her hair. She took another quick step back just as Simon and Moe bounced into the room.

The boy was wearing X-Men pajamas, Brad saw. And smelled of toothpaste.

"All set?" Zoe gave her son a bright smile. The blood was still roaring in her head. "Mister, ah, Brad and I were just going to have coffee."

"Yuck." Simon walked to Zoe and tipped his head up for a kiss good night.

"I'll be in, in just a little while."

"Okay. 'Night," he said to Brad. "We're going to have a rematch, right?"

"You bet. Hold on a minute, will you? I want your opinion on something."

Before Zoe realized his intent, Brad pulled her into his arms and kissed her. It was a restrained kiss, comparatively, and she froze like a statue, but it was still a kiss.

Then he eased back, keeping one arm firm around her waist while he raised an eyebrow at Simon. "So?"

The boy's eyes were long like his mother's, tawny like his mother's, and held a world of speculation. After a long five seconds, he crossed those eyes, poked a finger in his mouth, and made gagging noises.

"Uh-huh," Brad said. "Other than the gag reflex, do you have any problem with me kissing your mother?"

"Not if you guys want to do something that gross. Chuck says his brother Nate likes to stick his tongue in girls' mouths. That just can *not* be true. Can it?"

With what he considered heroic control, Brad kept his face very sober. "It takes all kinds."

"I guess. I'm going to take Moe into my room so he doesn't have to watch if you guys are going to do something gross again."

"See you, kid." As Simon and Moe padded off, Brad turned and grinned at Zoe. "Want to do something gross?"

"I think we'll just have coffee."

Six

MEETINGS, PROJECTIONS, AND PLANS FOR EXPANSION
kept Brad tied to HomeMakers for a couple of days. He couldn't
complain, as it had been his idea to come back to Pleasant
Valley, to make it his home base while overseeing the northeast
quadrant of his family's business, revamping the Valley store and
expanding it by fifteen thousand square feet.

That meant paperwork, conference calls, adjustments in staff
and procedure, consultations with architects and contractors,
haggling with or being wooed by suppliers.

He could handle it. He'd been raised to handle it and had
spent the last seven years in the New York offices learning the ins
and outs of being a top executive of one of the country's biggest
retail chains.

He was a Vane, the fourth generation of the HomeMakers
Vanes. He had no intention of dropping the ball. In fact, he
fully intended to slam-dunk that ball by making the first
HomeMakers store the biggest, the most prestigious, and the
most profitable in the national system.

His father hadn't been thrilled by his decision. B. C. Vane III
considered it based on sentiment. And so it was, Brad thought.

And why not? His grandfather had built the humble hardware store, then gambled everything to push it outward, had developed it into a successful, consumer-friendly outlet for home improvement needs, into a staple of the Laurel Highlands.

And through guts, guile, and vision, had built a second store, then a third, then more, until he'd become a symbol of American enterprise with his face on *Time* magazine before his fiftieth birthday.

So it was sentiment, Brad thought, but that was leavened with a good dose of the Vane guts, guile, and vision.

He studied his hometown as he drove through the downtown area. The Valley was prospering in its quiet, steady way. The real estate market was strong in the county, and when people bought homes here, they tended to dig in and stay. Retail was up, and steadily above the national average. And tourist dollars maintained a nice healthy stream into the local economy.

The Valley prized its small-town ambience, but being an hour from Pittsburgh lent that ambience a sheen of sophistication.

For vacationers it offered hiking, skiing, boating, fishing, and charming inns, good restaurants. The flavor of country, all within an easy commute from the bustle of the city.

It was a good place to live, and a good place to do business.

Brad intended to do both.

Maybe he hadn't intended to be quite so pressed, but he hadn't expected to come back and find himself spun into a search for mystical keys. And he hadn't expected to fall for a cautious single mother and her irresistible son.

Still, it was simply a matter of setting goals, establishing priorities, and taking care of the details.

He parked his car and walked into the *Valley Dispatch* to handle a few of those details.

He got a kick out of thinking of his friend running the local paper. Flynn might not project the image of a man who could, or would, ride hard on a staff, whip a daily through deadlines, and concern himself with advertising, content, and the price of paper. And that, Brad mused as he headed up to editorial and Flynn's office, was why his old buddy was so good at his job.

He had a way of pushing people to do things, and to do them his way, without letting them feel the nudge.

Brad wound his way around desks and reporters, through the cacophony of phones, keyboards, and voices. He smelled coffee, baked goods, and somebody's pine-scented aftershave.

And there was Flynn, within the glass walls of the editor in chief's office, sitting on the corner of his desk in a striped shirt, jeans, and banged-up Nikes.

Invoking the privilege of a thirty-year friendship, Brad strolled straight in through the open door.

"I'll cover that meeting personally, Mr. Mayor." Flynn jerked his head toward the phone on his desk, and the speaker light.

Grinning now, Brad slid his hands in his pockets and waited while Flynn finished the call.

"Sorry. Didn't realize you were on the phone."

"So what's a mature executive such as yourself doing in my humble office this morning?" Flynn asked.

"Dropping off the layout for next week's insert."

"Those are some fancy threads for a messenger boy." Flynn fingered the sleeve of Brad's suit.

"I have to head into Pittsburgh later, for business." He dropped the file on Flynn's desk. "And I wanted to talk to you about doing a ten-page, full-color pullout for the week before Thanksgiving. I want to hit Black Friday hard."

"I'm your man. You want my people to talk to your people. I like saying that," Flynn added. "It sounds so Hollywood."

"That's the idea. I'm generating this locally rather than out of corporate. It's specific to the Valley store, and I want it classy and convenient. Something the consumer can slide out and into a purse or pocket to bring along while shopping. And I want it exclusive. I want it in the *Dispatch* on a day without any other inserts, flyers, tip-ins."

"There's a flood of inserts the week before Black Friday," Flynn pointed out.

"Exactly. I don't want this one lost in the shuffle. It runs alone."

Flynn rubbed his palms together. "That's gonna cost you, bunky."

"How much?"

"I'll talk to advertising, we'll work up a price. Ten-page, full-color?" Flynn confirmed as he made a note. "I'll get back to you on it tomorrow."

"Good."

"Wow, look at us, doing business. Want coffee to go with that?"

Brad looked at his watch, gauged the time. "Yeah. There's something else I want to talk to you about. Can I close this?"

Flynn jerked a shoulder as Brad gestured to the door. "Sure." He poured coffee, sat back on the desk. "Is this about the key?"

"I haven't heard anything for a couple of days. The last time I saw Zoe I got the impression she didn't want to talk about it. At least not to me."

"So, you're wondering if she talks to me, or more likely to Mal and then Mal talks to me. Not so much right now," Flynn told him. "Malory's take is that Zoe's waiting for the other shoe to drop, and she's on edge wondering when Kane might make a move."

"I've been working with the clue. The way I read it, it's Zoe who has to make a move. I'm going to see her Friday night, but we might want to brainstorm beforehand."

"Friday night?" Flynn sipped his coffee. "Is that a social event?"

"Simon's coming over to fool around." Restlessly, Brad wandered the office as he spoke. "He's bringing his mother."

"Sneaky."

"You do what you can. That's one great kid, and he's not as complicated as his mother is."

"My impression is she had a rough road, and blazed the trail out of it on her own. Which eases right into the theme of her clue."

"She's an amazing woman."

"How stuck on her are you?"

"All the way." Trying to settle, Brad leaned against the windowsill. "Problem is, she doesn't trust me. I'm making progress, though. At least she doesn't freeze up or go on the defensive every time I look at her these days. But sometimes she looks at me like I've just dropped in from another planet and I have not come in peace."

"She's a package deal. Women who are part of a package have to be more careful. If they're smart. Zoe's smart."

"I'm nuts about that kid. The more I'm around him, the more I want to be. I'd like to know the story on his father."

Flynn shook his head at Brad's questioning look. "Sorry, my sources are very closemouthed on that subject. You could try the direct approach and ask her yourself."

Brad nodded. "One more thing, then I've got to take off. Are you going to write the story?"

"The Daughters of Glass," Flynn said aloud, looking off into middle distance as if reading a headline written on air. "Dateline Pleasant Valley, Pennsylvania. Two Celtic gods visited the scenic Laurel Highlands to challenge three local women to locate the keys to the legendary Box of Souls."

He laughed a little, lifted his coffee again. "It'd be a hell of a story. Adventure, intrigue, romance, money, personal risk, personal triumph, and the power of the gods, all right here in our quiet hometown. Yeah. I thought about it—to write it, and do it right. When I first got into this, I thought, Jesus, *Jesus*, this could be the story of the century. Of course, I could just as easily be hauled off and put in a padded room, but that wouldn't have stopped me."

"What did?"

"It would put them on the spot, wouldn't it? Again. Some people would believe it, many wouldn't, but everybody would ask them questions, hammer at them for answers and statements. They—well, none of us—would ever be able to live a normal life after that."

He looked down into his coffee, gave another little shrug. "And that's what this is about, at the base. All of us being able to live the way we want to, the way we're entitled to. It's different if Jordan writes it, turns it into a book. Then it's fiction. But I won't be writing it up for the paper."

"You were always the best of us."

Flynn paused with his coffee mug halfway to his lips. "Huh?"

"The most clear-sighted, the most clear-hearted. That's why you stayed in the Valley, at the paper, when you wanted to go. Maybe that's why Jordan and I could leave. Because we knew you'd be here when we got back."

It was a rare thing for Flynn's tongue to tie itself in knots, but it did so now. "Well" was all he could manage.

"I've got to get to Pittsburgh." Brad set his coffee aside and rose. "Call me on the cell if anything comes up while I'm gone."

Still speechless, Flynn only nodded.

ZOE MEASURED AND MIXED Mrs. Hanson's color. Her neighbor liked strong red highlights in the brown. Zoe had come up with a combination of toners that suited them both, and had been doing Mrs. Hanson's cut and color once a month for three years.

She was the only client Zoe serviced at home. Memories of growing up with hair on the floor and chemicals in the air had caused her to vow never to turn her home into a business.

But Mrs. Hanson was different, and the hour or so Zoe spent once a month doing her hair in the kitchen was more like a visit than a job.

She still remembered the day she'd moved into this house, how Mrs. Hanson, whose hair had been an unfortunate boot-black color then—had come over to welcome her and Simon to the neighborhood.

She'd brought chocolate chip cookies, and after taking a long look at Simon, had nodded in approval. Then she'd offered her services as official sitter, claiming that with her own sons grown up she missed having a boy around the house.

She was the first friend Zoe made in the Valley, and had become not only a surrogate grandmother to Simon but a mother to Zoe as well.

"I saw your young man come by the other night." Mrs. Hanson's blue eyes twinkled in her pretty face as she perched on the stool in Zoe's kitchen.

"I don't have a man, young or old." Zoe parted hair, dabbed the gray roots with color.

"Handsome young man," Mrs. Hanson continued, undaunted. "Looks like his father some, who I knew a bit when he was the same age. Those roses he brought you are holding up well. Look how nice they've opened up."

Zoe glanced at the table. "I've been trimming the stems and changing the water to keep them fresh."

"Just like having a sunbeam on the table. Yellow roses suit you. It takes a smart man to know that. Simon's full of Brad this and Brad that. Tells me he's good with the boy."

"He is. They get along like a house afire." As she worked, Zoe's brows knit. "Bradley seems very fond of Simon."

"I imagine he's very fond of Simon's mama, too."

"We're friends—or I'm working my way up to that. He makes me nervous."

Mrs. Hanson gave a quick hoot of laughter. "Man looks like that, he's supposed to make a woman nervous."

"Not that way. Well, yes, that way." Zoe laughed and scooped more color onto her brush. "But just altogether nervous."

"He kiss you yet?" At Zoe's long silence, Mrs. Hanson let out a satisfied cackle. "Good. He didn't look slow to me. How was it?"

"I had to check after to make sure the top of my head was still there, because it felt like it'd blown clean off."

"About damn time. I was a little worried about you, sweetheart. Working day and night, seemed to me. Never taking time for yourself. Last little while, I see those nice girls you've taken up with, and handsome Brad Vane coming around, it does my heart good."

She reached back to give Zoe's hand a pat. "Still working night and day, especially now that you're putting that business together, but I like seeing it."

"I wouldn't be able to have this business without you watching Simon after school so many afternoons."

Mrs. Hanson made a dismissive sound and waved Zoe's words away. "You know very well I love having that boy around. He's like one of my own. I don't see nearly enough of my grandchildren what with Jack moving down to Baltimore and Deke off in California. I don't know what I'd do without Simon. He brightens up my day."

"He thinks of you and Mr. Hanson as his grandparents. It takes a weight off me."

"Tell me how things are coming with the salon. I just can't wait until you open up for business, put that tightassed Carly's nose out of joint when you start stealing her customers. I heard from Sara Bennett that the new girl Carly hired to replace you isn't working out"

"That's too bad." But she said it with a snicker. "I wouldn't wish her bad luck, except for the way she fired me. Saying I took money out of the till," Zoe continued, firing up. "Calling me a thief."

"Easy there."

"Oh, sorry," Zoe apologized when she realized she'd given Mrs. Hanson's hair a tug. "I start seeing red whenever I think about it. I did good work for her."

"Too good. And too many of her regulars wanted you doing their hair, not her. Came down to jealousy, and that's that."

"You know Marcie? She does nails there? I called her up a couple days ago, just to feel her out. She's going to work for me."

"You don't say."

"We've got to keep it quiet until I'm all set up. I don't want Carly firing her, putting her out of work before I open. But she's ready to give her notice as soon as I say. And she's friends with a stylist working out at the mall who's getting married first of the year and wants to find something closer to town. So I said how about *in* town, and Marcie's going to have her come see me. She says she's really good."

"Sounds to me like you're putting it all together."

"It feels right, you know? I got Chris on board to do massages and some of the body treatments. And my friend Dana? She's hired this woman to work in her bookstore, and she has this friend who just moved back to the Valley and used to work at a spa out in Colorado. I'm going to be talking to her, too. It's so exciting—as long as I don't think about the payroll."

"You're going to do fine. Better than fine."

"The plumber was in today, setting things up for my shampoo sinks. I got the lights in, and I'm going to be working on the stations. Sometimes I just look around up there and think this has got to be a dream."

"You don't have to earn dreams, Zoe. And you've earned this."

SHE HAD EARNED IT, Zoe thought later as she washed out the color brush and bowl. Or she was earning it. Still, so much of it was like a gift. She promised herself she would never take it for granted.

She would do good work. She would be a good partner, and a good employer. She knew what it was to work for someone who was more interested in filling up the spaces in the appointment book than in the basic needs of her operators. Someone who'd forgotten what it was to stand on your feet hour after hour until they burned, until the small of your back ached like a bad tooth.

But she wouldn't forget.

Maybe this wasn't the road she'd expected to take, all those years ago when she was a young girl who imagined having pretty things and a quiet life that she would earn by using her brain.

But it was the road she'd taken, and she was making it the right road.

"You could go back, change it all."

She turned from the sink and looked at Kane. Surprise, shock, even fear were buried under thick layers of fog. She knew they were there but couldn't quite feel them.

He was beautiful, with a dark beauty. The black hair and deep eyes, the sharp bones sculpted under pure white skin. He was taller than she'd pictured. Not powerfully built like Pitte, but with a graceful, elegant body that she imagined could move as swiftly as a snake.

"I wondered when you would come." Her voice sounded hollow, as if formed more in her mind than with her mouth.

"I've watched you. A pleasant pastime." He stepped closer, and his hand brushed her cheek. "You're very lovely. Too lovely to labor as you do. Too lovely to spend your life working on the appearance of others. You always wanted more. No one understood."

"No. It made Mama angry. It hurt her feelings."

"She never knew you. She used you like a slave."

"She needed help. She did her best."

"And when you needed help?" His voice was gentle, his face full of understanding. "Poor young thing. Used, betrayed, discarded. And a lifetime of payment for one reckless act. What if it had never happened? Your life would be so different. Don't you wonder?"

"No, I—"

"Look." He held up a sphere of crystal. "Look at what could have been."

Helpless to do otherwise, she looked, and fell into the scene.

And swiveled in a deep leather chair to gaze out a wide corner window at the spears and towers of a great city. She had a phone to her ear and a satisfied expression on her face.

"No, I can't. I'm leaving for Rome tonight. A little business, a lot of pleasure." She glanced at the slim gold watch on her wrist. "The pleasure is a little bonus from upstairs for bringing in the Quartermain account. A week at the Hastier. Of course I'll send you a postcard."

She laughed, swiveled back to face the office as her assistant brought in a tall, slim china cup. "I'll talk to you when I get back. *Ciao.*"

"Your latte, Ms. McCourt. Your car will be here in fifteen minutes."

"Thanks. The Modesto file?"

"Already in your briefcase."

"You're the best. You know how to reach me, but as of Tuesday I'm off the clock. So unless it's dire, pretend I've gone to Venus and can't be reached."

"Count on it. Nobody deserves a vacation more than you. Have a wonderful time in Rome."

"I plan to."

Sipping her latte, she turned to her computer, brought up a file to check some final details.

She loved her work. Some people would say it was just numbers, accounting, black or red ink. But to Zoe it was a challenge, even an adventure. She handled finance for some of the biggest and most complex corporations in the world, and she handled it very well.

A long way from doing books for Mama's hair business, she mused. A very long way.

She'd studied hard to earn that scholarship to college, worked hard to complete her degree and secure an entry-level position with one of New York's most prestigious international banking firms.

And then she'd worked her way up. A corner office on the fiftieth floor, her own staff, all before she hit thirty.

She had a beautiful apartment, an exciting life, a career she loved sinking her teeth into day after day. She'd traveled to all those places she'd wondered about when she snuck out to walk the woods at night as a girl.

She had what she'd never been able to explain to her family that she needed. She had respect.

Satisfied, she logged off, sipped the last of the latte. She pushed away from the desk, picked up her briefcase, tossed her coat over her arm.

Rome was waiting.

Work would come first, but then it was play. She was planning to carve out a nice chunk of time for shopping. Something in leather, something in gold. A sortie to Armani or Versace. Maybe both. Who deserved it more?

She started toward the door, then stopped, turned back. There was a nagging sensation, a tug at the back of her mind. She was forgetting something. Something important.

"Your car's here, Ms. McCourt."

"Yes, I'm coming."

She started for the door again. But no. No, she couldn't just leave.

"Simon." Her head spun, so viciously she had to brace a hand on the wall. "Where's Simon?"

She rushed through the door, shouting for him. And fell back through the crystal and onto her kitchen floor.

"I WASN'T EVER AFRAID," Zoe told Malory and Dana. "Not even when I landed on the floor. It was more, 'hmmm, how about that.'"

"That's all he said to you?" Dana demanded.

"Yes. He was very smooth." Zoe said as she worked on attaching her stations to the wall. "Very sympathetic. Not frightening at all."

"Because he was trying to seduce you," Malory concluded.

"That's the way I see it." Zoe gave the station a test shake, nodded. "'Wouldn't you like things to be this way, instead of the way they turned out?' He made it seem like it was just a matter of stepping this way instead of that."

"The fork in the path." Dana set her hands on her hips.

"Exactly." Zoe lined up the last screw, then drilled the hole. "Here's the chance to have a high-powered career, a spiffy life, fly off to Rome for a week. All you have to do is one little thing. Not get pregnant at sixteen. He figured out he can't threaten me with Simon, so what if he just eliminates him from the equation."

"He's underestimating you."

Zoe glanced up at Malory. "Oh, yeah, he is, because nothing in that crystal ball comes close to what I have with Simon. And you know what? It doesn't come close to what I'm doing here, with both of you."

She smiled and pushed herself to her feet. "I was wearing really great shoes, though. I think they were Manolo Blahnik, like what's-her-name, Sarah Jessica Parker, wears."

"Hmm. Excellent and sexy shoes, or a nine-year-old boy." Dana tapped a finger on her chin. "Tough choice."

"I think I'll be sticking with Payless for the time being." She stepped back to study the completed station. "He doesn't scare me." She let out a laugh, then set down the drill. "I was so sure he would, but he doesn't."

"Don't let your guard down," Malory warned her. "He's not going to take a simple 'no thanks' for an answer."

"That's the one he's going to keep getting. Anyway, he's made me think about the clue again. Choices. The moment of truth, you called it, Malory, in the paintings. I guess I had one, the night Simon was conceived, or when I made the decision to have him. But I think there has to be another, either one that I've already made or one I have to make."

"We can make a list," Malory began and made Dana laugh.

"How did I know she would say that?"

"A list," Malory continued with a bland look for her friend, "of important events and decisions Zoe's made, and of minor ones that had important results. Just the way she thought about the Valley as a forest with paths. This time it's her life as the forest. We look for intersections, connections, how one choice led to others, how any of them pertains to the key."

"I've been playing around with that already and I was thinking . . . " She lined up the next station, pulled out her measuring tape, then just set it down. "The decisions you made, the things both of you did that led you to your keys, involved Flynn and Jordan. Brad and I are the only ones left, so it follows that mine's going to involve him. That puts him on the front line with me."

"Brad can handle himself," Dana assured her.

"I'm certain he can. And I can handle myself. I'm just not sure I can handle him. I can't afford to make a mistake, not about the key, not about myself and Simon."

"Are you worried that being closer to Brad, forming a personal relationship with him, could be a mistake?" Malory asked her.

"Actually, I'm starting to worry that not being closer to him might be a mistake. That's making it harder to be practical."

"You're going over there tonight." Malory said. "Why don't you take a tip from Simon just this once and enjoy being with someone who so obviously enjoys being with you?"

"I'm going to try." She picked up the tape again. "It helps to know I've got a chaperon. Two, actually, counting Moe."

"Sooner or later, no matter how fond Brad is of Simon, he's going to want to see you alone."

Zoe passed Dana the measuring tape and picked up her drill. "Then I'll worry about that, sooner or later."

More sooner, later, and right this minute, Zoe thought when she was alone again.

She knew that with a physical attraction this intense, they were bound to come together. But she could, and she would, decide the time, the place, the tone. The rules. There had to be rules, just as there had to be an understanding between them before that intimate step was taken.

If Bradley Vane was indeed one of her forks in the road, it was vital to be certain that neither of them ended up lost, alone, and bleeding at the end of the trail.

Seven

SIMON'S EXCITED CALL INTERRUPTED ZOE'S DEBATE OVER earrings. Should she go with the big silver hoops, sort of carefree sexy, or the little marcasite drops she'd splurged on last summer, more demure and sophisticated?

These were the details that set the tone for a woman's mood, her outlook, her intentions for an event. A man might miss them, she thought as she held one of each pair up to her ears, but a woman knew why she was wearing a particular pair of earrings, Or shoes. Or why she'd chosen a particular bra.

These were the building blocks for the dating ritual. She set both earrings down and pressed a hand to her stomach. God, she was dating.

"Mom! Come quick! You gotta *see* this."

"Just a minute."

"Hurry up! Hurry, it's pulling in the driveway. Man. Oh, *man!* Come on, Mom!"

"What is it?" She darted toward the living room in her bare feet. She couldn't decide on the shoes until she'd decided on the earrings. "For heaven's sake, Simon, we have to leave in a few minutes, and I'm not—" Her jaw dropped, mimicking her son's as she looked out the front window with him at the black stretch limo sliding in behind her ancient hatchback.

"It's the biggest car I've ever seen in my whole *life*."

"Me too," Zoe replied. "He must be lost."

"Can I go out and see?" He grabbed her hand, tugging on it as he did when particularly frantic. "Please, please, please! Can I go touch it?"

"I don't think you should touch it."

"A man's getting out." Simon's voice dropped to a reverent whisper. "He looks like a soldier."

"He's a chauffeur." She laid a hand on Simon's shoulder as they peeked out the window together. "That's what they call people who drive limousines."

"He's coming to the *door*."

"He must need directions."

"Can I just go out and look while you tell him how to get someplace? I won't touch it or anything."

"We'll ask." She took Simon's hand and walked to the door.

Simon was right, she thought as she opened the door. He did look like a soldier—tall and straight, with a military bearing in his black uniform and cap.

"Can I help you find someone?" she asked him.

"Ms. Zoe McCourt? Master Simon McCourt?"

"Ah." She tugged Simon a little closer to her side. "Yes."

"I'm Bigaloe. I'll be driving you to Mr. Vane's this evening."

"We get to ride in that?" Simon's eyes went wide and bright as twin suns. "*Inside?*"

"Yes, sir." Bigaloe gave Simon a quick wink. "In any seat you like."

"Sweet!" He pumped a fist, gave a hoot, and would have charged to the limo if Zoe hadn't hauled him back.

"But we have a car. And a dog."

"Yes, ma'am. Mr. Vane sent this."

Zoe looked down at the note Bigaloe held out, recognized the stationery. "Simon, you stand right here," she ordered, and released his hand to open the envelope.

The single sheet of letterhead read:

Don't argue this time either.

"But I just don't see why ..." She trailed off, undone and defeated by the desperate plea in Simon's eyes. "We'll be out in just a minute, Mr. Bigaloe."

"You take your time, ma'am."

The minute she closed the door, Simon threw his arms around her waist. "This is so awesome!"

"Yes. Awesome."

"Can we go now? Can we?"

"All right. Get your jacket, and the present we made for Bradley. I need my purse." And my shoes, she thought. It looked like it would be the marcasite earrings tonight.

The minute they were out of the house, Simon made a beeline for the car, then skidded to a halt to wave wildly at the Hansons, who stood on their front porch.

"We get to ride in a limousine!"

"Isn't that something?" With a wide grin, Mrs. Hanson waved back. "Just like a rock star. I want to hear all about it tomorrow."

"Okay. This is Mr. Bigaloe," Simon announced when the driver opened the door. "He's going to drive us to Brad's house. That's Mr. and Mrs. Hanson. They live next door."

"Pleased to meet you." Bigaloe tipped his cap, then offered a hand to Zoe. "The dog can ride up with me, if that suits you."

"Oh. Well, if he's no trouble."

"Look at that, John." Mrs. Hanson gave her husband's hand a quick squeeze. "Just like Cinderella. Just hope our girl's smart enough not to go running off when the clock strikes."

There were little glass vases with fresh flowers beside the tinted windows. And little lights, like faerie lights, streamed along the floor and the roof.

There were a television and a stereo, and buttons to work everything on a panel just above her head.

Everything smelled like leather and lilies.

Simon was already crawling over the long seat along the side to poke his head through the opening to the limo's cab and peppering Bigaloe with questions.

Zoe didn't have the heart to stop him. And it gave her a moment to try to adjust.

After that moment she gave up. It would take her a year to adjust.

Simon came sliding back. "Moe likes it up front, and Mr. Bigaloe's letting him stick his head out the window. And Mr. Bigaloe says I can touch anything, because I'm the boss. And I can have a soda from the ice place over there if you say so, 'cause you're the boss of me, and I can watch *TV*! In the car. Can I?"

Zoe looked at his bright and dazzled face. On impulse, she caught that face in her hands, gave him a loud, smacking kiss on the mouth. "Yes, you can have a soda. Yes, you can watch TV in the car. And look, look up here. You can make the lights go on and off. And there's a telephone."

"Let's call somebody."

"You do it." She picked up the phone and offered it. "Call Mrs. Hanson. Won't she love that?"

"Okay. I'm going to get a soda, and turn on the TV, *and* call her so I can tell her."

She giggled with him, and played with the controls, and drank a ginger ale just so she could say she had.

When they arrived at Brad's, she took Simon's hand before he could reach for the door handle. "Mr. Bigaloe's supposed to come around and open it," she whispered. "That's part of his job."

"Okay." When the door opened, Simon popped out and looked up at Bigaloe. "That was really good. Thanks for driving us."

"It was a pleasure."

"I guess you could tell it was our first time in a limo," Zoe said when he helped her out.

"I don't know when I've enjoyed driving anyone quite so much. I'll look forward to taking you home when you're ready."

"Thank you."

"Wait until I tell the guys." Simon grabbed the leash and let Moe pull him to the door. "They're not going to believe it."

Before Zoe could tell him to knock, he was pushing the door open and shouting for Brad. "Brad! We watched TV in the car and called Mrs. Hanson and had sodas. And Moe rode up front."

"Sounds like a busy ride."

"Simon, you're supposed to knock. Moe!"

The dog had already made a dash for the great room and the sofa.

"He's all right," Brad told her as Moe leaped on the cushions and stretched out like a furry sultan. "We're getting used to him around here."

"We brought you a present." Dancing in place, Simon thrust the box into Brad's hands. "Mom and I made it."

"Yeah? Let's go back to the kitchen and open it up. Just let me get your coats first."

"I can do it. I know where they go." Simon yanked off his jacket and bounced on his toes until Zoe handed him hers. "Don't open it until I'm there."

"Okay."

"I want to thank you for sending the car," Zoe began as they started toward the kitchen. "Simon's never going to forget it. It was a big thrill for him."

"Did you enjoy the ride?"

"Are you kidding?" She let out a laugh that was still tinged with wonder. "It was like being a princess for twenty minutes. Except we played with all the buttons and the television, so I guess it was more like being a kid for twenty minutes. But you didn't have to do something like that, go to all that trouble."

"It wasn't any trouble. I wanted to do it. I knew Simon would get a kick out of it, and I didn't want to worry about you driving home in the dark. And," he added as he pulled a bottle out of a silver bucket, "I wanted you to be able to relax and enjoy this really nice champagne."

"Oh. Even without the note you sent it would be hard to argue about all that."

"Good." He released the cork with a cheerful little pop and was pouring the second flute when Simon ran in with Moe behind him.

"You gotta open the present now. It's a homewarmer present."

"Housewarming," Zoe corrected, and hooked her arm, the way she often did, around Simon's shoulder. "A belated one, to welcome you back to the Valley."

"Let's see what we've got." He undid the bow, feeling a bit foolish, since he already knew he would save the lacy white ribbon and the little spray of tiny red flowers she'd tucked into it. She'd stamped or stenciled silhouettes of those flowers on the simple brown box, and had nestled the gift inside on a bed of white tissue sprinkled with glitter.

"You sure know how to wrap a present."

"If you're going to give somebody a gift, you should take the time to make it nice."

He took out the tri-colored candle in a squat, clear jar. "It's great." He sniffed. "Smells terrific. You made this?"

"We like to make stuff, right, Mom? See you have to melt the wax and then add the smelly stuff and junk. I picked out the smells."

"For the holidays," Zoe explained. "The top layer's apple pie and the middle's cranberry, with Christmas tree at the bottom. There's a tile in there to set it on. The bottom of the jar gets hot."

He took out the white tile with cranberries painted on each corner.

"Mom painted the berries, and I put the glaze stuff on."

"It's terrific." He set the tile on the counter and the candle on top. Then bent down to hug Simon. When he straightened, he grinned at the boy. "You may want to look away."

"How come?"

"I'm going to kiss your mother."

"Gack." Though Simon covered his face with his hands, there was a warmth in his belly.

"Thank you." Brad laid a light kiss on Zoe's lips. "All clear, kid."

"Are you going to light the present?" Simon demanded.

"I am." Brad took a long, slim tool out of a drawer and lit the wick. "Looks great. Where did you learn to make candles?"

"Just something I picked up. I've been experimenting. I'm hoping to get good enough to carry a line of candles and potpourri and that kind of thing in the salon."

"I would carry something like that at HomeMakers."

Zoe stared at her candle. "You would?"

"We'll be stocking a lot more items like decorative candles after the expansion. You'll have to show me some of the others you've done, and we'll talk."

"Is it okay if I go in the game room?" Simon asked. "I brought back *Smackdown*, so we can have our rematch."

"Sure. There's another game loaded. You can switch it."

"Are you going to come play now?"

"I've got to start putting dinner together, but you can go work up an appetite. I want you hungry. I had the frog legs flown in special."

"Uh-uh."

"Giant frog legs. From Africa."

"No way."

"Or we can just have steak."

"Frog steak!"

"Naturally."

On a mock scream, Simon tore out of the room.

"You're awfully good with him," Zoe said.

"He makes it easy. Why don't you sit down and—" He broke off when Simon's shouted "Holy cow!" burst out of the game room. "He found the new game."

"Bradley."

"Hmm?"

"I have to ask you for a promise. Don't say all right yet," she cautioned, turning her glass round and round by the stem as she studied his face. "It's important, and if you take the time to think about it first, I'll believe you'll keep your word."

"What do you want me to promise, Zoe?"

"Simon—he's so attached to you. He's never had . . . somebody like you pay attention to him, not this way. It's getting so he's depending on you paying that attention. I need you to promise that whatever happens with us, whatever way it turns out, you won't forget him. I'm not talking about riding in limos. I'm asking you to promise that you won't stop being a friend to him."

"He's not the only one who's attached, Zoe. I can make you that promise." He offered his hand. "You've got my word."

She took his hand, squeezed it as the tension that had built inside her while she made her request dissolved again. "All right. Well." She looked around the kitchen. "What can I do?"

"You can sit down and drink your champagne."

"I ought to be able to help with those African frog legs."

He cupped the back of her neck with his hand, kissed her, not quite so lightly, not quite so casually as he had when Simon had been in the room. "Sit down, and drink your champagne," he said again, flicking a finger at her earlobe. "Nice earrings."

She gave a quick, baffled laugh. "Thanks." Though she still felt as if she should be helping, she perched on a stool at the bar. "Are you really going to cook?"

"I'm going to grill, which is entirely different. All the Vane men grill. If they didn't they'd be drummed out of the family."

"You're going to grill? In November?"

"We Vanes grill year-round, even if we have to chip through the ice, brave blizzards, risk frostbite. However, it happens I have this very handy deal right here on the range."

"I've seen those in magazines." She watched him fire up the built-in grill on the stovetop. "And on TV, on some of the cooking shows."

He tucked potatoes already wrapped in foil around the flame. "Just don't tell my father I used this instead of standing outside like a man."

"Lips are sealed." She sipped champagne while he went to the refrigerator and pulled out a tray of hors d'oeuvres. "You made these?"

He considered for a moment as he set the platter on the counter in front of her. "I could lie and really impress you, but instead I'll dazzle you with my honesty. They're from Luciano's, and so's the chocolate bomb for dessert, and the lobster tails."

"Lobster tails? Luciano's?" She selected one of the canapés, slipped it between her lips, and moaned as the flavors melted on her tongue.

"Good?"

"Amazing. It's all amazing. I'm trying to figure out how Zoe McCourt came to be sitting here drinking champagne and eating canapes from Luciano's. It doesn't seem real. You *are* trying to *dazzle* me, Bradley. And it's working."

"I like seeing you smile. Do you know the first time you really smiled at me? When I gave you a stepladder."

"I smiled at you before that."

"Nope. Not really. God knows I wanted you to, but you seemed set on misunderstanding and taking offense at every second word out of my mouth."

"That's—" She cut herself off, then let out a laugh. "Probably true."

"But I cagily won you over, or started to, with a fiberglass stepladder."

"I didn't know it was a ploy. I thought it was considerate."

"It was a considerate ploy. You need more champagne."

She debated with herself while he went to get the bottle. "You intimidated me."

"Excuse me?"

"You intimidated me, still do, a little. And the house intimidated me. The first time I came here, to meet Malory, and saw you. I walked into this big, beautiful house, and there was the painting you'd bought."

"After the Spell."

"Yes. It was such a shock to see that, and to be here. My head was spinning. I said something about having to get back home for Simon, for my son, and you looked down at my hand, saw I wasn't wearing a wedding ring."

"Zoe—"

She shook her head. "And you got this look on your face. It set me off."

"Apparently you started misunderstanding me right from the get-go." As an afterthought, he topped off his own glass. "I'm going to tell you about the painting, and that's going to give you a very big advantage in this relationship we're starting."

Dating. Relationship. Her head was going to start spinning again. "I don't know what you mean."

"You will. When I saw that painting for the first time, well, that was a stunner. There's Dana, my best friend's kid sister. Someone I cared about a great deal."

He leaned against the bar, casually elegant in his black sweater, with her homemade candle flickering between them. "Then there was Malory. Of course, I didn't know her yet, but there was something that made me stop and think, made me look a little closer."

He paused, and tucked two fingers under Zoe's chin. "Then there was this face. This incredible face. I could hardly breathe for looking at it. I was undone by that face. I had to have that painting. I'd have paid anything for it."

"It's part of the connection." Her throat was dry, but she couldn't lift her glass to drink. "You were meant to have it."

"That may be true. I've come to believe it's true. But that's not the point I'm making. I had to have the painting because I had to be able to look at that face. Your face. I knew every angle of it. The shape of the eyes, the mouth. I spent a lot of time studying that face. Then you walked into the room that day, and I was staggered. She woke up, and she walked out of the painting, and there she is."

"But it isn't me in the painting."

"Ssh. I couldn't think. For a minute I couldn't hear anything but my own heart beating. While I was trying to think, while I was trying not to grab you just to convince myself that you weren't going to vanish like smoke, everyone was talking. I had to speak to you, to pretend everything was normal when the world had done a very fast one-eighty on me. You can't imagine what was going on inside me."

"No. I guess—no," she managed.

"You said you had to get home for your son, and you might as well have stabbed me in the throat. How could she belong to someone else before I get a chance? So I looked down, saw you weren't wearing a ring, and I thought, Thank God, she doesn't belong to someone else."

"But you didn't even know me."

"I do now." He leaned in, took her lips with his.

"Man. Are you going to do that all the time now?"

Brad eased back, brushed a kiss against Zoe's forehead, then turned to Simon. "Yes. But I don't want you to feel left out, so I'll kiss you, too."

Simon made spitting noises and danced to safety behind his mother's stool. "Kiss her if you've got to kiss somebody. Are we going to eat soon? I'm starving."

"Big fat steaks about to go on the fire. So, kid, how do you like your frog?"

AFTER DINNER, AND THE video rematch, after Simon's eyes drooped shut as he sprawled on the game room floor, Zoe let herself slide into Brad's arms. Let herself float into the kiss.

There was magic in the world, she thought. And this night had been some of hers.

"I have to take Simon home."

"Stay." He rubbed his cheek against hers. "Just stay, both of you."

"That's a big step for me." She rested her head on his shoulder. It would be so easy, she knew, to stay. To just let herself be held this way. But big steps should never be easy.

"I'm not playing games with you, but I have to think about what's right." For all of us, she thought. "I meant what I said about wondering how I've ended up here. I have to be sure about whatever happens next."

"I'm not going to hurt you. I'm not going to hurt either of us."

"I'm not afraid of that. No, that's a lie. I am. But I'm afraid I could hurt you. I didn't tell you what happened last night. I didn't want to talk about it in front of Simon."

"What is it?"

"Can we go in the other room? In case he wakes up."

"It was Kane," Brad said as he walked her into the great room.

"Yes." And she told him.

"Is that what you wanted, Zoe? To live in New York, work in a high-powered job?"

"Oh, I don't know about New York. Could just as easily have been Chicago, or Los Angeles, anyplace that seemed important. Anyplace that wasn't where I was."

"Because you were unhappy, or because there were things you wanted to do?"

She started to answer, then stopped. "Both," she realized. "I don't know that I thought about being unhappy, but I guess I was a lot of the time. The world just seemed so small and set where I lived. The way I lived."

She looked out the windows, across the lawn to the dark ribbon of river. "But the world isn't small, and it's not set. I used to think about that, to wonder about all that. The people and the places out there."

Surprised at herself, she turned back to see him watching her, quiet and steady. "Anyway, that's off the track."

"I don't think so. What made you happy?"

"Oh, lots of things. I don't mean to sound like I was sad all the time. I wasn't. I liked school. I was good in school. I liked learning things, figuring things out. I was especially good with numbers. I did Mama's books and her taxes. I took care of the bills. I liked doing it. I thought maybe I'd be a bookkeeper, or even a CPA. Or work in banking. I wanted to go to college, and get an important job, move to the city. Have things. Have more, that's all. Have people respect me, even admire me, because I knew how to do things."

She gave a little shrug, wandered to the fireplace. "Used to irritate my mama, the way I talked about it, and how I was fussy about what belonged to me because I wanted to keep it nice. She said how I thought I was better than anybody else, but that wasn't it."

Her brows drew together as she stared at the flames. "That wasn't it at all. I just wanted to be better than I was. I figured if I was smart enough, I could get that good job and move to the city, and nobody'd look at me and think, There's that trailer trash from over in the hollow."

"Zoe."

She shook her head. "People did think that, Bradley. They did because it was true enough. My daddy drank too much and ran off with another woman, left my mother with four children, a stack of bills, and a double-wide. Most of my clothes were what somebody'd given us out of charity. You don't know what that's like."

"No, I don't. I don't know what it's like."

"Some people give you things out of goodness, but a lot of them do it so they can feel superior. So they can sit smug and say, Look what I did for that poor woman and her children. And you see it on their faces."

She glanced over at him, her cheeks flushed with the heat of both pride and shame. "It's hateful. I didn't want anybody giving me anything. I wanted to get it for myself. So I worked, and I squirreled money away, and I made big plans. Then I got pregnant."

She looked back toward the archway to make certain Simon was still out of earshot. "Didn't realize I was until I was into my second month. Thought I had the flu or something. But it didn't go away, so I went to the clinic and they told me. I was about nine weeks already. God, nine weeks along, and too stupid to know it."

"You were a child." And one he ached for. "You weren't stupid, you were a child."

"Old enough to get pregnant. Old enough to know what that meant. I was so scared. I didn't know what was going to happen. I didn't tell my mother, not right away. I went to the boy. He was scared, too, and maybe he was a little angry. But he said we'd do the right thing. I felt better after that. I felt calmer. So I went home and told Mama."

She drew a deep breath, pressed her fingers to her temples. She hadn't meant to speak of all of this, but now that she'd begun, she would finish. "Oh, I can still see her, sitting there at the table with the fan blowing. It was hot, awfully damn hot. She looked at me, and leaned over and slapped me.

"I don't blame her for that," she said when Brad swore. "I didn't blame her then, I don't blame her now. I'd been sneaking out behind her back to be with that boy, and now I had to pay the price for it. I don't blame her for the slap, Bradley, I had it coming. But I blame her for after. For finding satisfaction in knowing I'd gotten in trouble, the same as she had with me. For making sure I knew I was no better than she was, for all my ideas and plans. I blame her for making me feel cheap, and making the baby I was carrying into a punishment."

"She was wrong." It was said simply, in a matter-of-fact tone that had Zoe's breath hitching. "What happened with the father?"

"Well, he didn't do the right thing, as he'd called it. I don't want to talk about that right now. There's this business in my clue about forks on the path. I chose my direction back then. I quit school, and I went to work. I got my GED and my beautician's license, and I left home."

"Wait." He held up a hand. "You went out on your own, alone, when you were sixteen? And pregnant. Your mother—"

"Didn't have any say in it," she interrupted. She turned, facing him with the fire snapping behind her. "I left when I was six months gone because I was not going to raise my baby in that goddamn trailer. I took my direction," she said, "and maybe that path started me on the road to the Valley, and the Peak, and all of this."

Maybe she had to say it all, she thought now. Maybe she'd needed to go back, step by step so she could see it all.

And so he could.

"I wouldn't be here if I'd chosen another, if I hadn't loved a boy and made a baby with him. I wouldn't be here if I'd gone on to college and gotten that good job, and flown off to Rome for the week. I have to figure out what that means, about the key. Because I gave my word I'd try to find it. And I have to figure out if that's why I'm here, with you. Because God knows, it doesn't make any sense for me to be here otherwise."

"Whatever brought you here, it makes perfect sense."

"Were you listening?" she demanded. "Did you hear a word I said about where I came from?"

"Every word." He crossed to her. "You're the most amazing woman I've ever met."

She stared at him, then lifted her hands in exasperation. "I don't understand you at all. Maybe I'm not supposed to. But there's something we both have to consider. Because the world isn't small, and it isn't set. And, Bradley, there isn't just one world for us to worry about here."

"It circles around," he said with a nod. "And it intersects."

"And because it does, are you the choice I'm supposed to take or the one I'm supposed to turn away from?"

He smiled, but it was sharp and it was fierce. "Try to turn away."

She shook her head. "And if I turn toward you, and something starts between us, something real, what happens if I have to choose again?"

He laid his hands on her shoulders, slid them up until they

framed her face. "Zoe, something's already started between us, and it's very real."

She wished she could be so sure.

When she rode home through the night sprinkled with the light of a quarter moon, nothing seemed quite real.

Eight

"Champagne and lobster and limos, oh my," Dana exclaimed as they maneuvered the wrought-iron baker's rack they'd bought into its place in their communal kitchen.

"Very classy," Malory agreed. "Maybe Brad will give Flynn lessons on how to prepare dinner for a woman."

"That's part of the problem. I'm the beer, burger, and station-wagon type. It was wonderful, absolutely wonderful, but the way a really good dream is."

"What's wrong with that?" Dana demanded.

"Nothing." Zoe puffed out her cheeks, slowly expelled air. "But I'm starting to get some very serious feelings about him."

"I repeat. What's wrong with that?"

"Let's see, where should I start? We're barely from the same planet. I'm trying to get a business started, which is going to involve every minute I can squeeze out of the day, and that's after raising Simon, for about the next ten years. I have three weeks left to find the last key to the Box of Souls, and if we were playing Hot and Cold right now, I'd have frostbite on my ass."

"You know, you never hear about people getting frostbite on the ass," Dana commented. "I wonder why that is."

She selected one of the fancy tins of tea she'd decided to carry and set it on a shelf of the rack. Turned her head this way, that way to critique its position.

"On a more serious note." Malory's voice was dry as she placed a hand-thrown bowl from her new stock on a shelf. "Neither the business nor Simon is a reason not to have a man in your life, if you're attracted to the man. If you believe he's a good man."

"Of course I'm attracted to him. A woman in a coma would be attracted to him. And he is a good man. I didn't want to believe he was, but he's a very good man."

Zoe put one of her scented candles on the shelf. "It would be less complicated if he wasn't. Then I could probably carve out just enough time for a hot, sweaty affair, and we'd both walk away from it without any regrets."

"Why are you already thinking about walking and regrets?" Malory asked her.

"I've had one constant in my life, and that's Simon. I've got another now, with both of you. They're both like miracles. I'm not banking on a third."

"And people call me pessimistic," Dana muttered. "Okay, here's an idea." She set another canister on the rack. "Consider Brad a big boy, so if you both decide to have that hot, sweaty affair, you're both responsible for the outcome. Oh, and don't forget to fill us in on all the deets. Next, remember that you may be up to bat for this round of the quest, but the three of us are still a team, which means you're not the only one courting frostbite at the moment."

"Good points." Malory agreed as she put a hand-painted tray on the rack, then nodded in approval at the apothecary bottle of hand lotion Zoe added. "I think it's time for an official meeting. We'll put six very good heads together and see what kind of storm we can come up with."

"Maybe it'll break the logjam in my head." Zoe added a dish

of fancy soap, another candle, then stepped back as Malory set a long, slim vase and a pair of white porcelain candleholders on the rack.

"Not such a jam," Dana disagreed. "You're pursuing theories, thinking things through, lining things up. It's taking on form, like this rack. A little here, a little there, then you step back and look at the whole, see what needs to be added or adjusted."

"I hope so. Needs books," Zoe commented, with a nod toward the rack.

"First shipment next week." Dana moved beside her, rested an elbow on Zoe's shoulder. "Jeez, I know it's just a kitchen rack, but, damn, it looks terrific."

"It looks like us." Pleased, Malory slid an arm around Zoe's waist. "And you know what's going to look even better? When people start buying."

UPSTAIRS, ZOE STOOD ON the stepladder to hang the storage cabinets above her shampoo bowls. As she worked, she ticked through the chores she'd set for herself that week.

She needed to log some more time on the computer. Not only for research but to try her hand at designing the menu of services for the salon and day spa.

She wondered if she could get paper close to the same color as her trim. Something distinctive.

And she was going to have to decide, once and for all, on her prices. Did she undercut the rates of her competitor in town by a few dollars, or did she charge a few dollars more and make a reasonable profit?

She was using higher-end products than the other salon in town, and they cost more money. She was certainly offering her customers a more attractive atmosphere.

And the other salon didn't serve the customers—clients, she corrected, "clients" was more sophisticated. The other salon didn't serve its clients iced mineral water or cups of herbal tea as she planned to do. And it didn't give them a heated neck roll filled with relaxing herbs while they had their nails done.

She hung the cabinet, swiped her forearm over her brow, and started to back down the ladder.

"What a wonderful color."

Caught off guard, Zoe grabbed the ladder and stared down at Rowena.

"I didn't hear you . . . " Pop out of thin air?

"Sorry." Rowena's eyes danced as if she guessed Zoe's thoughts. "Malory and Dana told me to come right up. I've been downstairs admiring what you three have done. I wanted to see your space. As I said, the colors are wonderful."

"I wanted them to be fun."

"You've succeeded. And what did I interrupt?"

"Oh, I was just finished. Storage cabinets, for shampoos, conditioners, that sort of thing. My shampoo bowls will go right here."

"Ah."

"And, well, the stations for the stylists." She gestured. "The stationary hair dryers over there, the reception counter, the waiting area. I'm going to put in a sofa, a couple of chairs, a padded bench. And that room that angles off down there, that's for nails. I ordered this heated massage chair for what I'm calling the Indulgence Pedicure. The standard pedi will be good, but this one's going to be a knockout. It'll include—you couldn't possible care."

"On the contrary." Rowena wandered over to look at the area, then moved through to another room. "And this?"

"One of the treatment rooms. Massages or facials. Across the hall's for the wraps. I'm going to offer a detoxifying wrap and a really terrific paraffin job. And I'm using the big bathroom for exfoliating treatments."

"It's very ambitious."

"I've been planning it in my head for a long time. It's hard to believe it's really happening. We plan to open by December first. Rowena, I haven't neglected the key. I just haven't figured it out."

"If it was easy, it wouldn't be important. You know that," Rowena added, giving Zoe an absentminded pat on the shoulder as she wandered back to the main salon. "None of this was easy."

"No, but it was just work. Step by step." She smiled a little as Rowena turned, lifted a brow. "Okay, I get it. Step by step."

"Tell me, how's your son?"

"Simon's fine. He's with a friend today. We had dinner at Bradley's last night."

"Did you? I'm sure that was enjoyable."

"I know there are things you can't tell me, but I'm going to ask anyway. It's not for me that I'm asking. I'm not afraid to take my lumps."

"No, I don't imagine you are. You've had plenty of them."

"No more than my share. I agreed to do this thing, just like Malory and Dana did. But Bradley didn't sign on. I want to know if something's making him have feelings for me, feelings I'm supposed to use to find the key."

Rowena stopped at a mirror, fussed with her hair in a timeless female gesture. "Why would you think that?"

"Because he's infatuated, with the painting, with Kyna's face in his painting, and I just happen to look like her."

Rowena plucked a bottle of shampoo from a carton, examined it. "Do you think so little of yourself?"

"No. I'm not saying he couldn't be, that he isn't, interested in me. In who I am. But the painting was the start of it for him."

"And he bought the painting, chose his path. The path led to you." She replaced the bottle. "Interesting, isn't it?"

"I need to know if the choice was his."

"I'm not the one to ask. And you're not ready to believe him, should he answer." She took out another bottle, opened it to sniff. "You want me to promise you he won't be hurt. I can't do that. And I believe he would be insulted if he knew you asked such a thing."

"Then he'll have to be insulted, because I had to ask." Zoe lifted her hands, let them fall. "It probably doesn't matter. Kane's hardly bothered with me. We thought he would come out, guns blazing, but he's barely flicked at me, like he would a fly. He doesn't seem to be very concerned that I'll find the key."

"And so by ignoring you, he erodes your self-confidence. You make it easy for him."

Zoe was surprised by Rowena's dismissive tone. "I didn't say I was giving up," she began, then stopped, let out a breath. "Jesus, he's got a better handle on me than I realized. He's playing me. Most of my life people either ignored me or told me I couldn't do what I wanted to do most."

"You've proved them wrong, haven't you? Now prove him wrong."

A FEW MILES AWAY, at the Main Street Diner, Brad shifted so Flynn could slide into the booth beside him. Across the table, Jordan had his long legs stretched out and was already studying the two-sided laminated menu.

"That menu hasn't changed in about sixty years, pal," Flynn pointed out. "You ought to have it down by now. Got held up," he added and since Brad's coffee was already there, helped himself to it.

"How come you always sit beside me and drink my coffee? Why don't you ever sit over there and drink his?"

"I'm a sucker for tradition." He smiled up at the waitress as she sidled over with a mug and the coffeepot. "Hi, Luce, I'm going to have the meat loaf sandwich."

She nodded, noted it down. "Heard you were down at the council meeting this morning. Anything up?"

"Just the usual hot air."

She snickered, glanced at Jordan. "How about you, big boy?"

When she walked off with their orders, Flynn settled back, twitched his head toward Brad. "So, did you hear that Mr. Bigshot Vane here sent a mile-long limo to pick up his date for dinner last night?"

"No shit? Show-off."

"It was only half a mile long, and how the hell do you know?"

"Nose for news." Flynn tapped a finger on the side of his nose. "My sources, however, were unable to confirm if said show-off scored."

"I took the kid in *Smackdown*, but he whipped my ass in *Grand Theft Auto*."

"Struck out with the mother," Jordan concluded. "I bet the kid got one large charge out of riding in that limo."

"He did. So did Zoe. Did you hear what she said the other day? She's never lain in a hammock?" His face clouded as he took his coffee back from Flynn. "How can somebody go their whole life and never lie in a hammock?"

"And now you want to buy her one so she can lie in it," Flynn decided.

"I guess I do."

"Which makes you, let's see"—Jordan stared at the ceiling—"oh, yes, that would be toast." Then he sobered. "She's a terrific woman. She deserves a break, somebody to take some of the weight."

"Working on it. With your mother, if somebody had come along who was serious about her, would that have bothered you?"

"I don't know. Nobody ever did—or she didn't let anybody. I can't say for sure. I guess it would have depended on who it was, and how he treated her. You that serious?"

"It's heading that way, for me."

"That brings us back around," Flynn commented. "The three of us, the three of them. Pretty damn tidy."

"Maybe sometimes things are meant to be tidy."

"I know all about that. I happen to be engaged to the queen of neat. But I think it's something we have to think about. What part you're meant to play in this production we're in," Flynn stated matter-of-factly.

He let that stew while their sandwiches were served.

"I've been thinking about it," Brad said. "It seems to me most of the clue deals with things that happened to her, or things she did before she met me. But those things brought her here. Then if we assume I'm part of it, those same clues could apply to things that happened to me, or things I did, before I met her. Those things brought me back here."

"Different paths, same destiny." Jordan nodded. "It's a theory. Now your paths have crossed."

"What you do now, that's a question," Flynn put in. "But also where. The goddess with a sword indicates a battle."

"She won't be fighting it alone," Brad promised. "The sword's sheathed in the paintings. In mine it's sheathed and placed with her in the coffin, and in the one at the Peak it's sheathed and at her hip."

"It's sheathed in the stone in the portrait Rowena did of Arthur, too. The one I bought," Jordan added.

"She never had a chance to draw it." Brad brought the image of the still, white face in the painting into his mind. "Maybe we're supposed to give her that chance."

"Maybe Malory should take another look at the paintings," Flynn suggested. "See if she missed anything. I don't—"

"Hold that thought," Jordan told him as his cell phone beeped. He flipped it out, smiled at the number on his readout. "Hey, Stretch." He lifted his coffee. "Uh-huh. It so happens my associates are with me in my office at the moment. I can do that," he said after a minute, then tipped the phone away from his ear.

"Meeting, six o'clock, Flynn's place. I have nods of assent," he said into the phone. "That works for me. Zoe's making chili," he told his friends.

"Tell Dana to tell Zoe I'll pick her up."

"Brad says to tell Zoe he'll pick her up. We were going to swing by and give you guys a hand this afternoon . . . Okay, I'll just see you at home, then. Oh, hey, Dane? So, what are you wearing?"

He grinned, then shoved the phone back in his pocket. "Must've gotten disconnected."

WHILE THE CHILI WAS simmering, Zoe spread her notes and papers over the kitchen table. The house was quiet for a change. It was time to take advantage of it.

Maybe she'd tried to be too organized, mimicking Malory's style. Or she'd depended too much on books, trying to follow Dana's lead. Why not try impulse and instinct with this task as she did with other projects?

What did she do when she wanted to pick new paint for the walls, or new fabric for curtains? She spread out a bunch of samples and flipped through them until something popped out at her.

And then she knew.

Here she had her own carefully written notes, copies of Malory's, of Dana's. She had Jordan's detailed flow of events, and the photographs Malory had taken of the paintings.

She picked up the notebook she'd bought the day after her first visit to Warrior's Peak. It didn't look so shiny and new now, she thought. It looked used. And maybe that was better.

There was a lot of work inside this notebook, she reminded herself as she flipped pages. A lot of hours, a lot of effort. And that work, those hours, that effort, had helped both Malory and Dana complete their parts of the quest.

Something in here was going to help her complete her part, and finish it.

She opened the notebook at random, and began to read.

Kyna, the warrior, she'd written. *Why is she mine? I see Venora, the artist, in Malory, and Niniane, the scribe, in Dana. But how am I a warrior?*

I'm a hairdresser. No, hair and skin specialist—must remember to pump that up. I worked for it. I'm a good worker, but that's not the same as fighting.

Beauty for Malory, knowledge for Dana. Courage for me. Where does the courage come in?

Is it just living? That doesn't seem like enough.

Considering, Zoe tapped her pencil on the page, then earmarked it by folding down a corner. She flipped through the section until she came to a blank sheet.

Maybe just living is enough. Didn't Malory have to choose to live in the real world—sacrificing something of beauty, and Dana had to learn to see the truth, and live with it? Those were essential steps in their quests.

What's mine?

She began to write quickly now, trying to see the pattern, trying to form one. As the ideas and possibilities clicked in her mind, she wore her pencil down, tossed it aside, and reached for another.

When that went dull, she pushed away from the table to take the pencils to the sharpener.

Satisfied with the points, she stuck one behind each ear and turned to the stove to stir the chili and think.

Maybe she was on the right track, maybe she wasn't—and she sure as hell couldn't see the end of the road. But she was moving somewhere, and that was important.

With her mind wandering, she lifted the spoon to taste, then stared at the dull reflection in the range hood.

Her hair was a long spill down her shoulders, adorned with a wide gold band with a dark center stone, diamond-shaped. Her eyes were more gold than brown. Very clear, very direct.

She could see the green of her dress—a dark forest color, and the brown leather of a strap over her shoulder. The silver glint of a sword hilt at her hip.

There were trees, misted with morning, pearly gleams from dewed leaves, wavering beams of early sunlight. And through the trees were paths.

She could feel the smooth wood of the spoon handle in her hand, smell the steam from the simmering pot.

Not a hallucination, she told herself. Not imagination.

"What are you trying to tell me? What do you want me to see?"

The image moved back, so Zoe saw the whole of her—the slim build, the booted feet. For another moment they stood, staring at each other. Then the figure turned, walked through the mist, into the forest, and with a hand on the hilt of her sword, strode down a rough path.

"I don't know what that means. Damn it." Frustrated, Zoe rapped a fist against the range hood. "What the hell does that mean?"

With a sharp twist of her wrist, she turned off the burner. She'd just about reached the end of her patience when it came to gods.

BRAD PULLED UP IN Zoe's driveway a little earlier than he needed to. He imagined men who were riding on that fast wave of love, lust, infatuation—whatever the hell he had—tended to be early to see the women with whom they were obsessed.

It didn't surprise him to see Zoe step out of the house before he could do more than turn off the ignition. He'd been around her long enough to know she was dependable.

She was also loaded with a backpack, an enormous shoulder bag, and a huge cooking pot.

"Let me give you a hand," he called as he climbed out of the car.

"I don't need a hand."

"Yes, you do, unless you've got an extra one stuffed in that bag." He took the pot, mildly surprised when she tried to tug it back.

"You know, once in a while, it'd be a nice change if you actually listened to what I say." She yanked open the back door of his big, shiny SUV and tossed the backpack inside. "Even nicer might be if you bothered to ask instead of just ordering, or assuming."

"Why don't I just give this back to you,"

She yanked the pot out of his hands, then bent to wedge it on the floor of the back.

"I didn't ask you to come by here and pick me up. I don't need to be picked up and hauled around. I have a car."

Love, lust, infatuation, he thought, they could all be put in the backseat, just like the chili, when irritation took the driver's seat.

"You were on the way. It didn't make sense to take two cars. Where's Simon?"

"He's having dinner and staying the night with a friend. Should I have checked with you first?" She stormed around the car, then just balled her fists when he beat her there and opened the door for her. "Do I look helpless? Do I look like I can't figure out how to open a damn door on some fancy car?"

"No." He slammed it shut. "Go ahead," he invited, and stalked around to the other side.

He waited until she'd whipped the seat belt across, shoved the buckle into place. "Would you like to tell me what crawled up your ass?" He spoke in the most pleasant tone, the same danger-ously pleasant tone his father used when he was about to slice an opponent into small, bloody pieces.

"My ass is my own business, and so are my moods. I'm in a bad mood. I have them. If you think I'm sweet and accommo-dating and easy to manipulate, you're mistaken. Now are you going to drive this car, or are we just going to sit here?"

He turned the car on, threw it in reverse. "If you've formed the impression that I believe you to be sweet, accommodating, or easy to manipulate, you're the one who's mistaken. What you are is prickly, stubborn, and oversensitive."

"You would think that, wouldn't you, just because I don't like being told what to do, how to do it, when to do it. I'm just as capable and as smart as you are. Maybe more, since I didn't grow up having somebody catering to my every wish and demand."

"Now just a damn minute."

"I've had to fight for everything I've got. Fight to get it," she snapped out, "and fight to keep it. I don't need somebody coming along on his white charger, or his limousine, or his big Mercedes, and rescuing me."

"Who the hell's trying to rescue you?"

"And I don't need some—some Prince Charming-looking man coming around trying to get me stirred up either. If I want to sleep with you, I will."

"Right now, honey, take my word, I'm not thinking about sex."

She sucked in air and gritted her teeth. "And don't call me honey. I don't like it. I especially don't like it in that snotty private-school tone."

"'Honey' happens to be the most polite thing I can currently think of to call you."

"I don't want you to be polite. I don't *like* you when you're polite."

"Is that so? Then you're going to love this."

He whipped the car to the curb, ignored the furious blast of horns behind him at the move. He hit the buckle of the seat belt with one hand, grabbed her sweater with the other. He yanked her forward, then knocked her back against the seat again with a kiss that had nothing to do with romance and everything to do with temper.

She shoved, she struggled, she steamed. In those few furious moments, it was her strength pitted against his, and the point was made, brutally, that she was outgunned.

When he released her, snapped his belt back into place, her breath was ragged.

"Fuck Prince Charming." He swung away from the curb.

No, he didn't look like a storybook character now, she thought. Unless it was one of those warlord figures who blazed through villages taking exactly what they wanted. The kind who dragged a woman up onto his horse and rode away with her while she was still screaming.

"I thought you weren't thinking about sex."

He spared her one hot look. "I lied."

"I'm not going to apologize for the things I said. I've got a right to speak my mind. I've got a right to be irritable and angry."

"Fine. I'm not going to apologize for what I just did. I've got the same rights."

"I guess you do. I wasn't really mad at you. I am now, but I wasn't. I was just mad in general."

"You can either tell me why, or not." He pulled up at Flynn's. Waited.

"Some things that have happened. I'd rather get into it all with everyone, all at once. I'm not going to apologize," she said again. "If you keep getting in my way, you're going to make the handiest target."

"Same goes," he said, and got out of the car. "I'm carrying

your goddamn pot." He yanked open the door, hauled it up. "Deal."

She stared at him, standing there in the brisk fall evening, in his gorgeous overcoat, holding her big stewpot. And looking, she thought, as if he'd just as soon dump the contents over her head as not.

She let the laugh bubble in her throat, then let it out as she retrieved the backpack. "It's kind of nice, when I'm being a jackass, to have somebody kick and bray right along with me. That pot's pretty full. Mind you don't tip it and spill chili on that lovely coat."

She started toward the door. "Fuck Prince Charming," she said and laughed again. "That was a good one."

"I have my moments," he muttered and followed her inside.

WHEN THE CHILI WAS simmering on Flynn's new stove, Zoe looked around the living room. Malory's touch was everywhere now, she noted. The tables, the lamps, the vases and bowls. The art on the walls or set around the room. There were fabric swatches on the arm of the couch and what looked like antique fireplace tools standing by the hearth.

There was a scent of fall flowers and of female.

Zoe remembered the first time she'd come into this room. Two short months—a lifetime—before. There'd been nothing but the big, ugly couch, a couple of crates standing in for tables, and some boxes yet unpacked.

The couch was still ugly, but the fabric swatches told her Malory was going to deal with that. As she would, in her organized and creative way, deal with the rest of the house.

She and Flynn had become a couple, Zoe thought, and were making the house into a home.

A reminder of how they'd come to this point hung over the mantel. Zoe moved closer, looking up at the portrait Malory had painted while under Kane's spell. The Singing Goddess, standing near a forest while her sisters looked on. It was brilliant and beautiful, and full of innocent joy.

And the key that had been on the ground at Venora's feet had been pulled out of the painting, brought into three dimensions by Malory's will, and used to open the first lock.

"It looks good there," Zoe said. "It looks right there."

She turned back. They were waiting for her, she knew, and she had to struggle against nerves. Both Malory and Dana had taken their turn at the head of a meeting. Now it was hers.

"I guess we'd better get started."

Nine

"I BROUGHT ALL MY NOTES," SHE BEGAN, "IN CASE WE need to look through them. Or in case I get turned around and need them. I spent most of last week thinking about this on my own and not talking about it with everyone, not very much. I think that was a mistake. Or maybe not a mistake, but it's time to do this now."

She blew out a breath. "I'm not real good at this kind of thing. I'm just going to say the things I think, and y'all can pitch in whenever."

"Zo?" Dana picked up a beer from the table, handed it to her. "Relax."

"Trying to." She took a quick sip. "I think Kane hasn't pushed at me very hard so far because he just sees what's on the surface. We learned from everything that happened before that he doesn't really understand what we are, inside. I think that's why he hates us. He hates us," she murmured, "because he can't see what we are, and he can't get a good hold on what he can't see."

"Well put," Jordan said, which helped her relax a little more.

"Here's what I think he sees with me. A woman from a ... 'disadvantaged' is what they call it. A disadvantaged childhood.

Poor is what it is, but people don't like saying 'poor.' I don't have much formal education. I got pregnant when I was sixteen, and I made a living doing hair. Mostly doing hair, with some waitressing and whatnot thrown in to make ends meet. I don't have Malory's class and culture."

"Oh, really, that's—"

"Wait." Zoe held up a hand to halt Malory's sharp protest. "Just hear me out. I don't have that, and I don't have Dana's education or confidence. What I've got is a strong back and a son to raise. All of that's true. But all of that isn't, well, all. And here's what he doesn't see, or understand."

She sipped again to wet her throat. "Determination. I didn't settle for being poor. I wanted more, and I found ways to get more. Then there's my word. I made a promise that night up at the Peak, and when I make a promise, I keep it. And I'm no coward. I think Kane has barely bothered with me because he doesn't see that, and even more because he's had enough time to watch me, or study me, or whatever the hell he does, and he was smart enough to figure out I might think less of myself, and my chances of doing this if he made it seem like he wasn't all that worried about me."

She took a deep breath. "That's his mistake. He's not going to win by making me feel I'm not worth the fight."

"You're going to kick his ass," Dana stated.

Her eyes brightened, and though she didn't realize it, her smile was a warrior's. "Oh, I'm going to kick his ass, and when I'm done, I'm going to squeeze his balls blue."

Deliberately, to make her grin, Flynn crossed his legs protectively. "Any specific angles on how you're going to go about that?"

"A couple. With Dana and Malory, they had to take steps, make choices, even sacrifices. They reflected the clues, and . . . " She glanced back at the portrait. "And the goddess they stood for. So, I have to think how what I've done, or have to do, reflects mine. The puppy and the sword. That's what she has in the painting at the Peak. She nurtures and she defends, I guess. I've got a son I've been nurturing and defending for more than nine years."

"Not just him," Jordan put in. "Your nature is to nurture and defend anyone you care about, anyone who needs it. It's instinctive, and that makes it one of your strengths. Another thing Kane wouldn't understand about you is you care about the women in that painting, care enough to go to the wall for them."

"Friendship," Brad added with a gesture toward the painting. "Family, and the preservation of those things. Those are essential elements in your life."

"I guess we're on the same page, then, because I was thinking that one of the basics of the quests, so far, has been living life the way you really want to live it, taking whatever steps and risks you need to, being willing to sacrifice and work to make it happen."

It sounded good when she said it out loud, Zoe decided. It sounded solid. "For me, I decided to have a child. A lot of people told me I was making a mistake, but I knew in my heart I wanted the child, and I wanted to do right by him. I left home because I knew I'd never be able to do right by him if I stayed. I was scared, and it was hard. But it was right for me, and for Simon."

"You chose the path," Brad said quietly.

"I chose it. And there was some of that loss and despair that Rowena talked about in the clue. You can't raise a child without some loss and despair. You sure as hell can't raise one alone without them. But you get all the joy, too, and the pride and the wonder. I chose to come here to the Valley because that was what I wanted for myself and for Simon. Then I had to decide if I was going to keep plugging away for a paycheck or take a chance and make something of my own. I didn't have to do that one alone, and see, those other choices made it so I didn't have to."

She crouched down to take some papers from her backpack. "See this? I made this up. It's like a chart, kind of a map."

She handed it to Malory first. "See, there's where I grew up—not all that far from here, really. Only about sixty miles across the state line. And there's the names of my family, and people who had an impact on me—one way or the other. Then I sort of routed out other places I lived, and worked, and the names and all that. Until I ended up here, with all of you. See, I was thinking, some of it's just living. What you do, and what happens to you while you're doing it."

Malory raised her eyes from the chart, met Zoe's. "You worked at HomeMakers."

"Just part-time. Three nights a week and Sunday afternoons, for about three months before Simon was born." She turned to Brad. "I didn't even think about it before. Just didn't."

"What store?"

"The one outside of Morgantown, off Highway 68. They were really good to me there. I was six months along when I went in looking for the extra work. I went into labor working cash register number four. I think that means something. I went into labor when I was working for you."

He took the chart as it was passed to him, looked at it, noted dates. "I was in that store doing some troubleshooting in March of that year." He tapped the chart. "I remember it because someone came into the meeting apologizing for being a few minutes late. It seemed one of our cashiers had gone into labor and he'd wanted to be sure she got off to the hospital safely."

The chill that danced through Zoe wasn't fear. It was excitement. "You were there."

"Not only there, but when I came back to finish up the next day, it turned out I'd won the baby pool. I'd taken a boy, seven pounds, and gone with twelve hours of labor."

She let out a shaky breath. "Pretty close."

"Close enough to earn me a couple hundred dollars."

"That is way spooky," Dana commented "Where do we go with it?"

"Some of it's going to be where Zoe and I go with it." He looked back at the chart. "You didn't go back to work at the Morgantown store."

"No. I picked up a few extra hours a week at the salon where I was working, and they let me bring the baby in. As friendly as they are at HomeMakers, you can't work the cash register with a baby under the counter."

He'd been there, Zoe thought again. Their paths had crossed at the most important moment of her life. "I didn't want to spend the money for a sitter," she continued. "More, I guess, I wasn't ready to let him out of my sight."

Brad studied her face, trying to imagine her—imagine both of them on that day, nearly ten years before. "If I'd done my tour of the floor sooner rather than later, I might have seen you, spoken with you. I decided to do the offices and take the meetings first. One of those little choices that change what comes after for quite some time."

"You weren't meant to meet then." Malory shook her head. "I know it goes back to sounding like destiny and fate, but those shouldn't be discounted. Even with our choices. You weren't meant to meet until you were both here. Paths, crossroads, intersections. Zoe's got them there on her chart."

Malory eased forward, tilting her head so she could read it along with Brad. "You could add your roads on there, Brad. From the Valley to Columbia, back to the Valley, to New York, to Morgantown, wherever else, then back here. You'd find other intersections and crossroads. And for both of you they've led here. It's not just geography."

"No." Brad tapped a finger on the names Zoe had listed near her hometown. "James Marshall. Is that Simon's father?"

"In the technical sense. Why?"

"I know him. Our families did some business. We bought some land from his father, though the son ran the deal. A nice chunk of commercial property near Wheeling. I closed the deal before I left New York. It was one of the levers I used to move back here and take over this area."

"You met James," Zoe whispered.

"Met him, and spent enough time with him to know he doesn't deserve you, or Simon. I need another beer."

Zoe stayed where she was a moment. "I'm going to check on the chili. Just, ah, give me a few minutes, and I'll dish it up."

She hurried toward the kitchen. "Bradley."

He kept walking, then yanked open the refrigerator, got his beer. "Is that why you were pissed when I picked you up?" he demanded. "You'd made your chart, started thinking it through and saw just how tight the connection is with me?"

"Yes, that was part of it." She linked her fingers, then pulled them apart. "It's like another brick, Bradley, and I haven't figured out if it's like having that brick put down on a walk to give me a good, solid path or like having it mortared into a wall that's closing me in."

He stared at her, astonished fury pulsing around him. "Who's trying to close you in? That's a hell of a thing to put on me, Zoe."

"It's *not* you. It's not about you. It's about me. What I think, what I feel, what I do. And damn it, I can't help it if it makes you mad that I have to decide if it's a wall or a walk."

"A wall or a walk," he repeated, then took a slug of beer. "Christ, I actually understand that. I'd rather I didn't."

"It made me feel pushed, and I get mad when I'm pushed. It's not your fault or your doing, but it doesn't feel like it's mine either. I guess I don't like dealing with what's not my fault or my doing."

"He was a stupid son of a bitch for letting you go."

She let out a sigh. "He didn't let me go. He just didn't hold on to me. And that stopped making me mad a long time ago." She moved to the stove, took the lid off her pot. "There was something else that happened. I'm going to finish making this meal, and I'll tell you and the others about it over dinner."

"Zoe." He touched her shoulder, then opened a cupboard to look for plates. "About those bricks? You can always knock a wall down, and build a nice walk out of it."

THEY ATE IN THE kitchen, crowded around the table, as the dining room was a long way from meeting Malory's standards. Over beer and chili and hot bread, Zoe told them about what she'd seen in the steamy shower mirror and the range hood.

"I thought I imagined it the first time. It just seemed too strange not to be my imagination—and it was only for a couple of seconds. But today ... I saw her," Zoe confirmed. "I saw her where I should've been."

"If Kane's trying another angle," Dana began, "I'm not following it."

"It wasn't Kane." Zoe frowned down at her plate. "I don't know how to explain how I'm so sure it wasn't, except to say it didn't feel like him. There's a feeling when he touches you."

She lifted her gaze, met Dana's, then Malory's for confirmation. "Maybe not as it's happening, but after, and you know. It wasn't from him. It was warm," she continued. "Both times it was warm."

"Rowena and Pitte may be adding a few flourishes." Flynn spooned up more chili. "They said Kane had broken the rules with Dana and Jordan, so they compensated."

"It may cost them," Jordan added.

"It may. So it could be they've decided to compensate more. In-for-a-penny sort of thing."

"Doesn't play for me," Bradley disagreed. "If they were going to go over the line again, this soon in Zoe's quest, why not do something solid, something tangible? Why so cryptic?"

"I don't think it was from them either." Zoe pushed food around on her plate. "I think it was from her."

"From Kyna?" Fascinated, Malory sat back. "But how? They're powerless."

"Maybe she is. We don't know how all this works, really, but say she is. Her parents aren't. I started thinking what if someone had Simon trapped somewhere? I would just about go crazy. If there was a way to get him out, I'd do anything I could."

"It's been three thousand years," Flynn pointed out. "Why wait?"

"I know." Zoe took a piece of bread, broke off a chunk. "But time's different for them, right? Didn't Rowena say that? And besides, maybe there wasn't anything that could be done before this, before Kane changed things by spilling blood, mortal blood."

"Keep going," Jordan prompted when she stopped. "Spin it out."

"Well. If Kane changed the nature of the spell by breaking the rules of it, and if that opened—well—like a chink in the curtain, wouldn't loving parents try to send some light through that chink? They wanted me to see her. Not just in a painting but more personally."

"To see her in you," Bradley finished. "To look in the mirror, and see her in you."

"Yes." Zoe let out a relieved breath. "Yes, that's how it feels to me. It's like they wanted her to tell me something. She can't just say, 'Oh, Zoe, the key's under the planter of geraniums on the porch,' but it's like she's trying to show me something I have to do or somewhere I have to go to find it."

"What was she wearing?"

"Jesus, Hawke." Dana jabbed him hard.

"No, seriously, let's look at the details. Was she dressed the way she is in the paintings?"

"Oh, I see." Zoe pursed her lips. "No. She was wearing a short dress, dark green." She closed her eyes to bring it back. "And boots. Brown boots that came right up to the knee. She had on the pendant, the one the legend says her father gave each of them, and this little headband, I guess they call it a circlet? A gold Wonder Woman sort of thing with a diamond-shaped jewel in the center. Dark green, like the dress. And the sword at her hip. Oh!"

Her eyes popped open again. "She had one of those ..." Impatient with herself she waved a hand back between her shoulder blades. "Quivers. That's what it is, the thing for arrows. And there was a bow strapped over her shoulder."

"Sounds like the lady was going hunting," Jordan concluded.

"Into the forest," Zoe continued. "She took the path into the forest to hunt. A hunt's like a quest."

"Maybe the forest in the quest is more literal than we assumed," Dana considered as she ate. "I'll do some research on forests—books and paintings—as well as the local woods around the Valley. Something might pop."

"If you can describe the scene to me, I can try to sketch it," Malory suggested. "It might help for all of us to see it as you did."

"All right." Zoe gave a decisive nod. "That feels positive. It's been like time is slipping away from me, but this feels positive. She had such strong, sad eyes," she said quietly. "I don't know how I could live with myself if I didn't help her."

She was lost in thought as Brad drove her home, and stared up at the waxing moon. It seemed as if she could almost see it growing fuller and whiter, marking her time.

"I don't know that I ever paid attention to the phases of the moon before. You just looked up, and it was full or a sliver or cut in half. I never thought to notice whether it was getting bigger or smaller. But now I don't think I'll ever not know. I'll know just where the moon is in its cycle, without ever looking at the sky.

"I've got less than three weeks left."

"You've got a chart, you've got a sketch. You've got a vision. You can't put the puzzle together without the pieces. You're gathering the pieces."

"I'm counting on it. It helped, talking it through, but it's all running around in my head now. And nothing will settle long enough for me to pick it apart again. I can't bend words into answers the way Dana does, or draw out images into answers like Malory. I have to, I don't know, get my hands around it, and work it into place. I don't have anything to get my hands around yet. It's frustrating."

"Sometimes you have to walk away from the pieces. Then come back and walk around them, look at them from a different angle."

He pulled into her drive. "I'm staying here tonight."

"What?"

"You're not staying here alone, without even Simon in the house in case something happens." He got out, took her pot from the back of the car. "I'll sleep on the sofa."

"I've got Moe," she began as the dog jumped up to race to the door.

"Last time I checked, Moe couldn't dial a phone or drive a car. You might need someone to do both." He paused by the door, waiting for her to unlock it. "You're not staying here alone. I'll sleep on the sofa."

"There isn't—"

"Don't argue."

Jiggling her keys, she took a good, hard look at him. "Maybe I like to argue."

"There wouldn't be any point in it, but if that's what you want to do, let's do it inside. It's dark, it's getting cold, and Moe's becoming a little too interested in what's left in this pot."

She opened the door and headed straight to the kitchen. "Just set that down. I'll take care of it." She got out one of the storage containers she used for leftovers, then shrugged out of her coat, tossed it over a kitchen chair. "It may not have occurred to you that I let Simon spend the night with a friend because I wanted some time alone."

"It occurred to me. I'll stay out of your way." He took off his own coat, then picked up hers. "I'll go hang these up."

Saying nothing, she began transferring leftover chili to the container.

He meant it for the best, she knew. And it wasn't as if she minded having a strong, capable man in the house. She simply wasn't *used* to having a strong, capable man in the house. Especially one who told her what was going to be done.

That was part of the problem, she considered, sealing the container. She'd been piloting her own ship for so long that having anyone take the wheel, however well intentioned, put her back up.

If that was a flaw in her character, she was entitled to a few flaws.

Part of the problem, she thought again as she took the pot to the sink to wash it. The other part, and the bigger chunk of the problem, was having a man she was attracted to in the house when there was no nine-year-old buffer between them.

And that, she realized, setting the pot to drain, was just dead stupid.

She went into the living room. He was sitting in a chair, paging through one of her magazines. Moe, having given up hope of chili, was sprawled over his feet.

141

"If you want reading material," she began, "I can do better than a magazine on hairstyles."

"It's okay. Great-looking models. Can I ask you a couple of questions? The first has to do with the availability of a blanket and pillow."

"I happen to have those items in stock."

"Good. The other, brought to mind by this redhead with the eyebrow ring is . . . just how do I put this?"

"You're interested in an eyebrow ring?"

"No. No, I'm not. But it happens that some time ago, I noticed . . . you were wearing these jeans that rode a little low and this shirt that rode a little high, so I couldn't help but notice you had this silver bar—that you had your navel pierced."

She cocked her head. "That's right."

"I wondered if you always wear it."

She kept her expression very sober, very serious. "Sometimes I wear this little silver hoop instead."

"Uh-huh." Unable to help it, he glanced at her belly, imagined. "Interesting."

"Before I came to the Valley, I worked a second job at a body-piercing and tattoo parlor. I was putting away all I could for a down payment on a house. As an employee, it was free, plus it helped in dealing with customers if you'd gone through it yourself. And no," she added, reading his thoughts, "the only body parts I was willing to have pierced were my belly button and my earlobes. Do you want something to drink? A snack?"

"No, I'm fine." Unless he counted the saliva that wanted to pool in the back of his mouth. "Tattoos? Did you get one?"

She smiled now, friendly as a Sunday school teacher. "I did. Just a little one."

She knew he was wondering what, and more, where. She would just let him wonder for now. "You don't have to sleep on the couch, Bradley." She watched his eyes narrow and focus on her face, and even from three feet away, felt his body tense. "There's no need for that when there's just the two of us here." She waited one long beat. "You can use Simon's bed."

"Simon's bed." He repeated it, as if speaking a foreign language. "Yeah. Right. Good."

"Why don't you come on upstairs, and I'll show you where everything is?"

"Sure." He set the magazine aside, gave Moe a nudge to roll him over and off his feet.

"There are plenty of clean towels in the bathroom closet," she began, enjoying herself as she started upstairs. "And I've got an extra toothbrush in there that you can use."

He kept his hands at his sides as he walked up behind her, and tried not to torture himself with images of tattoos and belly rings. He failed miserably. "I've got a staff meeting at eight-thirty in the morning, so I'll be out of your way early."

"I'm an early riser, so you won't bother me."

She nudged open the door of Simon's room. There were bunk beds with navy-blue spreads, and bright red curtains at the window. Shelves painted to match the spreads were full of the things boys collected. The action figures, the books, the rocks and model cars. A red desk, Simon-sized, was under the window and held a Superman lamp, school-books, and more of the flotsam and jetsam of a young boy.

It was neat but far from regimented, with a corkboard loaded with drawings and photographs and pictures cut out of magazines. There were shoes that had been kicked off, ball caps hooked on the posts of the top bunk, a book bag on the floor with some of its contents spilling out. And a scent, faint, of wildness that was all boy.

"It's a great room."

"We have a go-round periodically on cleaning it. I won the last one, so it's still in pretty good shape."

She leaned back against the doorjamb. "No problem sleeping in here?"

"No, this is fine."

"I appreciate you being a gentleman, not trying to take advantage of the situation and putting any moves on me."

"I'm staying because you shouldn't be alone, not to take advantage of anything."

"Mmm-hmm. I just wanted to be sure of that, and since I am, I'm going to tell you something. I'm not a gentleman." She stepped forward and pressed her body hard against his. "I'm going to take advantage of the situation." She clamped her hands on his butt, squeezed. "And I'm putting the moves on you. What're you going to do about it?"

His system spiked; his pulse scrambled. "Weep with gratitude?"

Laughing, she bit down on his bottom lip. "Cry later. Get your hands on me," she demanded and ravished his mouth. "All over me."

He fisted his hand in the back of her sweater, anchoring himself before he jumped out of his own skin. The taste of her, hot, ripe, flooded him, even as that tight, sexy body pressed and pumped against him.

Then his hands rushed under the sweater to take the long, smooth back, the dip of waist, the subtle flare of hip. More, his frantic brain could only think. More.

She arched and purred as his hungry lips fed off her throat.

His belly jumped when she dragged at the buckle of his belt.

"It's been a while for me." Her voice was thick, her fingers busy. "You'll have to excuse me for being in a hurry."

"No problem." In one fast move, he swung her around until her back was against the wall. "That's really no problem."

He yanked the sweater over her head, and tossed it aside. His hands were on her breasts before it hit the floor.

Gasping, she worked her hands between them, fighting to keep her mouth on his as she hurried to unbutton his shirt. God, she wanted the feel of him against her. The feel of him inside her. Her skin was alive again, the blood running hot under it, her heart pounding in a rhythm she'd forgotten could be so fast, so hard, so thrilling.

Desperate, she pushed his hand down, held it firmly between her legs. Her head fell back, exposing the line of her throat to his lips, his teeth, her hips moving as she pressed his hand to denim, and the heat under it.

It was like holding raw nerves. Nerves with edges of jagged glass. They scraped at his own, all but tore him open. And the scent of her, something exotic that whispered of midnights, shadows, secrets, slithered through his system like a drug. Until everything he touched, tasted, everything he knew was Zoe.

The need for her was like a lightning strike to the heart.

He yanked at the button on her jeans, dragged the denim down. Even as she struggled to step clear he was plunging his fingers into the heat. He watched the shocked pleasure rush over her face as she poured into his hand.

"Don't stop." Her mouth was frantic and fevered under his, and her nails scraped wickedly down his back before digging into his hips.

She rode it, that wild whip of sensation that snapped through mind and body, rode it shuddering and craved more. It burned through her, fueled her until she thought she would go mad from the sheer force of her own greed.

She ground herself against him in urgent demand, and cried out when he drove, hard and deep, inside her. And still it wasn't enough. Her hips pistoned in a brutal bid for speed, she groaned her desire for it over the sharp sound of flesh striking flesh, striking the wall, striking flesh.

He rode with her, in that fast, sweaty race toward release until his vision blurred and his blood screamed. Then drove them both, quivering, to the finish.

Her heart was still thundering when she dropped her head to his shoulder. She gulped air, felt it catch, then tear its way into her lungs and out again.

She was, she realized dimly, naked, sweaty, and pinned to the wall outside her son's room. She should be horrified. She wasn't, she thought. In fact, she was delighted.

"You okay?" His voice was muffled, and she felt his lips move against her hair.

"I think I was a lot better than okay. I think I was fantastic."

"You were. You are." He'd just taken her against the wall. Or she'd taken him. "Can't think yet," he admitted, and braced a hand against the wall so he could remain upright. "You went for the hoop today." He ran his other hand down her body until he could skim a finger over the ring in her belly button. "It's so fucking sexy. I had no idea."

He eased back just enough to watch her laugh. "We moved pretty quick. I seem to have missed your tattoo."

Dazzled, delighted, she touched his hair. "You're a funny guy, Bradley Charles Vane IV. All worked up over belly rings and tattoos."

"I never had this reaction to them on anyone else. Where is it?"

"I'll show you. First, I ought to tell you I'm not finished using you tonight." She leaned in, ran her tongue in a slow, wet line along the side of his throat. "But you may want to lie down for the next round."

"Am I still standing?"

She laughed again, then eased around him, tapping a finger to her left shoulder blade as she walked toward the room across the hall.

"Wait." He put a hand on her arm, coming close behind her to study the image. "It's a faerie."

"That's right. Sometimes she's a good faerie." Zoe looked over her shoulder, a small smile playing around her lips. "Sometimes she's wicked. Why don't you come in here with me and see just which she is tonight?"

Ten

ZOE FACED THE DAY WITH ENERGY TO BURN AND FRESH ideas springing inside her head. While the coffee brewed, she hummed and scrambled some eggs.

There was a man in her shower, she thought with a mile-wide grin. A gorgeous man who'd kept her busy half the night. She didn't know the last time she'd felt so ... *healthy* on less than four hours' sleep. Her body felt wonderfully loose and limber, and so did her mind. She was damn sure she could tackle anything that came her way, one-handed.

People who said sex wasn't important, she decided, obviously weren't having any.

She piled eggs onto a plate, added a slice of toast just as she heard Brad walking into the room. "Right on time," she said and turned to offer the plate.

"You didn't have to fix me breakfast."

"Don't want it?" She picked up a fork, scooped up some eggs.

"I didn't say I didn't want it." He grabbed the plate from her, then the fork. "You having any?"

"Maybe." She stepped forward, opened her mouth.

Willing to join the playful mood, he fed her a bite of eggs while they stood in front of the stove.

"Go ahead and sit down," she told him, and poured the coffee. "Eat while it's hot. You said you had an early meeting."

"Maybe I should cancel it." He leaned over to press his lips to the base of her neck. "We could have breakfast in bed."

"The only way you get breakfast in bed around here is if you're sick." She eased away so she could lay a hand on his brow. "Nope. Eat, go home and change, and get to work."

"You're awfully strict. But you make really good scrambled eggs. You got plans for the day?"

"This and that." She snagged a piece of toast, then sat across from him to butter it. "Next time you get a chance, you'll have to come by Indulgence. We're down to the details, and it's really starting to shine."

"That's the first time you've asked me to come by."

"It's the first time I've slept with you, too."

"I like to see it as a pattern emerging."

"Might be."

"I'm not interested in being with anyone else. Not in bed, not over morning eggs."

"I don't sleep around," she said in a serious tone.

"That's not what I said, and not what I meant." Reminding himself to be patient, he took her hand firmly. "I'm telling you that you're the only woman I'm interested in. Got that?"

"I'm being—what did you call it—prickly and oversensitive."

"Yeah, but you still make great eggs."

"I'm sorry. This sort of thing hasn't been . . . I was going to say a priority for me, but the fact is it just hasn't been. Period. I'm feeling my way."

"Try this: 'Bradley'—by the way, my mother's the only other person that always calls me Bradley. It's kind of nice. Anyway, 'Bradley, I'm not interested in anyone else either.'"

Her smile bloomed. "Bradley, I'm not interested in anyone else either."

"That works for me."

It was working for her, too. And that was just a little scary. "You said once I should ask you why you came back to the Valley. I'm asking you."

"Okay." He picked up the jar of strawberry preserves she'd set out and spread some on his toast. "HomeMakers is more than a business. It's more than tradition. It's family. If you're a Vane," he said with a shrug, "it's HomeMakers."

"Is that what you wanted?"

"Yeah, good thing for me. There were a lot of things to learn, to understand, to train for. I had to go out of the Valley to really get my teeth into the organization, to see it as a whole, beyond its beginnings."

She studied him. He was dressed casually, and his shirt was a bit wrinkled from her hands, from lying on the floor all night. Still, he exuded power and confidence. The kind, she supposed, that was bred in the bone.

"You're proud of it. Of your family, and the beginnings."

"Very much. It's grown, and it's still growing. We've done some really good things—again, not just business. Programs, projects, the layers my grandfather and my father built onto the base of it. I wanted to come back here, to the start, and make something for myself. I intend to make a mark, and I intend to make it in the Valley."

He set his coffee aside. "And I'd better get to it. Are you heading out now?"

"Soon. I've got some chores and errands." She picked up his plate before he could and took it to the sink, then turned to face him. "You'll make your mark, Bradley. You're the kind of man who does. The Valley's lucky to have you back."

For a moment he was simply speechless. "That's the nicest thing you could say to me. Thanks."

"You're welcome. Now go to work," she told him, and kissed him. "And make your mark."

A homey send-off, he thought, and one he could get used to. He wrapped his arms around her, pulled her close, then took the kiss several layers deeper.

Her eyes were blurry when he let her go—something else, he decided, that he could get used to. "Thanks for breakfast. See you later."

She waited until he'd strolled out before she let out a long breath. "Wow. That oughta hold me."

A glance at the stove clock had her moving quickly to put the kitchen back in order. It was time, she thought, to get to those errands.

Or rather, to start down the path she'd decided to take first.

Armed with her chart and her notes, she got in her car and drove toward her past.

Maybe this was part of the quest, she decided, dealing with and understanding the past while building a future. Or maybe it was just something she had to do to understand the route to the key.

Either way, she was heading to what had once been home.

She'd traveled these roads before, Zoe remembered, but always with some reluctance and not a little guilt. This time, she hoped, she was heading toward discovery.

THE HILLS WERE ALMOST colorless now, just the drab grays of denuded trees, the dull, dead browns of fallen leaves. And those trees speared up into a dreary November sky.

She turned onto the back roads, following the winding, narrow ribbon through fallow fields, past little houses planted on tiny lawns.

Every mile took her back.

She'd walked this road, many times. Early mornings when

she'd missed the school bus because she'd been unable to get everything done in time. She had run across that field, a shortcut, and could remember how green it had smelled in early summer.

Sometimes she'd raced across the field when she sneaked out to meet James, raced with her heart flying in front of her in the soft spring air to where he'd parked on the side of the road to wait for her.

The fireflies had danced in the dark; the high grass had tickled her bare legs. She'd believed everything was possible then, if you only wanted it hard enough.

Now she knew the only things that were possible were what you worked for. And even when you did, they could slip away from you.

She pulled to the side of the road, not far from where a boy had waited for her. And ducking through the wire fence, she walked across the fallow field toward the woods.

They'd been her woods as a child. Her forest, full of quiet and secrets and magic. They'd been hers still as she'd grown older. A place to walk, to think, to plan.

And it was there, she believed, on a red blanket spread over pine needles and crunching leaves, that she'd conceived the child who had changed the course of her life.

There were still paths beaten through the trees, she noted. So there were still children who played here, or women who walked, men who hunted. It hadn't really changed. Maybe that was the point. The forest didn't change, not as quickly, not as overtly, as what and who walked in it.

She stood still for a moment, breathing in the quiet, the November scents of rot and damp. Trying not to think, she let her instincts choose her direction.

Loss and despair, joy and light. She'd known all of those here. Blood from the loss of innocence? Fear of the consequences, hope that love would be enough?

She sat on a fallen log and tried to visualize the roads of her life that led from here, and the key that waited on one of them.

She heard the tap of a woodpecker, and the sigh of wind through empty branches.

And then she saw the white buck standing, watching her with eyes of sapphire blue.

"Oh, my God." She sat where she was, afraid to move. Afraid to breathe.

Both Malory and Dana had seen a white deer, she remembered, what Jordan had called a traditional element of a quest. But they'd seen the buck at Warrior's Peak, not in a narrow strip of West Virginia woods.

"This means I was right, I was supposed to come here. It must mean I'm right. But what do you want me to do? I want to help. I'm trying to help."

The buck turned his head and walked away down the rough path. With her knees trembling, Zoe rose to follow.

Had she once dreamed of this? she wondered. Not this exact thing, not of following the path of a white buck, but of magic and wonder and the wish to do something important.

Dreamed, she admitted, of doing something that would take her away from here, away from the tedium and the despair of not being able to see the world beyond these woods.

Had she looked to James for that? Had she loved him, or simply seen him as an escape?

She stopped, pressed a hand to her heart in a kind of shock. "I don't know," she whispered. "I really don't know."

The buck looked back at her, then gathered himself, leaped over the rocky banks of a small creek, and bounded away.

Hoping that she understood, Zoe took the left fork, walked out of the woods and onto the packed gravel of the trailer park.

Like the woods, it had changed little. Different faces, perhaps, different units here and there. But it was still lined with homes that would never grow roots.

She heard radios, televisions—the hum and blare of them dancing out of windows—the sound of a baby crying in short, fitful wails, and the gun of an engine as someone drove out of the park.

Her mother's place was a dull, pale green, with a white metal awning over the side door. The car parked next to it had a dented fender.

She hadn't taken the summer screen off the door yet, Zoe noted. It would make a harsh squeaking sound when you opened it, a slapping sound as you let it go. She climbed the stacked cinder blocks her mother used as steps, and knocked.

"Come on in. I'm setting cup."

The screen squeaked as Zoe opened it, and the inner door stuck a bit as she turned the knob. She gave it a little shove, and let the screen slap closed behind her as she went inside.

Her mother was in the kitchen, where she made her living. The short counter by the stove was crowded with bottles, bowls, a plastic box full of colorful rods for setting a perm, a stack of hair towels, frayed at the ends from countless washings.

The coffeepot was on, and a cigarette smoked in an ashtray of green glass.

She looked too thin, was Zoe's first thought, as if life had carved her down to the bare essentials. She wore snug jeans and a skinny black top that only emphasized the sharp angles. Her hair was cut short, and she was wearing it in a hot red these days.

Her bedroom slippers scuffed the floor as she poured coffee with her back to the door. And were worn, Zoe knew, for comfort.

She was setting up to do a perm, and would be on her feet for a while.

The television across in the living area was tuned to one of the morning talk shows that seemed to thrive on anger and grief.

"You're running early or I'm running late," Crystal said. "I haven't had my second cup of coffee yet."

"Mama."

Mug in hand, Crystal turned.

She'd made up her face already, Zoe noted. Her lips were red, her lashes thick with mascara. Despite the cosmetics, her skin looked tired and old.

"Well, hell, look what the wind blew in." Crystal lifted the mug and drank as her gaze slid past her daughter. "You bring the boy?"

"No. Simon's in school."

"Nothing wrong with him?"

"No, he's doing fine."

"With you?"

"No, Mama." She stepped over, kissed Crystal's cheek. "I had something I had to do out this way, and I thought I'd come see you. You've got an appointment coming?"

"'Bout twenty minutes."

"Can I have some coffee?"

"Help yourself." Crystal scratched her cheek as she watched Zoe reach overhead for another mug. "You just happened to have business out here? I thought you were starting your big fancy place over there in Pennsylvania."

"I am, though I don't know if I'd call it big and fancy." She kept her voice upbeat and struggled to overlook the suspicion, and the criticism, in her mother's. "Maybe you could drive over sometime and take a look. We should be open in just a few more weeks."

Crystal said nothing. Zoe hadn't expected her to. She just picked up the cigarette and took a long drag.

"How's everybody?"

"Getting on." Crystal shrugged a shoulder. "Junior's still

working for the phone company, doing right well. He knocked up that woman he lives with."

Zoe's cup clattered against the counter. "Junior's going to be a daddy?"

"Seems like he is. Says he's gonna marry her. I expect she'll make his life a misery."

"Donna's all right, Mama. They've been together more than a year now. They're going to have a baby," Zoe said softly, and smiled at the idea of her baby brother being a father. "Junior was always good with babies. He's got a gentle way with them."

"Like a baby's just gonna make everything all peaches and cream. 'Least Joleen's not looking to start popping them out right off."

Determined, Zoe kept the smile on her face. "Are she and Denny settling in all right?"

"They both got work and a roof over their heads, so they got nothing to complain about."

"That's good. And Mazie?"

"Don't hear from her much now she's got that place of her own down in Cascade. Thinks she's pretty high and mighty since she went to business school and works in an office."

What made you so sour? Zoe wondered. What turned you so hard? "You should be proud, Mama. Proud that all four of your children are making their way. You gave us the means to."

"Don't see any of them coming around here thanking me for working my ass off more'n twenty-five years so they could have food in their bellies and clothes on their backs."

"I'm here to thank you for it."

Crystal let out a snort. "What do you want?"

"I don't want anything. Mama—"

"You couldn't get away from here fast enough. Nothing was ever good enough for Queen Zoe. Got yourself pregnant from that highfalutin Marshall boy thinking you'd buy your way into the good life. He shook you off right quick, didn't he, and what'd you do but take off hoping to land in another pot of gold."

"Some of that's true," Zoe said calmly, "and some of it isn't. I wanted to get away from here, I wanted something better. I'm not ashamed of that. But I never thought of my baby as a ticket to a better ride. I worked hard for you, Mama, and I worked hard for Simon and for myself. And I made something. I'm still making something."

"That don't make you better. That don't make you special."

"I think it does. I think it makes me better than the people who don't buckle down and take care of their own. That's what you did. You took care of your own, the best you could, and that makes you special. I know how hard it is to raise a child," she continued while Crystal stared at her. "How hard, and how scary it is to raise that child, and worry about him and work to figure out how to pay the bills and just keep it all going with nobody to help."

Another car started up, with a frantic backfire. "I only have Simon, and there were times I just didn't know what I was going to do next, times when I didn't know how I'd make it to the next morning, much less the next week. You did it with four of us. I'm sorry if I made you feel I didn't appreciate it. Maybe I didn't appreciate it enough when it was going on. I'd like to thank you for it now."

Crystal stubbed out her cigarette, folded her arms across her chest. "You pregnant again?"

"No." With a laugh, Zoe rubbed her hands over her face. "No, Mama."

"You just stop in here, out of the blue, to say thanks?"

"I can't say I knew that's what I had in mind when I got up this morning, but yes. I just want to say thanks."

"You always were a strange one. Well, you said it. Now I've got a customer coming in."

Zoe let out a little sigh of defeat and set her coffee mug in the sink. "I'll see you Christmas, then."

"Zoe," Crystal said as she turned for the door. After a brief hesitation, Crystal stepped over, gave Zoe an awkward hug. "You always were a strange one," she repeated, then walked back to the counter and began separating rods.

With tears pricking her eyes, Zoe stepped out, let the screen door slap shut behind her. "'Bye, Mama," she mumbled, and walked back toward the woods.

She didn't know if she'd accomplished anything more than a kind of backtracking, but it felt right—just as the brief, self-conscious hug from her mother had felt right. She'd taken a step toward healing a personal wound, and finding the key.

She had to understand herself, didn't she? She had to understand why she'd made the choices she'd made, and where they had led her, before she would understand what choice she had to make to find the key.

Eager to move forward, she hurried down the path. She would drive to Morgantown, go by the rooms she'd rented, go by the salon and the store where she'd worked, the hospital where Simon was born. Maybe there was unfinished business there, too, something to resolve, something to see.

She'd lived there nearly six years, the first years of her son's life. But she hadn't forged any strong ties. Why was that? She'd been friendly with the people she'd worked with, had spent time with her neighbors and a couple of other young mothers.

She'd had relationships with two men while she'd lived there, men she liked. But it was all so transient.

Because, she realized, that had never been her place. It hadn't been a destination but a stopping-off point.

She hadn't known it then, but she'd been heading to the Valley. To Malory and Dana. To the Peak, to the key.

Had she been heading to Bradley, too, and was he to be as essential to her life as the rest?

Or was he just another crossroads, there to lead her from one point to the next?

Move forward, she told herself. Move forward and see.

She checked her watch, measuring the time it would take her to drive, to spend the time she needed in Morgantown, then get home again.

She should be able to manage it and still get back before Simon got home from school. But she should stop and call, just in case. She should let Dana and Malory know she wouldn't be in to work.

She would go in early the next day to make it up, and she could work that night on the slipcovers for the sofa, maybe swing by HomeMakers at some point the next day and pick up the shelving she wanted. If she could get that together, and the next shipment of her supplies came as scheduled, she could . . .

Her busy thoughts trailed off as she stopped and turned in a circle.

She'd detoured off the path, she realized, which served her right for letting her mind wander. The undergrowth was thicker here, and armed with thorns that would play hell with her pants and jacket if she wasn't careful.

She looked up to try to judge her direction by the sun, but the sky had gone to pewter, with a few angry clouds crawling across the dull plate of it.

She would just go back the way she'd come for a bit, she decided. It hardly mattered, as the woods were no wider than a football field, creating a wedge between the field and the trailer court.

Annoyed with herself, she stuffed her hands in her pockets and started back. The air had chilled while she walked, and the scent it carried was more of snow than rain. She walked quickly, in a hurry to be on her way as much as to keep warm.

The trees looked bigger, closer together than they should have, and the shadows much too long for so early in the day. There was no tapping woodpecker now, no rustling from squirrels running about their business. The woods had gone quiet as a tomb.

She stopped again, baffled that she should be so disoriented in a place where she'd run tame as a child. Things changed, of course, everything changed. But hadn't it struck her when she'd come into it how little this place had changed?

Her stomach dropped as she stared down at the long, deep shadows crossing her path.

How could there be shadows when there was no sun to cast them?

As the first flakes of snow fell, she heard the low, throaty growl from deeper in the trees.

Her first thought was bear. There were still bear in these hills. As a child she remembered seeing their tracks and their droppings. Once in a while they would wander into the court at night and bang around in the garbage if it hadn't been stored properly.

Even as her heart fluttered at the base of her throat, she ordered herself to be calm. A bear wasn't interested in her. She had no food, she posed no threat.

She simply had to get back to the court, or out to the field and her car.

She walked backward for a time, scanning the trees in the direction of the growl. And began to wade through a creeping fog that was edged with blue.

Turning on her heel, she walked quickly now through the thickly falling snow, and dug in her back pocket for her penknife.

As weapons went, it was pitiful, but she felt better with it in her hand.

She heard the growl again, closer, and on the other side. She quickened her pace to a jog and gripped her shoulder bag with her free hand. It had weight and a long strap. It could suit up as another weapon if necessary.

She set her teeth to keep them from chattering. Around her the snow fell so fast and hard, it filled in her footprints almost as soon as they formed.

Whatever stalked her matched her pace, turned as she turned. It had her scent, she knew. Just as she had its—strong and wild.

Briars seemed to spring up, straight out of the ground fog to block her path, with stems thick as her wrist, with thorns that glinted like razors.

"It isn't real. It's not real," she chanted, but those thorns tore at clothes and flesh as she fought through them.

And now she smelled her own fear, and her own blood.

A vine whipped up like a snake to wrap around her ankle and send her face-first onto the ground.

Panting, she rolled onto her back. And saw it.

Perhaps it was a bear, but not one that had ever wandered these woods or foraged for food in the garbage.

It was black as the mouth of hell, with eyes of poisonous red. When it snarled, she saw teeth long and sharp as sabers. As she hacked desperately at the vine with her pocketknife, it rose on its hind legs and blocked out the world.

"You son of a bitch. You son of a bitch." Tearing free of the vine, she sprang to her feet and began to run.

It would kill her. Tear her to pieces.

She sucked in the breath to scream as she darted left, and let one rip. She heard its answering call behind her, and it sounded like laughter.

Not real, not true, she thought frantically, but deadly all the same. It toyed with her, wanting her fear first, and then . . .

She was not going to die here. Not this way, not on the run. She was not going to leave her child without a mother to satisfy and amuse some hell-bent god.

She bent down, scooped up a fallen branch on the fly, then spinning around, she held the branch like a club and bared her own teeth.

"Come on, you bastard. Come on, then."

She held her breath and reared back as it lunged.

The buck came out of nowhere, one high leap out of the air. The rack speared into the bear's side, gored it. The sound of rending flesh and the furious howl was horrible. Blood gushed, splattering red over white as it turned to swipe the buck with those vicious claws.

The buck made a sound that was almost human as his white flank bloomed with blood, but he charged again, rack to claw, pivoting to range his body in front of Zoe's like a shield.

Run! She heard the command explode in her head, jerking her out of the shock of watching the battle. She shifted her grip on the branch and, using all her strength, swung hard.

She aimed for the face, and aimed true. The force of the contact had her arms vibrating, but she swung again.

"See how you like it," she muttered mindlessly under her breath. "See how you like it." And slammed wood against flesh and bone.

The bear screamed, stumbled back. As the wounded buck bunched, dipped its head for a killing charge, the bear vanished in a swirl of filthy mist.

Gasping, Zoe went down on her knees in the bloody snow. Her stomach clutched, had her retching uselessly. When the nausea and the wracking shudders eased, she lifted her head.

The white buck stood, knee-deep in the snow. The gouges on his side glistened with blood, but his eyes were steady and unblinking on hers.

"We've got to get out of here. It might come back." She pushed to her feet and, swaying, dug into her shoulder bag. She came up with a pack of tissues. "You're hurt, you're bleeding. Let me help you."

But he stepped back as she approached. Then he bent his forelegs, lowered his great head in what was unmistakably a bow.

And vanished, in a shimmer of light.

The snow was gone, and the path to the field was clear once again. She looked down where the blood had stained the ground, and saw a single yellow rose.

She bent to retrieve it, and let herself weep a little as she limped out of the trees.

"THEY'RE JUST SCRATCHES, BUT some of them are nasty." Malory pressed her lips together hard as she swabbed the cuts on Zoe's flesh. "I'm glad you came straight here."

"I thought ... No, I didn't think." She was feeling a little drunk, Zoe realized, a little light-headed and punchy now that she was back. "I just drove here, didn't even consider going home first. Jesus, I hardly know how I got here. It's all one big blur. I needed to see you and Dana, tell you about it, make sure you were both all right."

"We weren't the ones off in the woods alone, fighting monsters."

"Hmm." Zoe tried to ignore the sting of antiseptic.

She'd driven back to the Valley in a fog that had kept her numb. She hadn't started to shake until she'd walked through the doors of Indulgence.

She'd had to shower. She'd needed hot water, soap. Clean. The need for it had been so urgent that she'd asked her friends to come up to the bathroom with her so she could explain while she washed.

Now, wearing only her underwear, perched on a stool in the bathroom with Malory tending her hurts and Dana off to get her some clean clothes from home, it all felt like a dream.

"He couldn't even come after me like a man. Fucking coward. Guess I showed him."

"Guess you did." Overcome, Malory dropped her forehead to the crown of Zoe's head. "Oh, God, Zoe, you could've been killed."

"I thought I was going to be, and I have to tell you, it seriously pissed me off. I'm not trying to make light of it." She gripped Malory's hand. "It was awful. It was just awful—and, and *primal*. I wanted to kill. When I picked up that branch, I was ready to kill. I was hungry for it. I've never felt like that before."

"Here, let me get these cuts on your back. This one just missed your faerie."

"Good faerie today." She winced at the burn. "The buck, Mal. He saved me. If he hadn't charged that way, I don't know what might've happened. And he was bleeding, he was hurt. Hurt a lot more than I am. I wish I knew if he's okay."

She snorted out a laugh. "I was going to mop him up with a bunch of Kleenex. How dopey is that?"

"I bet he didn't think it was." Wanting to take inventory of her friend's hurts, Malory stepped back. "There. That's as good as it's going to get."

"My face isn't too bad, is it?" She got up cautiously, turned to the mirror over the sink. "No, it's okay. I guess I'm snapping back if I'm worried about my face."

"You look beautiful."

"Well, some lipstick and blush would help." She shifted her gaze, met Malory's in the mirror. "He didn't beat me."

"No, he sure as hell didn't."

"I got somewhere. I don't know exactly where, but I did something right today, took some step, and it's got him worried."

She turned around. "I'm not going to lose. Whatever it takes, I'm not going to lose."

IN THE HIGH TOWER of Warrior's Peak, Rowena mixed a potion in a silver cup. However troubled her mind, her hands were quick and sure. "You'll need to drink all of this."

"I'd rather a whiskey."

"You'll have one after." She glanced over to where Pitte stood, scowling out the window. He was stripped to the waist, and the gouges on his side were red and raw in the light.

"Once you've taken the potion, I should be able to treat the wound, and draw the poison out. Even with this, you'll be tender for a few days."

"And so will he. More than tender, I'd say. More of his blood spilled than mine. She wouldn't run," he recounted. "She stayed and fought."

"And I thank all the fates for it." She stepped over, held out the cup. "Don't frown at it. Drink it, Pitte, all down, and you'll not only have whiskey, but I'll see that there's apple pie for dessert."

He had a weakness for apple pie, and for the look in his lover's eyes. So he took the cup, tossed back the contents. "Damnation, Rowena, can you make it any more foul?"

"Sit now." She opened her hand, held out a thick glass. "And drink your whiskey."

He drank, but he didn't sit. "The battle lines have changed again. Kane knows now we won't stand back and do nothing, bound by the laws he's already broken."

"He risks all now, too. He banks on the power he's gathered, what he's twisted and surrounds himself with. If the spell can be broken, Pitte, if he can be defeated, he won't go unpunished. I have to believe there is still justice in our world."

"We'll fight."

She nodded. "We've made our choice, too. What will you do if this choice keeps us here? If this choice means we can never go home again?"

"Live." He stared out the window. "What else?"

"What else?" she replied, and laying her hand on his wound, she cooled the burn.

Eleven

HE HAD TO WORK AT BEING CALM, TO STRAP HIMSELF down so he didn't march into Zoe's house and start spewing orders. That, Brad knew, was his father's way.

And it was damned effective.

Still, as much as he loved and admired his father, he didn't want to *be* his father.

All he really wanted at that moment was to assure himself that Zoe was all right. Then to make sure she stayed that way.

And there was Simon to think of, Brad reminded himself as he pulled up in front of Zoe's house. He couldn't go shoving his way in, spouting off about how reckless she'd been in running off on her own, putting herself in the crosshairs, with the boy around. He wasn't going to frighten a child while venting his own fears and frustrations.

He would just wait until Simon was in bed, *then* vent.

An instant before he knocked, barking exploded inside the house. One thing you could say for Moe, nobody snuck up on you when he was around. He could hear the boy's shouts, his laughter, then the door swung open.

"You should ask who it is first," Brad told him.

Simon rolled his eyes even as Moe leaped up to greet Brad. "I looked out the window and saw your car. I know all that stuff. I'm playing baseball, bottom of the seventh." He grabbed Brad's hand and pulled him toward the living room. "You can take over the other team. You're only two runs down."

"Sure, bring me in when I'm two down. Listen, I need to talk to your mom."

"She's up in her room, sewing something. Come on, I've only got a few minutes before she calls the game and sends me to the showers."

The kid was a gem, Brad reflected, with eyes that made you want to give him the world. "I really have to talk to your mother, so why don't we schedule a game for later in the week? Head to head, pal, and I will rock your world."

"As if." He might have thought about arguing, but gauged his ground. If Brad kept his mother talking, she *might* forget when his hour was up. "A whole nine innings? You promise?"

"Absolutely."

His smile went sly. "Can we play at your house, on the big TV?"

"I'll see what I can do."

With the crowd in the video bleachers cheering again, Brad started toward Zoe's room. He heard the music before he reached the doorway. She had it on low, and he could just catch her voice as she murmured more than sang along with Sarah McLachlan. Then the voices were drowned out by the hammering hum he recognized as a sewing machine.

She was working with a portable set up on a table in front of the side window. The framed photographs and painted chest he remembered she kept on it were moved to her dresser now to make room for the machine and what looked like miles of fabric.

It was an essentially female room—very Zoe-esque. Not fussy, not fancy, but very feminine in its little touches. Bowls filled with potpourri, pillows edged with lace, the old iron bed given a luster with pewter paint and a colorful quilt.

She'd framed old magazine ads for face powder, perfume, hair products, and fashion and had them grouped on the wall in a kind of quirky, nostalgic gallery.

She sewed, he noted, like someone who knew what she was doing, in a steady, competent rhythm while her foot—clad in a thick gray sock, tapped to the music that jingled out of the clock radio by the bed.

He waited until she'd stopped the machine and begun to rearrange the material.

"Zoe?"

"Hmm?" She shifted in the chair and gave him the blank look of a woman whose mind was considerably occupied. "Oh. Bradley, I didn't know you were here. I didn't hear you . . . " She glanced at the clock. "I was trying to get these slipcovers finished before it's time to get Simon ready for bed. I guess I'm not going to make it."

"Slipcovers?" His train of thought took a detour. "You're making slipcovers?"

"People do." Irritation sizzled under the tone as she tugged the material. "I'm covering a sofa for the salon. I wanted something friendly and fun, and I think these big hydrangeas do the trick. Color works, too. And there's nothing wrong with homemade."

"That's not what I meant. I'm just amazed that I know somebody who would have a clue how to sew something like this."

Her back went up. She knew it was stupid, but it went up anyway. "I imagine most of the women you know have seamstresses, so they don't have to know one side of a sewing machine from another."

He walked over to lift a length of the fabric, and studied her speculatively. "If you're going to be determined to misinterpret everything I say, we're going to fight about something entirely different from what I came over to fight about."

"I don't have time to fight with you about anything. I need to get this done while I have the chance."

"You'll have to make time. I've got—" He broke off, scowled over at the clock radio as the alarm went off.

"I can't make what I don't have," she shot back and rose to turn off the alarm. "That's set so I know when it's time to get Simon up here for his bath. That process takes the best part of half an hour, if he cooperates. And it's Monday, and we read together for half an hour before bed on Mondays. After that, I've got at least another hour of sewing, then—"

"I get the picture." Just, he thought as he put his hands in his pockets, as he knew when a woman was determined to brush him off. "I'll handle Simon's bath and the reading."

"You'll ... what?"

"I can't sew, but I know how to bathe and how to read."

She was so baffled she couldn't make her way around the words and into a sentence. "But it's not—you're not ... " She paused, did her best to pull her thoughts together. "You didn't come over here to take care of Simon."

"No, I came over to yell at you—which you already know, which is why you're annoyed. But I can yell later. I imagine Simon's got the bath-and-bed routine down. We'll do fine. Finish your slipcovers," he said as he started out of the room. "We'll fight when we're both done."

"I don't—"

But he was gone, and already calling for her son.

It was pretty tough to stick to an offense with a man who figured her out that neatly. But still. She started to go after him, then stopped herself. Simon was already launching into his "five more minutes" plea.

Her lips quirked in a very smug mother's smile. Why not just let Bradley get a taste of the nighttime ritual of convincing a nine-year-old he needed to wash and go to bed? Odds were the man would throw up his hands in defeat long before it was done.

Which meant he would be too frazzled to worry about arguing with her—or lecturing her about going off on her own that morning.

Which she'd had a right to do, she reminded herself. More, she'd had an obligation. But she just didn't have the time or inclination to get into all that tonight.

So, Simon would wear him out, he'd go on home, and she'd have a quiet evening to finish her work and plan her strategy for the next few days.

Plus, she decided as she walked back to the sewing machine, she might just get the slipcovers knocked out.

She listened to their voices, the odd harmony of man and boy, then set up for the next running seam. One of them would shout for her when they hit impasse.

She heard laughter—maniacal on Simon's part, and smirked. Figuring her time was going to be very limited, she concentrated on the task at hand.

She lost track of time, and didn't surface until she realized just how quiet her house had become. No raised voices, no barking dog.

Concerned, she pushed away from the machine and hurried to the bathroom across the hall. It appeared that a very wild, very wet war had been waged. Towels were sopping up some of the water on the floor, and there was a skim of froth in the tub, telling her Simon had opted for bubbles along with the convoy of plastic vehicles and army of plastic men scattered in the tub.

Bradley's suit jacket hung on the hook on the back of the door. Absently, she took it off, smoothing the bump the hook had put in the collar.

Armani, she noted when she glanced at the label. That was

surely a first. Italian designs didn't generally hang on her bathroom hook.

Carrying it with her, she walked toward Simon's room. She could hear him reading—his voice taking on that weight it did when he was sleepy.

Careful to be quiet, she peeked in the door. Then simply stood, staring, with the suit jacket clutched to her heart.

Her son was in bed, on the top bunk. He wore his Harry Potter pajamas, and his hair was shiny from its shampooing.

Moe was stretched out on the bottom bunk, his head on the pillow, and already snoring.

And the man whose jacket she held was up in the bunk with her boy, his back braced against the wall, his eyes—like Simon's—on the book.

Simon was nuzzled up against him, his head resting on Brad's shoulder while he read *Captain Underpants* out loud.

Her heart simply fell. She didn't try to stop it, wasn't capable of launching any sort of defense. In that single moment, she loved both of them with everything she had.

Whatever happened tomorrow, she would always have this picture of them in her mind. And so, she knew, would Simon. For that single moment, she owed Bradley Vane more than she could ever pay.

Not wanting to disturb them, she eased back and slipped quietly down to the kitchen.

She put on coffee, got cookies out of the jar. If he was going to yell at her, they might as well be civilized about it. When they were finished, and she was alone, she would try to think clearly once more. She would try to figure out what loving Bradley meant.

Because she was listening for him, she heard him come down the little hall. She reached for the pot to keep her hands busy, and was pouring the coffee when he came in.

"He give you much trouble?"

"Not especially. You finish the sewing?"

"Close enough." She turned to offer him the mug, and her heart bobbled again. He was barefoot, with the sleeves of his beautiful blue shirt rolled to his elbows. The cuffs of his pants were damp.

"I know you're angry with me, and I guess you think you've got some reasons to be. I was going to be angry back, and say all these things about running my own life and doing what I promised to do."

She ran her hand over the shoulders of the jacket, which she'd draped on the back of a chair. "Since I've been thinking about it for a while, I had some pretty good stuff to say. But I just don't feel like saying it now. So I wish you weren't angry."

"I wish I wasn't either." He glanced at the table. "So, are we going to sit down and argue over coffee and cookies?"

"I don't think I can argue with you, Bradley, not after you put my boy to bed that way." Emotion swamped her. "But I'll listen while you yell at me."

"You sure know how to punch the stuffing out of a good fight." He sat, waited for her to sit across from him. "Let me see your arms."

Saying nothing, she pushed up the sleeves of her sweatshirt to reveal the cuts and scratches. When the silence dragged out, she tugged them down again.

"It was just briars, that's all," she said quickly. "I've had worse from gardening in my own yard."

She stopped, struck to silence by the cold glint in his eyes when they shifted to her face. "It could have been worse. A hell of a lot worse. You were alone, for Christ's sake. What possessed you to go driving off to West Virginia and tromping around the woods by yourself?"

"I grew up there, Bradley. I grew up in those woods. It's not wilderness once you cross the Pennsylvania border." To give herself something to do, she lit the three-wick candle she'd made for the kitchen table, one that smelled of blueberries. "My mother lives there in the trailer court beside those woods. Simon was very likely conceived in those woods."

"You want to go visit your mother or your childhood stomping grounds, that's fine. But these are not normal circumstances. You didn't say a thing to me about going there this morning."

"I know I didn't. If I had, you'd have wanted to go with me, and I didn't want you to. I'm sorry if that hurts your feelings, but I wanted to go on my own. I needed to."

He swallowed the resentment, though it scorched his throat. "You didn't let Dana or Malory know where you would be either. You took off without telling anyone, and you were attacked."

"It didn't occur to me to tell anyone. That makes you mad," she said with a nod. "You'll just have to be mad, then. I made an agreement. I gave my word, and I'm trying to do what I promised to do, and you can't sit there and tell me you wouldn't do the same. Going back there this morning was part of that. I think I was supposed to go. I think I needed to."

"Alone?"

"Yes. I've got some pride and some shame along with the rest of it. I'm entitled to what I feel, Bradley. Do you think I wanted to take you along, in your Armani suit, to that broken-down trailer'?"

"That's not fair, Zoe."

"No, it's not fair, but it's the truth. My mama already thinks I've got airs or something. If I'd gone in there with you ... Well, just *look* at you."

She waved a hand and nearly laughed at the exasperation on his face. "You got rich boy all over you, Bradley, in or out of that Italian jacket."

"For Christ's sake," was all he could think to say.

"You can't help it, and why should you? Besides, it suits you. It wouldn't have suited her, and I needed to see her, to talk to her. There were things I needed to say that I couldn't have said with you there. Or with Malory or Dana either. I needed to go back there for myself, and for the key. It was for me to do."

"What if you hadn't gotten out again?"

"I did. I'm not going to say I wasn't scared when it all started to happen. I've never been so scared." Instinctively, she rubbed her arms as if chilled. "It was like an ambush, the way everything changed, the way he came at me. It was almost like a storybook, and that's what made it so frightening."

She looked past him now, back to where she'd been. "Lost in the woods, and being hunted by something . . . not human. But I fought back. That's what I was supposed to do. In the end, I hurt him more than he hurt me."

"You beat him with a stick."

"It was bigger than a stick." Her mouth curved a little as she saw the temper was easing on his face. "It was a good, sturdy branch about this thick." She demonstrated by holding her hands apart. "And between being scared and spitting mad, I whaled the hell out of him. Of course I don't know how it would've turned out if the buck hadn't waded in. But I don't have to, because he was there, and Kane was there. That tells me I did something right by being there."

"Don't go back alone, Zoe. I'm asking you. I walked in here tonight fully intending to tell you. But I'm asking."

She picked up a cookie, broke it in two, then offered him half. "I was thinking I'd drive into Morgantown tomorrow, go by the place where I lived, where I worked, where Simon was born. Just see if that's the next turn. If I could get going first thing in the morning, I could get back by around two, three at the latest, then squeak out a little time at the salon. Maybe you could go with me."

He simply pulled out his cell phone, punched in a number. "Dina, it's Brad. Sorry to call you at home. I need you to clear my schedule for tomorrow." He waited a beat. "Yeah, I know. Reschedule it, will you? I have some personal business to take care of, and it's going to take most of the day. I should be able to swing in after three. Good. Thanks. 'Bye."

He clicked the phone off, tucked it away. "What time do you want to leave?"

Oh, you are a very special man. "About quarter to eight? As soon as Simon goes to school."

"All right." He bit into the cookie. "I guess you need to go back up, finish the sewing."

"Not just yet. I thought I'd take a break. Do you want to sit on the couch and neck while we pretend to watch TV?"

He caressed her cheek. "I definitely do."

ZOE WALKED INTO INDULGENCE the next afternoon carting an enormous box. She dumped it inside the door and looked around.

Malory and Dana had been busy in her absence. There were paintings on the walls, and what she recognized as a batik. The table she'd refinished stood along the short wall on the left of the door and held one of her candles, a tall teardrop-shaped paperweight of icy blown glass, and a trio of books tucked between bookends in the shape of more books.

Someone had installed the new ceiling light and laid a pretty rug, dancing with poppies.

Delight and guilt tangled inside her. She pushed up her sleeves, preparing to dive into work as she searched out her friends.

She didn't find them in Malory's section, but her jaw dropped as she wandered through. It had been two days since she'd taken a look at the main level, but it didn't seem possible so much could have been done in that time.

Paintings, pencil sketches, sculptures, and framed prints decorated the walls. A tall, narrow case held a collection of glass art, a low, long one displayed colorful pottery. Rather than a counter for transactions, Malory had chosen an antique desk for the first showroom. She'd kept the counter in the second, where she would offer gift-wrapping services.

There were shipping cartons yet to be opened, but it was clear that Malory's vision was focused. Zoe smiled when she saw there was already a slim Christmas tree, with handcrafted ornaments hanging on the boughs.

She circled around, moving through the kitchen and into Dana's store.

Books lined more than half the shelves. An old break-front held teacups, coffee mugs, tins.

All this, and she hadn't been there to share in the fun or help with the work.

Hearing the floor creak overhead, she dashed for the stairs and up them.

"Where is everybody? I can't believe what y'all got done while I . . ."

She trailed off, stunned speechless when she saw her salon.

"We couldn't wait." Dana swiped a hand over her cheek, then patted the chair she and Malory had just assembled. "We thought we'd have them all done before you got back. Just about made it."

Slowly, Zoe crossed the room, ran a hand over the cushy leather of one of her four styling chairs.

"And they work. Look." As Malory pumped her foot on the circle of chrome at the base of the chair, it rose. "It's fun."

"Hey." Dana dropped into the chair, spun it. "This is fun."

"They came," was all Zoe could say.

"Not only that, but look over there." Malory pointed to the three glossy shampoo sinks. "They installed them this morning."

She dragged a dazed Zoe over, and turned on the water. "See? They work, too. It's a beauty parlor."

"I can't believe it." Zoe sat on the floor, covered her face with her hands, and burst into tears.

"Oh, honey." Instantly, Malory untied the kerchief from her head and offered it as a hankie.

"I have shampoo sinks. And chairs," Zoe sobbed into the colorful square of cotton. "And—and you have paintings and statues and carved wooden boxes. Dana has books. Three months ago I had a lousy job working for a woman who didn't even like me. Now I have chairs. You put them together for me."

"You refinished the table," Malory countered.

"And found the baker's rack for the kitchen. Worked out all the track lighting, regrouted the bathrooms." Dana bent down to pat Zoe's head. "We're in this together, Zoe."

"I know, I know, that's just it." She mopped her face. "It's beautiful. All of it. I love it. I love you. I'm okay."

She sniffled, then let out a long breath. "God, I want to shampoo somebody." Laughing now, she sprang up. "Who wants to go first?" At the shout from downstairs, she shook her head. "Shit. Forgot. That's the boy from the flea market with my sofa. I paid him twenty dollars to haul it over here. I have to help him bring it up."

When she ran out, Malory turned to Dana. "She's got a lot building inside there."

"Yeah, she does. I wonder if any of us considered the pressure there'd be on the one who went last. Then you add in how close we are to finishing this." She held out her arms to encompass the salon. "She's got to be ready to pop."

"Let's make sure we're there when she does."

They went down to lend a hand with the sofa. When it was in place, Malory stepped back, cocked her head.

"Well . . . it's nice and long. And . . . " She searched for something else positive to say about the dull brown object. "It has a nice high back."

"'Ugly as homemade sin' is the term you're after," Zoe supplied. "But just you wait." She started to open the box she'd brought up with her, then stopped. "Go on downstairs till I'm done."

"Done what?" Dana kicked the couch lightly. "Burning it?"

"Go on. Give me ten minutes."

"I think it's going to take longer," Malory warned.

The minute she was alone Zoe set to work. If there was one thing she knew, she told herself, it was how to go about making silk purses out of sows' ears.

When the transformation was complete, she stepped back, hands on hips.

And by God, she'd done it again. She went to the top of the stairs to call down.

"Come on up. Tell me what you think and be honest."

"The burning idea wasn't honest enough for you?" Dana asked. "Mal and I can do it for you if you're running short of time. Don't you have to get home for Simon?"

"No. I'll tell you about that after." She grabbed Dana's hand, then Malory's, and pulled them back into the salon.

"My God, Zoe. My God, it's beautiful." Astonished, Malory walked over to study the sofa. The dull brown lump was now a charming seat blooming with deep pink hydrangeas on a soft blue background. The cushions were plumped, and cheerful bows encircled the arms.

"It's more of a miracle," was Dana's take.

"I want to make a couple of footstools, use the same fabric, or maybe one of the accent colors. Then I'm going to get some padded folding chairs and make covers for them—just a drape thing, like you see at weddings, with a bow on the back."

"Maybe you could knit me a new car while you're at it," Dana suggested.

"It looks great, Zoe. Now are you going to sit down on it and tell us what happened today?"

"I can't sit yet. You sit. I want to see how somebody looks on it."

She wandered, studying the sofa from different angles. "It's just the way I wanted it to look. Sometimes I get a little spooked, because everything's going so right for me. And I start worrying that because it is, I'll mess up with the key. I know how stupid that sounds."

"Not really," Dana told her as she snuggled into the couch. "I tend to worry about what's going to mess up when things are at their best."

"I thought—I hoped—that I might *feel* something by going back to Morgantown. I, well, we went by my old apartment, and the salon where I worked. The tattoo parlor. Even went into HomeMakers. But it wasn't like yesterday. There wasn't this sense of urgency or understanding."

She walked back to sit on the floor in front of the sofa. "It was good to see some of it again, to remember. But it didn't grab at me. I lived there nearly six years, but it was—I realized it was like a transition. I never meant to stay. I worked there and I lived there, but my mind was always looking ahead.

"To here, I guess," she said quietly. "Where we were going to go, as soon as I could make it happen. Simon was born there, and that was the biggest thing in my life. But nothing else I did there, nothing else that happened to me there, was all that important. It was just . . . a gathering place."

"Then that's what you found out," Malory said. "The key isn't there for you. If you hadn't gone, spent the time looking, you wouldn't know that."

"But I still don't know where it is." Frustrated, she tapped a fist on her knee. "There's this sense inside me that I should be able to see, that I've got my head turned, just a little, in the wrong direction, and I'm worried that I'll be going along, doing what I have to do just every day, and miss it because I don't just turn my head and look in the right place."

"We all got discouraged, Zoe," Dana reminded her. "We all looked in the wrong direction."

"You're right. It's just that so much is happening on this side, it makes what's happening on the other seem so little. This place, and how I feel about it—how I feel about you. It's so big. Then I think how am I supposed to pull this key out of the air—then the next minute I know I can. I know I can if I only look the right way."

"You've been back to where you started," Malory reminded her. "And you've looked at where you waited, isn't that a way to describe your time before coming here?"

"I guess it is."

"Maybe you should look where you ended up. Where you are now."

"Here, you mean? Do you think it could be here, in this house?"

"Maybe, or somewhere else important to you. Someplace you had, or will have, that moment of truth. That decision."

"All right." Thoughtfully, Zoe nodded. "I'll try to focus on that for a while. I'll work here while Simon's with Brad."

"Brad has Simon?" Dana echoed.

"That's the other thing." She shot Dana a baffled look. "We're coming back and I said something about picking him up from school, bringing him back here with me—trying to work out how I was going to manage this and that, and Brad says he'll pick him up. Saying no, that's all right, doesn't make a damn bit of difference. He'll pick him up at school, take him to HomeMakers for a bit, then over to his place, as it appears they've made some arrangement to play video baseball anyway. And why don't I just do whatever I have to do, and he'll drop Simon home about eight. Oh, and don't worry about dinner," she added with an airy wave of her hand. "They'll order pizza."

"Is that a problem?" Malory asked.

"Not a problem so much. It sure won't be for Simon, and I could use the time. But I just don't want to start depending on somebody. It's just another way to get into trouble. I don't want to start depending on him. I don't want to be in love with him. I don't want that, and I can't seem to help it."

With a sigh, she rested her head on Malory's knee. "What am I going to do?"

Malory stroked her hair. "Whatever comes next."

Twelve

Zoe stayed behind after her friends had gone home. She wanted to feel the building around her, the way she'd felt the woods the day before. What had it been about this house that had pulled her?

She'd been the one to find it. She'd been the one to crunch the numbers, even though a part of her hadn't believed she could make it work.

Still, despite the doubts, despite the odds, she'd pursued it, had plotted out in her head what had been a kind of fantasy at first. A kind of hope that had become her reality.

She'd been the first one of the three of them to walk through it, to begin to see what could be done. How it could be done. To stake a claim, she supposed, as she trailed her fingers over the wall in the central hall of the second floor.

Hadn't she stood here while the realtor had been yammering away about potential and commercial value and interest rates and known this was the place to build her future? She'd seen the dull beige walls, the chipped molding, the dusty windows, and had envisioned color and light and possibilities, if only she dared risk it.

Didn't that make it a moment of truth?

The house was one more thing that had drawn her together with Malory and Dana, that had made them a unit. Just as the quest united them. As they were each a key. Interlocked in the search for those answers to yesterday and tomorrow.

Kane had come here, to tempt and threaten both of her friends. Would he come here to tempt and threaten her? Her fear of him was a living thing that beat inside her.

She stood at the top of the stairs, looking down at the door. She had only to walk down the steps, go through that door, and step back into a world she understood and recognized and, to some extent, controlled.

Cars driving by on the street, people passing on the sidewalk. Ordinary life, going its ordinary way.

Inside she was alone, just as she'd been alone in the woods. Just as she was alone every night when she turned off the lamp beside her bed and laid her head on the pillow.

Those were her choices, and she couldn't fear what she had chosen to do with her life.

She turned away from the steps, turned away from the door and the world outside it, and walked the silent hall of what she'd claimed as hers.

Ice skated along her skin as she approached the door to the attic. They'd all avoided going up there since Malory's experience. Nor did they talk about it. It was a portion of the house that had ceased to exist for them, one they had—in a very real way—surrendered.

Wasn't it time to take it back? If the house was to be theirs, completely theirs, they couldn't pretend a part of it didn't exist.

Malory had reached her decisive moment there, and had won. Yet they had deserted this field as if they'd suffered a loss.

It was time to change that.

She reached out, turned the knob. Opened the door. It helped to flick the switch—an ordinary, everyday act. The light was more comforting than the dark, and that was human. But she walked up, struggling not to bolt when the stairs creaked under her weight.

Dust tickled her nose, and she could see it spin in motes in the shaft of light from the bare bulb. The place needed a good cleaning, and among the abandoned items the previous tenants had left behind, there was considerable trash that could be turned to treasures.

A dresser that needed to be stripped or painted, lamps without shades, a rocking chair with a broken runner, boxes gathering dust, books gathering mildew.

Spiders had been busy up here, she noted, and mice were likely making cozy nests inside the unfinished walls. It needed to be swept out. Traps should be set. This was good, practical storage space going to waste.

She remembered what it had been like filled with blue mist, and a cold that chilled to the bone.

Better, she reminded herself, to remember there had been victory here. Nevertheless, she walked to the window and shoved it open to let the chilly evening air chase the musty smell away.

Being up here, alone, was a major step, she decided. Not only a kind of reclamation but proof to herself that she wouldn't be blocked by fear. Next time, she promised herself, she would bring a broom, a dust cloth, and a scrub bucket. But for now she could take the time to look through what had been left behind and see what could be kept and used, and what needed to be hauled away.

There was an old birdcage that could be cleaned up and painted. She would find a use for that. And the metal pole lamp, the lopsided end table. The books were likely full of silverfish, so she made a mental note to take a look, box up whatever was too far gone, and cart it away herself to spare Dana the distress.

She found an ancient Raggedy Ann doll with a torn shoulder. Someone had loved it once, she thought. Maybe with a good wash and a few stitches someone would love it again. She tucked it in the crook of her arm as she pushed through boxes, shoved pieces of furniture out of the way.

She considered the long oval mirror with beveled edges a treasure. Yes, it needed resilvering, but it was a really nice shape. They could hang it from a ribbon in the central area or, better yet, use it in place of the medicine cabinet in the powder room on the main floor.

With the doll still resting in her arm, she tilted the mirror against the wall and stepped back to visualize.

She saw herself in the flyspecked glass, standing in the hard, unfiltered light, dust in her hair, on her cheek, with a wounded rag doll cradled in her arm.

Like the mirror, like the doll, she mused, she wasn't anything special to look at, at the moment. But potential was the important thing. She was looking a little tired around the eyes, but that was nothing a ten-minute break with cucumber eye pads wouldn't fix. She knew how to buff herself up, appearance wise. That was just routine, and a few tricks of the trade.

And she knew how to keep herself in tune inside, too. As long as she considered herself a work in progress, she wouldn't stop trying to learn, to become, to make more of herself.

She wasn't a sad Raggedy Ann who needed to be tended to. She knew, very well, how to tend to herself and those who needed her.

Kyna needed her, she thought. Kyna and her sisters needed her to find the last key to unlock their prison. She couldn't, wouldn't, give up until she'd done everything possible.

"Whatever it takes," she said aloud. "I won't walk away."

The glass misted as she watched, a thin sparkle dancing over the pocked surface. Through it she saw herself. Then it was no longer her but a tall, slim young woman in green robes, a puppy in the crook of her arm and a sword at her side.

Fascinated, she stepped forward, reached up to touch her fingers to the mirror. And watched them slide into the glass. Shocked, she snatched them back, fisted her hand over her speeding heart.

The image in the glass remained, looking back at her. Waiting.

She wanted to bolt, could feel her legs tense for the rush to the door and away. But hadn't she just promised? Whatever it takes. Closing her eyes for a moment, she struggled to steady herself. What Malory had told her about Brad applied to just about everything there was in life, didn't it? You just did what came next.

Zoe gathered her courage, clutched the doll for comfort, and walked into the mirror.

She stood with her sisters under the bright wash of sunlight with the scent of the garden rioting in the air. Birds sang in a kind of desperate joy that lifted her heart.

In her arm, the puppy wriggled and twisted himself to lick her jaw. She set him down to romp for a bit and joined her laughter with her sisters'.

"We should teach him to dance." Venora fluttered her fingers over the strings of her harp while the puppy leaped clumsily at a passing butterfly.

"What he'll do is dig in the garden." Bending, Niniane petted the pup's head. "And be in constant trouble, just as he should. I'm so glad you found him, Kyna."

"He looked like he was waiting for me." Madly in love already, she crouched, tickling the pup's soft, fat belly. "Sitting on the path of the forest as if saying, 'It's about time you got here to take me home.'"

"Poor little thing. I wonder how he got lost."

Kyna glanced at Venora. "I don't think he was lost. I think

he was found." She lifted him up, stood to turn in a circle while he yipped and wriggled with joy. "We'll take care of you, and protect you. And you'll grow big and strong."

"Then he'll protect us," Niniane said and reached out to give the puppy's tail a gentle tug.

"We have more than enough guards already." Rubbing her cheek against the pup's head, Kyna turned to look back across the garden to the two figures who embraced under the blossoms of a tree. "Rowena and Pitte are either watching us, or watching each other."

"Our father worries too much." Niniane set down her quill and lifted her face to the sky. A perfect bowl of blue. "How could we be safer than here, in the heart of the kingdom?"

"There are those who would strike the heart, if they dared." Unconsciously, Kyna laid a hand on the hilt of her sword. "Who would harm our parents, our people, and our world, even the world beyond, through us."

"I don't understand the need for hate when there's such beauty. And such love," Venora added.

"As long as there are those like Kane and his followers there will be a battle between what is good and what is evil. So it is in all the worlds," Kyna told them. "There must be warriors as well as artists and bards, rulers and scholars."

"There's no need for a sword today." Niniane touched Kyna's hip.

"For Kyna there's always a need for a sword," Venora said with a laugh. "But only look. Love is surely as valiant and true a weapon as steel." She plucked her harp as she studied Rowena and Pitte. "See how they are together, as if they need nothing but each other. One day we'll find that."

"But the man I love must be as handsome as Pitte," Niniane said, "and clever of mind."

"And mine will be all that, but with the soul of a poet." With a flutter of her lashes, Venora pressed a hand to her heart. "Yours, Kyna?"

"Ah, well." Kyna tucked the puppy in the crook of her arm again. "Handsome, of course, and clever of mind, with that poet's soul—and a warrior's heart. And he must be the most skilled of lovers."

They giggled together, as sisters do, gathered close, and didn't see that perfect bowl of sky begin to boil black in the west.

Venora shivered. "It grows chilly."

"The wind," Kyna began, and the world went mad.

She whirled, her sword singing as she drew it from its sheath, as she stepped between her sisters and the shadow that spilled out of the woods.

She heard the screams, the vicious lashing of the wind, the shouts of those who ran to defend. She saw the sly slither of a snake on the tiles and the crawl of a blue mist.

And Kane, his eyes black with power in his handsome face, stepped out of the shadows. He raised his arms toward that boiling sky, his voice like thunder.

Even as she charged, sword held high, the pain ripped through her like vicious fingers, tearing at her heart and dropping her to her knees.

She saw him smile an instant before she was yanked from her own body.

In the attic, under the harsh light of the overhead bulb, Zoe stood again, with an icy pain in her chest and tears spilling down her cheeks.

"I HURT FOR THEM." Zoe pressed her hands together on her kitchen table. "I felt what she felt—the emotions, the sun, the warm fur of the puppy, but I was still apart from it. I don't know how to explain."

"A kind of mirror image?" Brad suggested, and nudged the

wine he'd poured her a little closer. She'd held on, putting Simon to bed, but whatever she'd been feeling had showed in her eyes.

He'd sensed it, and he suspected Simon had, too, as the boy had gone to bed without even a token protest.

But now she was pale, and she struggled to keep her hands from trembling.

"Yes." It seemed to relieve her to have a name for it. "Like that, like a reflection. I walked into the mirror, like Alice," she said with wonder. "And I knew them, Bradley. I loved them, just as she did. They were sitting in the garden, enjoying the puppy and the sunlight, a little amused, a little envious of the way Rowena and Pitte were so absorbed in each other, and talking, just young girls chatting about the kind of men they would fall in love with. Then it was dark and cold and terrifying. She tried to fight."

Overcome again, Zoe brushed fresh tears from her cheeks. "She tried to protect them. It was her first and last thought. He—he reveled in their pain. He celebrated her failure. I could see it on his face. She couldn't stop it. Neither could I."

She picked up her wine, took a small sip.

"You shouldn't have been up there alone."

"I think I did have to be alone. I understand what you're saying, but I think, I feel, this was something I had to experience on my own. Bradley." She pushed the wine aside, reached across the table for his hand. "He didn't know I was there. Kane didn't know. I'm sure of it. It has to mean something that I was brought there without him knowing it. I think it means she's still fighting, or trying to."

He sat back, considered. "Maybe it's possible, that with the first two locks opened the daughters are able to get something through. Their thoughts, their feelings, their hope. It could be enough to connect to you, especially if they had help."

"Rowena and Pitte."

"It's worth finding out. If you can get someone over to stay with Simon, we'll go up and ask them."

"It's nearly ten now. We wouldn't be able to get up there and back before close to midnight. I don't want to ask anyone to come over at this time of night."

"Okay. I will." He rose, picked up the kitchen phone.

"Bradley—"

"Do you trust Flynn with Simon?"

"Of course I do," she said as he dialed. "But he shouldn't have to leave his own house and come baby-sit."

Brad merely lifted a brow. "Flynn, can you come over to Zoe's and stay with Simon? We've got to run up and see Rowena and Pitte. I'll fill you in on that later. Great. See you and Malory." He hung up the phone. "Ten minutes. That's what friends do, Zoe."

"I know that." Agitated, she pushed at her hair. "I just don't like putting people out because I've got the jitters."

"A woman who walks into a mirror shouldn't get the jitters driving up to the Peak."

"I guess not."

MAYBE IT WASN'T THE jitters so much as anticipation, she decided as they drove through the gates at the Peak. There was a new sense of urgency now that she, in some very real way, had been inside the skin of the woman in the portrait.

The girl, she corrected herself. She'd felt all that innocence and hope and courage—the sheer youth of it. For that time in the mirror, she'd known the goddess, heart and soul.

And her own heart ached from it.

She glanced up at the moon as she got out of the car. It was their hourglass, she thought. And time trickled steadily away while they waited.

It was Pitte who came to the door, opening it before they'd

crossed the portico. He looked relaxed, Zoe noted, and less formal than usual, in a stone-gray sweater.

"I'm sorry to come by so late," she began.

"Is it?" He took her hand and had her flushing by bringing it to his lips. "There's no hour you're not welcome here."

"Oh." Flustered, she looked at Brad to see him watching Pitte steadily. "That's very nice of you. But still, we'll try not to keep you long."

"As long as you like." He kept her hand in his and drew her inside. "The nights grow cold. We've a fire in the parlor. Your son is well?"

"Yes." Had she ever had a real conversation with Pitte before? Zoe wondered. "He's sleeping. Flynn and Malory are with him. Bradley drove me up because ... I have some questions about things that have happened."

"She was attacked," Brad said flatly as they stepped into the parlor.

Rowena rose quickly. "Are you injured?"

"No. No, I'm fine. Bradley, you shouldn't scare people that way."

"She was attacked," Brad repeated. "And though she got off with scrapes and bruises, it could've been considerably worse."

"You're angry," Pitte acknowledged. "So would I be, if she were mine. Even a warrior," he said to Zoe before she could speak, "should appreciate having a champion."

"Sit, please." Rowena gestured to the sofa. "Tea, I think. Something soothing. I'll arrange it." But she went to Zoe first, cupped Zoe's face in her hand and kissed her cheeks. "I'm in your debt," she said softly. "And there is no payment full enough."

Staggered, Zoe simply stood as Rowena glided from the room. Then she looked at Pitte. "It was you. In the woods. The buck in the woods. It was you."

He touched her again, just a skim of fingertips over her cheek. "Why didn't you run, little mother?"

"I couldn't. You were hurt." Her legs trembled, so she lowered to the couch. "I was too scared, and too mad to run. And you were hurt."

"She rushed him, with a tree branch for a club," he told Brad. "And she was magnificent. You are a fortunate man."

"She's not as convinced of that as I am. Yet."

Confused, Zoe pressed her fingers to her temples. "You were in the woods, watching out for me. The buck ... it had your eyes."

He smiled when Rowena came back into the room. "I might not have been there, if Rowena hadn't nagged at me."

"Would he have killed me?"

"He has spilled human blood." Pitte settled into a chair. "He might have spilled yours."

"Would he—could he have killed you?"

Pitte's chin angled just enough for arrogance. "He would have tried."

"Might have been a bit more effective to come as yourself, with a shotgun," Brad pointed out.

"I can't battle him in human form while he takes the form of an animal."

"You were badly hurt," Zoe remembered. "Your side was gouged."

"And has been tended. Thank you."

"Ah, here's the tea. He grumbled when I tended him." Rowena scooted forward to lift the teapot the servant set on the table. "Which is a good sign. Were Pitte seriously wounded he would say nothing."

"I was right to go back there. I feel, most of the time, I feel I'm not doing enough. But I was right to go back there."

"The path is yours to take." Rowena offered Zoe a cup. "Your man is worried for you. I understand," she said to Bradley and poured a second cup. "I can promise you we'll do all we can to keep her safe."

"You put protection around Simon. Put protection around her."

Rowena's face mirrored sympathy as she held out the second cup. "There is no key without risk. There is no end to risk without the key. She needs your faith in her. It's as vital as a shield and a sword."

"I have all the faith in the world in Zoe. And no trust whatsoever for Kane."

"You're wise on both counts," Pitte acknowledged. "He may be licking his wounds for the moment, but he's not finished. With either of you."

"He hasn't bothered with me," Brad pointed out.

"A canny foe chooses the time and the field. The more she cares for you, the harder the blow. After all, the surest way to the soul is through the heart."

As Zoe's cup rattled in its saucer, Brad nodded to Pitte. "Let's worry about what is for now, and handle what comes as we get to it. You're the keeper of the keys," he said to Rowena. "The rules have changed, you've said so yourself. Give her the key, and end it."

"He negotiates." Obviously pleased, Pitte sat straighter. "There is a contract."

"Which stated nothing about danger to life and limb," Brad said easily. "The terms of which were voided when attacks were made on the people involved."

"They waived recompense for any injuries beyond our control."

"There wasn't full disclosure."

Rowena let out a sigh. "Must you get him started?" she said to Brad. "I'm sure both of you would enjoy a good wrangle over contracts and terms and what have you. And the fact is, I would agree there would no longer be the penalty of a year of your lives, as stated in the contract, if Zoe decides to end her quest. Pitte would agree as well, though he would enjoy arguing the terms first for form."

"And entertainment," he added.

"I can't give her the key," Rowena continued. "Once the quest was accepted, once it was begun, it was out of my hands. I can't touch the keys until they're found by the ones chosen to find them, or until the time has elapsed. Such is the nature of this."

"Then tell her where it is."

"I can't."

"Because it's not anywhere until I find it," Zoe said softly as it settled clearly into her mind. "It's not there," she said, looking over at Rowena now, "until I know."

"You have all the power in this, and have only to understand how to use it."

"Did I send myself through the mirror? Or did you?"

"I don't understand."

"The mirror in the attic at Indulgence. Kyna was in it. We looked at each other, then I stepped through, and I was there, in the garden of the painting. I was part of her."

Rowena clamped a hand over Zoe's wrist. "Tell me all. Exactly as it was."

As she did, Rowena's gaze never left her face. The fingers dug into her flesh until she could feel the blood gathering to bruise.

When she was done, Zoe felt those fingers tremble once before they dropped away. "A moment," Rowena said in a thick voice, and rose to stand facing the fire.

"A *ghra*." Pitte crossed to her, lowered his cheek to the top of her head.

"Is it bad?" Shaken, Zoe reached out, searching for Brad's hand.

"I feared the worst for my world. That Kane would defy all

law and go unchecked. That he would spill the blood of mortals and not be punished. Oh." Rowena turned, pressed her face to Pitte's chest. "My heart was dark and full of fear."

"A battle rages, there can be no doubt. And I am trapped here." Frustration scraped through Pitte's words.

"Here is where you're needed." Rowena stepped back from them. Her cheeks were damp with tears. "This battle must be won as well."

She moved to Zoe again. "There is new hope."

Opening her purse, Zoe pulled out a tissue, offered it. "I don't understand."

"I didn't see this, nor did Kane. Didn't anticipate it, nor did he. If she was able to show you, to let you touch what she is, he was able to reach her."

"Who?"

"The king. It is not only Kane who can use war to his own ends. If we can win on this ground, the king will win on his. You've been given a gift, Zoe. For a few moments you were a goddess, the daughter of a king." Her face glowed. "You weren't only shown what they are, what they lost, you touched it. Kane can never break that bond."

"She tried to fight, but she couldn't. She drew her sword," Zoe said, and could feel—even now—the way it had all but flown out of its sheath. "But he struck her down before she could use it."

"The battle's not done." Gently now, Rowena touched her hand. "In your world or in mine."

"She knew him. She understood—when it happened, she understood, and she looked him in the face."

"She touched you, lived in you for those same few moments, knew, I think, what you knew. That was your gift to her."

"I'm not going to leave her there. I hope she knows that."

*

BRAD HUNG BACK AS they started to leave, and turned to Pitte while Rowena walked Zoe to the door. "If he hurts her I'll come for you, whatever form you take."

"I would do the same, were our situations reversed."

Brad glanced toward Zoe, kept his voice low. "Tell me what to do to make him come after me."

"He will, because you're linked. All of you are linked. Make her love you, and it will be the sooner."

Thirteen

SLEEP, ZOE DECIDED, WASN'T GOING TO BE A PRIORITY for a while. The way she had things planned, it wasn't even going to make the top five. She had a son to raise and she didn't feel as if she'd been giving him the time or attention he deserved. She had a business to get organized, and that was going to eat up considerably more time.

She was having her first serious adult relationship with a man, and she hadn't had the time to figure out how she'd gotten into it, much less how to enjoy it.

She had a quest, and if she didn't cross the finish line in under two weeks, all was lost. What was trapped inside a glass box had for a miraculous moment lived inside her. She was prepared to sweat blood to save it.

So sleep would just have to wait until she could work it into her schedule.

She spent a day at Indulgence interviewing her prospective employees, working out potential hours and a pay scale. She spent the evening with Simon, helping him design a birdhouse for a school project, giving his hair a trim, and just enjoying his company.

Most of the night was split between paperwork and household chores she'd let slide for too long.

She crunched numbers, she juggled them. She stretched them, and she compressed them, but the results were the same. The start-up costs had devoured her capital at a staggering rate. A great deal of that had to do with her own determination to start up with style, she admitted. But she'd be damned if she would allow anything to dull this dream.

So, she would be running close to the bone, she acknowledged as she studied the spreadsheet she'd created on the computer. She had run close to it before. If they managed to have their opening the day after Thanksgiving, *and* if they actually had paying customers, they would quickly start to offset the outlay. In dribbles, but a dribble could become a trickle and a trickle a flood.

Those weeks before Christmas were the prime cut in retail, and just what Indulgence needed to get it off the ground.

If there was one thing she knew how to do, it was how to stretch a dollar. She'd make it. She would need to eke out another two years on her car without any major repair bills, please God.

She could nip at corners a little here, a little there, without it affecting Simon. Six months, maybe a year, and Indulgence was going to make such a big difference in their lives. It would give them the stability she so desperately wanted for her son. And it would give her the pride and respect she so desperately wanted for herself.

It was where she'd been heading since she'd walked out of that trailer at sixteen. A major intersection among the many in her life. One more direction. Considering, she sat back. What about the others?

If Indulgence was one of her crossroads, so was the house she lived in, the house she'd saved for and was paying for every month with her hard-earned money. It seemed to Zoe that if both a trip back to her roots and an exploration of the attic at Indulgence could churn up power and forces, then scrubbing her own kitchen floor might do the same thing.

She tidied her papers, shut off the laptop, and got out her scrub bucket.

She'd picked this house first because she could afford it. Barely. And she'd known, just as she'd known when she stepped into the house that had become Indulgence, that this was her place. The home she would make for Simon.

It hadn't been much to look at then, she recalled as she soaped the floor on her hands and knees. Dirt-brown paint and a weedy yard hadn't added up to much of a presentation. Inside, the carpets were worn and the plumbing questionable, the kitchen linoleum a disgrace and the walls pocked with nail holes.

But the size had been perfect and the price right.

She'd scraped, she'd painted, she'd dug, she'd planted. She'd scavenged from yard sales and flea markets, and even the town dump.

She hadn't slept much back then, either, she recalled as she sat back on her heels. But it had been worth every hour. She'd learned a lot about herself and what she could do.

Smiling, she ran a finger over the shining square of vinyl. She'd laid that floor with her own hands. She'd watched for sales and had hunted up the clean white pattern at HomeMakers.

She'd bought the exterior and interior paint at HomeMakers, too, she realized. And some of the plumbing supplies, as well as the light fixture in the upstairs bath.

In fact, there wasn't a room in the house that didn't owe something to HomeMakers. That had to mean something.

It had to mean Bradley.

He was everywhere she looked, Zoe mused. And even when she wasn't thinking of him, he was in there, circling around in her mind. Being involved with him was thrilling, and just a little frightening. But being in love with him ... that was just impossible.

More, it was dangerous for him. She hadn't missed what Pitte had said. The more she cared about Bradley, the more he could be hurt. She didn't question that he was part of the quest, that he would be a part of her life somehow. But she wouldn't let her own fantasies about what could be, if only things were just a little different, put him in Kane's path.

It was enough to have a man like him care about her, and care so much for her son. She wouldn't be greedy and ask for more.

With the floor done, she glanced at the clock on the stove. It was nearly three-thirty in the morning. She had a spotless kitchen, a balanced checkbook, a menu design, and a price list. But if she'd taken another step toward the key, she didn't know it.

She decided to get a little sleep and start fresh in the morning.

BRADLEY SAT BY THE red glow of the campfire and drank lukewarm beer. The temperature didn't matter. When you were sixteen it was all about the beer. His father would skin him if he found out—and he nearly always found out. But nothing could spoil the freedom of a hot summer night.

He didn't intend to sleep. He was going to smoke another cigarette, drink the rest of his beer, and just be.

It had been Jordan's idea to camp up here in the hills, close to the shadows of Warrior's Peak. The spooky old place had always pulled at his friend, so he was forever making up stories about it and the people who might have lived or died there.

And Brad had to admit that the house was fascinating to look at. Interesting to think about. When you did, you had to wonder who the hell would build such a big-ass monster on a mountain-top in Pennsylvania. It was kind of creepy, but cool.

Still, he would leave the Peak to Jordan. He much preferred the rambling wooden house by the river. Even when he thought about moving to New York after college, or traveling around, he couldn't really imagine living anywhere but the River House.

Not for keeps.

But college, New York, and for keeps were all a lifetime away. A million summers away. Right now, he liked being exactly where he was, a little buzzed on beer by a campfire in the woods.

Being so high in the hills only added to the adventure of driving up there with Jordan and Flynn, climbing over the high stone wall like a gang breaking into prison instead of out.

He had to work on Monday. Good old B. C. didn't tolerate malingerers. Vanes pulled their weight, even during summer vacation, and that was okay. But he had the whole weekend to hang out with his friends. To tromp around in the woods, in the wild grass, to know there was no one to tell them not to.

He understood all about responsibility—to family, to the business, to the Vane name. One of these days he would make his own mark—like his grandfather, like his father had. But sometimes a guy just had to get away from all that and have a beer, a couple of burnt hot dogs, and a night around a campfire with good friends.

He didn't know where the hell they'd gone off to, but he was too lazy to find out. He sipped the beer, ignoring the little voice in his head that said he didn't actually like the sharp, yeasty taste all that much. He smoked a cigarette and watched the fireflies put on their nightly light show.

The hoot of an owl was just creepy enough to give him a thrill, and the steady hum of insects added a nice backdrop to his thoughts about how soon he might talk Patsy Hourback into the backseat of his car. So far she was being very strict about limiting their activities to tonsil-diving kisses and the occasional tantalizing handful of breast—on top of her shirt.

He really wanted to get that shirt off Patsy Hourback.

The trouble was, she wanted him to say he loved her first, and that was just way too intense. He liked her, a lot, and he had a serious case of lust going for her, but love? Jesus.

That was scary, long-time-in-the-future stuff. He didn't love Patsy, and didn't see his feelings going in that direction. When he took that fall it would be ... later—that was for sure. It would be a hell of a lot later, and with someone he couldn't quite see yet. Someone he didn't even *want* to see yet.

He had a lot of things to do first, a lot of places to go.

But meanwhile, his just-in-case condom was burning a hole in his wallet, and he really wanted a shot at Patsy Hourback.

He finished the beer and contemplated having the second of his share of the six-pack. But it wasn't much fun drinking it by himself.

The rustle in the brush made him grin. "That must've been the longest piss in history, especially when you've got that little dick to work with."

He waited for the rude comment or insult, then frowned when the woods settled into silence again. "Come on, guys, I heard you out there. You don't come back, I'm going to drink the rest of the beer myself."

The answer was another rustle, from the opposite direction. He felt a chill creep up his spine, but defended his manhood by reaching for the second beer. "Yeah, that's going to scare me. Jesus, it must be Jason in his hockey mask! Help, help. You two are so lame."

He snorted, popped the top on the beer, and took a long swallow for form.

The growl came out of the dark, and was wet and hungry.

"Cut it out, Hawke, you asshole." But the order squeezed out, thin and jumpy, from a throat that had snapped shut. His hand inched along the ground in search of one of the sharpened sticks they'd used to roast the dogs.

The scream ripped through the silence, horrible and packed with fear and pain. Brad shot to his feet, the stick clutched in his hand like a sword. He whirled in a circle, fear gnawing at his belly as he searched the shadows.

For a long, long moment, there was no sound but his own raging heart.

When the scream came again, it was his name.

Fireflies flashed in mad flicks of light as Brad sprinted toward the sound. It had been Flynn's voice, a desperate high-wire sound of terror, of agony, that couldn't have been faked. There was another call, equally urgent. This one from Jordan, from behind him, and it seemed to shatter the night.

Torn, panicked, he spun back. A thrashing sounded in the dark, rushed toward him with a force that couldn't have been human. Suddenly the night was full of sound. The wind roared through the trees, limbs crashed to the forest floor around him. And cries came from every direction at once. As he ran, the summer heat turned to bitter, biting cold and a mist spilled over the ground, rising like a river until it was nearly to his knees.

Fear was wild in his belly—for his friends, for himself.

He burst out of the trees into the high grass that spread beneath the spears and towers of Warrior's Peak.

The moon, fat and full, rode overhead. In its light he saw his friends, sprawled in that high grass. Torn to pieces. Mindless prayers ripped from his throat as he raced forward.

He slipped on blood, and worse, went down on his hands and knees in a gruesome skid near Flynn's body. His stomach heaved as he clutched at his friend and his hands came away wet and warm.

The blood dripped from Brad's fingers in the clear light of that perfect white moon.

"No." He said it softly, in a voice that shook. Closing his eyes, he gathered himself, dug as deep as he could. "No." His voice strengthened as he opened his eyes and forced himself to look again. "This is bullshit."

While Brad stared, fighting grief and fear, Flynn turned his head on his torn neck and grinned. "Hey, asshole. Guess what? You're next."

Though his heart scrambled inside his chest, Brad pushed to his feet and repeated. "Bullshit."

"It's really gonna hurt." Still grinning, Flynn rose. There was a chuckle, hideously juicy, as what had been Jordan did the same. They started toward him in lurching steps.

"We're all meat," Jordan said, and winked at Brad with the single eye that remained in its socket. "Nothing but meat."

He could smell them, smell the death, as they closed in. "You're going to have to do better, Kane. A hell of a lot better, because this is bullshit."

It did hurt, a shocking, stunning pain that radiated from his chest to every cell of his body. Brad bore down on it, used it, and forced his lips into a smile as he stared at the horror-movie images of his friends.

"You guys are seriously messed up." He managed what passed for a laugh, fought not to pass out.

And woke shuddering with cold in his own bed.

Rubbing a hand on his throbbing chest, he sat up, took a deep gulp of air. "Well, it's about fucking time."

"So, WE REALLY LOOKED gross?"

Flynn offered Brad a sunny smile. They sat with Jordan at Brad's kitchen table. He'd waited until morning to call, though it had been a very long two hours alone with the images of his experience chasing through his head.

He'd told them nothing but that he needed them to come. And, of course, they had.

Now, in the bright light, with the scent of coffee and toasted bagels, the entire experience seemed overblown and sloppy. Too many nightmares piled into one, in Brad's opinion, for it to hold solid.

"Let's see, most of your throat was gone, and a good part of your chest was missing. And you," he said to Jordan, "your left eye was dangling pretty effectively out of its socket, and some of your face was torn away."

"Could only be an improvement," Flynn commented.

"I think I slipped on some of your brains," Brad told him. "Not that you'll miss them."

"Flynn slips on his own brains half the time," Jordan shot back. He studied Brad over the rim of his mug. "You hurt?"

"Chest throbbed like a bitch for about an hour, and I came back with the mother of all headaches, but that's about it."

"So the question hangs, how did you get back?"

"First, I had more time to prepare, knowing what happened to each of you. More time to figure out what might be coming and what to do about it. I had this little thing going in my head, what you could call a key word that I had planted there to snap me out. It worked."

Flynn bit into bagel. "And the word is?"

"'Bullshit.' It's crude," he continued as Flynn sprayed crumbs. "And it's human and to the point. And the other thing is, well, he was sloppy. I can't say it wasn't effective, especially at first. I felt sixteen. Hell, I was sitting by the campfire, drinking warm beer and thinking about Patsy Hourback's body."

"She did have a great body," Jordan recalled.

"Anyway, I was pretty obsessed with Patsy that summer.

Actually I was mostly obsessed with sex, but Patsy was the headliner. So in the beginning of it, I was back there, in the woods by the Peak. Then Flynn starts screaming like a girl—"

"How do you know it wasn't Jordan?" Insulted, Flynn sulked over his bagel. "How come I have to scream like a girl?"

"Take it up with Kane," Brad suggested. "At that point, I was just whacked out. You were both screaming and calling for me. But it started to go off, just a little. The wind, the fog, the cold. It was overkill, and it started to click in my head. When I saw you, the two of you lying there, I lost it again for a minute. Then I was sliding on Flynn's brains, or maybe his intestines."

"Trying to eat here," Flynn complained.

"It was too much, you know? And it wasn't holding. I wasn't sixteen anymore, not in my head. He'd lost the grip, I guess you could say. And I knew it was him. I knew it was bullshit."

Brad rose to get the coffeepot. "Going over it for the last couple hours, I figured out what he was trying to do."

"Separate us," Jordan said.

"Got it in one. Isolate me—sitting alone while you two are off together. Then finding you mauled when you'd been calling to me for help."

"Then having us turn on you," Flynn finished. "The zombie twins. Pits us against you. How are you going to trust, much less work with, a couple of guys who try to eat your brains? I've seen the movies," he added. "That's what zombies do."

"He wanted me to feel alone and alienated, and threatened."

"Maybe worse," Jordan added. "If you hadn't yanked yourself out, we might have done some damage. When he tries for you again, he'll be more direct."

"That's okay." Brad picked up his coffee. "So will I."

"I think you need more than your dashing good looks when you're taking on a sorcerer, pal," Flynn pointed out.

Nodding, Brad picked up the knife beside his plate, flipped a thumb over the tip. "Even sorcerers bleed."

"Are you planning on telling Zoe what happened?" Jordan asked.

"Yeah. We stick together on this, until it's done. I thought I'd run by Indulgence this morning."

"She's not going in until afternoon," Flynn told him. "Malory said she had things to take care of at home first."

"Even better."

HE FINISHED UP A call on his cell phone as he pulled in behind her car, then took a minute to plug in the new appointment on his Palm Pilot. Thinking of the meeting with his architect, the expansion plans, and the changes he wanted to implement in the design, he walked to the front door and knocked.

All of that dropped right out of his head when she answered.

She was wearing jeans ripped at both knees and one of those belly-baring tops. It was the bar today, he noted. That erotic little silver bar glinting in her navel.

Her feet were bare, with toes painted an Easter-egg pink, thin and enormous silver hoops swung at her ears. And she held a rag that smelled strongly of lemon.

"I've been cleaning," she said quickly. "I just finished in the bedroom." As if realizing she held her polishing rag, she stuffed it into her back pocket. "I needed to have some time around here before I went in today."

"Okay." He stepped in, managed to take his eyes off her long enough to look around the living room. Every inch of wood gleamed, every piece of glass sparkled. "You've been busy."

"Cleaning gets my mind going, and I was thinking about the house. That maybe the house is part of it. And if I took the time, paid attention to it, to everything in it, things might—What is it?" Flushing a little under his unblinking stare, she rubbed at her cheek. "Is my face dirty?"

"Your face is perfect. It's the most perfect face I've ever seen."

"That's nice to hear after I've been chasing dust bunnies."

"Simon in school?"

"Yes." Her eyes widened as she recognized the glint in his. "Well, for heaven's—it's almost ten in the morning. Don't you have to work?"

"I do." He stepped forward as she backed up. "But I made a little time because I needed to talk to you. Looks like talk's going to have to wait."

"We can't just . . . " Could they?

"I bet we can. Let's try this."

He scooped her right up, and her stomach did a long, lovely roll as he started back toward her bedroom.

"Golly." She couldn't quite stop the nervous giggle. "Just like in a romance novel. Except I'd be wearing something sexier than old jeans."

She smelled of her furniture polish and ripe plums. "There's nothing sexier than old jeans when you're in them."

"Oh, that's good." Delighted, she nuzzled his neck. "That's really good." She nipped at his earlobe. "I've got laundry going. It sort of backed up on me the last few days. So . . . I'm not wearing anything under these jeans."

He turned his head, looked into her laughing eyes. "Oh, yeah, then talk definitely has to wait."

Her arms linked around his neck as he laid her on the bed, and she drew him in, welcoming. "This must be my reward for doing all my chores," she murmured.

"I've thought about making love with you again ever since I made love with you."

He took her lips with his, rubbed gently, then sank deep.

It was like her own personal miracle, Zoe thought as she let herself float on the moment. Being swept up and away by a man who could make her feel as precious as diamonds.

He kissed her as though he could spend his life doing nothing else but mating his lips and hers. He would spend time in the warmth even when she could feel the need for heat pulsing from him. The quiet joy of it, of him, wound around her heart in soft, silky ribbons.

He touched her as though her body was a delicate treasure he would never tire of exploring. Each caress with those marvelous hands soothed, stirred, and promised. The sweet wonder of it slid through her blood like wine.

Here, in the morning sunlight, was patience that glided over her in long, almost lazy strokes. She let herself rise under them and drift down again as the world outside went on its busy way without her.

Stealing time for each other added a gauzy layer to intimacy.

He toyed with flesh exposed by ripped denim, skimmed his fingers along where her blouse rode up. Heard the low sound of arousal as he traced the silver bar. When his lips nibbled down her throat, she turned her head and sighed.

All the worries, all the fatigue that had dogged her melted away.

He could feel her yield to him, to the pleasure, hear her breathing thicken as he took his time. Could she know what it meant to him to be with her like this, with the sun streaming through the windows and the house empty and quiet around them?

Could she know how much he needed her when he was only beginning to understand it himself?

He hadn't known until that moment just how much he had to give, so desperately wanted to give. What he was, what he had, what he felt, what he imagined. His mouth covered hers again, and he offered all.

Her heart bounded into her throat, her hands clutching his shirt as emotions engulfed her. More than pleasure, more than the promise of it flooded through those seductive sensations. Trembling, she slipped under.

This was what he needed—the utter surrender to each other. Where there was no one and nothing but the two of them. "I want to look at you." He rained kisses over her cheeks before easing her top over her head. "Just to look at you."

Watching her, looking into those heavy, dazed eyes, he slid the denim down.

Smooth skin and subtle curves, long, almost balletic limbs. Those slumberous eyes and that siren's mouth. She was, he thought, such a fascinating combination of the fragile and the exotic.

Bending, he pressed his lips to the top of her thigh, gliding them slowly down over sensitive flesh as she shuddered.

He teased closer to the heat with his tongue. "I want you to lie there. And let me do things to you."

She couldn't have stopped him. She was already steeped in need, awash in sensation. When the first shock of heat slammed through her, she wrapped her fingers around the iron bars of the bed and let him take her anywhere he wished.

Here was glory and wonder. Those hands, so exquisite in their patience, unlocking every secret. That mouth tender and thorough, devouring her by inches. She bowed up as the orgasm catapulted through her, and still he didn't stop.

Emotion careened against emotion, feeling against feeling until it seemed her senses were alive with light, her skin shimmering with it. And each time the ache built again, she welcomed it.

He was lost in her, aware of nothing but what she gave, and what he was compelled to take. Each time her body shuddered, there was more.

He rose over her. She encircled. He slid into her. She surrounded.

Slowly, still slowly, to drain every drop of pleasure even as it drenched them. The rise and fall of bodies, the beat of blood, the trip of pulse locked the world outside of that sun-filled room.

Somewhere time ticked away, cars rumbled past on the street, a dog barked at squirrels in a backyard, but she knew nothing but him. Heard nothing as she teetered on the edge of the world but her name, spoken almost like a prayer.

Then her own cry of joy as she leaped with him.

No one, at any time or in any place, Zoe decided, had ever felt better than she did right here and now. No one had ever been more completely seduced or thoroughly pleasured.

Drifting in the afterglow, she stroked her fingers through Brad's hair.

His head rested between her breasts, and his hand covered hers at her side. It was the sweetest combination of sensations she'd ever felt.

"I'm so glad you dropped by." she said sleepily, and smiled when she felt his lips curve against the side of her breast.

"Glad you happened to be home."

"This is all so ... *gorgeous.* Lying here, all naked and satisfied at ... " She turned her head to check the clock. "Mmm, ten minutes to eleven in the morning. Better than winning the lottery."

He lifted his head and grinned at her. "And then some."

"You're so handsome. I keep thinking you look like one of those slick-looking guys in my hairstyle magazines."

He grimaced. "Please."

"Really. You could use a trim, though." She spread her fingers in his hair. "I could take care of that for you."

"Ah ... Maybe sometime. Or other."

She gave the hair she held a friendly tug. "I'm very good, you know, at what I do for a living."

"I'm sure you are. Absolutely." To distract her, he pressed a kiss to her collarbone, then rolled aside. "I really did come by to talk to you."

"You can talk while I give you a trim. Hairdressers are like bartenders. We're trained to talk and work at the same time."

"I bet. But this probably isn't the best time. We should get dressed."

"Coward." She sat up, wrapped her arms around her updrawn knees.

"I'll accept that for the moment." He rose to find his pants. "Zoe, last night—well, more accurately early this morning—I had an experience."

The playful mood vanished as she scrambled to her knees. "Are you hurt? Did he hurt you?"

"No." He picked up her top, held it out. "You're going to need to stay calm while I tell you."

He dressed while he related the story.

Her initial fear had abated. He was unhurt, she could see that for herself. And he was steady, God knew. Maybe just a little too steady.

"You think he was using Jordan and Flynn against you—or wanted you to think they were against you."

"That sums it up."

"He doesn't understand people, or love, or friendship. He doesn't understand you, that's for certain, if he thought that would make you feel isolated or frighten you off. It just made you more involved."

The faintest smile ghosted around his mouth. "You seem to understand me."

She studied his face. "I don't know that I do, but I do understand how you are with Jordan and Flynn. Why did he pick that night? Because you were young, because it was near the Peak? Everything means something now. We're so close everything means something."

He nodded, pleased that their thoughts were running along the same lines. "I think it was both. While we were young, and more easily molded. Before we knew you or Mal, before Jordan looked at Dana as someone other than Flynn's sister. That was the night Jordan saw Rowena walking on the parapet at the Peak."

He paused, smoothed the cuffs of his shirt. "I was sixteen that night, Zoe. The same age you were when you left home."

"Oh." She wrapped her arms around herself as if she'd just felt a chill. "You think that means something?"

"I don't think we can afford to discount anything as coincidence. It was an important night for me, and for Flynn and Jordan. Didn't seem like it at the time, really. Just one of those reckless summer nights. But we were on that brink where you step away from childhood, toward manhood. You were the same age when you took your step."

"It was different for me."

"Yeah. But maybe if Kane could have twisted what happened that night, at least in my mind, he could have twisted how I think about it now. And what I did after. How I feel about Flynn and Jordan has a lot to do with why I'm back here, and how I met you."

"So if he'd driven a wedge between you, even had them hurt you—well, not them but what you believed was them, it might have weakened what we all have. Or even destroyed it."

"I think that was part of the plan."

Uneasy, she pressed her lips together. "He failed, so he'll be angry."

"Yeah, he'll be angry. I don't think any of us should spend much time on our own for the next few days. I want you and Simon to stay at my place."

"I can't—"

"Zoe, take a minute." Already prepared for objections and excuses, he stepped closer and laid his hands on her shoulders. "Whatever has to be done to finish this is going to involve both of us. We should stick together as much as we can. And beyond that, I want you with me. Both of you."

"That's the tricky part. How am I supposed to explain to him that we're staying with you?"

"He knows enough about what's going on to accept it. And do you really think he's going to object to the idea of easy access to my game room?"

"No. No, I don't." She eased out from under his hands, got to her feet. "Bradley, I just don't want him ... I know what this sort of thing is like for a child. After my father left us, there always seemed to be a man moving in for a little while."

His face went stony. "This isn't like that. It's more important than that on every possible level. Zoe, you and Simon aren't temporary in my life."

Her breath clogged. "You need to slow down."

As impatience pumped through him, his voice toughened. "Maybe you need to speed up. You don't want me to tell you what you mean to me, what I feel for you?"

"How can either of us think clearly about that?" Desperate for breathing room, she moved over to twitch at the curtains. "You don't know what I'm going to mean or what you're going to feel after this is done. We're caught up in something now, and it—it magnifies everything."

"I was caught up in you the first instant."

"Don't do this." Her breath hitched now as it squeezed around her heart. "You don't know how this could hurt me."

"Maybe I don't. Tell me."

"I can't do this now." Though she damned herself for a coward, she turned back toward him and shook her head. "Neither can you. We both have to go."

He caught her chin in his hand, laid his lips on hers. "We're going to talk about this, and a great deal more. But let's deal with living arrangements for now. If you don't want to stay at my place, I'll stay here. But I'd like you to think about doing it my way. I'll come by after work, and we'll sort it out."

Fourteen

By twelve-thirty, Zoe was installing the track lighting in Dana's bookstore. They'd made the decision to concentrate on one area of the building that afternoon until the final details in that section were complete. In a fast contest of rock, paper, scissors, Dana had won the round.

"It makes sense to me." Dana filled a small spin rack with greeting cards. "There's more room at Brad's place, and he has a cleaning service. He's also been known to cook in a pinch. You could concentrate on the key, and your salon, and let everything else go until the end of the month."

It was logical, Zoe admitted. It was even sensible. But ... "It's not as simple as that. How can I follow through on the idea that my house may be a part of this if I'm not *in* my house?"

"Has that taken you anywhere?" Malory asked her.

"No, it doesn't seem as if it has, but it's only been a couple of days since I started working that angle."

When this was met with silence, Zoe lowered her arms and sighed. "Okay, I know I should have felt something by now if it was important. But I can't be positive."

"Sounds like avoidance to me," Dana said out of the side of her mouth.

In defense, Zoe slanted her a long, steely stare. "It is not avoidance. It's . . . caution. And it's not the same as Jordan staying in your apartment while the two of you wait to move up to the Peak, or Malory moving in with Flynn. You're engaged. And I've got Simon to think about."

"Brad's crazy about Simon," Malory pointed out.

"I know that." She lifted her electric screwdriver to finish attaching the track to the ceiling. "But that doesn't mean we should pack up and move in. I don't want Simon confused about me and Brad—the sex—or getting used to that big house and all the *things,* and the attention, and the, well, the everyday accessibility to Brad."

Malory stopped shelving books. "Is it just Simon that you don't want getting confused?"

"No." She let out a sigh as she passed Dana the screwdriver. "I'm trying to be comfortable with my feelings, to keep them within reasonable limits. There are a lot of reasons for that."

"I'm looking at you, and I'm not seeing a woman who puts limits on herself."

Zoe took the light Malory held up, then clicked it smoothly onto the track. "You think I should do this."

"I think you should do what makes you happy. And sometimes doing what makes you happy is harder and scarier than doing what's safe."

Though she was a long way from certain about what would make her happy, or what was just going to scare her brainless, Zoe broke routine and picked Simon up from school.

"I thought I was going over to Mrs. Hanson's."

"I know." In a now practiced move, Zoe eased her shoulder out of the way as Moe shoved his face through the seats to greet Simon. "I called her. I wanted to talk to you."

"Am I in trouble?"

"I don't know." Brows arched, she asked, "Are you?"

"No, I swear. I didn't do anything."

She parked the car, waved to Mr. Hanson, who was in his front yard raking leaves.

"Okay, then. Let's go inside and have a snack and chat."

"Moe." Loving the game, Simon piled out. "Cookie!" he shouted and laughed himself silly as Moe raced like mad for the front door.

"Mom?"

"Yeah?"

"Do you think, when Moe has to go back home, Flynn will let him come visit?"

"I bet he will." She paused at the door while Moe vibrated. "Simon, I know you want a dog of your own. Why haven't you asked me?"

"Maybe we can't afford one yet."

"Oh." On the little clutch in her heart, she opened the door and let Moe bullet toward the kitchen and cookies.

"They cost money to buy. Even if you get them from the pound, I think you have to pay something. And you gotta buy food for them and toys and stuff. And they need shots from the vet. But I'm saving up so we can get one. Maybe next year we can get one."

Not trusting her voice, Zoe nodded. She hung up her coat, and Simon's, using the time to compose herself. When she got back to the kitchen, Simon had already dumped his book bag on the floor and pulled a biscuit out of the box for the now desperate Moe.

She poured Simon a glass of milk and got out an apple to slice to keep her hands busy while she talked.

"You know I'm trying to do something important, trying to find a key."

"For the magic people."

"Yes, for the magic people. I'm trying really hard, and

sometimes I think, well, today I'll find it. And others, I don't think that at all. I'm pretty sure I'm going to need help."

"Do you need me to help you?"

"In a way." She put the apple slices on a plate, added some grapes. "Bradley wants to help me, too. And the magic people told me it's important that he help."

"He's pretty smart."

"You like him a lot, don't you?"

"Uh-huh." He reached for an apple slice as she set the plate down. "You do, too, right?"

"Yes, I do. Bradley thought he might be able to help me better if we stayed at his house for a little while."

His face inscrutable, even to his mother, Simon watched her as he munched apple. "Live there, with him?"

"Well, stay at his house for a little while. Like a visit."

"Moe, too?"

At the sound of his name, Moe grabbed his beloved tennis ball in his teeth and wedged his wide head under Simon's arm.

"Yes, I'm sure Moe could come."

"Sweet." After giving the ball that Moe had dropped at his feet a kick to send the dog chasing it, Simon reached for a grape. "He likes it over there. It's fun."

"We'd be guests, Simon, so you and Moe—" This time she gave the ball a kick. "You'll have to be on your best behavior."

Simon nodded as Moe skidded across the floor, rapped smartly against the back door, then retrieved the ball. "Okay. Will you and Brad sleep in the same bed and have the sex?"

"What?" It came out in a squeak.

"Chuck says his parents have it in their bed, and it's right in the next room. He says his mother makes noises like it hurts."

"Oh, my God."

Munching grapes, his eyes sharp on his mother's face, Simon sent the ball and Moe across the room. "Does it hurt?"

"No," she said weakly, then cleared her throat. "No, it doesn't hurt. I think we'd better, you know, pack if we're—"

"Then how come she yells and stuff, and makes noises like it does?"

Zoe could actually feel the blood draining from her face, then flashing back again like fire under the skin. "Well. Um. It's just that some people get..." Oh, please, God, help me out here. "You know how when you're playing a game or watching one on TV and you're excited, so you . . . you yell or make noises."

"Yeah. Because it's fun."

"Because it's fun. Sex can be fun, but you have to be old enough, and you need to care about each other and want to share this with each other."

"Guys are supposed to wear a condom so you don't make each other sick or have babies before you want to." Nodding sagely, Simon finished off the grapes. "Chuck's father has some in the drawer by his bed."

"Simon McCourt, you have no business going into Mr. Barrister's drawer."

"Chuck did. He got one and brought it to show me. They look funny. But Brad has to wear one if he's going to have the sex with you, so you don't get sick."

"Simon." She had to close her eyes a moment. "Simon," she repeated. "We're not going to stay with Brad so we can have the sex. And when two people, two adults, have the kind of relationship that includes ah, being together that way, it's very private."

"Then Chuck's mom shouldn't be so loud."

Zoe opened her mouth, closed it again, then just laid her head on the table and laughed until she cried.

WHEN BRAD ARRIVED, SHE had a suitcase packed for each of them, a duffel stuffed with items Simon considered essential to his survival and another filled with what she considered essential to hers. In addition, she had the cooler loaded with perishables from her refrigerator and some of Simon's favorite cereals and snacks. Beside it was the best part of a twenty-five-pound bag of dog food along with a box crammed with Moe items.

"Are we going on safari?" Brad asked as he scanned the luggage.

"You asked for it," Zoe reminded him.

He nudged the cooler with his toe. "You know, I actually have food at my place."

"This will spoil if it isn't used. And speaking of spoiling, I don't want you to feel you have to cater to Simon, or to me, for that matter. He'll need to have rules and chores just as he does here. If he gets out of line, just let me know and I'll deal with it."

"Anything else?"

"Yes. I'm happy to fix meals for all of us, and we'll split the expenses for food."

"You want to cook, I'm all for it, but you're not going to worry about paying for half a loaf of bread."

"Don't *you* argue. I pay my own way or we don't go." She grabbed her coat, shoved her arms through the sleeves. "I won't pick up after you, but I will pick up after myself and Simon. Whenever you need quiet or privacy, don't be shy about saying so."

"Maybe I should write some of this down." He patted his pockets as if searching for a notepad. "I'm afraid there's going to be a quiz."

"You may find this hilarious now, but you haven't lived under the same roof with a nine-year-old boy and a dog before. You may need therapy by the end of the month. So, if you reach a point when you've had enough, just say so."

"Is that it?"

"One more thing. Simon and I had a discussion earlier, and I think we need to address—"

She let it drop as Simon rushed down the stairs with Moe. "Mom, I almost forgot the slime dragon."

"Simon, it's only for a few days. You don't need to take everything you own."

"Let's have a look." Brad held out a hand and took the hard plastic dragon. He found the mechanism, pressed it and watched a ribbon of pale green slime slide out of the dragon's snarling mouth. "Cool."

"I give up. Simon, let's start loading all this in the car."

IT TOOK CONSIDERABLE TIME and persuasion to settle Simon down for the night. Zoe couldn't blame him for jumping out of his skin with delight and excitement. The room he would use at Brad's was double the size of the one at home and boasted an entertainment center with its own TV.

Though she laid down the law in that area, she intended to keep her ear cocked for the sounds of the television post-bedtime.

She unpacked her own things, laying clothes in the cedar-scented drawers of an antique mahogany dresser, setting out toiletries on the acre of pale green countertop in the adjoining bath.

"Don't get used to it," she warned herself as she trailed her fingers over the delicate white lace of the spread accenting the four-poster she would sleep in.

It's just for a few days, she thought. Like a chapter in a faerie tale.

She looked up at the honey-colored wood that formed the coffered ceiling and wondered what it would be like to wake in the morning in this bed, in this room.

She zipped her empty suitcase as Brad knocked on the jamb of the open door.

"Find everything you need?"

"All that and more. It's a gorgeous room, like being inside a warm biscuit." Crouching, she scooted the suitcase under the bed. "It's tempting to have a few jumps on the bed like Simon."

"Help yourself."

Though she smiled, her eyes were troubled. She gestured to the yellow roses on the dresser. "Were you so sure you'd get your way?"

"I was sure of your common sense, and your commitment to follow through on the quest."

"You've got a way about you, Bradley." She trailed her fingers over the bedspread again. "A smooth way about you."

"Regardless, I wanted you and Simon as safe as possible. If I'd had to bully you to get you here, I would have. I appreciate you sparing us both that."

"If you'd bullied me, I'd've gotten my back up, which would've canceled out my common sense. Anyway, it's smarter to stick together."

"Good. Are you going to let me sneak in here in the middle of the night?"

Though she tried for a cool stare, she felt her lips twitch. "It's your house."

"It's your choice."

She let out a laugh, shook her head. "A smooth way. We have to talk. Can we go downstairs?"

"Sure." He held out a hand, and though he noted her hesitation, he kept it extended until she stepped forward and laid hers in it. "How about a glass of wine by the fire?"

"That would be lovely. Everything here is lovely. I'm terrified Simon's going to break something."

"Stop it. The day I was moving back, Flynn stopped by with Moe. The first thing that dog did was run through the house and break a lamp. It wasn't a national tragedy."

"I guess I'm just jumpy, between one thing and another."

"Go in and sit down. I'll get the wine."

There was a fire already blazing. He must have seen to that while she was unpacking. Like the rest of the house, the room looked settled and warm and *interesting*. All the little pieces, the things she imagined he'd collected on his travels, the art, even the way it was all placed.

It spoke of a man who knew what he wanted and was used to having the best.

She wandered over to study a painting of a Paris street scene, the sidewalk café with its cheerful umbrellas, the rivers of flowers, the dignity of the Arc de Triomphe in the background.

A far cry from her framed postcards.

And he'd sat at one of those busy cafés, drinking strong black coffee out of a tiny cup, while she'd only dreamed of it.

Brad came in with a bottle of wine in one hand and two glasses held by the bowls in the other. "I bought that a couple of years ago." he said as he joined her. "I liked the movement, the way the traffic's bunched up on the street. You can almost hear the horns blasting."

He tipped wine into one of the glasses, waited for her to take it. "We Vanes can't seem to stop collecting art."

"Maybe you should think about having a museum."

"Actually, my father's working on something. A hotel, a resort. He could fill it with some of his art, and have an excuse to buy more."

"He would build a hotel just so he has a place to put his art collection?"

"That, and enterprise. Art, wood, and capitalism are the Vane bywords. He's angling to find the right piece of land here in the Highlands, where it all began." His shrug was a gesture of easy confidence. "But if he doesn't, he'll find it elsewhere. Once B. C. knows what he wants, he doesn't take no for an answer."

"So you come by it honestly."

"I'll take that as a compliment. He's a good man. A little

formidable, but a good man. A good husband and father and a hell of a businessman. He'll like you."

"I can't imagine," she said faintly.

"He'll admire what you've done with your life, what you've made. And what you're still building. He'd say you have grit, and there's nothing he respects more."

She expected a man like B.C. Vane would grill her like a hamburger patty if he ever discovered she was involved with his son.

"Do you love them? Your parents?"

"Very much."

"I don't know if I love my mother." It spilled out before she knew she meant to say it, before she knew she thought it. "What an awful thing to say. I want to, but I don't know if I do."

Shocked by her own words, she lowered herself to the arm of a chair. "And my daddy, I haven't seen him in so many years. I don't even know him, so how could I love him? He left us. He left his wife and his four children, and he never came back."

"That was tough on you. Tough on your mother."

"On all of us," Zoe agreed. "But especially on Mama. It didn't just break her heart, it shriveled it up until it was all dry and brittle and there wasn't any juice left for us. When he left, she took off after him. I didn't think she was going to come back."

"She left you alone?" The sheer outrage of it vibrated in his voice. "She left four children alone?"

"She was wild to get him back. She was only gone a few days, but ... oh, God, I was scared. What was I going to do if she didn't come back?"

"Wasn't there anyone you could've called, gone to for help?"

"My mama's sister, but she and Mama fought all the time, so I didn't want to call her. I didn't know if I should call any of my daddy's family, the way things were. The fact was, I didn't know what the hell to do, so I didn't do anything except mind the kids and wait for her to come home."

He couldn't fathom it. "How old were you?"

"Twelve. Junior was only a year younger than me, and he wouldn't mind me. Joleen, she was a couple years younger than him, so she'd've been eight, I guess, and she cried for a whole day. I never saw anybody cry like that before or since," Zoe said with a sigh. "Mazie, the baby, was five, so she didn't really understand what was going on, but she knew something was up. I couldn't hardly take my eyes off her for a minute. I didn't know what I was going to do if we ran out of food or money to buy more."

She shifted to sit in the chair, dangling the wineglass between her knees. "But she came back. I remember thinking how tired she looked, and how hard. But she was going to look more tired, more hard before it was done. She did her best for us. She did all she could, but I don't know that she ever loved us again. I don't know if she could."

She looked up at him then. "Those are the people I come from. I wanted you to know."

"Are you telling me that because you think it'll change my feelings for you? That if I find your parents irresponsible and selfish I'll stop loving you?"

Wine sloshed over the rim of her glass when her hand jerked. "Don't say that. Don't say something about love when you don't even know me."

"I know you, Zoe. Do you want me to tell you what I know? What I see, what I feel?"

She shook her head. "God. I don't know what I'm supposed to do. I don't know how to make you understand how this twists me around. How I'm afraid if I let go again, I could end up dried up inside, too."

"The way you let go with James Marshall?"

She sighed. "I loved him. Bradley, I loved him so much. It was like being inside a crystal bowl, where everything was so shiny and bright. It wasn't just something reckless, something careless between us."

He sat down with her. "Tell me. I need to know," he said when she hesitated. "And if that's not enough, going back over it, with me, might be one of the steps toward the key."

"I'm not ashamed." She spoke quietly. "It's not that I'm ashamed, but that some of it—the things that happened, the things I fett—have always been just for me. But you deserve to hear it."

He touched the back of her hand, then let her go. "How did you meet him?"

"I guess you could say it was through our mothers. Mrs. Marshall, she had my mama do her hair. Sometimes she'd have Mama come out to her house before a party, or before she was going somewhere special, to do her up. Maybe I'd go along, give Mrs. Marshall a manicure, or do the shampoo. She was nice to me. She was always very kind, and not snooty. Well, not very," she corrected.

"She would talk to me, and she'd answer questions if I asked about the pictures on the walls or the flowers on the dresser. She'd ask me about school, or boys. And she'd always slip me an extra five dollars when my mother wasn't looking.

"James was off at school. I'd see him once in a while, but he never noticed me. And I'd look at his pictures on Mrs. Marshall's bureau. He was so handsome, like a knight or a prince, so maybe I fell a little bit in love that way. Girls do."

"So do boys," Brad added.

"Maybe. They gave a lot of parties in the big house. Mrs. Marshall, she loved giving parties. She hired me to help with the serving for some of them, and even bought me a good black skirt and a white blouse so I'd look nice. They had a party in the spring, and James was home from school. He noticed me."

She looked down at her wine as if she'd forgotten it was there.

Gathering her thoughts, she took a slow sip. "He followed me back to the kitchen, and he was talking to me, flirting. I was so shy, and he made me clumsy. But he was so sweet about it. After it was over, and things were cleaned up, he drove me home."

She lifted her shoulders, let them fall. "I wasn't supposed to take rides from boys, so I shouldn't have let him drive me. I knew his mama wouldn't like it if she found out. And mine? She'd've skinned me. But I couldn't help it. Just like I couldn't help seeing him again. Sneaking out to see him, because his parents and my mama, they wouldn't have allowed it. That only made it more exciting, more wonderful. Like Romeo and Juliet. I was young enough, and so was he, to think like that. To slide right into love without thinking about anything else."

She looked at Brad, and could read his thoughts. "You're thinking he took advantage of me, that he was using me, but it wasn't like that. Maybe he didn't love me, not the way I loved him. But he thought he did. He was only nineteen, and caught up in the romance of it the same as I was."

"Zoe, at nineteen, with his background, his lifestyle, he knew a lot more about . . . life than you did."

"Maybe. Maybe that's true, especially since I didn't know much of anything. But he didn't push me, Bradley. I don't want you to think that. He didn't insist or demand, and he wasn't any more to blame than I was. It just happened."

"And when you told him you were pregnant?"

She took a breath, long and slow. "I didn't even know I was for over two months. I wasn't very smart about that kind of thing. It was September before I was sure, and he was away at college. When he came home one weekend, I told him. He was angry, and he was scared. And I guess, looking at it from here, I can see it was already fading for him. Here he is, off at college with all those exciting things happening, and some girl at home he's already losing interest in comes up pregnant."

"Yeah, his bad luck."

She had to smile a little. "You're awfully hard on him."

"A hell of a lot harder if I had the chance." Annoyed, he got up to pour another half glass of wine. "Maybe part of it's jealousy. But the bigger part is knowing he let you go through this alone."

"He said we'd do the right thing, that he'd stand by me. I believe he meant it, even though he was scared and angry. I believe he meant it when he said it."

"Words are cheap."

"Yes, they are." She nodded slowly while Brad wandered around the room. "Someone like you, you'd have meant them, and you'd have followed through with them. Not everyone's built the same. And sometimes the right thing isn't what you think it is. I'm where I am because he didn't follow through, so it was the right thing. For me and for Simon."

"All right. What happened next?"

"He was going to tell his parents, and I had to tell my mama, then we'd do what we had to."

"But he didn't do it."

"Oh, he told his parents, just like I told my mother. Mama was mad, but a part of her was smug. I could see that part on her face when I told her. The part that was thinking it served me right for acting like I was better than the rest of them, and now I'd find out just what was what. Still, when Mrs. Marshall came around, Mama stood up for me."

Her chin came up now, a gesture of pride. "Mrs. Marshall said I was a liar and a cheat, a tramp who'd tricked her son into sneaking around behind her back. I wasn't going to drag her boy down in the gutter, and if I was pregnant it didn't mean the baby was his. Even if it was, she wasn't having him pay the rest of his life for falling in with me. She said more, things about how she'd taken me into her home, trusted me, and I was no better than a thief and a whore. She tossed a check for five thousand dollars down on the table and told me that was all I'd ever get. I could use it for an abortion, or whatever, but I'd never get another penny, and if I tried to get more, tried to see James again, she'd see to it that my family paid for it."

"You were carrying her grandchild."

"She didn't see it that way. She couldn't. And she would have made my family pay. She had the money and the power, and I had nothing to fight back with. She sent James away. I don't know where. I wrote him a letter that September, to the college, asking him what to do, what did he want me to do. He never answered, so I guess that was answer enough. I took the money, and the savings I'd squirreled away, and I left. I wasn't going to raise my baby in that trailer court. I wasn't going to raise him anywhere near the Marshalls. After Simon was born, I sent James another letter, with a picture of the baby. It came back unopened. So I put that aside, and I promised myself I'd look after my own. And I wasn't going to look for somebody to make things better, or different, or show me what to do. I wasn't going to look for somebody to tell me they loved me and they'd do the right thing."

He came back to sit, took the glass of wine she'd neglected out of her hand and set it aside. "You've proved you can make a good life for yourself and Simon. On your own. Do you have to go on proving it?"

"If I let this happen between us, and you walk away ... I'm not brave enough to risk it. Maybe I would be if it was just me. But it's not."

"You don't believe I'm in love with you."

"I believe you think you are, and I know that no one would stop you from doing the right thing. Even if it wasn't right for you. So I'm going to ask you to wait until this month is over, until everything's less romantic and exciting, then see how we are together."

She was holding up a mirror, he thought, reflecting back what was between them to what had been between her and James. He struggled to find some understanding through the resentment. "I want to ask you one thing. Just one. Do you love me?"

"I can't help but love you, but I *can* help what I do about it."

Fifteen

SHE'D GONE OFF IN THE WRONG DIRECTION. ZOE WAS sure of it now. She'd gone back to Indulgence, searched through all three floors alone, cleaned every inch of the attic, stared in the mirror. But she found nothing to guide her. No sudden flash of light or inspiration.

No key.

She'd gone back to her house, and had spent a full hour sitting alone in the living room. Though she felt foolish, she closed the curtains, lit candles and tried to push herself into some state of knowledge or perception.

Instead, she almost fell asleep.

She was tired, frustrated, and irritable, and probably in no state to open herself to intuition.

She decided to go back to the beginning and try again. She made the arrangements for Simon before she approached Bradley.

He'd been polite since they'd moved into the guest rooms. A little cool, Zoe thought as she walked toward the office he kept in his home. But she couldn't blame him.

She knocked, then eased the door open when he called out to come in.

"I'm sorry to bother you, but ... oh." The enormous blueprints tacked up on a display board pulled her into the room. "These are your plans, for the expansion."

"Mmm. Couple of changes yet, but we're almost there. We'll break ground in March, as soon as the weather cooperates."

"You're adding all this to the lawn-and-garden section?"

"Doubling it. Homeowners want trees, shrubs, flowers, and vegetables, and the means to plant and maintain them." He tapped his fingers on his thigh, studying her as she studied the plans. "Then there's garden decor. And this section here will carry several new lines of outdoor furniture."

"It's very ambitious."

"I'll make it work. When something matters, you keep at it until you make it work."

"I know you're angry with me."

"Some. Mostly frustrated. You heading into town?"

"No, not today. I just talked to Flynn. He's going to keep Simon for a while today. He's missing Moe anyway, and Simon won't mind spending most of his Saturday romping around with Flynn and the dog. And I'm ... I want to go back to West Virginia, to the woods. To see if I missed something before. I'm telling you because I don't want you to worry or be upset."

"I'll drive you."

"Yes." Her stomach unknotted. "I think that's a good idea. I have a stop to make on the way back, but I need to talk that over with you, too. If we could get started soon, I'd appreciate it."

"Give me five minutes."

"Thanks. I'll go get Simon and Moe together."

When she left, Brad took a hunting knife out of a locked drawer and unsheathed it to test the edge.

*

She ordered herself to stay relaxed as they drove out of the Valley. "Um. One of the things I wanted to talk to you about is Thanksgiving. Malory mentioned that you were staying here for the holiday."

"It isn't the time to leave."

"No." Thanksgiving was the day before her deadline. In less than a week, all the sand in that hourglass would have drained. "I wondered if you'd like it if we, all seven of us, had Thanksgiving together at your house. Malory's dining room isn't ready yet, and yours is bigger anyway. I could handle the cooking, and—"

"Yes." He reached over, touched a hand to hers. "I'd like that very much. If you're handling the cooking, I'll take the gathering. Make me a shopping list."

"That'll help. There's not much time."

He looked at her, understanding perfectly. "There's time enough."

"I'm holding on to that. There's another thing I thought you might help me with. I want to go by the pound, pick out a pup for Simon. After Thanksgiving, after ... everything's over, I can go get it. They said they'd hold one for me for a week."

"Why not just take it now?"

"Oh, that'll be fine—a boy, a huge dog, and a new puppy running around your house. A puppy who'll pee on your rugs and chew everything that isn't nailed down. We'll wait till we're home again."

"Logical," Brad said, and let it drop.

She directed him off the main road, along the winding ones, and asked him to park beside the field as she had done before.

"It's beautiful country."

"It is." She stepped out of the car and into brisk air that immediately pinkened her cheeks. "I love the hills. I never wanted to live anywhere that didn't have hills. And trees."

She ducked under the fence. "I played in those woods there when I was little, and I used to sit in them and dream when I was older."

"What did you dream of?"

"Oh, all the places I'd go, the things I'd see, the people I'd meet."

"Boys?"

"Not so much. Or not as soon as most girls, I guess. I used to think if there was one thing I wasn't going to do it was get myself tied down to a man and a bunch of babies so I'd never do or have anything special. Maybe Mama was right to be smug."

"No, she wasn't."

"I was just so sick of taking care of my sisters and my brother, of helping to run things. Worrying about bills and how to make a meal stretch. By the time I was twelve the last thing on my mind was boys or weddings or babies. I didn't even play with dolls."

He took her hand as they approached the trees. "What did you play with?"

"Tools and paints. I liked to fix things. I gave my dolls to Joleen and Mazie. There wasn't any point pretending to take care of somebody when I already was. Oh, God, I wanted out of here. I wanted out, so bad, Bradley, then when James came around—I didn't hope to get pregnant. But ... I'm not sure I didn't figure somewhere in my head that it had to be a man and babies after all, and that was the only way I was going to get out and get more."

"What if it was?" He stopped as they reached the edge of the trees. "What if it was, Zoe? You were sixteen."

"I'm not anymore, and I want you to know that I don't look at you and think you're a way I can get more." She gripped both of his hands, hard. "I need you to know that before we walk through these woods."

"I don't think that. Hell, I can hardly get you to take more when I knock you over the head with it." To soothe them both, he lifted her hand, pressed his lips to it. "But I'd take it from you. I want more from you."

"If I could give it to anybody, it'd be you." She wrapped her arms around him, pressed close. "You're the best man I ever met in my life, and that's what scares me most."

"It's about time you let me worry about myself."

"A few more days," she murmured, then pulling back, took his hand again and walked into the woods.

"I saw the white buck on the way through," she told him. "But nothing else. It felt good to walk here again. Peaceful. Simon was conceived in here. It's a good place, an important place for me."

"For both of us, then."

She walked the way she'd walked before, but there was no white buck, and no sense of import. When they came to the edge where the gravel began, she stopped again.

"I've got to go over and see my mother. You don't have to come."

"You don't want me to meet her?"

Staring at the trailers, she blew out a breath. "Maybe you'd better. Saturday's a busy day for her. She'll probably have customers, so we won't stay long."

He saw some children playing on a rusted swing set, and a Doberman mix tethered by a thick chain that barked at them as if it'd already tasted blood. From a trailer to the left came the sounds of voices raised in a vicious argument. And to the right, a little girl was perched on a rickety step, singing her baby doll to sleep.

She looked up and offered Bradley a slow and beautiful smile. "Time for Cissy's nap," she told him in a whisper.

He crouched, angling his head around to look at the doll. "She's very pretty."

"She's my sweet baby girl."

As she spoke, the door opened behind her. A young woman stepped out, a dishrag in her hand and a cautious look in her eye.

"Can I help you?" She laid a hand on the little girl's shoulder.

"Just admiring Cissy," Brad said.

"I'm Crystal McCourt's daughter, Zoe." Understanding the mother's caution, Zoe stepped up to touch Brad's arm. "We're just dropping by to see her."

"Oh." She relaxed visibly. "Nice to meet you. You gave me a start, is all. Chloe knows she's not supposed to talk to strangers, but she can't seem to help it. She trusts everybody. Tell Mrs. McCourt I said hey, and thank her again for cutting Chloe's hair so nice."

"I will." As Zoe walked away, she heard the woman say, "Come inside with Mama, sweet baby girl."

"Some people make a good life here," she said quietly. "They plant little container gardens and have picnics in the summer."

"And some people live in palaces and can't make a good life. It's not where, it's how. And it's who."

Maybe, Zoe thought, that was one more thing she was meant to remember.

"That's ours. Hers. Ours." She dropped the hand she'd used to gesture to the dingy green double-wide. "I'm ashamed that I'm ashamed of this. And I hate myself for hating that you see this. She always said I had too much pride. I guess she was right about that."

"I guess you're not perfect, then. Maybe I don't love you after all."

She tried to laugh, but it got stuck in her throat.

"Are you going to introduce me to your mother, Zoe, or should I just go up and knock on the door myself?"

"She won't like you."

"You're not taking into account my incredible charm."

Noting the amused and confident tone, Zoe merely slid her gaze up to his face. "That's one of the things she won't like about you." Resigned, she started forward. She heard the chattering inside as she reached the door. Young voices, at least two.

Saturday morning drives into Saturday night, she thought. Date night. A couple of girls wanted to get done up for a night on the prowl. She knocked on the metal frame of the screen, squeaked it open, then gave the inner door a good nudge with her shoulder.

Three girls, she noted. One with her hair already plastered with stripper. Somebody was going blond. The second had her short do already coated and setting up, and a third waited her turn and was holding out a fashion magazine to show off a hairstyle.

They sounded like an excited flock of birds, then fell into silence, then into snorting giggles when they spotted Brad behind Zoe.

The place smelled of bleach, dye, smoke, and last night's dinner.

Crystal finished setting an egg timer on the counter, turned. Her eyebrows raised high. "Wind blew you back a second time in one month, and it ain't even my birthday." Her gaze shifted to Brad and held, speculatively.

"I was out this way. I wanted you to meet my friend, Bradley."

"Bradley. That's a silver-dollar name."

"It's nice to meet you, Mrs. McCourt."

"Too many people in here." She grabbed her cigarettes and her hot-pink Bic. "Go on outside."

"Ladies," Brad said to the girls, and the giggles erupted again as he stepped back.

"I can see you're busy," Zoe began.

"Good Saturday business today." When the door shut behind her, Crystal flicked on her lighter, blew out a stream of smoke. "The Jacobson girl wants her hair blond. Wants to be Britney

Spears. Had herself a nice head of chestnut brown, too, but it's no never mind to me if she wants to ruin it."

"Is that Haley Jacobson? She was just a little thing the last time I saw her."

"She's sixteen. Same age as you when you ran off. She keeps sashaying around like she does, she'll get herself in trouble same as you did."

"I stopped thinking about it as trouble a long time ago." Zoe knew the girls were there, too, and that as her mother hadn't bothered to lower her voice, that they heard every word. "Simon's the best thing that ever happened to me."

"You said you weren't breeding again." The line etched between Crystal's eyebrows deepened as she shot another look at Brad. "You come to tell me different?"

"No. Bradley's, he's ..."

"Zoe and Simon are important to me," Brad said smoothly. "I wanted to meet you. Zoe told me you raised four children, mostly on your own. That must be where she gets her courage."

Fancy name, fancy looks, fancy talk, Crystal thought as she chuffed out smoke. "Doesn't take courage to raise kids. It takes a strong back."

"I imagine it takes both. You have a beautiful and amazing daughter, Mrs. McCourt. You must be very proud."

"Bradley. Silver-dollar name and a fancy manner. You want to take her on, that's your business." As if it didn't matter to her one way or the other, she jerked a thin shoulder. "She's a good worker, and she breeds well. Doesn't whine much."

"I'll keep that in mind," Brad said equably, and made Crystal laugh in spite of herself.

"Maybe she's got better taste this time around. You don't look to be too much of an asshole."

"Thanks."

"You never tried to wiggle out of work," she said to Zoe with a hint of affection. "I'll give you that." On impulse, she reached out, touched Zoe's hair. "Good cut—got style. Anyway, you never were stupid, either. You got a chance for the high life here—'cause this one looks like the high life to me—you'd be a fool not to take it. A woman's got to take what she can get."

"Mama."

"I say what's on my mind, always have, always will." Crystal dropped the cigarette, crushed it under her shoe. "I gotta get back inside. Get a ring on your finger this time," she told Zoe, then tipped her chin at Bradley. "You could do worse."

She dragged the screen open, went back inside. And shut the door.

"It never comes out right. It just never does." Tears flooded Zoe's eyes and were ruthlessly blinked back. "We need to go."

She started toward the woods almost at a jog, kept her head down when Brad took her arm. "She doesn't understand you."

"That's not news to me."

"She doesn't understand the light inside you. Or that it's not about what you can get, it's about what you want to make. She doesn't understand you, so she doesn't know how to love you."

"I don't know what to do about it."

"You keep trying, and it's going to hurt you. You stop trying, and it's going to hurt you." He ran his hands up and down her arms for comfort. "I understand you, Zoe, so I know which choice you'll make."

She looked back toward the trailer. "I'll come back at Christmastime and maybe . . . just maybe." Because she thought they both needed it, she worked up a smile. "I told you she wouldn't like you."

"She did too like me. She's already caught in my web." He bent to kiss her lightly on the lips. "Just like her daughter."

"Me, I'm hell on cobwebs." She took his hand again, and they walked into the woods.

"Why do they call them cobwebs? They're not made out of cob."

"There's a question for Dana. She'll look it up somewhere—I don't know where she finds half these things—and give you a whole lecture on it. I never knew anybody so smart with words. It was always numbers for me. Now I'm friends with Dana, who knows everything about books, and Malory, who knows everything about art. I've learned a lot from them in the last couple months. Sometimes it all seems like some kind of dream."

She paused, looking around as she spoke. "And I'll wake up one morning and it'll all be the way it was. I'll be working for that bitch Carly again and I won't even know Dana or Mal. I'll pick up the newspaper and read Flynn's column, but I won't know him. Or I'll see one of Jordan's books and wonder what he's like, because I won't know."

She looked up at Brad, touched her fingers to his cheek. "I won't know you. I'll go pick up something at HomeMakers, and I won't think of you because none of this happened."

"It's real." He curled his fingers firmly around her wrist so she could feel his grip, so he could feel her pulse. "This is real."

"But if it wasn't, if I'm in bed having some long, complicated dream, I think I'd wake up heartbroken." She looked back in the direction of her mother's trailer. "Or worse. Whatever happens next, wherever all of this ends, I couldn't stand it if I'd missed knowing you. Kiss me." She leaned in, rose on her toes. "Will you?"

He drew her close, and laid his lips on hers gently. Letting the moment spin out. When she sighed, when she linked her arms around his neck, it was more lovely than any dream.

She felt something shift inside her with an ache so sweet it brought the tears rushing back. The air was cool, his mouth so warm. Love, beyond what she'd ever hoped for, was here.

She felt his hand stroke her hair, smooth it all the way down her back. His slim young body pressed to hers with his need quivering through it, and into hers.

She eased back, looked into bright blue eyes, and let a tear trickle down her cheek. "James." She said it softly, cupped his face in her hands.

"I love you, Zoe." James's voice—a little breathless, eager, fell on her ears. "We were meant to be together. You'll never feel this way about anyone but me."

"No, I won't." Swamped with the love that poured from a sixteen-year-old girl's heart, she pressed his hand to her lips, to her cheek, held it there. "Nothing will ever be the same, not for either of us."

"We'll run away together. We'll be together forever."

She smiled, very gently. "No, we won't." She kissed him again, with no regrets, then stepped back. "Good-bye, James."

Brad hauled her upright when her knees gave way and continued to shake her, to say her name, as he had since he'd felt her leave him.

Her eyes had blurred, her cheeks had paled.

She'd called him James.

"Look at me. Look at me, goddamn it."

"I am." Limply, her head rolled back, and though her vision grayed with the effort, she fought to focus. "I'm looking at you. Bradley."

"We're getting out of here." He started to scoop her up, but she pressed a hand to his chest.

"No. It's all right. I just need a second. Let me take that second sitting down."

She slid down, sat on the ground with her forehead pressed to her updrawn knees. "I'm a little dizzy. Just need to get my bearings."

He pulled the knife from the sheath under his jacket and took a long scan of the woods before crouching in front of her. "You clicked off, like someone had flicked a switch inside you. You called me James."

"I know."

"You slipped away. You weren't with me, you were with him. Looking at him." With love. "You said nothing would ever be the same."

"I know what I said. He took me back. Kane took me back, but I knew it." Steadier, she lifted her head. "I knew it, almost as soon as it started. I felt ... I'm not ashamed of what I felt, and I'm not sorry for it. That would mean I'm ashamed and sorry about Simon. But I can be sorry Kane used you that way."

"You cried for him." Reaching out, Brad caught a tear on his fingertip.

"Yes, I cried for James. And for what might've been if he'd been stronger, maybe if we'd both been stronger. Then I said good-bye."

She laid her hand over Brad's, curled her fingers into his palm. "Kane wanted me to feel all those things I felt for James, and he wanted to use them to drive something between us. Has he?"

"It pissed me off. It hurt." He looked down at their joined hands and, after a moment, turned his over so their fingers linked. "But no, he didn't drive anything between us."

"Bradley." She started to lean in, wanted to touch her lips to his. And saw the knife. Her eyes went huge. "Oh, God."

"He can be hurt," Bradley said simply. "If I get the chance, I'm going to hurt him." Standing, he sheathed the knife, then held a hand down to her.

She moistened her lips. "You better be careful with that thing."

"Yes, Mom."

"Still a little pissed, aren't you? I know who you are, Bradley. I know who I am. He tried to make me forget that, but he couldn't. That has to mean something. I felt exactly like I did when I was sixteen and with James. My body, my heart, my head. He ran his hand down my hair. I wore it long then, and he used to do that. Run his hand all the way down my hair when he kissed me. That kind of thing's inside me, in those memory boxes. Kane can get into those."

It took a supreme act of will, but Bradley forced himself to think beyond the personal, toward the quest. "What did he say to you? James—what did he say to you?"

"That he loved me, that I'd never feel about anyone else the way I did about him. That's true, I won't. I shouldn't. But Bradley, I *knew*."

She spun around now, and her face shone. "Even when I was standing there with hair halfway down my back and his face in my hands, I knew it wasn't real. Just a trick. And *I* used it."

She pressed her palms together, tapped the sides of her fingers against her mouth as she turned in a circle. "This place. I had to come back here. More, I had to come back here with you. But the key isn't here." She dropped her hands. "It's not here."

"I'm sorry."

"No." She shook her head, twirled again, with a brilliant smile. "I know it's not here. I feel it. I don't have to wonder, I don't have to come back hoping or looking, because I've done what I needed to do here. Or we have."

She jumped into his arms, hard and fast enough to knock him back a full step. Laughing, she hooked her legs around his waist and gave him a noisy kiss. "I don't know what it all means, but I'll figure it out. For the first time in days, I believe I'll figure it out. I'm going to unlock that box, Bradley."

She pressed her cheek to his. "I'm going to unlock it, and they're going to go home."

WHEN THEY PULLED UP at Flynn's, Zoe aimed a steely look at Brad. "This is on your head, I want to make that clear."

"You did. About six times already."

"I'm not going to have any sympathy for you or your belongings."

"Yeah, yeah. Blah blah."

She stifled a laugh, kept her face stern as she followed him toward the house. "Just remember who tried to be practical."

"Right." He shot her a grin as he pushed open the door. "You were a goner as soon as you looked into those big brown eyes."

"I could've waited a week."

"Liar."

The laugh escaped as she set the puppy down and let him race down the hall. "This ought to be interesting."

Moe shot out of the kitchen, then skidded to a halt. His eyes rolled, his body braced. And the little pup, a ball of brown and gray fur, yipped in joy and leaped up to nip at Moe's nose.

Brad grabbed Zoe's arm before she could run forward. "But what if—"

"Have a little faith," Brad suggested.

Moe quivered, sniffed the pup as it jumped and tumbled. Then he collapsed, rolling over on his back in an attitude of bliss as the puppy climbed all over him and chewed on his ears.

"Big softie," Zoe murmured, and felt her own smile spread, big and foolish, as Simon wandered out from the kitchen.

"Hey, Mom! We're having subs for lunch. Me and Flynn made them, sand . . . " He trailed off, his eyes going round as the puppy deserted Moe to charge him.

"Whoa! A puppy. Where'd he come from?" Simon was already down on the floor, laughing as the pup licked his face, tumbling back as Moe tried to horn in. "He looks like a bear cub or something."

Buried in dogs, Simon twisted enough to look at Brad. "Is it yours? When'd you get him? What's his name?"

"Not mine. He's just been liberated. And he doesn't have one."

"Then who—" He went very still, and those long gold eyes fixed on his mother's.

"He's yours, baby."

In that moment she knew the puppy could chew through her house like a plague of termites and she would never regret it. She would never forget that flash of stunned joy on her little boy's face.

"To keep?" Simon's voice shook as he managed to get to his knees. "I can keep him?"

"I think he's counting on it." She walked over to kneel down and ruffle the pup's cloud-soft fur. "You're going to have to be very responsible, and make sure he's fed right and taught, and loved. Puppies are a lot of work. He's going to depend on you."

"Mom." Too overcome to be embarrassed that Brad looked on, Simon threw his arms around his mother and buried his face against her shoulder. "I'll take good care of him. I promise. Thanks, Mom. I love you more than anything, ever."

"I love *you* more than anything, ever." She answered his fierce hug with one of her own, then managed a watery laugh when both dogs tried to wiggle between them. "I think Moe's going to like having a friend."

"It's just like a big family." Simon lifted the puppy high.

The newcomer expressed his delight by peeing on Simon's knee.

Sixteen

ZOE RUBBED THE EXFOLIATING CREAM OVER DANA'S CALF and grinned as her friend let out a long, heartfelt moan.

"I really appreciate the two of you giving up your Sunday afternoon to be my guinea pigs."

This time Dana grunted. Malory sat on a stool in the treatment room and rubbed her fingers over her newly scrubbed and polished skin. "I can't get over how good it feels."

"I wasn't worried about the results—these products are great. But I want to be sure the whole experience works."

"Works for me," said Dana's slurred and muffled voice.

Zoe glanced around, scanning the shelves of products, the glowing candles, the neat stack of mint-green towels on the counter, the clear crystal she'd hung from the ceiling over the padded table.

It was, she thought, exactly right.

"Of course, when we're doing this for real there won't be three people in here talking. You want us to be quiet, Dana?"

"You don't even exist in my little world. That stuff smells as good as it feels."

"It's good we're doing this." Malory sipped some of the lemon water Zoe had chilled in a squat glass pitcher. "If we're going to open on Friday, we want to work out as many kinks as possible, in all three areas."

Swallowing hard, she pressed a hand to her belly. "God, we're going to open on Friday. Even if it is a kind of dry run for the grand opening on December first, it's happening."

"Big day, all around," Zoe said.

"You're going to find the key." Malory touched her shoulder. "I know it."

The connection—Malory's hand on her, hers on Dana—bolstered her. "That's another reason I wanted to do this today. I needed some time with just the three of us."

She glanced up at the crystal again. It certainly seemed she'd become a bit more mystical-minded over the last few months. "To recharge my energy. My girl power."

"Rah-rah," Dana cheered and made Zoe laugh.

"With what happened yesterday I feel more confident, but this little voice keeps sneaking in asking me why the hell I think I can do this."

"Is it Zoe's voice," Dana asked her, "or Kane's?"

"It's Zoe's, which makes it more irritating. Yesterday, there was this rush of excitement, of energy, when I realized what was going on, that I knew what it was and could control it. But I need to move it from there."

"You went back to a beginning, and an ending." Curious, Malory examined the bottles and tubes neatly lined up on Zoe's shelves. "And with the three of us here today, we're going back to basics. Both Dana and I had periods during our part of this when we felt discouraged and lost."

"Check," Dana confirmed. "And when we went off on tangents that dead-ended. Or seemed to."

"Seemed to." Turning back, Malory nodded. "But without those tangents would we have gotten on the right track? I don't think so. It's something I've thought about a lot," she added, leaning back on the counter. "A quest isn't linear, it isn't straightforward. It circles and it winds and overlaps. But every step, every piece, has its place. Let's take yours."

"Dana has to rinse off."

"Then hold that thought." Wrapped in the bath sheet Zoe provided, Dana headed for the shower.

"You've got some ideas." Zoe walked over to rinse her hands. "I can see it."

"I do, actually. It might be easier for me to see, well, the forest for the trees, because I'm not in it the way you are. And the experience I had in the attic here was similar to what happened to you yesterday. In that I knew what was going on, and controlled it. And part of me, a little part, wanted to stay in that illusion and let the rest go."

Zoe looked back, saw the sympathy, the understanding on Malory's face. The tension in her shoulders dissolved. "I really needed to hear that. So much. I didn't want James, Mal, not really, but part of me remembered how much I *had* wanted him."

"I know. I know exactly."

She could, Zoe thought. She and Dana were the only ones who really could. "Part of me felt that same way, had that same yearning. And it would've been so easy to drift back there and believe everything would turn out differently."

"But you didn't drift back."

"No." She began changing the cover on the treatment table, adjusting the pad, smoothing the cotton. "Everything but that one little part knew I didn't want it to turn out differently. I didn't really want the boy who couldn't stand by me or his own child. But I had to remember him, really remember him, and what I felt for him. So I could say good-bye."

"Do you want the man who's willing to stand by you, and your child?"

"I do." There was a flutter under her heart as she selected the lotion for Dana. "But I don't seem to trust either of us to make it work. Lie on your back," she said when Dana came back in. "And there's more than that, than not trusting us."

Efficiently, she adjusted the towel that covered Dana from breast to crotch, then warmed the lotion in her hands. "If I take that last step with him, how much danger will that put him in? It's kind of a quandary. If you love someone, you want to protect them. If I'm going to protect him, I can't let myself love him. Not all the way."

"If you love him, you ought to respect him enough to know he'll protect himself."

Zoe stared at Dana. "I do respect him."

"I don't think you do. You keep wondering if and when he's going to let you down, let Simon down. When he's going to walk. You're talking to somebody who's been there. You're thinking you shouldn't give him a hundred percent because you'll need something in reserve when he takes a hike. I'm not saying you don't have a right to that. You've got a lot on the line."

"And what's most on the line for Zoe? Personally," Malory qualified. "The single thing you won't risk?"

"Simon."

"Exactly."

"I know Bradley won't hurt him." Zoe massaged the lotion in, working her way down Dana's body. "But the more Simon looks to him for the sort of things a boy looks for from a father, the more of a jolt it'll be if things don't work out. He's had to deal with not having a father. Ever. Not like a divorce or even death, but never having one. However much I've smoothed it for him. however much he knows I love him, and I'm there for him, he's always known there was someone who didn't, who refused to be there. I don't want him to ever feel unwanted again."

"And to keep that from happening, you'd sacrifice. You'd

fight," Malory added. "Whatever it took, whatever it cost you, you'd fight. Because of all the choices you've made, Simon is the most important. He's your key."

"Simon?" Zoe repeated as Dana sat up. "Oh, sorry, over on your stomach. My mind's churning."

"Mal's clicked on something." Dana rolled over, but propped her head on her fist. "We're the keys, the three of us. That's been emphasized over and over. But of the three of us, Zoe's the one who has—you could say—re-created herself in a child. Simon's part of Zoe. Zoe's the key, ergo, Simon's the key."

"Kane can't touch him." Fear wanted to leap up and choke her. "Rowena said she'd protected him."

"Count on it." Dana looked over her shoulder. "If he could do anything about Simon, he'd have tried by now."

"I think it might be more than Rowena that protects him," Malory added. "I think whatever can be done from the other side is being done. Someone's children were already harmed. They won't let it happen again. Between all that, and us, nothing touches Simon."

"If I believed otherwise, I'd walk away from this in a heartbeat." Zoe paused as she caught Malory's nod. "Which Kane has to know, so he would have done anything he could to threaten my son. He hasn't, because he can't. Okay." She let out a long breath. "Okay, let's work from there. If Simon's the key, or part of it the way he's part of me, doesn't that take me back to choices I've made regarding him? Having him was a choice, keeping him was a choice—the best ones I ever made. But I've been back there. And though I think going back mattered, I don't have the key."

"You made other choices," Dana pointed out. "Went in other directions."

"Been over some of those, too. It's been a kind of journey, I guess," she continued as she finished slicking the lotion on Dana.

"Remembering, seeing it again, thinking about it all. It's been good for me, all in all, because it validated my choices and let me see that the mistakes I made weren't all that big. You want to roll over? I'll get you your robe."

"You came here to the Valley," Dana began. "You got a job, you bought a house. What else?"

Malory held up a hand while Zoe helped Dana into her robe. "I'm not going to say all of that's not important, and maybe going through some of the details is one of the answers. But we could look at this from a different angle. What if some of the answers have to do with Simon's choices?"

"He's a kid," Dana pointed out, rubbing a hand on her forearm to admire Zoe's work. "His biggest choice is which video game to play."

"No." Thoughtfully, Zoe shook her head. "No, children have a lot of choices. Right or wrong. Some of those choices stick with them, and push them in a certain direction. What friends they make. Maybe they read a book about a fighter pilot and they decide they want to fly. Right now, in a hundred different ways, Simon's deciding what kind of a man he'll be."

"Then maybe you need to take a closer look at some of those decisions," Malory suggested.

A DECISION SIMON WAS particularly pleased with at the moment was his choice of Homer as a name for the pup. It combined some of his favorite things into one—baseball, a cartoon character, and a dog. Outside in the crisp fall air, watching Moe chase a tennis ball and Homer chase Moe, Simon figured life didn't get any cooler.

Plus, the guys were coming over pretty soon to watch the game while his mom and her friends did girl stuff. He could eat potato chips till he puked.

He snatched up the ball Moe dropped at his feet, then did a

lot of dancing and fake throwing to make the dogs totally nutso before he hurled it toward the trees.

When he went to school the next day, he'd tell all his pals about Homer. Maybe, if it wasn't too goofy, he could get Brad to take a picture so he could show everybody.

He looked back toward the river while the dogs rolled around together. He really liked it here. He liked his house, too, and the yard and all. And living next to the Hansons. But, boy, he really liked it here, with the woods to explore and the river right there.

If they were going to stay longer, it would be so cool to have his friends over. Man, they would freak over the game room. And they could build a fort in the woods, and maybe go tubing on the river in the summer. If his mom didn't wig out over the idea.

Maybe he still could, even after they went back home. He could ask Brad, and then Brad would help him work on Mom. That was cool, too, having another guy so they could double-team her.

It was sort of like having a father. Not that he cared about that, but it was probably like it. Sort of.

Anyway, it was going to be totally awesome to have Thanksgiving here, with everybody piling into the house, and the guys all arguing about the game, and eating pumpkin pie until they busted their guts.

His mom made really good pumpkin pie, and she always gave him little pieces of the dough to make dough people with.

He wondered if Brad would think that was lame.

He looked over, then ran toward the house as Brad came out. "Hey! You want to throw the ball some? Moe's teaching Homer how to fetch."

"Sure." He snugged the knit cap he'd brought out over Simon's head. "Getting cold."

"Maybe it'll snow. Maybe it'll snow six feet and there won't be any school."

"We can always dream." He picked up the ball and winged it in a way Simon desperately admired.

"If it snows six feet, can you stay home from work?"

"If it snows six feet, I'll make a point of staying home from work."

"And we can have hot chocolate and play ten million video games."

"That's a deal."

"Do you wear a condom when you have the sex with my mother?"

All the blood in Brad's head drained out of the soles of his feet. "Do what?"

"Because if you don't, you could make a baby. Would you marry her if you made a baby?"

"Holy Mother of God."

There was a tickle at the back of Simon's throat, a kind of sick nervousness. But he couldn't stop the rush of words—they *had* to be said. "The guy who made me with her, he didn't marry her, and I think it hurt her feelings. I have to look out for her now, so if you're not going to marry her if you make a baby, you can't have the sex." Because his belly was jumping, Simon looked down and gave the ball a good kick. "I just wanted to say."

"Okay. Wow. Okay, I really think I need to sit down." Before even the jelly his knees had become melted away. "Why don't we all go inside and do that ... the sit down thing."

"I'm the man of the house," Simon said in a small voice.

"You're a hell of a man, Simon." In a gesture he hoped bolstered them both, Brad laid a hand on the boy's shoulder. "Let's go inside and sit down and talk about this."

Brad prayed for wisdom, and whatever else would help while they peeled off their jackets. He figured the kitchen was best so they could occupy themselves with drink or food, or anything to make the discussion less horrendous for both of them.

Though he wanted a beer in the worst way, he poured them both a Coke. "About sex," he began.

"I know about sex. Mom said it doesn't hurt, but sometimes people yell and stuff because it's fun."

"Good," Brad managed after a moment, and worried that he could actually hear his brain cells dying. "Your mother and I ... Ah. Adults, healthy, single adults often have relationships that—the hell with this. Look at me."

He waited until Simon lifted his head. All the doubts, the defiance, the determination were printed clearly on his face. Just, Brad thought, like his mother's.

"I'm in love with your mother. I make love with her because she's beautiful, and I want to be with her that way. I want to be with her in every way because I'm in love with her."

"Is she in love with you back?"

"I don't know. I'm hoping."

"Do you hang around with me so she'll be in love with you?"

"Well, you know, it's a pretty big sacrifice for me, seeing as how you're so ugly, and you smell so bad. Plus you're short, and that's really annoying. But whatever works."

Simon's lips twitched. "You're uglier."

"Only because I'm older." He laid his hand over the boy's. "And somehow, despite your many flaws, I'm in love with you, too."

Emotions rushed into Simon's throat and seemed to flood onto his face. "That's pretty weird."

"Tell me about it. I want both of you more than I've ever wanted anything."

"Like a family?"

"Exactly like that."

Simon stared down at the table. There were so many things he wanted to say, to ask, but he wanted to make it right. "Would you marry her, even if you didn't make a baby?"

So, it wasn't to be horrendous after all, Brad mused. "I'd like to make a baby, now that you mention it. But ... Hold on a minute, there's something I want to show you. I'll be right back."

Alone, Simon rubbed his eyes hard. He'd been afraid he would cry, blubber like a girl or something. When you were having a real man-to-man talk, like Chuck's father called them, you didn't start crying.

He took a drink of his Coke, but it didn't settle his stomach. Everything kept wanting to jump around inside of him. He struggled to calm down when he heard Brad coming back, and wiped at his face, just in case.

Brad sat down again. "This has to be just between us. Just the two of us, Simon. I need you to promise me."

"Like a secret?"

"Yes. It's important."

"Okay, I won't tell anybody." Solemnly, Simon spat on his palm, then held it out.

For a moment Brad could only stare. Some things, he thought—oddly comforted—never changed. He mirrored Simon's gesture, and they joined palms.

Saying nothing, Brad put a small box on the table and opened it, showed Simon the ring inside. "This was my grandmother's. She gave it to me when she and my grandfather had their fiftieth anniversary."

"Wow. They must be completely old."

Brad's lips quivered, but he kept his voice steady. "Pretty much. It was her engagement ring, and he gave her a new one on their fiftieth. She wanted me to have her first, and to give it to the woman I'd marry. She says it's lucky."

Lips pursed, Simon poked at the box and watched the ring beam. "It's really shiny."

Brad turned the box so he could study the old-fashioned ring with little diamonds in the shape of a small flower. "I think it's something Zoe would like. It's delicate, and it's different and it's proved itself. I'm planning to give this to her on Saturday."

"How come you're waiting? You could give it to her when she gets home."

"She's not ready. She needs some more time." He looked back at the boy. "She needs to find the key, Simon, by Friday. I don't want to push her, or do anything that distracts her before then."

"What if she doesn't find it?"

"I don't know. We have to believe she will. Either way, I'm going to give her this on Saturday and ask her to marry me. I'm telling you now not only because you're the man of the house and deserve to know my intentions, but because you and Zoe are a package deal. You're entitled to your say in this."

"Will you take good care of her?"

Oh, you marvelous child. "The very best I can."

"You have to bring her presents sometimes. You can make them, like I do, but you can't forget. Especially on her birthday."

"I won't forget. I promise."

Simon scooted his glass around in circles. "If she says yes and you get married, will her name be like yours?"

"I'm hoping she'll want that. Vanes are really proud of our name. It'd mean a lot to me if she took it."

He scooted the glass again, watched it intensely. "Will mine be like yours?"

Everything inside Brad lit up like one big candle of love. "I'm hoping you'll want that, too, because it'll tell everyone how you belong to me. Simon, if she says yes, and we get married, will you call me Dad?"

Simon's heart pounded so hard, he heard it ringing in his ears. He looked up, smiled. "Okay."

When Brad held out his arms, he did what came naturally and went into them.

*

THERE WERE SO MANY things to think about, and all of them seemed to want to jumble in her head as she drove along the river. The day was almost over, and that left only five more. Five more days to find the key, to open that final lock. Five days to search her mind, her heart, her life.

Nothing was the same as it had been. And when the week was up, everything would change again. All these new directions, she thought, so many roads, when before her route had been so direct.

Earn a living to make a home. Make that home so her son could have a happy, healthy, normal life. However arduous it had been from time to time, it had been relatively uncomplicated. You got up every morning, took the first step, and kept going until you got everything done.

Then you did it again, in some variation, the next day.

It had worked, and worked well.

But it was true, wasn't it? she admitted as she slowed to make a turn. It was true that under it all she'd still wanted more. The little things, the pretty things she saw in magazines. She'd found ways to have them by learning how to make them. Nice curtains, a table arrangement, a garden that lasted from spring till frost.

And the big things. The college fund she'd started for Simon and built on a little each month. The business she'd begun.

So however direct her route, she'd always had her eye out for a detour.

Well, she'd taken one now.

She pulled up at Brad's, saw Flynn's car, Jordan's. It made her smile. Her detour hadn't just brought two women she'd come to love into her life, it had brought three interesting men. And in less than three months, they had become more like family to her than her own.

She parked, waited for the guilt to creep in at that thought. When it didn't, she sat back and considered. No, she didn't feel guilty at all. She'd *made* this family, she realized. And through some miraculous twist of fate they understood her in a way her own never had. Probably never would.

She could love her mother, her sisters, her brother, she shared hundreds of memories and moments with them—good and bad. But she didn't feel, couldn't feel, the same connection, the same intimacy with them as she did for the family she'd made.

They were her more, she thought.

Nothing would ever take away what they'd built together over the past three months. Whatever happened next, she would always have her more.

Almost giddy with the sensation, she stepped out of the car and started toward the house. It felt good to stride up this walk, easy and natural to head for the front door not knowing quite what to expect when she opened it.

Dogs running, three men and a boy in a football coma, a male-generated disaster in the kitchen. It didn't matter what she found, because whatever it was, she was part of it.

Struck, she stopped. She was part of it, part of what went on inside this house. And the man who owned it. Slowly, she walked back to the banks of the river and turned, and looked.

She remembered the first time she'd seen the house, how she'd stopped her car just to stare and admire. She hadn't known Brad, hadn't really known any of them yet. But the house had caught her.

She'd wondered what it would be like to live there, inside something so wonderfully designed. To have some part in that perfect spot, woods and water, to call her own. And when she'd gone inside, she'd been drenched in delight and wonder. The warmth and the space had pulled her along. She remembered standing at the window in the great room and thinking how incredible it would be to live there, and to be able to look out that window whenever she liked.

Now she did. She could.

Her quest had brought her here, her and her son, to live inside that house with the man who owned it. With the man who loved her.

He loved her.

Breathless, Zoe pressed her fingers to her lips. Was this an intersection, she wondered, or a destination?

Eager to know, she ran toward it. She flung open the door, then held herself still, trying to interpret what she felt.

Ease, she thought, and comfort. And excitement, anticipation. A wondrous mix of the soothing and the giddy. Here, she thought. Yes, there was something here. Something that might be hers.

Moe dashed up, and she laughed as he bounded to plant his paws on her shoulders in greeting. "You'll never learn." She gave him a happy rub before pushing him down, and scooped up the puppy jumping over her feet.

"Let's go find our men." She tucked Homer on her shoulder like a baby, patting his back as she headed toward the noisy game room.

They were, as she'd suspected, sprawled everywhere in an intensely male Sunday afternoon tableau. The football game must have ended, but there was a new contest under way as Flynn took on her son in what appeared to be a vicious round of Mortal Kombat.

Jordan was slumped in a chair, a beer bottle dangling from his fingers, his long legs stretched out on a rug that was littered with potato chip shards, portions of the Sunday paper, and dog hair.

Brad had copped the couch, and with a bowl of nachos balanced on his belly looked to be catching a nap, despite the ringing sounds of battle from the screen and the floor.

Flushed with love for all of them, Zoe headed toward Jordan. He gave her a lazy smile, then cocked a brow as she caught his dark hair in her hands and bent down to give him a long, hard kiss.

"Hello, handsome."

"Hello, gorgeous."

With a laugh for his perplexed expression, she swung around. She crouched by Flynn and as Simon goggled, hooked her arm around Flynn's neck, tipped him back like a dance move and pressed her lips enthusiastically to his.

"Jeez, Mom."

"Wait your turn. Hi, cutie," she said to Flynn.

"Hi, back. Did Mal have whatever you did?"

She grabbed Simon, wrestling him into her arms as he pretended to struggle. She peppered kisses over his cheeks, then did an exaggerated *mmmmm* on his lips. "Hello, son of mine."

"Did you drink stuff, Mom?"

"No." She gave him a quick tickle in the ribs, then got to her feet.

Brad stayed as he was, but his eyes were open now and on hers. With a slow smile, she pushed up her sleeves one at a time as she crossed the room.

"I wondered if you'd get around to me."

"Saved you for last."

She picked up the nachos, set them on the table. She sat at his hip, and grabbed a handful of his sweatshirt. Yanked. "Come here, and bring that sexy mouth with you."

Behind her, Simon rolled around on the floor making gagging noises until Moe sat on him.

She ended the kiss with a teasing nip on his bottom lip and a whispered "We'll finish this later." Then gave him a light shove to send him flat again.

"Well." She rose, brushed her palms together as if completing a task. "Y'all be sure to pick up in here when you're done. I've got some work to do upstairs."

She sauntered out, feeling like the queen of the world.

Seventeen

BRAD WASN'T SURE WHAT HAD GOTTEN INTO HER, BUT HE was pretty sure he liked it. Whatever had put that brilliantly sexy look on her face and had turned her voice into a laughing purr couldn't be bad.

He wondered what sort of strange and exotic female rituals she and the others had performed while he'd been watching football.

He wondered if they would perform them once a week.

The first chance he got, he was going to corner her and see that she made good on that promise to finish what she'd started with that long, smoldering kiss.

But from the looks of things, it wasn't going to be soon.

By the time Flynn and Jordan left, Simon claimed to be starving to death. The fact that the boy had been eating steadily all day didn't seem to matter. He was starving, the dogs were starving. They would all keel over and *die* if they didn't eat soon. To hold them off, Brad thrust what was left of a bag of corn chips in Simon's hands and chased the three of them outside.

But from Zoe there hadn't been a peep in over an hour. The

woman had swept in, stirred him up, then swept out again, leaving the taste of her lingering on his lips.

Simon wasn't the only one who was starving.

Unwilling to wait for her to wander his way again, Brad went upstairs and knocked on her closed bedroom door.

"Come on in."

He opened it and saw her sitting on the bed, surrounded by stacks of paper and notebooks, library books and her borrowed laptop. She still looked sexy—he doubted she could look anything but—and very focused.

"What's up?" he asked her.

"The desk couldn't hold all this. It's a big bed." She had a pencil behind her ear and was idly chewing on another one. "I'm going through everything one more time, start to finish. I've got all this energy all of a sudden and all these ideas." She shook herself as if she couldn't hold them all comfortably. "I'm trying to organize them, but one thing just keeps slapping into another."

Watching her, he walked over to sit on the side of the bed. "You look excited."

"I am. It just sort of struck me as I was driving back, and I thought if I went back through each clue, each quest, each ... Where's Simon?"

"He's outside with the dogs."

"It's getting late. I wasn't paying attention. I'd better throw something together for dinner, and get him in and settled down."

"Take a minute. Tell me where you're heading with this."

"That's one of the things I need to figure out. Where am I heading? I'll tell you while I see about dinner."

"You don't have to see about dinner," he said as she wound through her stacks and off the bed. Reaching out, he snagged the pencil from her ear, tossed it on her papers. "There's enough left over down there to forage through."

"I think better when I'm busy, and foraging isn't part of the deal. And I like fussing around in that kitchen of yours," she added as she started out. "That's one of the things I need to talk to you about."

"You want to talk to me about the kitchen?"

"That's part of it. Part of the whole." Catching his expression of pure male distress, she chuckled. "Don't panic, I'm not pulling a Malory on you. Your kitchen's wonderful just as it is. The fact is, this is the most wonderful house I've ever seen."

She trailed her fingers along the rail on the way downstairs. "Everything about it is just as it should be. I love my place. It means so much to me. There are still some mornings I wake up and just hug myself because it's mine."

She stepped into the kitchen. And let out a very long, very audible breath.

"We, ah, foraged considerably earlier."

"So I see." There were dishes, glasses, bottles of soda and beer, bags of chips and other jetsam of a male afternoon spread over the counters and table. "Well." So saying, she rolled up her sleeves.

"Wait a minute. Just wait." More than a little embarrassed that he'd let the state of the house get quite so out of hand, he grabbed her arm. "If we're talking about deals, you're not supposed to pick up after me."

"I'm not picking up after you." After brushing him off, she plucked up a half-empty bag of taco chips and rolled up the end. "I'm picking up after all of you, which balances out you having Simon underfoot all day while I was off doing something else. Do you have any clothespins?"

"Clothespins?" He struggled to find the connection. "You're going to hang out wash?"

"No. These chips'll stay fresher if you clip them closed. You can buy those plastic spring things they make for it, but clothespins work just as well."

Amused, he slid his hands into his pockets. "I don't believe I have any of those in stock at the moment. We could order them for you."

"I've got my own. I'll bring some by." With quick, efficient moves, she had the bags rolled and stored, or crushed and thrown away. And started straight in on the dishes. "A man's got a beautiful house like this, he shouldn't let it get to be such a mess. I imagine the game room looks like an army was bivouacked in it."

He began to jiggle his change. "Maybe. I have a cleaning crew—" He broke off at the single steely look she sent over her shoulder. "Am I going to have to vacuum?"

"No, Simon is, to thank you for the day. Meanwhile, I was talking about houses. Flynn's got a great house. I imagine he bought it because it pulled some string inside him and made him comfortable. Made him at home. He didn't do a lot with it until Malory came along, but there was something about that place that told him this is the one, this is my place."

"Okay, I'm following that."

With the dishes loaded, she damped a cloth to wipe off the counters. "There's the Peak. That's a fantastic place. A magic one. But it's a home, too. It was a place that meant something special to Jordan even as a boy. Something he aspired to. He and Dana are going to make it their own."

She poured a couple of swallows of warm beer in the sink, tossed bottles into the recycle bin. Watching, Brad was certain he'd never seen a room put so quickly to rights.

"I could never live in a place like that," she continued. "It's too big, too grand, too everything. But I can see how it's right for them."

She got out a pot, measured water by eye and set it on the range. While she spoke, she pulled out vegetables and the sealed bag of beef she'd marinated that morning. "Then there's

Indulgence. As soon as I saw it, I knew, this is the place. The place where I could make something. Where Mal and Dana and I could make something. It was a crazy idea when you really think it through."

She julienned peppers and carrots with what looked to Brad like the skill of a veteran line chef. "How so?"

"Putting it all under one roof that way, with the bare minimum of seed money. Buying the place, too, instead of pushing just to rent. But I wanted to buy it, to have it, as soon as I saw it."

"You don't say it was a crazy idea for the three of you to go into business together so quickly after you'd met. Or that it was crazy to take on that much work."

"Those aren't the crazy parts for me." She cut strips of onions, minced garlic. "There was never any question for me about Malory and Dana. And work, that's just what you do. It was the place, Bradley. It held the same kind of magic for me as my house. That's why I thought, I really thought for a while that was where I'd find the key."

"You don't think so now."

"No, I don't."

She moved from one task to another without breaking rhythm, measuring out rice, cubing tomatoes, slicing beef. He thought it was like watching a kind of poetry.

"Malory's key was there. In the painting, yes, but she had to *do* the painting in that house. And Dana's was at the Peak—or in the book, in *Phantom Watch*, which was based on the Peak. When you look back through their clues, you can see them being led around to it. Through their connections with the place, through their connections with Flynn, and Jordan."

She drizzled olive oil in a skillet. "The painting for Malory. The book for Dana. But they needed the place, too."

"And for you?"

"For me, it's not a thing so much. It's a kind of journey with different paths. Some I took, some I didn't, and the whys of both, maybe. And it's a struggle, a kind of battle." She added garlic and onion to the sizzling oil. "Maybe it's understanding that the ones I lost were as important in their way as the ones I didn't. I think maybe you can't see clearly where you're going next if you don't see where you've been. And why."

He had to touch her, just to feel her under his hand for a moment. He brushed his fingers over her hair, down the long, lovely line of her neck. And got the absent smile of a busy woman in response. "Where are you going, Zoe?"

"I can't say I know that, not for sure. But I know where I am right now. In this house. In this house that pulled a string in me the first time I saw it. Here I am, cooking dinner in the kitchen, and Simon's out there playing with the dogs. I have a connection here. To this place. To you."

"Enough to stay?"

The beef she'd started to slide into the skillet slipped out of her fingers and plopped into the oil. "That's one sure way to scatter my thoughts." She picked up another slice, concentrated fiercely on the exact placement. "Bradley. I can't—I just can't step that far off the path. I made promises to myself when Simon was born. Promises to him."

"I want to make them to you."

"I've only got until Friday to do this," she said quickly. "Only a few more days. If I don't do this right, I feel like I may never do anything right again." She looked at him pleadingly. "I see her face in my sleep, Bradley. I see all of them, waiting for me to do this last thing."

"You're not the only one fighting a battle, Zoe. I'm in this as deep as you. And damned if I can figure out if loving you is a sword or a curse."

"Do you ever ask yourself, in some quiet moment, whether you think you love me because my face is in that painting?"

He started to speak, then stopped himself and gave her the plain truth. "Yes."

"So do I. One thing I do know is I don't want to lose you. I won't risk losing what we have now by making or asking for promises that neither of us may want to keep down the road."

"You keep waiting for me to let you down, Zoe. You're going to have a long wait."

Surprised, she turned around. "I don't. I'm not. It's—"

She broke off as Simon burst in the back door. "I'm *starving*."

"Dinner's in ten minutes." She reached out to stroke his hair. "Go ahead and wash up. I got off the track," she said to Brad as Simon zoomed out in a flurry of dogs. "I was working my way around to asking you if I could go through your house."

Irritation flickered over his face. "You try my patience, Zoe."

"I imagine I do," she said calmly, and turned back to finish sautéing the beef and vegetables. "And I wouldn't blame you for wanting to give me a good kick in the ass. But I've got a lot of important balls in the air right now, and I'm not going to drop any of them."

He remembered the way her face had glowed when she'd come home that afternoon. What was the point, he asked himself, in dimming that light because he was frustrated, even angry, that she didn't just leap into his arms and give him everything he wanted, all on one big plate?

"I reserve the right for the ass-kicking. Why ask me if you can go through the house when you're living ... when you're staying here?"

"I mean go through it like I did my own and Indulgence. Top to bottom, which would mean poking into personal spaces." She got out a platter, scooped her finished rice onto it. "I think the key's in this house, Bradley. No, that's not right. I know it is. I feel it."

Efficiently, she topped the mound of rice with the contents of the skillet. "Something just opened up for me today when I drove up here, and I know it. I don't know where or how, I just know it is."

He looked at her, looked at the platter. In under thirty minutes, he calculated, she had talked him through another stage in her quest, irritated him, amused him, fended off a proposal, and cooked a very attractive meal.

Was it any wonder she fascinated him?

"When do you want to start?"

THEY GAVE IT TWO hours after Simon was in bed, starting with the lower level. She searched every inch of the great room, moving furniture, rolling up rugs, going through drawers, into closets. Armed with a flashlight, she checked the fireplace, testing each stone, running her fingers over the mantel.

She started the same treatment on the dining room, then stopped and sent Brad an apologetic look. "Would you mind if I did this by myself? Maybe it takes doing it alone."

"Maybe you think you have to do too much alone, but all right. I'll be upstairs."

She was fumbling one of those important balls, Zoe admitted when he left her. And she was counting, maybe a little too much, on his patience. Still, she didn't know what else to do, or how else to do it.

For now, her wants, and his, would have to wait until she had completed her quest and what she loved was safe.

She moved to the buffet, ran her hands over the wood. Cherry, she thought. A warm, rich wood, and the curves of the design made the piece airy while the mirrored back added a sparkle.

He'd arranged a few pieces on it, a thick bowl of hazy green glass, a colorful tray that was probably French or Italian, a couple of fat candle stands, and a brass dish with a woman's face carved into the lid. Lovely pieces, artful, she thought. The sort of things Malory would sell in her gallery.

She lifted the lid on the dish and found a few coins inside. Foreign coins, she realized with delight. Irish pounds, French francs, Italian lire, Japanese yen. What a wonder that was, she mused, to have those careless pieces of such fascinating places tossed inside a dish.

He might not even remember they were there, and that was more amazing.

She closed the lid, and put aside the vague guilt of peeking into personal spaces as she opened the first drawer.

It was a silverware drawer, lined in deep burgundy velvet. She lifted out a spoon, turned it under the light. It looked old to her, like something that had been used for generations and kept polished and ready.

Perfect for Thanksgiving, she decided, and filed that away as she went carefully through each slot.

She found china in the base of the buffet, an elegant white on white. As she searched she began mentally setting the holiday table with the dishes and bowls, the platters and stemware she found stored in sideboards and servers.

She sighed over linens and damask and a set of bone-white napkin rings. But she found no key.

She was shaking out books in the library when the clock on the mantel chimed one. Enough, she told herself. Enough for one night. She wasn't going to let herself get discouraged.

The fact was, she realized as she switched off the lamps, she didn't *feel* discouraged. More, she felt on the verge of something. As if she'd made some turn, or crested a hill. Maybe it wasn't the last leg, she thought as she started upstairs. But she was focused on the goal now.

She checked on Simon, going in automatically to tuck him in. Moe lifted his head from the foot of the bed where he stretched out, scented her and gave one halfhearted slap of his tail before starting to snore again.

The puppy was snoozing with his head on the pillow beside Simon's. She supposed she should discourage that sort of thing, but she honestly couldn't see why.

They looked so cozy there together. Harmless and unharmed. If Simon was part of it, as Malory believed, then maybe the key was here, in this room where he was sleeping.

For a moment she sat on the edge of the bed, her hand idly stroking his back.

The light from the last quarter of the moon filtered through the window and washed pale light over her son's face. There was still light, she told herself, so there was still hope. She was holding on to it.

She rose and slipped quietly out of the room.

She glanced toward Brad's door. For what was left of the night, she would hold on to to him as well.

She went to her own room first and selected lotions and scents to prepare herself for him. She might not be able to give him all he wanted, or seemed to want, but she could give him this.

They could give each other this.

It pleased her to massage fragrant lotion over her skin, to imagine his hands and mouth trailing over her. It pleased her to feel completely like a woman again. Not just a person, not just a mother, but a woman who could give and take from a man.

There was a knowledge here she hadn't felt as a girl, a yearning and a confidence she felt with no one else.

Wearing only a robe, she carried a white candle that wafted the scent of night-blooming jasmine over the air.

She didn't knock, but eased silently into the dark of his room, across the thin silver stream of moonlight that drifted through the open curtains.

She hadn't come inside this room before, and wondered if he

would know, as she did, that this was another step for her. She saw the gleam of wood from the curved foot- and headboards, felt the soft brush of the rug under her bare feet.

She opened her robe, let herself tingle at the sensation of it falling away to pool at her feet. Carefully, she set the candle on the nightstand, lifted the covers, and slid into bed beside him.

She'd never watched him sleep before, she realized, and wanting to, she waited for her eyes to adjust to the shadow and light. She liked the way his hair fell over his forehead, and the fact that he looked no less powerfully handsome at rest than he did alert.

This time, Prince Charming would get the awakening treatment.

Interesting, she thought as she traced a finger lightly over his shoulder. She'd never seduced a man out of sleep before. It was a heady proposition and gave her, at least for the moment, complete control.

Should it be fast and hot and shocking? Slow and dreamy and romantic? Should it be sweet or smoky? It was for her to decide, her to create. And hers, ultimately, to give.

Easing the covers down, she shifted to range herself above him and held on to that secret erotic charge another moment before she began to use her mouth. Began to use her hands.

Slowly, she thought, slowly to tease him out of sleep and prolong this fascinating interlude. His skin was warm and smooth, his body hard and firm. And she could feast freely.

He dreamed of her, gliding out of forest shadows, with her body slim and free. Dreamed of her low laugh as she turned toward him, then away, as her fingers trailed over his cheek. As she lured him to follow her into the forest, where the moonlight-dappled ground was blanketed with flowers.

She lay back on that sea of blooms. Her arms, gleaming like gold dust in the scattered light, lifted.

Her lips met his, then drew away again to leave him with one tantalizing taste.

He awoke in stages, craving more. And found her.

Her mouth was on his again, and as she sighed his name, her breath became his breath. And when his caught on a moan, he all but drowned in the scent of her.

"There you are," she whispered and caught his chin lightly in her teeth. "I've been taking horrible advantage of you."

"You've got ten years to stop that, or I'm calling the cops."

Playfully now, she scraped her nails down his belly, and muffled a giggle when he bit off an oath. "Ssh. We have to be quiet. I don't want Simon to hear us."

"Right. Don't want him to know we're in here having fun." His mind was still scrambling, but he could see her face clearly enough, and the surprise that flashed over it. "He happened to mention it."

"Oh, God." She had to press her lips together and plaster a hand over them to stifle her chuckle. "Oh, my God."

"Ssh." Brad reminded her, and rolled over until he pressed her into the mattress. "Now where were we?"

"I was sneaking into your bed in the middle of the night and waking you up."

"Oh, yeah, I really liked that part." His grin was quick. "I'm awake now," he said and slid down to take her breast into his mouth.

A fireball of heat burst in her belly. "I'll say."

She arched, riding up on the joy of it, before she rolled over again. "But I don't think I was quite finished."

They grappled, burying themselves under the blankets, tangling in them. Struggling with laughter, biting back gasps, they tormented each other. Pleasured each other until bodies were damp and quaking, until the playful became the intense.

They rose up together, kneeling on the tumbled bed, locked

tight. Breath heaving, she bowed back, an erotic bridge, and locked her legs around him.

In the thin light of the last quarter of the moon, they joined. They completed. Fluidly, she came back to him, pressed heart to heart, mouth to mouth, so they were wrapped together as they emptied.

"Don't let go." She burrowed into his shoulder. "Don't let go yet."

"I'm never going to let go." All but delirious, he ran his lips over her hair, her cheek. "I love you, Zoe. You know it. You love me. I can see it. Why won't you say it?"

"Bradley." Why shouldn't she say it, and damn all the consequences? Why shouldn't she take what she so desperately wanted? She turned her head, rubbing her cheek on his shoulder.

And saw, in the fading moonlight, the portrait that hung over the bedroom mantel.

After the Spell. That was the name of it, Zoe remembered. The Daughters of Glass lying in their transparent coffins.

Not dead. Worse than dead, she thought with a shiver.

Why shouldn't she say it? They were one reason, she knew. But even they weren't the heart of it. Kane couldn't see what was inside her—not what was deep inside her. He could neither see nor understand.

So she would keep it there, and keep Bradley as safe as she could, a few days longer.

"You put the portrait here."

"Damn it, Zoe." He yanked her back, then snapped out another oath at the plea on her face. "Yes, I hung it here."

He let her go.

She touched a hand to his shoulder. "I know I'm asking you for a lot."

"You're fucking testing me."

"Maybe I am. I don't know." She dragged her fingers through her hair. "This has all been so fast for me. So fast and so big, sometimes it seems like I can't keep up with my own feelings. But I do know I don't want to hurt you. I don't want to fight with you. I have to take this at my own pace, and part of that's tied up with them." She gestured to the portrait before she rose and reached for her robe. "I can't help it."

"You think because there's some similarity between my background and James's, I'll turn away from you?"

"I did." She looked down as she belted her robe, then shifted her attention to him. "I did think that. And I thought maybe I was attracted to you because of those similarities. But I know better than that on both counts now. There's still a lot I have to work out, Bradley. I'm asking you to wait until I do."

He was silent for a moment, then reached over to flip a switch. Light washed over the portrait.

"When I first saw that, it was like being grabbed by the throat. I fell in love—in lust—whatever the hell it was, with that face. Your face, Zoe. When I first saw you, I had exactly the same reaction. But I didn't know you. I didn't know what was inside you. I didn't know how your mind or your heart worked, or what made you laugh, what irritated you. I didn't know you liked yellow roses and could handle a nail gun as well as I can. I didn't know dozens of the little details of you that I know now. What I felt for that face isn't a shadow of what I feel for the woman it belongs to."

She was afraid she wouldn't be able to speak. "The woman it belongs to has never known anyone like you. Never expected to."

"Get things worked out, Zoe. Because if you don't, I'm going to work them out for you."

She let out a small laugh. "No, never anyone like you. This is a big week for me, and by the time it's . . . " She trailed off as she looked at the portrait again.

Her heart began to thump. "Oh, God, could it have been that simple all along? Could it have been right there?"

Trembling, she walked toward the hearth, staring at the painting, her gaze riveted now to the three keys Rowena had painted, scattered over the ground by the coffins.

She stepped onto the hearth, held her breath, and reached up. Her fingers bumped canvas.

She tried again, closing her eyes first, imagining her fingers reaching *into* the painting, closing over the key as Malory's had done.

But the painting stayed solid, the keys only color and shape.

"I thought . . ." Deflated, she stepped back. "For a minute, I thought maybe . . . It seems so stupid now."

"No, it doesn't. I tried it myself." He walked to her and wrapped his arms around her waist. "A few times."

"Really? But it's not for you to find."

"Who knows? Maybe this one's different."

She kept her eyes on the portrait. "It isn't one of them. Rowena painted those keys, years ago. And they're, well, they're despair, aren't they? And loss. Not hope or fulfillment. Because they lie there where no mortal can find them, and no god can use them. It's not despair that leads to my key. It's getting through it. I understand that."

BUT WHEN SHE SLEPT that night, she dreamed she stepped into the portrait, walked beside the still and pale shells of the daughters inside their glass coffins. She dreamed she picked up the three keys and took them to the Box of Souls, where the blue lights beat sluggishly.

Though she put each key into its lock, none would turn.

It was despair she felt when those blue lights winked out, and the glass of their prison went black.

Eighteen

MALORY RUSHED INTO INDULGENCE THE FOLLOWING morning, waving one of several copies of the *Dispatch*. "The article! Our article's in the morning edition."

She looked right, left, up the stairs, then huffed out a breath when no one came running. Flynn's article on Indulgence, and its "innovative proprietors"—oh, she *loved* that part—was front-page news in the Valley, and she couldn't get a rise out of her partners?

With her coat flapping behind her, she hurried into Dana's section. As always, the sight of the color, the books, the pretty tables, the *things*, made her want to do a happy dance. So she boogied her way into the next room, grinning when she saw Dana behind the counter with the phone at her ear.

Adding a little bump and grind to the dance, she waved the paper, only to have Dana nod and keep talking.

"That's right. Yes, I have that in stock. I'll be happy to. I could—yes—well, I don't ... mmm-hmm." She mimed acknowledgment, delight, then did a bootie shake when Malory slapped the article on the counter in front of her. "Just let me transfer you to the salon."

She took a deep breath, stared at the new phone system. "Please let me do this right, please don't let me cut her off." She punched buttons, crossed her fingers, then hung up the receiver.

An instant later she heard the faint ring of the phone from upstairs. "Thank you, Jesus. Mal, you just won't believe it."

"Forget that. Look at this! Look, look." She jabbed her finger on the newspaper.

"Oh, that." When Malory's jaw dropped, Dana pulled a stack of the *Dispatch* from under the counter. "I bought five copies. I've read it twice. Would've read it again, but I've been busy manning this phone. Mal—God, there goes yours, I think."

"My what?"

"Your phone." Dana swung around the counter, grabbed Malory's arm, and dragged her to the other side of the house. "I got in ten minutes ago, and the phones were already ringing. Zoe said—never mind. Answer it."

"My phone's ringing," Malory murmured and stared at it as if it were an alien device.

"Watch this." Dana cleared her throat, picked up the receiver. "Good morning. Indulgence, the Gallery. Yes, one moment, please, let me put Ms. Price on the line."

Dana punched Hold. "Ms. Price, you have a call."

"I have a call. Okay." Malory wiped her palms on her coat. "I can do this. I did this for years for somebody else, I can do it for myself." She engaged the line. "Good morning. Malory Price."

Three minutes later she and Dana were doing a fast polka around the room and out into the hallway.

"We're a hit!" Dana shouted. "We're a hit and we haven't even opened the doors. Let's go up and get Zoe."

"Should we leave the phones?"

"Let 'em call back." Laughing like a maniac, Dana pulled Malory up the stairs.

Zoe sat, tipped back in one of her salon chairs, an expression of shock on her face. Still flying, Dana charged over and gave the chair a wild spin. "We kick ass."

"I have appointments," Zoe said dully. "I'm nearly booked solid for Saturday already, and there's two manis, a pedi, a cut and color, and two massages for Friday. I have a mother-daughter facial booked for next week. For next *week*."

"We need to celebrate," Malory decided. "Why don't we have any champagne around here? We could make mimosas if we only had champagne and orange juice."

"The phone was ringing when I walked in," Zoe continued in the same dazed voice. "It wasn't even nine o'clock and the phone was ringing. Everyone's saying how they read the article in the paper. I want to marry Flynn and have his babies. I'm sorry, Malory. I feel I must."

"Get in line." Malory grabbed the newspaper Zoe had on the station. "Look at us. Don't we look great?"

She held up the page that carried the photograph of the three of them, arms around each other's waists, as they stood in the hallway that linked their three enterprises. "Price, McCourt, and Steele," she read, "the beauty and the brains behind Indulgence."

"I have to say, he really did a solid job on the article." Dana leaned over Malory's shoulder to scan it again. "We come across great, but then, hey, that's a given. But he really got the point of our place across. The fun factor. Then there's the whole local women, revitalizing property, giving a boost to Valley economy, blah blah blah. That gets people interested."

"And we look really hot," Zoe added. "Which never hurts. I read the article before breakfast, then I had to pull over on the drive here and read it again."

"I'll have it framed," Malory said. "We'll hang a copy in the kitchen." She pulled a notebook out of her purse to write it down. "Oh, while I've got this out, we need to make sure we check on the refreshments we're serving at Friday's opening. I'll take the bakery. Dana, you've got the drinks, Zoe, the fruit and cheese."

"My phone's ringing again," Zoe said, and shocked everyone by bursting into tears.

"Uh-oh. You take her." Malory pointed at Dana. "I'll get that." She dashed to reception as Dana yanked tissues from the box on the station and pressed them into Zoe's hands.

"I'm sorry. I'm sorry. Why do I keep *doing* this?"

"Don't sweat it. Go on, let it out."

She couldn't stop, and only managed a choked sob and a wave of her hand when Malory came back.

"Let's go down to the kitchen and have some tea." Briskly, Malory pulled Zoe to her feet, and tucking an arm around her waist, led her out of the salon.

"Okay, good. God, what an ass." Zoe blew her nose fiercely. "I don't know what's wrong with me."

"It might be having a business about to open, a quest coming up on deadline, a man. And the combination of those bringing just a little hint of stress into your life. Here, now, sweetie, let's all take ten."

"I feel so stupid." Still sniffing, Zoe let Malory ease her into a chair in the kitchen. "What have I got to cry about? Everything's great, everything's wonderful." Tears flooded again, and she simply laid her head on the table and wept. "I'm scared out of my mind."

"It's all right." Standing behind her, Malory rubbed her shoulders while Dana put on the kettle for tea. "It's all right to be scared, honey."

"I don't have *time* to be scared. I have my own salon. I've been thinking about how I could build up to this for almost ten years, and now it's real. My phone's ringing. It makes me so happy, so why am I falling apart?"

"I'm scared, too."

Zoe lifted her head, blinked at Malory. "You are?"

"Terrified. When I first started reading Flynn's article, I got this buzzing in my ears and this metallic taste in the back of my throat. The happier I got, the louder the buzzing, and the more I had to keep swallowing back that taste."

"I keep waking up in the middle of the night." Dana turned from the stove. "I think: I'm opening a bookstore, and the butterflies wake up in my stomach and have a party."

"Oh, thank God." Outrageously relieved, Zoe pressed her fingers to her temples. "Thank God. It's okay when I'm busy, when I'm doing something or thinking about all the things I have to do. But sometimes when I stop and it all hits me, I want to lock myself in a nice dark closet and whimper. And at the same time I want to turn cartwheels. I'm making myself crazy."

"We're all in the same boat," Dana said, "and it's been christened *Neuroses.*"

Zoe managed a watery smile as Dana set colorful cups on the table. "I'm really glad both of you are crazy, too. I was feeling like such an idiot. There's more. I think I know where the key is. Not exactly," she said quickly when Malory's hands jumped on her shoulders. "But I think it's at Bradley's. There's something about the house, and when I turned that angle over in my head yesterday, it just seemed to open up. It feels right to me. And because it does, because it feels as if I'm one step away from finding it, I'm all twisted up inside."

"Because you're close to finding it?" Malory asked. "Or because it's Brad's?"

"Both." Zoe picked up her cup, held it in both hands. "Everything's coming to a head. The quest, this place. I've been so focused on both things since September that now that they're both so close to finished, I know I have to start looking beyond that, to what happens next. And I can't see it. Having this, well, these big purposes, pushed me along. Now I'm going to have to deal with the results."

"You won't have to deal with them by yourself," Malory reminded her.

"I know. That's another part of it. I'm used to dealing with things on my own. In my life I've never been as close to anyone, other than Simon, as I am to the two of you. It's like this incredible gift. Here are these two wonderful women, and they'll be your friends. Your family."

"Jeez, Zoe." Dana picked up one of the scrunched tissues. "You're going to get me started."

"What I mean is, I'm still getting used to knowing I've got you. To realizing I can pick up the phone if I need to, or just go by and see you. Come here and see you. That I can tell you I'm scared or sad or happy, or I need some help—anything, and you'll be there."

She soothed her raw throat with tea, set the cup down. "Then there's the guys. I've never been friends with men before. Not really. With Flynn and Jordan ... to be able to talk or hang out, flirt and know there's nothing there but friendship. To have Simon be able to be with them, to have that kind of adult male influence, it's another real gift."

"You haven't mentioned Brad," Malory pointed out.

"Working around to it. I'm nervous and excited about finding the key. About this certainty that I *will* find it, and that it's connected to Bradley. At the same time, the certainty that it's connected to him scares me as much as anything ever has."

"Zo, have you considered that it could be the fear that's blocking you from finding the key?"

She nodded at Dana. "Yeah, but I can't push through it. He thinks he's in love with me."

"Why do you qualify it?" Malory demanded. "Why can't you just say he's in love with you?"

"Maybe I want it too much. And I want it not just for me, but for Simon. I know that's part of it. Bradley's wonderful with

Simon, but it's all still, well, novel between them. The reality is this is a nearly ten-year-old boy, another man's son."

Saying nothing, Dana walked over, opened a cupboard, and took out their box of emergency chocolate. She set it on the table in front of Zoe.

"Thanks." Choosing a piece at random, Zoe let out a little sigh. "If Bradley loves me, he'll take Simon. He'd always be good to him, kind to him, I know that. But wouldn't there be something missing, that unbreakable connection?"

"I don't know." Malory pushed a hand through her curls. "But I'd say that's going to be up to them."

"Yes, but Simon's used to it being the two of us, having my attention focused on him, doing what I say—or trying to get around doing what I say. If this is going to work, he's going to need time to see Bradley as something other than a friend with a really cool game room. Time to adjust to having someone else have real authority over him, just as Bradley has to adjust to having a child, already half grown. If I just jump the way I want, it means taking both of them in with me, maybe before they're ready."

"That's sensible." Giving in, Malory took one of the chocolates. "It's logical. But sometimes this sort of thing isn't either one."

Zoe drew a breath. "There are other things. Rowena and Pitte, they said the more I cared about Bradley, the harder Kane would go after him."

"So you're protecting him by holding back." Dana lifted her brows. "That'll piss Brad off. I know that if it was Jordan, since I love the jerk, I'd probably try to do the same thing."

"I've been going over and over it in my head. This way, that way. If I do this, what could happen. If I do that." Zoe shrugged wearily. "There's too much at stake. Everything's at stake, so I can't just grab on to something because it looks so shiny and beautiful. Not without considering the consequences."

"Maybe you should add more to the mix." Malory laid a hand on Zoe's. "You might hesitate to grab that something shiny and beautiful because to hold it you have to give things up."

"What do I have to give up?"

"The house you made on your own, and the life. The family you made with Simon. The shape of everything you have now changes forever if you reach out and take something else. That's a scary proposition, Zoe. If you don't reach out, you may lose him. If you do, something else slips away. You have to decide which holds more value for you."

"It's not just me. Not even just me, Simon, and Bradley." Zoe rose, carried her cup to the sink. "My key has to do with courage. But is it having the courage to reach out for something or the courage to walk away from it? We've read about the gods, so we know they're not always kind. Not always just. And they want payment."

She turned back. "If we fail, the penalty—before it was revoked—would have been the loss of a year of our lives. We wouldn't even have known which one. It could even have been this year, right now. There's a fine sort of cruelty in that. Mal, you were given something you wanted all of your life. They let you hold it, taste it, feel it. But to find the key, you had to give it back. It hurt you."

"Yes, it hurt."

"And you nearly died, Dana, finding yours. They changed the rules, and you could've died."

"I didn't."

"But you might have, and do you think the gods would've shed a tear?"

"Rowena and Pitte . . ." Malory began.

"It's different for them. They've lived with us for thousands of years, and in some ways they're just as much pawns as we are. But the ones behind the Curtain, the ones watching through it, do they care if we live happily ever after?"

She sat again. "How did the three of us come together. How did we have the time to look for the keys? We lost our jobs. A job I needed, jobs each one of you loved. They took that away from us so we would be more useful, then dangled cash in front of us so we'd sign on the dotted line. The motivation may have been unselfish and noble, but they manipulated us."

"You're right," Dana agreed. "No argument."

"We got this place out of it," Zoe continued. "But *we* got it. We took the risk, we did the work. If this place is a miracle, we made it."

Nodding, Malory sat back. "Keep going."

"Okay. You and Flynn. You met him when you met him because he was connected. You fell in love with him, and he with you. But if you hadn't, even if you hadn't, you'd have made the choice you made up in the attic. You wouldn't have taken the illusion, however much you wanted it, and sacrificed souls. I know that because I know you. If you'd loved Flynn the way I do, as a friend, as a kind of a brother, you'd have done the same thing."

"I hope so," Malory replied. "I want to think so."

"I know so. Or you might have felt something for each other that was more transient, that faded after your month was up rather than growing deeper. It didn't matter to them whether you were happy, just whether you succeeded or failed."

"That may be true, but the things I experienced and the choices I made during that month were part of what built what I have with Flynn."

"But you built it," Zoe said. "Jordan came back to the Valley at this time because he was connected. He was a piece that had to be added. You needed to resolve your feelings for him, Dana, that was central. But you might have resolved them differently with the same results. You might have forgiven him. You might have realized that you didn't love him, but you valued your history together. The friendship more than the passion. You could've given up what was between you and still found the key. You're not thinking of orange blossoms because the gods smiled on you."

"Orange blossoms might be carrying it a little far, but okay, I follow you." Absently, Dana plucked a piece of chocolate, nibbled on it as she thought things through. "When you circle it back, it's what we were told from the beginning. Each of us is a key. So what we get out of it, or don't, in the end is of our own making."

"But they manipulate," Zoe added. "They put us together, tossed in the circumstances. Bradley may very well have come back to the Valley, it's his home, and he has ambitions here. But without all this, I would never have met him. Malory might have met Flynn at any time, but it's unlikely I'd have met Bradley Charles Vane IV. And what pulled him to me first? The portrait. Manipulating his feelings."

It riled her up just to think about it. With heat in her eyes, she chomped down on chocolate. "I know it's not a painting now. But the change in him is incidental to them. We needed to be pushed together so I could be led to—or away from—the key. Depending on whose side you're on. If I find it, if I don't, my usefulness is at an end, and so is his. Do you think it matters to them if that usefulness involves hurt, and pain, and loss?"

Her temper began to spike, giving her voice an edge. "If it means that his heart, or mine, ends up broken, they won't give a damn. Isn't it just as likely that heartbreak is what's necessary to that last step? Despair and loss, those are in my clue. And blood," she continued. "It won't be his. I won't risk that even to save three souls."

"Zoe." Malory spoke carefully. "If you already love each other, then haven't you already built your own end?"

"Have we? Or is that my illusion, and what I'll have to sacrifice? There's another part of the clue. How I'm supposed to look at the goddess, know when it's time to pick up the sword, when it's time to lay it down. Do I fight for what I want for me, or do I surrender it for the good of the whole?"

"Those are reasonable and logical suppositions, reasonable and logical questions." Dana held up a hand before Malory could object. "We don't have to like them, but we should give credence to them. Nobody promised we were all going to land in a big bowl of rose petals at the end of this. What we were promised was a big bowl of money."

"Screw the money," Malory shot back.

"I wish I could tell you to bite your tongue, but unfortunately I feel the same way. However," Dana pointed out, "while Zoe has posed those reasonable, logical suppositions, she's left out the parts about hope and joy and fulfillment. The intersecting paths that lead from one to the other."

"I'm sitting in the heart of that joy and hope and fulfillment right now, with both of you." Zoe held her arms out to encompass the room, the whole of what they'd built. "I'm not leaving them out, but I need to be realistic. I have to be, because I want to believe, almost more than I can stand, that when I come to the end of this, with that goddamn key in my hand, I'm going to have a chance for . . . for more."

"What's next, then?" Dana asked her.

"I need both of you to think about it. You're the only ones who have actually held one of the keys. Dana, you and Jordan and Flynn know Bradley's house almost as well as he does. I'll take all the help I can get."

She pushed to her feet. "But right this minute, we'd better start answering those phones again."

THERE WAS ONLY A sliver of moon left, just a thin slice of curve to float in the black sky. Though she wished, desperately, that a storm would blow in full of mean clouds that would cover even that, Zoe couldn't stop staring at the waning light.

She'd looked everywhere. There were times she was certain her eyes or her fingers had passed over that glint of gold. But she was unable to see or touch it.

Unless she did that within the next forty-eight hours, everything Malory and Dana had been through, all they'd accomplished, would be for nothing.

The Daughters of Glass would forever lie still and empty in their crystal coffins.

Bundled in a jacket, she sat out on the rear deck, trying to hold on to that last splinter of hope.

"It's here. I know it. What am I missing? What haven't I done that I'm supposed to do?"

"Mortals," Kane said from behind her, "look toward what they call the heavens and ask what to do, what to think."

As Zoe froze, he skimmed a fingertip along the base of her neck. She felt the touch like a line of ice.

"It amuses me."

His soft boots made no sound as he walked around her to lean casually back against the deck's railing.

He was so breathtakingly handsome, she thought. Made for the dark. For moonless nights, for storms.

"You've failed," he announced matter-of-factly.

"I haven't." The cold was creeping into her bones, so she had to fight the urge to shiver. "There's time left."

"It ekes away, minute by minute. And when that last sliver of moon is dark, I will have all. And you will have nothing."

"You shouldn't come here to gloat before it's over." She wanted to stand, to push herself defiantly to her feet, but her legs felt like rubber. "It's bad luck."

"Luck is a mortal belief, one of your many crutches. Your kind requires them." He slid his fingers down the silver chain of his amulet, began to swing it slowly side to side.

"Why do you hate us?"

"Hate indicates feeling. Do you feel anything for the bug you crush beneath your boot? You are less to me than that."

"I don't have conversations with the bug, either. But here you are."

Irritation rippled over his face, and steadied her.

"As I said, you amuse me. You, particularly, of the three Rowena and Pitte set on this doomed quest. The first ... she had style and a clever mind. The second, there was fire there and intelligence."

"They beat you."

"Did they?" He laughed, a soft, derisive sound as he swung the pendant. "Do you not consider that after so long I might wish some entertainment? To have ended it quickly would have been to deny myself the amusement of watching you, all of you, plot and plan and congratulate yourselves. To have ended it would have meant denying myself the pleasure of seeing you squirm, as you are now. You interested me simply because you lack the wit and style of your companions. Badly educated, poorly bred."

He shifted, lifting the pendant an inch higher. "Tell me, where would you be if not for that invitation to Warrior's Peak? Certainly not here in this house, with this man. A man who will, when the ... sparkle of this mutual goal has dulled, see you for what you are. He'll cast you off, as the other did. But you already know that."

The silver pendant's slow, steady movement made her head feel light. "You don't know anything about me. Or him."

"I know you're a failure. And when you fail in your quest, the others will know it as well. It was cruel of Rowena and Pitte to involve you in this, to expect so much of you. To toss you in with these people," he continued as mists began to scud—thin blue clouds—along the boards of the deck. "People who have so much more to offer than you. Cruel to give you a taste of what life might be so you'll spend the rest of your days thirsting for it."

"My friends—"

"Friendship? Another mortal delusion, and as false as luck. They'll desert you when you fail, and fail you will. A hand such as yours was never meant to turn the key."

His voice was soothing now as he straightened, as he stepped closer with the amulet swinging, swinging, a glittering pendulum. "I feel some sympathy for you. Enough to offer you some compensation. What, of the things Rowena and Pitte have so carelessly pushed into your life, would you like to keep? Your little business, this house, the man? Choose one, and I'll grant it to you."

He was hypnotizing her. She could feel herself drifting under, feel the mists crawling over her skin. So very, very cold. It would be so easy to slide down into those crooning promises, to take *something*. Her hands felt stiff and icy and useless, but she balled them into fists until she felt the prick of her nails biting into her palms.

With one vicious effort she tore her gaze from the pendant and looked into his face. "You're a liar." Her breath heaved out, ripped painfully from her lungs as she staggered to her feet. "You're a liar and a cheat."

He knocked her back. Though she didn't see the blow, she felt it like a strike of jagged ice across her face. Without thought, riding on temper, she leaped forward and raked her nails down his.

She saw the shock—one instant of utter disbelief that flashed into his eyes. She saw blood bloom in the grooves she'd sliced in his skin.

Then she was slammed back against the wall of the house, pinned there by a wild surge of wind so cold she saw crystals of ice, black as onyx, swirling through it.

And he stood, huge in his billowing black robes, with blood on his face. "I could kill you with a *thought*."

No, he can't, he can't. Or he would have. He's a liar, she reminded herself frantically. And a bully. But he could hurt her, God, he could hurt her. And she felt the pain, tearing and bright, in her chest.

"Go back to hell!" she shouted at him. "You're not welcome here."

"When this is done, you will lose all. And I'll add your soul to my winnings."

As if a switch had been flipped, the wind died. Zoe fell forward on her hands and knees, gasping for breath, shuddering in shock.

She stared, baffled, at the wood of the deck and struggled to clear her mind. When she lifted her head she saw the night had turned into soft, misty morning. Through the dawn haze, at the verge of the trees, stood a buck with a coat that seemed to gleam gold. The jeweled collar around his neck shot fire through the mist, and his eyes burned green fire.

Those mists drew together, like a curtain, and when they parted again, he was gone.

"I'm not done." She spoke aloud for the comfort of her own voice. Kane had tricked her out of time, hours of precious time, but she wasn't done.

And when she got to her feet, she looked down at her hands, saw there was blood on them.

His blood.

"I hurt him. I hurt the son of a bitch."

Tears tracked down her cheeks as she stumbled toward the house. Her vision wavered. She thought she heard someone shouting, a threatening growl, a slam. Shapes and sounds melted together into one dark void.

*

WHILE THE MIST SMOKED across the deck, it slithered over the bed where Brad slept. Chilled him. Trapped him. He turned in his sleep, reached out for warmth and comfort. Reached for Zoe.

But he was alone.

In the dark. The forest was dank with rot and alive with a bitter wind. He couldn't see the path, only the monstrous shapes of the trees, gnarled and twisted into nightmares. The thorns from wild briars ripped at his flesh, bit into his hands like greedy teeth.

He could smell his own blood, his own panic sweat. And something wilder.

He was being hunted.

There was sly movement in the brush, shadows. Not just hunted, he thought as he fought his way clear of the briars. Taunted. Whatever it was wanted his fear as much as it wanted his death.

He had to get out, get away, before what stalked him tired of the game. When it did, it would leap out and tear him to pieces.

Save yourself. There was a whisper in his brain, soft, soothing, as he stumbled into a clearing. *This is not your fight. Go home.*

Of course. That was it. He should go home. Dazed, disoriented, he stumbled toward a faint glow of light. Began to run toward it as he heard the howl of the predator behind him.

The glow was a door, and Brad's breath shuddered out in relief as he sprinted toward it. He would make it. He had to make it. He wrenched the door open even as he felt the hot breath of what pursued him at the back of his neck.

Light showered through the dark. And color, and movement. He stood in the doorway of his New York offices, his breath heaving from the run. Blood from his wounded hands fell onto the polished oak of the floor.

Through the wide triple windows, he saw the skyline, all those gleaming spears that rose into the morning sky.

A young blonde in a sharp black suit walked by, shot him a sunny smile. "Welcome back, Mr. Vane."

"Yes." His lips felt stiff. Why was it so cold in here? "Thanks."

Michael, his assistant, hurried up to him. He wore red suspenders over a blue shirt and carried a thick appointment book. "I have your schedule for the day, Mr. Vane. Coffee's on your desk. We'd better get started."

"I should . . ." He could smell the coffee, and Michael's aftershave. He heard a phone ringing. Confused, he lifted his hand, watched the blood drip from the puncture in his palm. "I'm bleeding."

"Oh, we'll take care of that. You just need to come in. All the way in."

"No." He swayed. Nausea roiled in his belly, sweat poured down his face with the effort. "I don't." Gripping the doorjamb for balance, he looked behind him, and into the dark. "This isn't real. This is just more bull—"

He broke off as he heard Zoe scream.

Whirling, he shoved away from the door.

"You'll die out there," Michael shouted after him, seconds before the door slammed. A bullet shot.

Brad plunged into the dark, calling for Zoe. He couldn't see, though he tore frantically through briars, he couldn't see anything but that unrelieved veil of black.

He couldn't find her, would never find her. And what was in the dark would kill them both because he hadn't held on to her.

She only wants your money. A rich father for her bastard son.

"That is such crap." Exhausted, sick, he fell to his knees. He was letting himself get roped in, letting himself believe the lies.

It had to stop.

He threw back his head, bunched his fists. "It's not real. It's not happening. Goddamn it, I *am* home. And so is she."

He woke, gulping in air, with the last tendrils of the mist

fading and Moe standing on the foot of the bed, snarling like a wolf.

"Okay, boy. Christ." Still a little shaken, he started to reach out for the dog, but felt the pain shudder through his hand. Turning it over, he saw the blood smeared on his palm, welling fresh from several punctures. "Well, some of it was real."

On a long breath, he shoved his bloodied hand through his hair. And the next instant was leaping out of bed. *Zoe.* If the blood was real, her screams might be.

He raced to her room, threw open the door. In the soft morning light he could that see her bed hadn't been slept in. Pushed by panic, he whirled to Simon's room, shuddered with relief when he saw the boy curled up with the puppy.

"Stay with him." Brad ordered Moe into the room. "You stay with him," he repeated, then tore downstairs to look for Zoe.

Shouting for her now, he burst into the great room just in time to see her stumble in from the deck.

When she opened her eyes, Zoe saw Brad's face, pale, with his hair tousled around it.

"You need a haircut," she mumbled.

"Christ Jesus, Zoe." He gripped her hand hard enough to rub bone against bone. "What the hell were you doing outside? What happened? No, quiet." He snapped himself back from the line of utter terror. "Lie still. I'll get you some water."

He hurried to the kitchen, filled a glass, then just braced his hands on the counter while he fought to steady his pulse.

Ordering himself to take slow, deep breaths, he washed the blood off his hands, then picked up the glass of water and went back to her.

She was sitting up now, and the color was back in her cheeks. He'd never seen anyone so white as she'd been when she'd come through that doorway.

"Take it easy," he ordered. "Sip slowly:"

She nodded, though it was hard to obey when her throat was on fire. "I'm okay."

"You're not okay." He didn't shout it, but there was a slapping edge to his voice. "You fainted. You've got a bruise on your face and blood on your hands. You're not fucking okay."

It was amazing how he did that, she thought. How he never raised his voice, but managed to have the temper and the authority to crush you into dust.

"It's not my blood. It's his." It steadied her to see it again. To know what she'd done. "I scratched his goddamn face. I have good, strong nails, and I tore that bastard's cheeks open with them. It felt great."

She handed Brad the empty glass, and because she thought they both could use it, kissed his cheek. "I'm sorry I scared you. I was ... oh!" On a sound of distress, she snatched his hand. "You're all scratched and cut."

"I had a little adventure in the woods while you were ... whatever you were doing."

"He worked on both of us," Zoe said softly. "But we're here, we're right here, aren't we?" She lifted his wounded hand to her lips. "Let's go clean up these cuts, and you'll tell me what happened to you. I'll tell you what happened to me, but first I want you to know something."

She took his face in her hands, looked into his eyes. "I want you to know it's going to be all right. Everything's going to be all right. Let's go in the kitchen. I want to wash my hands, bandage yours, and make some coffee."

She drew a breath and got to her feet. Her legs were steady, she noted with some pride. And her mind was set. "We'll talk about the rest while I work."

"Work?"

"I've got a turkey to stuff."

Nineteen

"I DON'T KNOW HOW YOU CAN BE SO CALM." MALORY washed fresh cranberries at the kitchen sink.

"Oh, I've roasted turkeys before." Zoe shot a grin over her shoulder and continued to prepare the yams.

"I don't know how she can be such a smart-ass," Dana commented, scowling at the mountain of potatoes she had yet to peel. "You'd think a pissing match with an evil sorcerer god, a fainting spell, and cooking for an army would spoil her mood, but oh, no, our Zoe's in some form today."

"It's Thanksgiving."

"Which forces me to broach the question." Dana frowned at her paring knife. "Why are the three of us doing all the work in here while the men laze around like kings?"

"I wanted the three of us to be alone for a while," Zoe told Dana. "This was the simplest way."

Dana set another potato aside. "So you say."

"And Bradley watching me like a hawk makes me nervous."

"A man's entitled when you swoon into his arms," Malory pointed out.

"I don't blame him. It's interesting, too, that he was there to catch me. Don't you think? Romantic, I guess, but interesting, too. He's upstairs asleep, and I'm out there for—I don't know how long. Hours. It felt like minutes, but it was hours."

She glanced toward the doorway to make certain no one was hovering. "Then he's not just asleep—Kane's got him running around in the dark, getting his hands all cut up. He tried to get him to go back to New York in his head, where everything's ordered, everything's normal."

"But he didn't do it." Malory set the strainer of cranberries in the sink. "At the threshold—a moment of decision, and he made his choice."

"He made it, and so did I when I ripped Kane's face. Those are decisions we can both feel pretty damn good about today."

"Wished I'd seen you do it." Dana attacked the potatoes again. "My one regret."

"It was great." Zoe assured her. "I don't know when I've done anything that's made me feel that powerful. But anyway, after all that, Bradley gets downstairs just in time to keep me from falling flat on my face."

Zoe brought her knife down with a thunk. "Kane tried to keep him away, to trap him in that illusion."

"Didn't want a man interfering," Malory said sourly, "while he bullied the little lady."

"No, and I think he didn't want us together while he tried to make me feel like a loser."

"Doesn't sound like you're feeling like a loser."

"He pushed all the right buttons, I'll give him that. But he's not the first one to push them, and I've learned how to push back. He pushed them because he's scared. Because I'm close. Because he knows I can beat him. So he worked on my insecurities and my feelings, then he tried to bribe me. And when it didn't work, he got pissy."

"Pissy." Malory stepped over to touch her fingers gently to the bruise on Zoe's cheek. "Honey, he clocked you."

"Maybe so, but I can promise you, he looks a lot worse." She threw back her head and let out a hoot. "If I'd been thinking straight, I'd've followed up. A good kick to the balls. If he has balls. I hurt him, and Bradley beat him. We've got him running scared. And that just makes my whole damn day."

She saw the flicker in Malory's eyes and sighed. "I know. I know I don't have much time left. Part of me wants to go running through this house like a mental patient trying to find the key. But that's not the answer. I don't know what is, only that isn't it. So I'm going to make Thanksgiving dinner, a wonderful Thanksgiving dinner. Because I do belong. I do belong with all of you, and I'm thankful for it."

Dana set the paring knife aside. "He did get to you some."

"Maybe he did," Zoe admitted. "He hit me where I live. Poor little Zoe McCourt who got herself knocked up by the first boy who smiled at her. The high school dropout scrounging for pennies so she can buy diapers for the baby she'll be raising on her own. What makes her think she can do anything that matters?"

She spooned her yams into a casserole dish. "Because I can, that's what. Let's have some wine."

"Well, now you're talking." Though Dana exchanged a look with Malory behind Zoe's back, she got out a bottle of Pinot Grigio.

"There are things I'm going to do today," Zoe said as she took glasses out of the cupboard. "Besides making this meal with you and eating it. Things I'm going to do, things I'm going to say. I've just got to work them all out in my head first."

She set the glasses down, tilting her head as she looked out the window and spotted Brad and Simon walking along one of the paths that wound through the garden shrubs toward the trees. "What in the world are they doing?"

Dana laid a hand on Zoe's shoulder as she leaned over to pour the wine. "I can tell you what they're not doing. They're not peeling potatoes."

"What's that he's carrying?" Absently, she lifted her glass of wine, shifted to get a better angle. Her son was dancing around Brad, and the dogs raced back and forth, hoping for a game. "It looks like . . . well, for heaven's sake."

She watched, dumbfounded, as Brad hung the bird feeder from a branch so that it dangled over his lovely ornamental shrubbery. Then he lifted her son so Simon could pour seed into the opening.

"For heaven's sake," she repeated. As if in a dream, she set the wine down and walked to the door. Walked outside.

"What the hell is that about?" Dana wondered.

"You've got me." With her nose all but pressed to the glass, Malory smiled. "What is that thing? Why are they hanging a boot from a tree?"

Zoe hadn't thought to get a jacket, but she didn't mind the bite of wind. It carried Simon's laugh to her as he raced away to play with the dogs. And her heart was too warm for the chill to touch it.

Brad stood on the path, his hands in his pockets, grinning at the bird feeder. Hearing her footsteps, he turned to greet her. "What do you think?"

She'd helped make it, guiding Simon through the steps of turning the flashy red cowboy boot into a bird feeder, steadying his hands as he'd cut the hole in the leather, watching him measure the strips of scrap wood to make the little pitched roof.

He'd been so proud of it, she remembered, so pleased that no one else in his class would have a project quite like his.

He'd told her they could hang it in the backyard at home after it was graded and given back.

At home, she thought.

"Simon gave it to you?" she asked carefully.

"Yeah. He got an A on it, you know."

"Yes, I know."

"We figured—what the hell are you doing out here without a coat?" On a huff of impatience, he stripped off his jacket. She stood silent as he shoved her arms into the sleeves of buttery-soft leather.

"I saw you from the kitchen. Saw you hanging this in your beautiful garden, behind your beautiful house."

"Okay." Obviously puzzled, he lifted his shoulder. "And?"

"He gave you his bird feeder, and you hung it." Tears tickled the base of her throat. "Bradley, this has to be the silliest-looking thing you've ever seen in your life. It's an old boot with a hole in it. You're going to see it every time you look out the window, and so's everyone else."

"That's the idea." He stepped back and just beamed at it. "It's terrific."

"Bradley, I have to ask you something. I was thinking, this morning, after what happened, I was thinking about how I might find the way to ask you. But I thought I needed to talk to Simon first, to explain to him and to see how he'd ... "

She looked back at the feeder and smiled. "But I can see I don't have to talk to him or explain. He's made his choice already."

"Ask me what?" He reached out to give the boot a little push, just for the pleasure of watching it swing.

"I wanted to ask you to marry me." She felt her courage evaporate when his hand dropped to his side, when he stared at her, but she picked it back up again with both hands. "I thought I should wait until all the rest was finished and I'd had a long talk with Simon and ... all sorts of things. And until I wasn't so scared about what would happen if I did ask. But I think I was wrong about waiting to ask, and about not telling you that I love you, so much. So much it made me more scared so I was afraid to trust myself, or you. Or even Simon. And God, I wish you'd say something and shut me up."

"Well. This is pretty sudden. Hang on a minute."

Of all the things she'd expected—the best and the worst—it hadn't been for him to stroll away, calling for Simon. Heat rose into her cheeks even as ice balled in her belly. She wasn't sure if that was the result of mortification, hurt, or temper. She tugged his jacket tight around her as he bent down to Simon.

She couldn't hear what was said, but it caused Simon to nod rapidly, give a little war whoop, then charge back to the house.

Hooking his thumbs in his front pockets, Brad walked back to Zoe. His expression was both polite and pleasant. "Let's see now, where were we? You're asking me to marry you because I hung the feeder Simon gave me in the garden."

"Yes. No. Damn it, Bradley, you don't have to make me sound like a fool. The only other people Simon's ever given things he makes to besides me are the Hansons, and that's because he thinks of them like grandparents. He gave this to you because he loves you, and I thought . . . You hung it."

"I happen to like it" He couldn't help grinning like a fool when he tapped a finger against the red leather boot. "I'm afraid you might be missing the artistic whimsy of the design. But be that as it may—"

"Don't you talk to me about artistic whimsy. Let me tell you something, Bradley Charles Vane IV, if you're not prepared to stand behind all that talk about being in love with me, then you don't know who you're dealing with."

The grin stayed plastered on his face as he looked at her. "Don't I?"

"Marriage isn't a joke to me, it's what I expect from the man I love and the one who claims to love me. My son deserves a father, not someone who just wants to play around at relationships. Neither of us is going to settle."

Brad nodded. "I guess that told me."

"I got it! I got it!" Simon bulleted out of the house. "It was right where—" He cut himself off at the warning look from Brad, but though he stared down at the ground, his shoulders shook with laughter.

"I'd like to know what's so damn funny."

"A little man business between me and Simon," Brad told her, deftly palming the box Simon had clutched in his hand. "You see, it happens Simon and I discussed a certain matter a while back, and—"

"You said you had to wait until . . . " Hunching his shoulders under Brad's bland stare, Simon scuffed a toe on the path. "Okay, okay, but hurry *up*."

"We came to an understanding," Brad continued. "And as questions on both sides were resolved, I thought it only right to show him this, so he could be sure of my intentions."

Brad lifted the box, opened the lid.

"It was his grandmother's and—golly, can't I say anything?" Simon complained when Brad shushed him.

"Let's see what your mother has to say first."

Looking at the ring was like looking at stars. Delicate and bright, and beautiful. She could only give a helpless shake of her head.

"You had plenty to say a minute ago," Brad pointed out. "Something about me standing up, and what you expect. But maybe I should answer your initial question. Yes." He took the ring from the box. "Absolutely yes. I'll be your husband, and love you every day for the rest of my life."

"Put it on her finger," Simon demanded. "You're supposed to put it on her finger, then you have to kiss her."

"I know the drill."

"You—the two of you—already talked about this?" Zoe managed.

"That's right. When a guy's taking on a father, there are things he needs to know." Brad exchanged a look with Simon, one that made Zoe's heart sparkle every bit as richly as the ring. "And when a man's being given a son, there are things he needs to say."

"It's man-to-man stuff," Simon told her. "You wouldn't get it."

"Oh." She felt the laugh bubble up through the tears in her throat. "Okay, then."

"Zoe? Give me your hand."

She looked at him first, looked into his eyes. "He's the most precious thing in the world to me." She laid her right hand on Simon's shoulder and gave Brad her left. "We're both yours now."

"We're each other's."

There was warmth as the ring slid onto her finger, a lovely jolt of it as it circled her flesh. "It fits. It's so beautiful. I've never seen anything more beautiful."

"I have." His eyes held hers as he kissed her.

"Can I call you Dad now?" Simon tugged on Brad's sleeve. "Can I, or do I have to wait?"

As Brad lifted Simon off his feet. Zoe's already full heart overflowed. "You don't have to wait. Neither do we." With his free hand, Brad pulled Zoe into his arms and made the three of them a unit. "We don't have to wait for anything."

As cheers sounded from the house, Zoe looked over. Everyone was on the deck, applauding.

"I sort of told them," Simon confessed. "When I went in to get the ring."

"Get back here!" Dana shouted between her cupped hands. "We need champagne and we need it now."

"I wanna watch it pop." Wiggling down, Simon ran for the house.

It seemed to Zoe that everything glowed as if it had been

washed with gold. With her hand clutched in Brad's she took the first step down the path toward the house.

Simon leaped onto the deck. The pup missed a step and tumbled, and Moe raced in circles around him. She saw Flynn give Jordan a friendly punch on the arm. And watched as Malory slid her arm around Dana's waist.

Brad's hand was warm against hers as their fingers linked.

And she knew.

"Oh! Oh, of course. How simple." The knowledge filled her like light, like that lovely gold light, had her spinning so her body pressed against Brad's, laughing at the sheer joy of it. "How perfect, and how simple. Hurry."

She ran, tugging him along the path. One she'd chosen, she thought, and that her child had chosen. One that changed everything, and led toward home.

"The key." Tears sparkled on her lashes, and still she laughed as she stepped onto the deck with the man she loved, with her child, with her family. "I know where it is."

She kept Brad's hand in hers as she crossed toward the door.

The kitchen door, she thought. The one used for family, for friends, for those who lived inside. The everyday door that would never be locked against her.

Crouching, she lifted the mat. Beneath it, the key was a glint of gold on wood. "Welcome home," she said softly, and picked it up.

"It's my home now, you see?" With the key resting in her palm, she turned to Brad. "I had to believe it, expect it, accept it. All of that. I faced him here, last night, when I was so low, so afraid, so tired. But I faced him, and he couldn't make me give up. And I found it because I fought for it. And for you, and for myself."

She curled her fingers around it. "We've beaten him."

The wind came up in one, long howl. It raged across the deck with enough force to hurl her back, to slam her down. Through the roar of it, she heard the shouts, the crash of glass.

She rolled, saw her friends scattered over the deck, saw Brad using his body to protect Simon from flying glass and debris. And saw the blue fog creeping over the ground toward them.

The key pulsed in her fist, a frantic heartbeat.

Kane would kill for it, she knew. He would destroy them all to stop that beat. Crawling on her belly, she reached Brad and Simon. "Is he hurt? Baby, are you hurt?"

"Mom!"

"He's all right!" Brad shouted. "Get inside. Get in the house."

Her home, she reminded herself grimly. The bastard wouldn't get inside her home again, would never, never touch what was hers. She slid the key into Brad's hand, closed his fingers tight around it.

"Protect them. Get Rowena. Dana and Malory can get Rowena."

If she gave them the chance, Zoe thought, and bracing herself, she rolled away and off the deck. She kept her fist closed tight as if she held something precious in it. Ignoring the shouts from behind her, she pushed herself to her feet. Bent double against the fury of the wind, she lurched toward the trees.

He would come after her, and that would buy time. As long as he believed she had the key, he would focus on her. The others were nothing to him now. Bugs, she reminded herself as she wrapped her arms around a tree trunk to gain her balance. He wouldn't waste time swatting bugs now.

Until the key was in the lock, the war wasn't over, so she would take the battle with her.

The mists twined around her ankles, seemed to pinch and tug so she panicked enough to kick out and scream. When she fell to her knees again, the stench of it filled her mouth, her lungs. Choking, she dragged herself up and ran.

The wind wasn't as fierce now, but the cold—oh, the cold was barbed and ate through the leather of Brad's jacket, into her sweater, into her flesh. Snow began to fall in fat, dirty flakes.

He was taking her back to that first illusion. She pressed a hand to her belly half expecting to find it full of child. But she felt only the quiver of her own knotted muscles.

Kane was toying with her now, she decided. His ego would demand it. Entertaining himself. Certain that he could strike her down at any time, take the key, and win.

Disoriented, she stumbled through the snow, only praying that she wasn't somehow circling back toward the house. They needed time. She'd found the key. If they could get it to the Box of Souls, Simon could open it. It had to be true. He was part of her. Her blood, her bone. Her soul.

Once the lock was open, they would all be safe. She had to keep Kane's mind off the others until it was done.

Black lightning shot out of the sky and lanced fire at her feet. She screamed, hurling her body away from the burn of it, gagging on the stink of its smoke.

When she scrambled up again, he was standing in her path, his black robes swirling inches above the dingy snow.

"A coward, after all." The marks from her nails still scored his cheek. "Leaving your own child, your friends, your lover, running like a rabbit to save yourself."

She let the tears come, wanting him to see them, mistake them for a plea. And she put her fisted hand behind her back as if hiding something. "Don't hurt me."

"Only hours ago I offered you your heart's desire. How did you repay me?"

"You frightened me." She needed a weapon, but was afraid to take her eyes off his to search for one.

"You should fear. You should beg. Perhaps if you do, I'll spare you."

"I'll do whatever you want, if you just leave me alone."

"Give me the key of your own will. Come here, place it in my hand."

Of her own will, she thought. That was the trick. He couldn't take it, even now. "If I give it to you, you'll kill me."

"If you don't . . . " He let the threat lie unspoken. "But if you give it, put it from your hand into mine, I'll spare your soul. Do you know what it is to live without a soul? To lie frozen and empty for millennia, while your . . . essence is alive and trapped and helpless? Will you risk that for something that has nothing to do with you?"

She took one step forward as if beaten. "Rowena and Pitte said you couldn't spill our blood, but you did."

"My power grows beyond them. Beyond all." His pupils seemed to whirl with color as she took the next step. "The king is weak and foolish, hardly more than a mortal in his grief and pain. The war is nearly won. Today it's finished, and I will rule. All who have fought against me, all who have sought to stop me will pay dearly. My world will be united again."

"It's pain that gives you power. And grief. Is that your soul?"

"Clever, for a mortal," he acknowledged. "Dark will always smother the light. I choose its strength, and while those who strive to preserve that light are distracted in battle and politics, in diplomacy and *rules* of combat, I use the dark. So I am here and do as I will until it is done. What little you, or they, do to stop me is no more than a delay. Now the key."

"You can't have it."

Rage exploded through him. She braced as he lifted a hand, prepared to try to duck the blow.

Brad leaped through the curtain of snow. She saw the glint of a knife, saw it strike, but couldn't see where. She hurtled forward, then flew back again as Brad was flung out against her.

"You dare."

307

She saw blood on Kane, bright red against the black. Then Brad shoved her behind him.

"Do you?" he countered. "Do you dare to fight a man, or can you only take on women?" Brad turned the knife in his hand.

"Or mortals," Pitte said and moved through the snow. "Will you battle one of your own, Kane, power to power, god to god?"

"With pleasure."

"Stay back, woman," Pitte snapped at Rowena even as she moved to stand beside him.

"Yes." Kane lifted his arm. "Back."

A shock wave struck the air. Zoe was lifted off her feet to tumble through it. She landed hard on her back by the river-bank. Jarred, she rolled over painfully. She saw Brad a few feet away, his mouth bleeding as he crawled toward the knife that had flown out of his hand.

Nursing her throbbing arm, she pushed herself to her knees. She saw Rowena now, lying still, perhaps dead, in the dirty snow. Whatever force Kane had thrown out, Zoe realized, had been aimed at her.

Pitte was still on his feet, bleeding, battling. The air sparked and smoked with power, sizzled with light, streaks of dark, and a terrible sound of rending.

"Stay down," Brad ordered, and he spat blood, gripped the knife.

Though he hurled himself at Kane, the wall of snow and mist repelled him. "Get to the Peak!" he shouted at Zoe. "Get it done."

"There's no time." Dark smothers the light, she thought as she crawled toward Rowena. She could feel it weighing down, feel it winning. Her fingers trembled as she grabbed Rowena's hand. It was so cold, but she felt the beat in the wrist.

A god could breathe, she thought. A god could die.

She gripped the hand frantically, looking back to where Pitte fell to one knee, spun, and avoided a killing blow by inches.

"Help me," Zoe demanded. "Help me stop him." She dragged Rowena's head up from the snow, shook her while Brad battered against the wall.

If she could revive Rowena, and Rowena could add her power to Pitte's, they could still win. Unwilling to use the snow that Kane had created, Zoe crawled to the river, dipped her hands in for water.

She saw the reflection in its surface, the young warrior goddess with her face. "Help me," she said again, plunging her hand into the water.

And drawing out a sword.

It gleamed silver in the dull light, and in the wind that whistled over it, it sang. Power, clean as water, ran down its length.

Gripping the hilt in both hands, Zoe struggled to her feet. And hoisting the sword over her head, she charged. A warrior's cry ripped from her throat—a sound not completely her own—had Kane spinning toward her.

There was a jolt, a kind of electric snap, as she burst through the wall. Sparks shot out from the shock of light. There were a thousand screams in her head, the singe of burning along her skin. As Kane threw up his arms to strike, she plunged the blade through his heart.

The ground heaved under her feet, and her arms shook from the sudden blast of cold. She saw his face change—the fury, the shock, even the fear drowning away as his eyes went red. His jaw lengthened, his cheeks hollowed as the illusion of beauty died.

His hair grayed and changed into thin coils, and as his lips peeled back she saw teeth as sharp as sabers.

Though she staggered from the strain, she kept her grip tight on the sword when he fell. Panting, she stood over him and watched a god die.

He faded into the mist, or it into him, until there was nothing but the shadow of him on the snow. Then the shadow melted and she stood holding a sword with its tip dug into the ground.

"Well fought, little mother." His voice riddled with pain, Pitte knelt in front of her, took her hand and kissed her fingers. "I owe you more than my life."

"Rowena ... she's hurt."

"I'll tend her." With obvious effort, he got to his feet, then simply smiled when she held out the sword to him. "It belongs to you now," he said and walked over to cradle his woman.

"Zoe." His face smeared with blood, with smoke, Brad touched her hair, her cheek, then with a strangled sound wrapped his arms tight around her. "Zoe."

"I'm all right. You're hurt. Are you hurt? Simon."

He tightened his hold as she tried to shove away. "Safe. I promise. I made sure he was safe before I came after you. Trust me."

She let the sword drop to the ground and locked her arms around him. "With everything I've got."

Twenty

It wasn't the way she'd planned to spend the great American holiday, but it seemed appropriate to celebrate it at Warrior's Peak.

The details of transporting everything, dealing with the food, the preparations, calmed her. Though she had expected the key to be the first order of business, Rowena had other ideas.

"This is an important ritual for you, for your friends." In the vast dining room Rowena laid plates on the grand table. "It must be observed."

"It's a gorge-fest," Zoe told her and, unable to help herself, stepped over to stroke Rowena's hair. "You don't have to do this. You still look a little pale. We've got plenty of hands around here. Why don't you lie down for a bit?"

"I want to have a part." Thoughtfully, Rowena circled a finger around the rim of a plate. "I need time to settle myself, and something to do until my mind's quiet again. You understand this."

"Yeah, I do." Surprised, and touched, Zoe rubbed Rowena's arm when she leaned against her.

"I thought, for a moment, I thought all was lost. His power

was so full of hate and fury. I wasn't prepared for it. Perhaps I couldn't have been. All I know, all I am ... but I couldn't stop him. Even Pitte would have fallen."

"He didn't. We didn't."

"No. I've learned a lesson in humility."

"Rowena, she gave me the sword. How could that be?"

"As I miscalculated Kane's power, so did Kane miscalculate the king's. His power, his patience, his purpose. He gave you Kyna's sword, through her image."

She began to set the table again. "I'm allowed to see this now. Allowed to see that the battle in my world, for my world, has never ended. Kane gathered strength while we searched here for the chosen. He bargained with the darkest of forces, traded his own soul for power, even as those who followed him used might or intrigue or sabotage to keep the king and those loyal to him focused on maintaining the balance behind the Curtain."

Her movements still a bit stiff, Rowena walked around the table. "Much has been lost since we were sent here. But there was never defeat. I feared that," she said, looking over at Zoe. "Perhaps my fear made me weak when I finally stood against Kane. But my king is not weak. Kane mistook his ability to love, his kindness, and his compassion for weakness and forgot his wisdom and his terrible power."

"I saw him," Zoe said softly. "I saw him, a gold buck with a jeweled collar. This morning, standing outside the house, watching me."

"He has watched us all, more closely than I knew. He waited, grieved, fought, planned, three thousand years for the ones who could free his children. You were the only ones who could. I was not shown this until now. All these years, the failures, the preparations, they were all leading to you."

Gently, she smoothed a napkin. "If you, any of you, had

turned away, there would have been no others. Had I known . . . had I known, I'm not sure I could have borne it. So, I was not to know."

Because her legs felt suddenly weak, Zoe reached out to the back of a chair. "That's a pretty big chance to take with three women in Pennsylvania."

Rowena's lips curved, but the smile didn't reach her eyes. "I would say the gods chose very well."

"The sword . . . I'd already found the key. I'd completed my quest. I understand that Kane tried to stop us from using it, that what had grown in him, or what he'd decided to use, allowed him to try to stop us from using it. But once I found it, the rest was really between the gods, wasn't it?"

"You'd done what you were chosen to do," Rowena agreed.

"Then why did he give me the sword? Why didn't he give it to you or Pitte? Or just take Kane out himself?"

"He would not battle Kane on this field, in this place. For such matters, a champion must be chosen."

"Pitte, then, or you."

"No."

"Why?"

Tears glimmered in her eyes for an instant, then were gone. When she spoke, her voice was very strong. "Because we are not forgiven."

She set the last of the flatware in place, stepped back to study the table. "This is not the time for sorrows. We have much to be thankful for. Tell me—I have spent as little time as possible in kitchens—what comes next?"

Something had to be done, Zoe thought. But she smiled because she knew Rowena wanted it. "Ever mash potatoes?"

"No."

"Come on. I'll teach you."

*

THEY GATHERED AROUND THE table with the fire roaring and the candles gleaming. Whatever unhappiness Rowena knew was well masked by laughter and conversation. Champagne sparkled in glasses that were never empty. Platters and bowls were passed from hand to hand in an endless carousel of abundance.

"You'll want plenty of these," Zoe told Pitte as she offered him the mashed potatoes. "Rowena made them."

His eyebrows shot up. "How?"

"The same way women have been doing it for a number of years."

From the other end of the table, Rowena angled her head. "Pitte is now debating whether to risk them. My brave warrior wonders if he'll be forced to eat paste and pretend it's ambrosia."

As if to demonstrate his bravery, or his love, Pitte piled a small mountain of potatoes on his plate. "You wear his ring," he said to Zoe, nodded at the diamond on her finger.

"Yes." To please herself Zoe wiggled her fingers and watched the ring shoot fire.

"You are a fortunate man," he told Bradley.

"I am. I've got to take that ugly midget along with her." He sent a wink toward Simon. "But I figure she's worth the sacrifice."

"So many weddings," Rowena announced. "So many plans. Have dates been set?"

"We've been a little busy," Flynn began.

Malory fluttered her lashes at him. "We're not busy now."

"Oh." He lost a little color. "Guess not. Well . . . I don't know. Um . . . "

All attention turned to him, had him squirming. "How come it's my deal? There are three of us in this boat."

"Looks like you're at the wheel, son," Jordan said and continued to eat turkey.

"Man. Christmas is coming. We could work with that."

"Too soon." Malory shook her head. "We have—hopefully—the holiday rush at Indulgence to deal with. And I haven't picked out my dress yet. Then there's the flowers, the venue, the theme, the—"

"That should only take three or four years, once you get started. Great potatoes," Flynn said to Rowena.

"Thank you."

"It certainly won't take three or four years. I'm a very organized, goal-oriented woman. Just because I want a big wedding and I want it perfect doesn't mean I can't pull it together in a reasonable amount of time. You can forget stalling, Hennessy."

"Valentine's Day."

"What?"

There was something wonderful about watching her big blue eyes go blank. "February fourteenth." Inspired now, he grabbed her hand, kissed it. "Marry me, Malory. Be my valentine."

"I think I'm going to be sick," Jordan grumbled under his breath and got a sharp elbow in the ribs from Dana.

"Valentine's Day." Everything inside Malory melted. "Oh, that's so perfect. That's so beautiful. Yes!" She scooted around in her chair to throw her arms around his neck. "And you'll never have any excuse to forget our anniversary."

"Always a catch."

"Okay, big guy." Dana used her elbow again. "Batter up."

"What's wrong with what he said? Except for the gooey parts."

"Yes!" Malory erupted again, face glowing. "Let's do it together. All of us. A triple wedding on Valentine's Day. It's perfect. It's . . . right."

"Works for me." Brad looked at Zoe. "What do you say?"

"I say it makes a lovely circle."

"Do I have to wear a suit?" Simon demanded.

"Yes," his mother said definitively.

"Figures." He grumbled it as wedding plans flew around the table.

WHEN THE MEAL WAS finished, they gathered in the room where the portrait of the daughters looked down on them. The fire burned in the hearth, red and gold flames. A hundred candles glowed with light.

"I'm nervous," Zoe whispered and groped for Brad's hand. "Kind of silly to be nervous now."

He brought her hand to his lips. "All in a day's work for you, champ."

She laughed, but her stomach did a quick flip when Pitte lifted the Box of Souls.

"An artist, a scholar, a warrior." He set the box on its pedestal while the blue lights inside pulsed. "Inside and out, mirror and echo. Through their hearts, their minds, their valor, the last lock can be opened."

He stepped to the side, a soldier, while Rowena moved to her place to flank the box. "Please," she said to Zoe, "send them home."

Her stomach calmed, and her heart beat steady as she crossed the room. She felt the shape of the key in her hand, and its warmth as she looked at the final lock. And the lights that fluttered inside the glass like wings.

She took one long breath, held it, then slid the key into the lock and turned it.

Heat spread along her fingers. Light burst, white and pure and bright. With wonder, she watched the lid of the box fly open, saw the glass seem to explode without sound and send crystals spiraling into the air.

The three blue lights soared free, spinning, spinning into a circle linked by the blur like the tail of a comet. The air sparkled, white and blue.

Dazed, she heard Simon shout out, "Hey, cool!" and reached up, fascinated, to touch one of those whirling lights.

For an instant, it lay in her palm. The beauty of it, the joy of it rushed into her with such force, such intimacy, she was staggered.

She stared, dumbfounded, as she saw both Malory and Dana standing as she was, hands outstretched, each with a pulsing blue light cupped in her palm.

We've touched souls, she realized.

Then the lights seemed to leap, rushing in a kind of joyful madness from hand to hand, spinning flirtatiously around the men, playfully around a laughing Simon, over the heads of the dogs, before they shot to Rowena and Pitte to hover where they'd both gone reverently to their knees.

"It's so beautiful." Malory gripped Zoe's hand, reached for Dana's. "I've never seen anything so beautiful."

Once more, the three lights rose in a perfect circle, then separated and arrowed toward the portrait. And into it.

The painting shimmered, its already rich colors deepened. Zoe swore, that for just a moment, she heard three hearts begin to beat once more.

Then all was still.

"They are free." Rowena's voice trembled with tears. "They are home."

She moved to the three women. "This is a debt that can never be paid. What we give you is a token only." She stepped closer to kiss each of them on the cheek in turn. "Please, sit. I know you have much to do for tomorrow, but we still have one or two things to discuss."

"I'm not sure I can talk sensibly right now." Zoe pressed her hands to her mouth and stared at the portrait. "Or ever again."

"Champagne." Rowena threw back her head and laughed.

"We'll have champagne to celebrate this great day. To celebrate our joy, and your fortune."

She spun away to fetch the flutes Pitte was already pouring. "Thanksgiving." Her face glowed as she handed out the glasses. "Oh, it's such a day for it. Life finds its way, doesn't it? And you have found yours."

"We'll get the business out of the way," Pitte began. "The funds will be transferred to your accounts immediately, as agreed."

"No." Dana sat down, sipped her champagne, and caught Zoe's smirk out of the corner of her eye as Pitte blinked.

"I beg your pardon?"

"Do you want more?" In a gesture of acceptance, Rowena lifted a hand. "Don't tell me a bargain is a bargain," she said before Pitte could speak. "If they want more than the agreed-upon amount, they'll have more."

"No," Dana said again. "We don't want more. We don't want any." She jabbed a finger in the air toward Brad. "Mr. Business?"

"The parties waive payment," Brad began. Enjoying himself, loving these women. "After discussing the contractual terms, an agreement was reached, unanimously, to refuse any further monetary remuneration."

He drew forth a paper he'd written up, hurriedly, at their instructions, which they had signed. And he, Flynn, Jordan—and Simon—had witnessed. "This document, though informal, is self-explanatory and valid."

He held it out, waited for Pitte to come over and take it.

"Payment was agreed," he began.

"That was before." Malory looked up at the portrait. "Before we knew you, or them. When it was a kind of challenging game. We can't take money for this."

"We took the down payment," Dana put in. "And we're not

giving it back because, well, it's gone." She shrugged carelessly. "But we're not going to get rich off their souls."

"The money means nothing to us," Rowena began.

"No." Zoe nodded. "But it means something to us, so we can't. Wherever we go from here, whatever we make, we'll do it on our own, and together. That's our decision and we ... we expect you to honor it," she finished.

"Honor," Pitte said slowly, "is beyond price. I am humbled by yours."

"Then let's drink." Grinning, Dana lifted her glass. "It'll be the first time I ever drank to turning down a million."

Rowena walked to Zoe's side. "If I could have a moment with you, in private."

She'd been waiting, and though Zoe stood, she stayed where she was. "You're going to offer me a boon, the way you did when Malory and Dana found their keys. Isn't that right?"

"Yes." Rowena quirked her eyebrows. "Here, there?"

"Yes, please."

"Very well. You know the debt is deep. As you were the last, you know most of all how deep, how impossible to pay. But whatever you want that I'm able to give is yours."

"Malory and Dana didn't ask for anything."

"No. Still—"

"But I'm going to."

"Ah." Pleased, Rowena took her hand. "What will you?"

"It seems to me that since we unlocked the box, that even if I ask for something you can't handle—"

"I can handle quite a bit," Rowena said with a laugh. "I promise you."

"But if you can't, that under the circumstances, there are others who know what happened here, what I did, and they could get it for me."

"You intrigue me." Rowena angled her head. "I believe you

can have whatever you like. As I told you, our king loves his daughters and would surely repay you for all you've done. What do you wish, Zoe?"

"That you and Pitte be allowed to go home."

Rowena's fingers went limp on hers, dropped away. "I don't understand you."

"That's what I want. It's what I decided to ask for even before I knew it was what they wanted." She gestured to the portrait. "They touched us, and the six of us were like one for that moment. It's what we want."

Pitte stepped forward to lay his hand on Rowena's shoulder. "We're responsible for our own prison."

"No, Kane is," Dana interrupted. "And I like to think he's writhing in hell. Whatever part you played, you've paid for. The daughters understand that."

"You told me you weren't forgiven," Zoe continued. "But those most hurt never blamed you. And you kept your bargain, your word, your honor for three thousand years. Whatever rules you broke were only to spare lives after Kane crossed the line. I'm asking that you not be punished for that."

"It's not something . . . " With a helpless look at Pitte, Rowena shook her head.

"I wouldn't argue with her." Giving Simon's hair a quick ruffle, Brad sent Zoe a warm look. "She's a very determined woman."

"And a generous one." Moved beyond measure, Rowena pressed her palm to her heart. "But we have no power for this thing you ask."

"The king does. Will he tell me no? Will he tell them no?" With her mind made up, Zoe pointed to the portrait. "If he does, he may be a god, but he doesn't know squat about justice."

"Careful." Weakly, Pitte held up a warning hand. "Even a warrior so well proven should have care when she speaks of a king."

There were times to lay down the sword, Zoe remembered. And there were times to fight. She drew herself up. "He gave me a sword, and I used it. I fought for his children, and I helped save them."

She turned in a circle, studied the faces of her friends, her family. "Everyone in this room worked and risked and struggled to free them, to send them home. This is what I want in payment. This is *my* balance. If he's any kind of a king, any kind of a father, he'll give it to me."

Thunder boomed, not only outside but seemingly in the room itself. The great house shook, and in the hearth flames leaped.

"Boy." Dana swallowed hard, and snuck her hand into Jordan's. "I hope that's a yes."

On a small cry, Rowena pressed herself against Pitte. The words she spoke were foreign, drenched in emotion, as his were when he whispered in response.

Utter peace settled over his face before he buried it in her hair.

"I'd say that's a big yes," Jordan decided. "You're a stand-up woman, Zoe."

"Well." She picked up her glass now, amused to see her own fingers tremble. "Whew."

"In all the years since I came here," Pitte said quietly. "In all the endless hours and days of longing for home, I never knew I would miss anything from this world. I will miss you." With Rowena tight to his side, he bent down to kiss Zoe. "I will miss all of you."

"We will not forget you." Rowena stepped away from Pitte to drop into a deep curtsy, then chuckled as Moe pranced over to lick her face. "And there is much I will miss. Take care of them, my handsome warrior." She kissed Moe's nose. "Take care of each other. The gods are grateful to you all."

She straightened, smiled beautifully. "Sisters, brothers. Friends.

Our thanks to you, and our blessings on you." She held out her hand for Pitte's.

Their fingers linked, and they were gone.

THE NEXT DAY, AT six-forty-five P.M., Dana closed the door of Indulgence, locked it. Turning, she grinned at her friends, then slid down into a heap on the floor.

"Are we sure that's everybody? Are we sure it's just us left in here?" Zoe demanded.

"It's just us," Malory assured her.

"Holy jumping Jesus!" She shouted it and leaped into the air. "We rocked!"

"We rocked, we rolled, we kicked retail ass," Dana said from the floor. "I've never been so tired in my life. I may just sleep right here until we open again in the morning."

"We are such a hit. Did you see? Did you see how it all worked?" Her voice giddy, Malory spun in a circle. "Just the way we hoped. One of your manicure ladies bought my blown-glass bowl."

"And two of your art customers came up and booked a full-day spa package."

"I sold books to everyone who's ever lived," Dana chimed in and pillowed her head on her hands.

"And I think every one of them came through my shop on the way to Zoe's salon. And they loved it. How many times today did you hear people saying how pretty everything was, how much fun, how this was the best thing to happen to the Valley?"

"I lost count." Dana lifted her head. "I'm going to need another bookseller. Joanne and I couldn't keep up."

"I'm going to have to order more supplies." Zoe sent a look up the stairs. "I should probably go up and do inventory now."

"Hell with that." Malory grabbed her arm. "We're celebrating. There's champagne in the kitchen."

"I've had more champagne these past three months than I've

322

had in my entire life." Dana blew out a breath. "But what the hell. Who's going to carry me back there?"

Zoe took one arm, Malory the other, and hauled her to her feet. "Thank God we don't have to go home and cook," Zoe said. "We've all got enough leftovers to deal. I can't wait to tell Bradley and Simon about today. What they saw this morning was nothing."

"I'm hoping to con Jordan into rubbing my feet for an hour." In the kitchen, Dana poked her head in the refrigerator for the champagne.

"Just don't forget, we need to start hammering out the wedding plans on Sunday. February's closer than you think."

"Slave driver." Dana came out with the bottle. "What have you got there, Zoe?"

"It was on the counter." The box she held was wrapped in silver paper, with a gold ribbon. Three gold keys dangled from the bow. "This isn't any of your wrapping paper, is it, Malory?"

"No. Gorgeous, though, I should find out where it came from. But it's nothing one of my customers left behind."

"Maybe one of the guys snuck in and left it for us," Dana suggested. She gave it a poke before she reached for glasses. "That would be kind of sweet."

"Only one way to find out." Zoe picked carefully at the seams of the paper. "I can't rip it, it's too pretty."

"Take your time. Builds anticipation." Malory leaned back on the counter while Dana opened the champagne. "God, I'm exhausted, but in the best possible way. Almost like having really great sex."

Malory glanced over at Zoe as Zoe lifted the lid. "What've we got?"

"There are three smaller boxes inside. And a note." She took the boxes out first. "They're for us. Each one has one of our names. Gosh, the boxes look like real gold."

Dana lifted hers, then yipped when Malory slapped her hand. "Don't open it yet. Let's read the note."

"Jeez, you're so strict. What does it say, Zoe?"

"Oh. Oh! It's from Rowena." She held up the note so they could all gather around it to read.

My dearest friends,

I know this finds you well and happy, and am glad of it. Pitte and I send our love, and our gratitude. There is still work to do in our world, but balance is being restored. Already, celebrations are begun. While shadows are never dispelled completely, it is due to them the light shines bright.

I send this as I sit in the garden and hear the voices that were silent for so long. There is joy in them, and in me.

These three gifts are from the daughters, who wish you to have a token, one that both cherishes and honors the link you shared with them.

Know that on the day of your weddings, there will be celebration here, on this side of the Curtain, and that the gods bless you and yours.

My love to you, to your men, and to all you hold dear.

Rowena

"She sounds ... peaceful." Malory sighed. "I'm so happy for her."

Zoe laid the note down, brushed her fingers over it. "We should open the boxes together."

They picked them up, nodded, then opened the hinged lids.

"Oh." As did the others, Zoe lifted out the pendant on a long gold chain. "The pendants they wore in the painting. The ones Rowena said their father gave them." She gently touched the deep green of the emerald cabochon.

"They're exquisite." Staggered, Malory stared at the rich sapphire. "Just beautiful."

"And personal," Dana finished, holding up her ruby. "A

kind of family heirloom. You know, it may be a little hokey, that something old, something new business for brides. But, these sure qualify as old. I think we should all wear them at the wedding."

"That's a wonderful idea. Zoe?"

"It's a perfect idea." She slipped hers over her head, kept her hand loosely fisted around the stone. "I think we should have a toast. Somebody think of something."

"To beauty," Malory said, lifting her glass. "To truth and to valor."

"To the Daughters of Glass," Dana added.

"And what the hell. To us." Zoe held out her glass.

As they clinked crystal together, the silver mist of the Curtain of Dreams slid gently closed.

For now.